Anthologies

EDGE OF DARKNESS
(with Maggie Shayne and Lori Herter)

DARKEST AT DAWN
(includes Dark Hunger *and* Dark Secret*)*

SEA STORM
(includes Magic in the Wind *and* Oceans of Fire*)*

FEVER
(includes The Awakening *and* Wild Rain*)*

HOT BLOODED
(with Maggie Shayne, Emma Holly, and Angela Knight)

LOVER BEWARE
(with Fiona Brand, Katherine Sutcliffe, and Eileen Wilks)

FANTASY
(with Emma Holly, Sabrina Jeffries, and Elda Minger)

Specials

DARK HUNGER
MAGIC IN THE WIND
THE AWAKENING

Titles by Christine Feehan

SPIDER GAME
VIPER GAME
SAMURAI GAME
RUTHLESS GAME
STREET GAME
MURDER GAME

PREDATORY GAME
DEADLY GAME
CONSPIRACY GAME
NIGHT GAME
MIND GAME
SHADOW GAME

HIDDEN CURRENTS
TURBULENT SEA
SAFE HARBOR

DANGEROUS TIDES
OCEANS OF FIRE

WILD CAT
CAT'S LAIR
LEOPARD'S PREY
SAVAGE NATURE

WILD FIRE
BURNING WILD
WILD RAIN

FIRE BOUND
EARTH BOUND
AIR BOUND
SPIRIT BOUND
WATER BOUND

SHADOW RIDER

DARK PROMISES
DARK GHOST
DARK BLOOD
DARK WOLF
DARK LYCAN
DARK STORM
DARK PREDATOR
DARK PERIL
DARK SLAYER
DARK CURSE
DARK HUNGER
DARK POSSESSION
DARK CELEBRATION

DARK DEMON
DARK SECRET
DARK DESTINY
DARK MELODY
DARK SYMPHONY
DARK GUARDIAN
DARK LEGEND
DARK FIRE
DARK CHALLENGE
DARK MAGIC
DARK GOLD
DARK DESIRE
DARK PRINCE

SHADOW
RIDER

CHRISTINE FEEHAN

JOVE BOOKS, NEW YORK

JOVE

An imprint of Penguin Random House LLC
375 Hudson Street, New York, New York 10014

SHADOW RIDER

A Jove Book / published by arrangement with the author

ISBN: 9780515156133

PUBLISHING HISTORY
Jove mass-market edition / July 2016

PRINTED IN THE UNITED STATES OF AMERICA

10 9 8 7 6 5 4 3 2 1

Cover illustration by Danny O'Leary.
Cover design by Judith Lagerman.
Cover photograph of brick © Lenatru / Shutterstock.
Text design by Kristin del Rosario.

Penguin
Random
House

For Alisha Roysum,
thanks for the major family support.
I can't tell you how much it means to me.

FOR MY READERS

Be sure to go to christinefeehan.com/members/ to sign up for my PRIVATE book announcement list and download the FREE ebook of *Dark Desserts*. Join my community and get firsthand news, enter the book discussions, ask your questions and chat with me. Please feel free to email me at Christine @christinefeehan.com. I would love to hear from you.

ACKNOWLEDGMENTS

With any book there are many people to thank. For her help with Italian translations, a huge thank-you to Lillian Pacini. Any mistakes made are strictly my own. Thanks to Domini, for her research and help with editing; to C. L. Wilson, Sheila English and Kathie Firzlaff, for the hours in starfish bouncing around ideas; and of course to Brian Feehan, who I can call anytime and brainstorm with so I don't lose a single hour.

CHAPTER ONE

Stefano Ferraro pulled on soft leather driving gloves, his dark blue eyes taking a long, slow scan around the neighborhood. *His* neighborhood. His family knew everything that happened there. It was a good place to live, the people loyal. A close-knit community. It was safe because his family kept it safe. Women could walk the streets alone at night. Children could play outside without parents fearing for them.

He knew every shop owner, every homeowner by name. The Ferraro family territory started just on the edge of Little Italy. He knew every inch of Little Italy as well, and those residing and working there knew him and his family. Crime stopped at the edge of the Ferraro territory. That invisible line was known by even the most hardened of criminals and no one dared to cross it because retaliation was always swift and brutal.

He glanced at his watch, knowing he didn't have a lot of time. The jet was fueled and waiting for his arrival. He needed to get into his car and get the hell to the airport, but something held him there. Whatever it was, the feeling he had was disturbing. The compulsion to stay was strong, and anytime that happened, every Ferraro knew there was trouble coming. He carefully and very quietly shut the door to his Maserati, rounding the hood, and then retreating to the sidewalk.

Urgency was always about work, and nothing ever interfered with the Ferraro family business. Nothing. He played hard when he played, but work was important and dangerous and he kept his head in the game when it was time to get down to business. He needed to get his ass moving, but he still couldn't force himself, in spite of all the years of discipline, to get into his car and get to the airport. The compulsion in him was strong, not to be ignored, and he had no choice but to give in to it.

A voice drifted to him above the normal sounds of the street. Elusive. Mysterious. Musical. He turned his head as two women rounded the corner just at the very edge of his territory and began walking deeper into it. He recognized Joanna Masci immediately. Her uncle, Pietro Masci, was a longtime resident in Ferraro territory, born and raised there. He owned the local deli, a very popular place for residents to buy their produce and meats. A good man, everyone in the neighborhood liked Pietro and respected him. Pietro had taken Joanna in when his brother died years earlier.

It wasn't Joanna who caught his interest. The woman walking beside her was dressed totally inappropriately for the weather. No coat. No sweater. There were rips in her blue jeans, which clung lovingly to her body. And she had a figure. She wasn't thin like most girls preferred; she actually had curves. Her hair was wild. Thick. Very shiny. She wore part of it pulled back from her face in an intricate thick braid, but the rest tumbled down her back in waves. The color was rich. Vibrant. A true black. He couldn't see her eyes from that distance, but she was shivering in the cold Chicago weather and for some reason, he had an entirely primal reaction to her constant shivering. His gut knotted and a slow burn of rage began in his belly.

It wasn't her looks that caught his interest or made him stand utterly still. It was her shadow. The sun was throwing light perfectly to create tall, full shadows. Hers leaked long tentacles. Thin. Like streaks reaching out toward the shadows around her. Everywhere there was a shadow, hers connected to it with the long feelers—with long tubes. His breath hitched. His lungs seized.

She was the last thing he'd ever expected to happen

because . . . frankly . . . a woman like her was so rare. He didn't know how to feel about it, but suddenly there was nothing else more important, not even Ferraro family business.

He had his cell phone out and punched in numbers without taking his gaze off of her. "Franco, I'm going to need to take the helicopter this morning. I have business to attend to before I can leave. Half an hour. Yeah. I'll meet you." He ended the call, still watching the two women and the strange shadow the stranger cast as he punched in another number. "Henry. I'm not going to use the car after all. Please return it to the garage for me." The Ferraro family had a temperature-controlled garage with a fleet of various cars and motorcycles. They all liked them fast. Henry took care of all the vehicles and kept them in top running order.

Stefano snapped the phone shut and stepped off the sidewalk to cross the street. He held up his hand imperiously and of course the cars stopped for him. Everything stopped for him when he demanded it.

Francesca Capello prayed she wouldn't pass out as she walked with Joanna toward the deli. She'd never felt so weak in her life. She was hungry. She'd made tomato soup using ketchup and water, but that was all she'd had to eat for the last two days. If she didn't get this job she was going to have to do something desperate, like ask the homeless woman she'd given her coat to where the nearest soup kitchen was.

Maybe it hadn't been such a great idea to give the woman her coat. Her clothes weren't the best for a job interview, but they were all she had. She needed the job, and she definitely wasn't looking very professional in her faded but very soft vintage blue jeans, a perfect fit, which was rare for her to find in the thrift stores. There were holes in the knees and one small one on her upper thigh, but some of the designer jeans featured rips. The tears in her jeans just happened to be from real wear.

"Wow, the deli's packed," Joanna observed as they stopped

in front of a glass door. She yanked it open and ushered Francesca inside.

Francesca thought she might faint from all the smells of food. Her stomach growled and she pushed on it with one hand, hoping to quiet it. People were three deep at the counter and every small table throughout the room was filled.

"Popular place," she observed, because she *had* to say something. She'd let Joanna do most of the talking because—well—she *couldn't* talk. She wasn't bursting into tears in front of her friend. Not after all Joanna had done for her.

"I told you." Joanna flashed a grin, caught her arm and tugged her through the crowd to the window on the far side opposite the door. "We can wait here until Zio Pietro has a couple of minutes."

Francesca didn't think he was going to be free anytime soon. Now all the smells blended together, making her feel nauseous. She didn't want to throw up right there in his deli. She was fairly certain that wouldn't get her the job, but her stomach was so empty.

Her lungs burned from holding her breath, waiting for Joanna's uncle to get free enough to come interview her. Joanna had promised her the job. Francesca had spent nearly every cent she had—the money she'd borrowed from Joanna—getting to Chicago, and into the tiny apartment right on the very edge of Little Italy. She had nothing left for food or clothing. She *had* to get this job. She could survive another week if she was very, very careful, but not much longer. She'd be living on the street with Dina, the homeless woman. She'd done that already once and it hadn't been fun. Truthfully, she wasn't altogether certain that her apartment was better than the street. Still, it had a roof.

Francesca couldn't stop shivering, no matter how hard she tried. The cold was biting and penetrated right to the bone. It didn't help that after the wild storm, there were puddles everywhere, impossible to avoid, and her shoes and socks were soaking wet. The soles were thin and the water had easily gotten inside her shoes. Not only were her feet wet, but her toes were numb.

Still, if she got the job, this was the perfect place for her. The neighborhood was small. Everything was in walking distance. She didn't own a car, or anything else for that matter. She was starting over, determined to rise from the ashes like the phoenix, but seriously, if Pietro didn't hurry up, she'd be on the floor soon.

If she didn't need food and to warm up so badly, she would have been happy with the evidence that the store was popular as a small specialty grocery and sandwich shop. Clearly, Pietro needed help. She could handle a cash register no problem. She could make sandwiches. She'd held a job in a deli while putting herself through school and she was certain this would be a piece of cake.

The door opened and a blast of cold air swept into the shop, chilling her further. She turned her head and froze. She had never in her life seen a man more gorgeous or more dangerous. He was tall, broad shouldered, tough as nails and totally ripped. His hair was jet-black and seemed messy, but artfully so, as if even it refused to disobey him.

He wore a three-piece dark charcoal pin-striped suit that had to have been tailor made in Italy or France and looked to be worth a fortune. His tie was a darker gray to match the thin stripes in his suit and was worn over a lighter shade of charcoal shirt. He wore butter-soft gloves and a long, dark cashmere overcoat. Even the shoes on his feet looked like he'd paid a fortune for them. He made her acutely aware of her shabby clothes.

She wasn't the only one who noticed him. The moment he entered, all chatter in the shop ceased. Completely. No one so much as whispered. No one moved, as if they were all frozen in place. Pietro came to attention. Beside her, Joanna took a deep breath. The atmosphere in the store went from friendly chatter and lighthearted gossip to one of danger.

His face was carved in masculine lines and set in stone.

He had a strong jaw covered by a dark shadow. He was easily the most gorgeous man she'd ever seen. His eyes were such an intense blue she almost didn't believe it was his natural color. The blue eyes swept the room, taking in everything and everyone. She knew they did. So did everyone in the room. Just like her, they were all staring at him. The eyes came back to her. Settled. Narrowed.

The impact was physical. Her breath rushed from her lungs. He could see right through her. She had far too many secrets for him to be looking at her and seeing so much. Worse, his gaze drifted over her, taking in the cropped sweater that molded to her breasts and just barely reached her waist. Her jeans rode a little lower than her waist so she had to resist pulling at the hem of the sweater, although her fingers automatically curled around the hem to do just that. The sweater was one of the few things she owned that was warm.

His gaze traveled down her holey jeans to her wet shoes and back up to her face. She wished the earth would open up and swallow her. The tension in the deli went up several more notches. Francesca knew why. Not only was this man gorgeous and dangerous, he was angry. A black wall of intense heat filled the room until no one seemed able to breathe. She could actually *feel* his anger shimmering in the air. The room vibrated with his fury.

She found herself trembling and shrinking back under that brilliant blue stare. She didn't understand why he'd singled her out, but he had. His diamond-hard gaze was fixed on her, not on any of the other customers—just her. She took a deep breath and let it out, tugging self-consciously on the hem of her sweater. When she did, his scowl deepened.

"Mr. Ferraro." Pietro stepped around the counter.

Pietro's shoulders were square, his face a mask of concern, his tone respectful. He looked as if he might faint any moment. Everyone did. Francesca didn't understand what was happening, but clearly Joanna was very aware. Her friend trembled and put one hand on Francesca's arm as if to steady herself.

They were all afraid of him. Francesca could see why—
he looked and felt dangerous. But every single person in the
store? Afraid? Of. This. Man. That was a little terrifying.
She wished fervently he would stop looking at her.

The man, Mr. Ferraro, stepped in her direction. He looked—
predatory. His gaze didn't waver. Not for one moment. If
she wasn't mistaken, he didn't blink, either. The crowd instantly parted, just like the Red Sea, leaving open a path
straight to her. She felt more vulnerable and exposed than
ever. She couldn't even ask Joanna who he was and why
everyone was afraid of him or even how they all knew him.
Or why his anger would be directed at her.

Everything in her stilled. Unless he knew. Oh, God. He
couldn't know. She had nothing left, nowhere to go. If she
didn't get this job, she'd be on the street again. Her face burned
under his scrutiny. She knew he saw everything. Her thrift
store clothes. Her wet shoes. Her lack of makeup. His suit
easily cost thousands, as did his coat. His gloves probably
cost more than her entire outfit when it had been brand-new.
What he spent on his watch could probably buy a car.

She felt her color rise, and she couldn't stop it. Her gaze
lowered, although she felt defiant. Just because he was
wealthy—and he was more than wealthy, anyone with eyes
could see that—he had no right to judge her.

God, but he was good-looking. Italian American. Olive
skin. Gorgeous blue eyes and thick black hair that made a
woman want to run her fingers through it. No man should be
able to look like he did. She tried to look away from him, but
something in his steady gaze warned her not to and she didn't
dare defy him. She couldn't imagine anyone crossing him. He
didn't exactly walk up to her. He stalked, like a great jungle
cat emerging from the shadows. Silent. Fluid. Breathtaking.

"Poetry in motion," she murmured under her breath.
She'd heard the expression, but now she knew what it meant,
how the words could come alive with a man moving.

He stopped abruptly. Right in front of her. Had he heard?
She felt more color creeping into her face. A deep red. She

was mortified to be singled out of the crowd. That was bad enough, but if he'd heard her . . .

"I'm Stefano Ferraro. You are?" It was a demand, nothing less.

She opened her mouth. Nothing came out. She actually felt paralyzed with fear. Of what she wasn't certain. Joanna's fingers dug into her arm hard, hard enough to get her to blurt out her name. "Francesca. Francesca Capello."

"Where the fuck is your coat?" His voice was pitched low. Soft. It sounded menacing, as if all his anger was directed at her because she didn't have on a coat.

She winced at his language and the abruptness of his completely shocking question. She tipped her chin up and instantly his eyes were on her face, following that gesture of defiance. "It isn't your business," she said, keeping her voice as equally low.

A collective gasp went up in the store, reminding her they weren't alone. She *felt* alone, as if there were only the two of them.

"It is my business," he returned. "You're shivering so badly your teeth are chattering. Where the fuck is your coat?"

She opened her mouth to tell him to go to hell, but nothing came out. Not one single word.

"She gave her coat to the homeless woman," Joanna supplied hastily. "On our way here. We were walking along Franklin and there was a woman sitting under the eaves there and she was cold so Francesca gave her coat to her."

"Dina," Francesca muttered.

"Dina?" he repeated.

"She has a name. It's Dina," she repeated, before she could stop herself. She knew she sounded snippy, but she didn't care.

"I'm well aware who she is," he said. "I'd like to know who you are."

Francesca was both horrified at his interest and mortified that she was in the spotlight. She sent up a little prayer for the floor to open up and swallow her right there.

This was met with silence so Joanna jumped to fill the breach. "She's a friend of mine, and I talked her into coming here to live from California. Uncle Pietro needed someone to help in the deli and she has tons of experience." The words tripped over one another in her haste to get the information out. "That's what we're doing now, applying for the job."

Francesca was well aware everyone in the store was staring at her, including Pietro. She was certain she looked homeless in her thrift store clothes, but really, the woman in the street had been freezing. Francesca, at least, had four walls to protect her—until the end of the month, and then she'd be sharing a cardboard box with Dina.

"I see." Stefano Ferraro said the words thoughtfully, his eyes still fixed on her. "You know her, Joanna? You vouch for her?"

Joanna nodded her head vigorously, her dark cap of hair flying around her face. Francesca could feel her trembling, which was unusual. Joanna had always had tons of confidence in herself. She'd been popular at school and always, always had an opinion to give. Everyone liked her, yet she was definitely shaking.

Stefano, still watching Francesca's face, pulled out his wallet, shoved a handful of bills into his coat pocket and then removed the coat. He held it open in front of Francesca.

Her lungs seized. She shook her head and tried to step back but she ran into Joanna's trembling body. Who was this man that everyone was so afraid of? Francesca knew the blood had drained from her face; she could feel it. She shook her head again, more vigorously so there could be no mistake the answer was a resounding, emphatic *no*.

Impatience crossed his face. "I don't have time to fuck around, *bambina*. Get your arms in the coat and come outside with me for a moment. We'll talk." He glanced at his very expensive watch. "I have about two minutes and then I have to be somewhere."

She considered stalling for the two minutes so he'd have to leave, but both Joanna and Pietro looked desperate. He had to be a criminal. Mafia. One of the strong-arm men who came in and took all the money from the stores, like on television. He looked far too elegant for that, but he also looked as if he could easily break bones and not break a sweat.

Joanna actually pushed her toward Stefano. Resigned, Francesca turned her back to him, slipping her arms in the sleeves. To her horror he reached around her to button up the long coat. *Around her.* Caging her in. Her back was against his chest and his arms were long, enclosing her while he buttoned the coat. She felt his warmth. His strength. For the first time that morning, she stopped shivering.

His arms felt enormously strong, his chest an iron wall. More, with every single breath she took in, she breathed him in. His scent. Very masculine. Spicy. He turned her around to face him and then stepped in close to her—too close— because again, she couldn't breathe. The coat was warm. Heaven. Soft. It smelled like him. And he smelled good. He actually made her weak in the knees, unless really, he had nothing to do with it and she was just hungry.

His hand slipped down her arm and his fingers shackled her wrist in a firm grip. She looked up at him, bracing her-self for the moment their eyes would meet, but he was look-ing at Joanna's uncle. He wasn't smiling, but he offered his other hand.

"Pietro. Good to see you. I trust you'll take good care of what's mine." His voice was low, sexy. She actually felt a strange answering vibration move through her body, like a song, a note tuned only to him.

He looked down at her again, and the impact of his eyes was enough to send her into a mini-orgasm. It was the truth whether she liked it or not. Joanna made a little sound in her throat, saving her, allowing her to turn her head toward her friend at Stefano's declaration. Pietro's head jerked up and his gaze shot to Francesca's face. Francesca frowned, trying to read the local language, but she had no idea what had passed as conversation between Pietro and Stefano Ferraro.

Gritting her teeth, she went with Stefano because it was time to give the man a piece of her mind and she couldn't do that in front of everyone. And also because he didn't really give her any other choice. Not only were Pietro and Joanna staring at her, but once again, everyone in the store was as well. She didn't like or need attention on her.

The blast of cold hit her as Stefano opened the door and allowed her to emerge first. She was too aware of him, of that hard, muscular body moving so close to hers. He kept her close with his grip, so that when she took a step, her body brushed against his continuously.

He stopped just outside the deli, to the right of the door, under the eaves. Her hands dropped to the buttons of his coat. Instantly his hand covered hers, preventing her from sliding the buttons open. His body blocked hers from the wind, crowding her. He put one hand to her belly and pushed gently until she took the three steps necessary for her back to be against the wall of the building, and then he easily caged her in.

"Use the money to eat something. Buy a decent pair of shoes. Do *not* give my coat away. I'm rather fond of it."

His voice was a little impatient, definitely authoritative, as if everyone in the world would obey his every command— and they probably did. She detested that she was standing in front of the world's hottest man and he could see she had nothing. Absolutely nothing. She wasn't taking anything from him, either.

"I am *not* taking your money or your coat," she snapped.

His hands kept hers trapped. His thumb slid over the back of her hand and even through the soft, buttery leather of the glove, the gesture sent a tingle of awareness down her spine.

"The coat is a loan, and the money . . ." He shrugged.

"I'm *not* taking it," she reiterated.

"Is there a reason why you're allowed to be kind, but I'm condemned for the same gesture?" he asked softly.

Her eyes met his and that was a mistake. A huge mistake. She felt as if she was falling into those hard, piercing eyes. She knew instantly he hadn't given her the coat because he was being kind. She just didn't know why he'd given it to her. Or why he'd taken an interest in her at all.

"Francesca?" he prompted.

She tried not to scowl at him. "No, of course not. It's just difficult to accept charity." She took a breath.

"It isn't charity."

That's what she'd been afraid of. Her gaze slid away from his. "I can't accept . . . That is . . . From you . . . Because you're . . ." *God.* She couldn't even talk. He was too close. Surrounding her with heat. Too handsome. Too dangerous. Too everything she wasn't and would never be.

His jaw hardened even more if that was possible. She had her eyes fixed on his very sexy five-o'clock shadow so she saw very plainly his impatience. Her belly tightened into little hard, apprehensive knots. She couldn't help herself; she pressed her hand deep to try to stop the tension coiling there. His gaze dropped to her hand and then came back up to her face.

"It's because I have money." He made it a statement.

His accusation stung, mostly because it was the truth. The color deepened in her face. He made her sound prejudiced. She hated that he called her on it, but the truth was, she would have been much more able to accept the coat from someone who had far less. She caught her lower lip between her teeth. Of course that wasn't the only reason, but she couldn't enumerate those reasons, either. That he was gorgeous, superhot. Or that he was dangerous and she thought he might be a member of organized crime.

"Francesca."

Her stomach somersaulted. He said her name low. Commanding. He was used to deference. Obedience. She took a breath.

"Look at me."

She let her breath out slowly and forced her gaze up his handsome face until her eyes collided with his. Then the breath slammed out of her lungs, leaving her fighting for air.

"Keep. The. Fucking. Coat." He bit out each word.

He scared the crap out of her. He wasn't touching her or threatening her, but she felt menace rolling off of him in waves. There was no use fighting him on it. He was going to get his way. Both of them knew it.

"Thank you." The words tasted a little bitter, but she managed to choke them out.

He nodded his head and glanced at his watch again. "Get something to eat," he added, turning away from her. "I'll be back for my coat."

She cleared her throat. "Mr. Ferraro?"

He spun back. Graceful. Impatient. "Got things to do, Francesca."

She didn't care. She had to know the truth. "Why is everyone afraid of you?"

His blue eyes held hers captive for so long she heard her heart pound. "Because I'm not a man you ever fuck with."

She blinked up at him, a little shocked at the honesty in his answer. She was fairly certain he was right. He'd brought an entire roomful of people to a standstill. No one had moved. No one had spoken. He definitely looked like a man no one would dare fuck with. Least of all her.

She cleared her throat. "I don't like that sort of thing."

He pressed one hand to her belly again, pushing her back against the wall, stepping in close to her until his heat and the scent of him surrounded her. "What sort of thing?" His gaze dropped to her mouth. Held there.

Her lips trembled, and a million butterflies took wing in her stomach. Her heart pounded. God. He was so close. Too close. He was taller than her by at least a head and a half. His shoulders blotted out the street behind him. He smelled— delicious. She didn't know a man could smell that good. It was freezing cold outside and he wasn't even shivering though she had his coat.

"The F-word sort of thing." She blurted it out, saying the first thing that came into her mind without thinking.

His eyebrow shot up. She hadn't thought that anyone really could do that. Shoot up one eyebrow. It was incredibly hot—at least on him.

"'The F-word'?" he repeated. "*Dolce cuore*, you can't even say *fuck*, for fuck's sake."

She felt the color creeping into her face, although she didn't know why. She wasn't the one spouting off inappropriate language to a complete stranger. She wasn't staring at his mouth, although she wanted to. She resisted, because that was what was polite. She wasn't pressing him against a wall and holding him there with a hand on his belly and another by his head. She wouldn't dare touch him.

There was nothing to say to that so she didn't say anything. She just stood there, waiting for him to release her.

He glanced at his watch again. "I really have to go. Eat. I mean it, Francesca. Don't give the money or the coat to anyone else. I'll know, and I won't like it."

She made a face. "Should I be afraid of you?"

For the first time amusement softened his features. "Only if it keeps you from giving away my coat and ensures you eat today." He reached out and bunched her hair in his hand and then allowed the strands to slip out of his fist. "Don't forget to buy a decent pair of shoes."

"I'll use your coat, but the money . . . I don't know when I can pay you back."

"Pietro pays a decent wage." He turned away from her.

"I don't have the job yet."

"You have the job." He lifted a hand and started down the street, moving easily, quietly. Looking more gorgeous than ever.

"Wait. How do I return the coat?" she asked a little desperately. He'd made it clear he wanted his coat back.

"I'll find you."

She watched him striding away. Watched how people on the sidewalk moved out of his way. He seemed to flow across the sidewalk, a force to be reckoned with. She felt a little bit battered, as if she'd been in the middle of the sea during a terrible storm. She didn't move, not for a long time. She huddled there in his long coat and forced herself to breathe deeply, trying not to feel faint.

Joanna caught her by the arm. "Oh. My. God. Did that just

happen? Tell me that didn't just happen." She practically shook Francesca in her shock.

Francesca glanced through the window of the deli. No one had moved. The attention of every individual in the store remained completely riveted on Stefano Ferraro. She ducked deeper into the warmth of the coat. The cashmere smelled like him. Was warm like him. Elegant like he was.

"What *did* just happen?" Francesca asked Joanna. "Because I have no idea."

"He just told Zio Pietro to hire you. *Ordered* him."

"He can't do that." Francesca frowned, alarmed.

"Yes, he can and he did. No one goes against a Ferraro. No one, Francesca."

"Great. Your uncle is going to blame me for having someone step in and tell him what to do in his own store."

"No, he won't. He's excited that he got to do a favor for Stefano. That's rare and it means something. You do a favor for one and they *all* feel they owe you. The entire family. That's huge, to have a Ferraro owe you. Zio Pietro was practically dancing around the shop."

"Why would that man get so angry because I didn't have a coat?"

Joanna looked confused. "I have no idea. I just know it's supercool that you attracted his attention. I've been around for years, since I was a little girl, and they all know my name and they know me, but they've never taken that kind of interest in me."

Francesca clenched her teeth. "Why would that be?" Already knowing the answer and not liking it.

"We don't exactly run in the same social circles. That family is total celebrity. Everyone knows them."

That didn't make Francesca the least bit predisposed to feeling better about Stefano Ferraro's interest in her. "I don't know them. I don't want to know them." Which wasn't altogether true. She'd heard the name. She knew the name was associated with an international bank and a very prestigious hotel as well as a racing team.

Joanna caught her arm and tugged in the direction of the deli's door. "Come on, it's cold out here. Zio Pietro wants to meet you."

"You said *them*. There's more than one of him?" She knew a Ferraro drove a race car, but surely the name wasn't that uncommon.

Joanna nodded solemnly. "And they're all that gorgeous. I kid you not. Stefano's the oldest. He has four brothers, equally hot. One sister, totally beautiful. When they walk around together, people just stare at them. That's how hot they are. Each one of them is supercool as well, which makes them all *scorching* hot. I'm a little in love with them, including their sister. That's how totally gorgeous they are."

Francesca couldn't help it. She started to laugh. She hadn't laughed in months. It was good to see Joanna again. She was not in the least complicated, nor did she want to be. She always found humor in everything and she loved to party, go to clubs and dance the night away.

"I can't believe Stefano Ferraro claimed you."

The statement tumbled out, leaving Francesca feeling weak and more confused than ever. As they entered the store, all eyes turned to her. The deli was eerily silent. Color infused her face. She wanted to turn and run.

"Joanna, come behind the counter and help out while I talk to your friend," Pietro ordered, beckoning to his niece.

Joanna squeezed Francesca's hand. "Zio Pietro, this is my best friend, Francesca Capello."

"Yes, yes, you talk about her all the time," Pietro said, beaming. He waved toward the customers. "Hurry, before they take their business somewhere else. I'll look after Francesca for you."

He indicated for Francesca to follow him and she did, winding her way through the throng of people, back behind the counter. Once behind the counter she was up close to the smells of the food and her stomach growled again. She found herself pulling the coat closer around her like a shield, trying to hide from all the eyes staring at her. Trying to hide the fact that she was *starving*. She followed Pietro through a narrow hallway to the rather messy office.

Pietro waved her toward a chair. "Sit. I'll get you an application, but that's just because I need your information. A mere formality."

She winced, wishing it were easy for the average person to get a new identity. She'd actually made inquiries, only to find out it would be impossible when she didn't have money and didn't know anyone in the criminal world—well, only one someone—so she'd remained Francesca Capello. Her fingers gripped the outside of the coat, gathering the material into her fist, holding so tight her knuckles turned white.

"Tell me how you know Stefano Ferraro. It sounded as if you just met, yet he said . . ." He trailed off, clearly looking for more information.

She looked across the desk at Pietro, her heart beginning to pound. She *needed* this job. She wasn't good at lying, but . . . She didn't know what to do, how to answer him. "I'm sorry, Mr. Masci. I never laid eyes on him before today." There. She told the truth. She found she was trembling from head to foot. She had to get the job. She leaned toward him. "Please. I'm a really hard worker. I've had tons of experience. Really." She just couldn't put down any references. Not a single one.

Pietro sat back in his chair, frowning at her. "You've never laid eyes on him before today?" He repeated her denial softly. Thoughtfully. "He *claimed* you. He asked me to take care of you for him. Do you have any idea what that means for us? How can you not know him?"

She was getting desperate. Food had been scarce for the last few weeks. Hiding in old buildings trying to stay alive when you were being hunted could make food not a first priority. The bus trip had been long. She had to save her money to try to get a place to stay. That didn't leave a lot for food.

"I met Joanna in school—in college. When . . . things happened to me . . . to my family, she was kind enough to help me out. I took a bus out here from California because she thought I could work in your store and build a new life here."

He put both hands on the desk. Flat. Leaning toward her. Eyes piercing. Her heart sank.

"Are you running from the law?"

Relief was so strong she wanted to cry. She shook her head. "No, sir. I'm not. I did get into some trouble back home, but I'm not in trouble with the law. I really need this job. I don't have much money left . . ." That reminded her of the folded bills Stefano Ferraro had stuffed into the pocket of his very warm coat.

"Why would Stefano Ferraro ask a favor of me for you? Does he know your family?"

She shook her head, feeling dizzy. "I swear to you, I don't know him. I don't know why he gave me his coat, or acted the way he did."

"He took you outside and had a conversation with you. What did he say?"

"Nothing. He didn't want me to give away his coat. He said I had to buy some shoes with the money. He was being kind."

Something in his eyes shifted. "The Ferraros are a lot of things, but they are not kind. He wants you taken care of. My niece has asked as well. I'll hire you. You can start tomorrow. Fill out the papers, and I'll go get you food. You look as if you haven't eaten in a while."

Francesca had to admit she didn't think Stefano had helped her out of kindness, but certainly Pietro's expression was kindly and she sagged with relief. She was going to put down the entire incident with Stefano as weird, treat it like he meant the gesture kindly. She wouldn't spend his money, but she'd wear his coat and then hang it carefully in her apartment until she figured out how to get it back to him.

She filled out the application, leaving just about everything blank. Her name. Her social security number. That was it. There was nothing else she could safely tell him.

CHAPTER TWO

Joanna tossed a handful of magazines onto the table in front of Francesca. "Check those out. Tell me I'm wrong about the Ferraro family."

Francesca sighed. She'd managed to eat two meals, thanks to Joanna and her uncle. She'd kept the meals small, and she was happy she had. The food sat in her stomach as if her body had forgotten how to process it. Her first day at work had been very successful and Pietro was pleased. The deli's customers had doubled in one day. She'd kept her head down and worked hard, avoiding the staring eyes. Pietro didn't care if they stared at his newest employee. He cared about the cash register, and it was full. That meant the tip jar was full as well.

Francesca smiled at Joanna as Joanna leafed through one of the glossy magazines to show her a headline. *Ferraro brothers. Fast cars and faster women.* There was a series of photographs of Stefano Ferraro standing by a race car with a huge smile and a large trophy, a woman in his arms, looking up at him. Four very hot men and an exceptionally beautiful woman circled him, all beaming at him. Joanna was right. They were gorgeous.

"Well, that lets me out. I don't own a car, and I couldn't be considered running in the fast lane no matter who was talking about me." Francesca should have been feeling relief, but the more she paged through the magazines and saw models, singers, actresses and heiresses adorning the arms of the Ferraro males, the more she felt a little sick.

"Wow. If you considered even a tenth of this stuff is true, they live life on the edge. Parties. Racing cars. Playing polo. What was he doing in your uncle's shop? I wouldn't think he would set foot in a place that was rated less than five stars."

"The Ferraro family owns most of the buildings in our neighborhood. Not the homes, but the apartment buildings, and all the store space. They're very hands-on. Their parents actually buy locally. They often come in and talk to Zio Pietro."

"You're telling me that these people are actually friends with all of you?" She couldn't keep the disbelief from her voice.

Joanna shook her head. "Not friends exactly. I'm not saying we run in the same circles. It's more like they're royalty and we all know them by sight. They keep an eye on things."

Francesca looked at the pictures of the ridiculously handsome faces with women on their arms—women dripping with diamonds—and she just couldn't see them walking around the neighborhood and frequenting the local shops.

"Are they mafia?"

Joanna gasped and looked around her. "Francesca! Sheesh. Are you nuts? You don't ask a question like that where anyone might hear you."

"Well. Are they?" she persisted.

Joanna looked uncomfortable. "They keep the neighborhood safe."

Francesca looked down at the open pages of the magazines again. They looked like playboys, yet if she looked really close, if she studied their faces, she could see the danger lurking under all that beauty. The bell over the door announced a customer and Francesca looked up as she stood. Her heart stuttered. Another Ferraro. Definitely. Not Stefano, but certainly one of his brothers. His sharp gaze moved around the store until it settled on her. Her stomach reacted, taking a little dive. She glanced at Joanna. Her friend sat frozen, her mouth open, her hand on the magazines.

Francesca carefully closed the covers and prayed those sharp eyes already dissecting the two of them hadn't seen what they were looking at. She forced her body to move, going straight to and around the counter. That helped, putting a barrier between them.

"May I help you?" Her voice came out a little strangled. She had secrets. Men like the Ferraros—jet-setters, men so rich they thought they owned everything in their world—could ruin her. She knew from experience that they wouldn't think twice about destroying anyone who got in their way.

"Hello, Joanna," the newcomer said, looking at Francesca, not Joanna. "You want to introduce us?"

Joanna jumped up so fast she nearly knocked over her chair. This time of day the deli was relatively quiet. Clusters of customers came in sporadically until the next big rush. Still, the few customers that were there ceased speaking, just as they'd done when Stefano had walked in.

"Of course. Giovanni Ferraro, this is my friend Francesca Capello."

Giovanni stuck out his hand. Francesca had no choice but to take it or seem rude. For all her declarations of the Ferraro family keeping the neighborhood safe, Joanna seemed anxious. Giovanni's hand closed around hers.

"You're new in our neighborhood." Giovanni made it a statement.

Francesca nodded. "Is there something I can get for you?"

"Mamma would like me to bring her some of Pietro's tiramisu. She's been craving it and couldn't get into the store today. Would you box me up six pieces?"

Francesca nodded. Relieved. He had a legitimate reason for coming to the store. What did she know? Joanna said the family frequented the store. Her weird encounter with Stefano made her nervous—that was all. She put together one of the carry boxes and lined it carefully, knowing Pietro would want the box to be extra special.

"How are you settling in to the neighborhood?" Giovanni asked. "Everyone treating you right?"

Francesca felt the tension in the store rise a notch. She lifted her gaze slowly to meet his. This was no casual visit. She didn't know why the innocent question tipped her off, but the Ferraro family continued to take an interest in her. Alarm bells began shrieking at her. Maybe even Chicago wasn't safe for her. She tried not to look as if she was freaking out. Joanna was. Her face had gone pale and she twisted her fingers together anxiously, waiting for Francesca's answer. The entire store seemed to be waiting.

"Everyone has been wonderful," she replied, and looked down at her work space, carefully placing each piece into the box.

"No complaints then?" he prompted.

Her heart jumped. She felt like she was walking on eggshells, one wrong move and something terrible would happen. She just didn't know what.

"None." She put the box on the counter.

Giovanni leaned close as he handed her the money for the tiramisu. "Buy some shoes." His voice was low. Just between the two of them.

Her gaze jumped to his. He refused to look away. She wasn't going to argue with him, but she wasn't spending Stefano's money. Not one cent. Not for anything. Pietro let her eat there at the deli and she was careful not to abuse that privilege, but she wasn't going hungry anymore, so she didn't need Stefano's money. The Ferraro family seemed to be obsessed with her getting new shoes.

"Don't piss him off," Giovanni advised. "Buy yourself the shoes. You can always pay him back. He'll be home soon and you don't want to get him riled."

"He sent you to check up on me?" she hissed.

He grinned at her, completely unrepentant. He looked nearly as gorgeous as his brother. And as arrogant. "We're watching over you," he admitted. "He'd beat the holy hell out of us if we didn't. So buy the shoes and keep me from getting a broken nose. I like mine the way it is."

She gave him the change. "Just wait right there. I've got his coat in the back and you can . . ."

Giovanni backed away from the counter. "Not going to happen, woman. You give him that coat in person. He'd kill me over that coat. Wear it. He'll be checking on that, too. Buy some shoes and wear the fucking coat. Put him in a good mood for a change."

What did that mean? Stefano looked like he was in a good mood when he was smiling for the cameras with all those women hanging on his arm.

Giovanni turned away from Francesca, which was just as well because she might have thrown something at him. "Joanna, you haven't been by the club for a while."

Joanna had closed the rest of the magazines, stacked them and turned them all over so only the back covers showed. Francesca was fairly certain it was too late. Giovanni had seen what they were doing. There was no doubt in her mind that he would report that to his brother as well.

"You been giving our competitors your business?" Giovanni's tone was teasing, but Joanna looked nervous.

"I love the club," she said, "but the price is a little steep, and I usually don't make it in even if I come up with the door fee."

Giovanni's face darkened. "What did you say?"

"It's all right, really. I understand. It's a hot spot. I don't exactly have the clothes . . ."

"That's bullshit." He pulled a card from his wallet and handed it to her. "Skip the fucking line and show that to the bouncer. They don't let you in, you call the number on that card and I'll handle it. You're one of ours. They let you in when you want in. Come this next weekend and bring Francesca. I'll be there and so will Stefano. We've got a meeting. If there's any trouble, just call."

Francesca was horrified. Shocked, too. Giovanni sounded really angry. Not because of her, but on Joanna's behalf, and that made Francesca like him a little better. He didn't like that Joanna had been refused entry into their club. Still, she was *not* going to some hot club. What was she going to wear? Her holey jeans? Not likely.

They watched Giovanni leave, and then Francesca came out from behind the counter. "What in the world was that?"

"I don't know, but clearly the family is watching over you," Joanna said. She held up the card. "Can you believe he gave me this? He was angry that they didn't let me in. He said to just jump the line, too. Can you imagine getting to do that? I've gotten into the club a couple of times but usually they turn me away at the door."

"That's terrible. Snobs."

"The Ferraros clearly aren't the ones being snobs," Joanna said, waving the card at her. "We can go dancing, Francesca."

"I can't go," Francesca protested. "I wouldn't have the money to get in, let alone something to wear. Seriously, Joanna, go with your other friends or by yourself. No way am I going out to a club, especially one the Ferraros frequent."

"Own. They own it. They have several businesses, and that's just one. The main family business is international banking. They also have the hotel, which is the bomb. Movie stars stay there. In any case, you *have* to come with me. They'll expect it." Joanna pressed the card against her heart. "I'll find you something to wear."

"No." Francesca threw herself into the seat beside Joanna. "They're watching me. He as good as said so. Why would they do that? Do you think they found out about . . ." She trailed off, and reached for Joanna's hand. "They run in the same circles. If they tell anyone I'm here, I'll have to run again and I don't have enough money."

Unbidden came the thought of the money Stefano had shoved into the pocket of his coat. It would be stealing to take it and disappear. She had the feeling if she did run, Stefano would find her. He would never allow her to steal from him and not hunt her down. She shivered at the thought.

She didn't want him coming after her. He would be relentless and she doubted if he had much mercy in him.

Joanna shook her head. "You're under Stefano's protection. That's what he meant when he said to my uncle to take care of what was his. Clearly the Ferraro family is looking out for you."

Francesca glanced around the room, took the stack of magazines, held them up and lowered her voice even more. "Are you crazy? I can't come under any scrutiny. You know that. No one can know anything about me. Having Stefano Ferraro showing me any interest, for whatever reason, even if he's just worried about my well-being, is dangerous."

Joanna looked crushed. "I *love* that club. Celebrities go there. Movie stars, Francesca. It isn't like they notice me, but I get to see them up close. Some of the NASCAR drivers go there as well. The bartenders do amazing tricks, just like you see in the movies, and the music is killer. Best dance place in Chicago."

"He said you could go anytime," Francesca reminded gently. "It didn't have anything at all to do with me."

Joanna sighed and nodded. "I guess you're right. What time do you get off?"

"Your uncle said five. It's nearly that now."

Francesca didn't have to look at the clock to know it was close to the end of her shift. Her feet were killing her, toes numb with cold. She was afraid she was going to get frostbite. She wished for a bathtub to soak in. The tiny apartment had only a shower, and the water wasn't very hot. Still, she wasn't about to complain. She had a roof over her head and Joanna's uncle paid her a much better wage than she'd anticipated, which meant if he kept giving her the hours he'd promised her, she could pay another month's rent.

If she just ate one meal a day at the deli, or grazed a little throughout the day, she'd save money. Electricity and water were included in her rent. She didn't have a cell phone or a car. She was on the lookout for thrift stores so she could see if she could find a few more outfits.

"Why the big sigh?" Joanna asked.

"Why would it be such a big deal to the Ferraro family for me to buy a pair of shoes?" The temptation was there. Her feet were so cold she wanted to cry, not to mention, because the shoes were too big, she had blisters from them constantly rubbing.

"Is it a big deal?"

Francesca nodded, leaning into her hand. "Giovanni told me to buy shoes or his brother was going to be angry. He said not to make him angry."

"He said that?" Joanna looked shocked.

"I don't understand why Stefano would care in the first place. It isn't his business. Does he go around the streets and search for people with holes in their shoes and demand they buy new ones? Does he have a shoe store that needs business? And why would he send his brother in here to make certain I actually buy the shoes?"

"Wow." Joanna fanned herself. "That's just . . . *wow.*"

Francesca rolled her eyes. "Don't start. It isn't *wow.* It's creepy. Maybe his brother has a shoe fetish and my shoes don't meet his standard for the neighborhood."

"It's *wow* and you know it. He's hot. He's rich. He's interested in you."

Francesca stiffened. "He is not. Not like that. Take another look in those magazines at what that man's type is. It isn't me. I'm no model. I'm short and have a lot of curves. All the running in the world isn't going to get rid of my . . ." She indicated her generous breasts. "Or my butt. Not to mention, I didn't see one Italian-American woman in the entire harem."

Joanna burst out laughing. "Maybe he's looking to add one."

Francesca couldn't help but laugh with her. "I don't think so."

"You are beautiful, Francesca," Joanna said, sobering. "Really, really beautiful. Your face is flawless. None of those models have anything on you. Your face. Your hair."

"My lovely figure," Francesca said sarcastically. "I'm not a size zero."

"You have a lovely figure. I've always been envious of that tiny waist."

Joanna was tall and willow thin. She easily could have been a model. She liked food and ate more than Francesca could imagine any woman eating without gaining weight, but she just didn't. Every one of their college friends envied her.

"I don't gain in my waist, just up top or my bottom. No pizza for me." Francesca *loved* pizza, and they were going out for her first Chicago pizza. Joanna told her the best place was right there in the Ferraro neighborhood. That's what she referred to it as—the Ferraro territory or neighborhood—as if they owned it all. Maybe they did. At least the buildings.

"You're going to eat pizza," Joanna said. "You won't be able to resist. This place makes the best. It's orgasmic."

Francesca burst out laughing again. "You're so crazy." Her smile faded. "Joanna. Seriously. Thank you. I don't know how I'm ever going to repay you. I felt so hopeless and I was terrified all the time." She was still terrified, but not so hopeless. And Joanna made her remember friendship, family and laughter.

"Don't be absurd. I'm so glad you've come. I have friends here, but not a bestie. You're my total bestie. In any case, you repaid me already. I have Giovanni Ferraro's card and I can skip the line and get into the club or call him."

Francesca smiled. "There you go. I'm good for getting you into clubs." She glanced at her watch. "I've got to get back to work. I'll wipe everything down and clean up for the next shift. Pietro should be back by then."

Joanna waited for her and they walked out together, Francesca wrapped in Stefano Ferraro's long cashmere coat. She'd considered leaving it in her apartment, but she didn't dare. Her apartment wasn't very safe. The lock was tricky and sometimes didn't actually lock. She'd told the owner and he'd promised to put a new lock in, but she wasn't leaving that coat where someone could walk in and steal it. Who knew that the responsibility of a coat would make her a little crazy?

It seemed silly to carry the overcoat to work, when it would keep her warm, so she wore it, inhaling Stefano's scent with every breath she took. She hung it carefully in Pietro's office rather than in the employees' little break room. Pietro didn't mind. In fact, he seemed happy that she was keeping the coat in his office.

She plunged her hand in the pocket. The money was there. All of it. She hadn't counted it, but she had a feeling she might faint when she found out how much he'd left her. "Where are we going, Joanna? I thought you said the pizza place was the opposite way?" They were heading away from Ferraro territory and the pizza parlor was deeper into it. They'd gone three long blocks, all businesses. Two streets over she knew residences started. They passed her apartment building. It marked the very edge of the Ferraro neighborhood and the next block was rather like her building, shabby in comparison.

"There's only one shoe shop open this late unless we go to the big mall and then we'd have to take the bus."

Francesca halted. "I don't know if I want to spend the money on shoes. Seriously, Joanna, I'd have to pay it back and I have to be careful so I can pay the rent. Having a roof over my head is more important than anything else right now. And I can try to find shoes . . ."

"*Don't* say it. You aren't going to find shoes at a thrift shop. No way. You aren't putting your feet into something someone's put their feet into."

"Seriously? Joanna, I don't have any money. I can't afford to be picky right now. If Stefano Ferraro is going to lose his mind because I didn't buy shoes and get all mad and punch out his brother, then I need to find a pair of shoes, but I don't have to spend his money on them."

"Punch out his brother?" Joanna echoed. "Did Giovanni say Stefano would punch him out?"

Francesca shrugged. "Something like that. He mentioned not wanting a broken nose."

"Oh. My. God. I'm falling even more in love with the Ferraro brothers. *All* of them. They're so hot. And cool. And *gorgeous*. I can perv on them for like forever." She caught Francesca's arm. "Here. This shop. Let's just go in. You can see if you can find something you like."

Francesca couldn't help herself. She was sick of having freezing feet, wet socks and toes that were numb from the icy cold. Once again her hand crept into the pocket to the neatly folded bills. She took a deep breath and nodded. It was an insane thing to do, owe Stefano money, but the temptation when her feet were killing her after standing on them all day was more than she could pass up.

It was embarrassing to try on shoes when hers were in such horrible condition. Joanna knew the manager and chatted all the while, allowing Francesca to remain silent. She couldn't look at the man. He was good-looking and flirted outrageously with Joanna. Apparently they'd gone to high school together. It took Francesca a few minutes before she realized Joanna was deliberately distracting him, knowing how embarrassed Francesca was over the state of her shoes. She felt very, very lucky to have such a good friend.

Shoving her wet socks into her wet shoes, she hastily pulled on the warm, dry socks Joanna handed her. Clearly, along with shoes, Joanna expected her to buy thicker socks. Having made up her mind, Francesca didn't waste time arguing. She pulled them on and then allowed the salesman to help her into the boots that had caught her eye. They were lined and felt like a miracle on her feet. They actually fit and when she stood up in them and walked around the store, she had to resist making noises that might have sounded a bit on the *orgasmic* side. She was *so* taking the boots. She didn't even care that they cost more than every article of clothing that she owned put together.

"I'm going to wear them out of the store," she announced. "You can throw my old shoes away, socks and all."

Joanna laughed. "That's the spirit. A splurge is definitely in order."

Francesca pulled the money from the pocket of the coat and walked with the salesman and Joanna to the counter. Every single step was heaven. Keeping her hands below the counter, so the salesman wouldn't see, she counted out the bills. Most were hundreds. There were a few twenties and two tens. She knew the color left her face and her heart nearly stopped beating before it began pounding.

She caught Joanna's arm and dragged her away from the counter. "Oh. My. God. Joanna. There's over a thousand dollars here. I've been walking around with that kind of cash in the pocket of the coat. What was he thinking?"

Joanna gawked at her. "Are you sure?"

Francesca nodded slowly. "Positive. I counted twice." She glanced toward the counter. The salesman was watching them closely.

"Is something wrong?"

For the first time, Francesca glanced at his name tag. Mario Bandoni was totally into Joanna. Even though he was asking Francesca if something was wrong, he was looking at Joanna with a softness in his eyes.

"No," Joanna answered for them. She snatched two of the hundred dollar bills from Francesca. "We'll take a couple more pairs of socks as well."

"Joanna," Francesca protested.

Joanna ignored her and handed the money to Mario. He flashed her a grin, disregarding Francesca's protest as well.

"You going to write your phone number down?" he asked Joanna.

Francesca walked across the room to stare out into the gathering dusk. There were two men standing just off to one side of the store talking together. A couple walked by, the man glancing over his shoulder warily several times at the two men still talking. Francesca realized she'd never seen a hint of nervousness when she'd walked home from work the night before, or when she'd walked to the deli in the morning.

She wondered at a family who could protect their territory so well that the residents felt that safe, even in the middle of a city. Pulling Stefano's coat closer around her gave her a strange sense of security. It shouldn't. He was a terrifying man. She didn't understand why he would give her a thousand dollars so casually. He didn't know her. For all he knew she would go on a shopping spree at his expense. She knew, now that Joanna was aware how much cash she had, that Joanna would try to talk her into buying decent clothes. She'd probably insist they go to the club.

"Where are you two heading?" Mario asked.

"Petrov's Pizzeria" Joanna said. "I plan on impressing Francesca with the best pizza in the world, although I didn't make reservations. I'm counting on Tito letting us in. He always finds me a table."

"Best pizza ever." Mario flashed a grin at Joanna.

"We're also thinking about hitting the Ferraros' club this weekend," Joanna said. "I've got a go-to-the-front-of-the-line pass. Do you like to dance?"

He laughed at her. "Joanna, come on. Who was the king of dancing in school?"

She wrote down her number. "Call me. We'll set something up." Waving her hand, she pulled open the door and they went back outside. She leaned into Francesca. "I'm *so* going to get lucky. I've always crushed on Mario. *Always.* He's so sweet. And I have to tell you, the man can dance like no one's business."

"Only you can walk into a shoe store and come out with a date," Francesca observed. "You could in college and apparently you're still as hot as ever. I don't think the man could describe me even if someone asked him to. He had eyes only for you."

"That's not true."

Francesca laughed. "Don't deny it. You've always been a man magnet, at least as long as I've known you. I'll bet you were the prom queen."

"You know I was, so you can't bet on that," Joanna protested, pushing at Francesca.

A hand caught Francesca's coat from behind, whirled her

around and slammed her so hard against the wall the breath was knocked out of her. She felt the hot burn of something against her throat. A man held her tightly, one arm shoved against her chest, the other holding the edge of a knife to her throat. She knew he'd made a very shallow cut there because not only did it burn but she felt the trickle of blood.

She should have thought about dying, but all she could think about, rather hysterically, was that she couldn't get blood on Stefano's coat. He loved that coat. He'd made a big deal about her returning the coat. She should *never* have worn it anywhere. Joanna let out a shocked scream that was hastily cut off. Francesca could see a second man with his arm around her throat and a hand over her mouth.

"Give me the money, bitch, or you're dead," the man with the knife snapped at Francesca. "Right now. Give it to me."

She was going to owe Stefano a new cashmere overcoat that had to have cost what a car might, as well as over a thousand dollars. She had stupidly counted the money in front of the window of the store. She'd been so careful not to let Mario see the wad of cash, but she hadn't thought about the window.

She couldn't think what to do. She couldn't let him have the coat or the money. She couldn't get blood on the coat. She started to struggle, which was the absolute stupidest thing she could have done, but she was more afraid of owing Stefano Ferraro than of having the mugger slit her throat.

One moment her assailant had a knife against her neck and the next he was on the ground and the knife was in the hands of a big, burly man. Her savior looked furious. He wasn't alone, either. His companion, looking every bit as scary, held a gun on the other man. He'd gently pulled Joanna to one side and then put her behind him, away from their assailants.

The first man, the one who had removed the knife, handed Francesca a handkerchief. She pressed it against the cut.

"Are you all right?" he asked. He kept a foot on her

assailant's neck, not allowing him to get up off the sidewalk. He wasn't gentle about it, either. "I'm Emilio Gallo. That's my brother, Enzo."

Francesca pressed back against the building, very, very scared. No, terrified. This was her worst nightmare, to bring trouble to Joanna.

"We work for the Ferraro family," Emilio continued, obviously trying to reassure her. "Cousins. First cousins." He kept trying to soothe her, not realizing he was making it worse. "What were they after?"

The moment she heard who they worked for, Francesca tore the coat from her back and tried to shove it at Emilio. "Take it. Really. You have to take it. Take the coat to him."

Emilio didn't move. He stayed as still as a statue, one fist closed around the knife, the other hand down at his side. Both men stared at her as if she'd lost her mind.

Joanna moved cautiously around Enzo to put her arm around Francesca. "Honey, it was just a robbery. That's all. Put the coat back on. You're shaking like a leaf. Here, let me help you." She took the coat from Francesca and held it out for Francesca to slip her arms back in. "There, honey, that will keep you warm." Joanna smiled at their rescuers. "Do you want me to call 911 and report this?"

"You go along. Another team will pick you up so you'll be safe. Mr. Ferraro will want to speak to these gentlemen in person."

Emilio was soft-spoken, but Francesca wasn't fooled. The two men were in a lot more trouble than they would have been if the police were called. A dark town car pulled to the curb, and Enzo shoved one mugger inside before Emilio dragged the one up off the ground and shoved him in. Francesca found it significant that neither of the muggers was tied up, yet they didn't attempt to fight; instead, they looked very scared.

Francesca's gaze clung to Joanna's, but she spoke to Emilio. "You aren't going to kill them, are you?" She couldn't keep the quaver from her voice.

"Francesca," Joanna hissed.

Francesca forced herself to look at Emilio. "Are you?" She tilted her chin. She didn't have a cell phone to call the police with, but Joanna did and she'd use it if she had to.

"I have no intentions of killing them," Emilio said. "Mr. Ferraro will want to talk to them."

She didn't ask which Mr. Ferraro because she was fairly certain she knew. Keeping the handkerchief pressed to the shallow wound in her throat, she let Joanna lead her away.

"He said there was another team on us," Joanna whispered. "As in bodyguards. When Stefano said you were his to my uncle, I had no idea what he meant. He's serious. Bodyguards? More than one *team* of bodyguards? That and his brother coming into the store to talk to you? What is going on, Francesca?"

"I have no idea."

"What did he say to you when he took you outside? Did he ask you out?"

"No. Of course not. He didn't show that kind of interest," Francesca denied. She ignored the intense chemistry that had arced between them. She'd felt it, but she wasn't positive Stefano had. "He just seemed worried that I didn't have a coat or shoes. He told me to get myself something to eat."

"He gave you all that money. You could buy some decent clothes with it. Clearly that's what he wanted you to do." Joanna snapped her fingers. "We could get you a killer dress for the club and heels to match."

"We nearly got robbed and you're thinking of spending the money? I'm going to ask your uncle to put it in his safe along with this coat. I nearly died when that mugger made me bleed and I thought I might get blood on Stefano's favorite overcoat."

Joanna burst out laughing. "That's scary crazy and so are you, Francesca. Held at knifepoint and even cut, but you aren't worried about being robbed, just a coat."

"Not *just* a coat," Francesca denied, with a small grin,

finally finding humor in the situation. "Stefano Ferraro's *favorite* coat. And after that I was worried about them taking his money and trying to figure out how I'd pay that back. I was considering stripping for a living."

Joanna's laughter went from forced to genuine. "Stripping?"

"I had four years of pole dancing for exercise in college. I believe you did as well. We were pretty good."

"*You* were pretty good," Joanna corrected. "You're great at dancing, too. You can move your body in a million different ways all at once. I forgot how envious I always got when you were on a dance floor."

"Muscle control and core strength. If you hadn't cut half the classes for a date, you would have managed the advanced classes."

Joanna shrugged. "I was studying anatomy. What can I say? I got pretty good at that." She took Francesca's arm. "So what do you think? Should we go spend money at the mall? Get a killer dress and go out to the club this weekend?"

"No way. I'm *not* spending one more penny. In fact, if I make enough money to pay the rent before he comes looking for his coat, I'll pay him back for the shoes and he'll never know I used any of his money."

Joanna's eyebrows nearly shot into her hairline. "You are so stubborn, Francesca. If I had an opportunity like you have, protection from the Ferraro family, and a thousand dollars to spend, believe me, I'd be counting myself lucky, not resenting it."

Francesca sighed. "I guess I do sound resentful instead of thankful. It's just that . . ." She trailed off, looking around her. They were back in Ferraro territory. Whatever Stefano and his brothers were, the neighborhood felt different. Safe. She couldn't imagine the attack happening on their ground. She couldn't deny that she could feel that difference. She hadn't felt safe in a very long time. Without thinking too much about the why, she snuggled deeper into Stefano's warm coat. "He's so wealthy. Not a little bit well-off, everything about him screams money. I don't like that type. They live so differently than mere mortals like us."

Joanna flashed a grin. "You got that right. Jetting off around the world at a moment's notice. It's no wonder they forget what it's like to live from paycheck to paycheck."

"They don't forget," Francesca corrected. "They've just never had to do it."

CHAPTER THREE

The moment the wheels touched down on the runway in Los Angeles, Stefano unbuckled his seat belt and looked across the narrow aisle at his two brothers. "Is everything set?"

Ricco nodded. "The Lacey twins are meeting us and bringing a couple of friends. We'll party with them at the local hot spot and be very visible."

Stefano shook his head. "The Lacey twins? Again? Seriously, Ricco?"

"They're hot right now. The roles they get are prime and the paparazzi follow them everywhere. They're perfect. We'll be splashed all over every gossip rag there is. By tomorrow morning, the Internet will blow up with pictures and speculation."

"You want me to believe you chose them because they'll give you a lot of exposure?" Stefano pinned him with a glare. "You like fucking them both."

"Well." Ricco grinned at him. "There's that. It also gives me a chance to practice the art of Shibari. I like to keep my skills sharp."

"You like to fuck them after you tie them up, and that's going to come back to bite you in the ass," Stefano declared, his voice mild, but there was nothing mild about the look he gave his brother. "It isn't like the gossip is going to go away when the pictures and articles are everywhere. You can't exactly deny it. You find your woman and how are you going to convince her one woman will be enough for you when you're always with two?"

The smile faded from Ricco's face, leaving it bleak, a stone mask. "The chances of that happening are like one in a million. This woman coming into our territory is a fluke, Stefano. We all know that. More, you have a long road ahead of you. Nothing guarantees that she stays."

Stefano went still inside. He knew Ricco was right, and he was also wrong. Fate was strange—one moment giving no hope and the next handing the world to a man. Not the world—a glimpse of what might be. He sighed. Who was he to lecture his brother? He'd done a few crazy things, but not publicly, not so if he ever found a woman to call his own, he would be ashamed. Binding a woman to him, forcing her to accept his life, was going to be a difficult enough task, but he *would* do it. Now that he knew there was a possibility of having her, he would make it a reality. There was no other choice for him—or for her.

"You have a point," he conceded in a low voice. "It is your life, Ricco, and what you choose to do is for you to decide. Just know that if your woman does walk into your life, asking her to live with our name, within the rules of our family, is a big enough curse. What else do you have to offer her?"

Across from him, Vittorio stirred. "Are you certain this woman is one that you can bind to you?"

Vittorio. Always the peacemaker in the family. Stefano smiled at him. It wasn't an easy smile because Stefano, even with his own family members, rarely felt like smiling, but it was there all the same because Vittorio was such a good man. Stefano was always proud of him. They needed to hear how the miracle had happened. They knew, from watching other family members, that finding a shadow rider outside the family was a rare phenomenon and none of them had ever believed it would happen to them.

Stefano knew his brothers needed hope. Ricco especially. He was wild. Sometimes out-of-control wild. Not with the family business, of course. Then he was stone cold and all about business, but he took risks. Too many. He was the best driver in the family, and they were all good, but Ricco often *needed* the adrenaline rush of fast speeds just to keep him sane.

In another family, Ricco would have been an artist. In their family, creativity was only about the ability to find ways to carry out their work. Ricco had turned to the erotic form of Shibari to satisfy both his need for creating art as well as his sexual needs. He was darker than his brothers, and more prone to violence and chance taking, yet his work was impeccable.

Stefano sighed. His brothers needed to know there was hope. "I felt an electrical charge in the air and found it disturbing. I thought it was a bad thing, a premonition of something coming that our family would have to deal with. The need to stay there was so strong, I couldn't leave. Even knowing we had to be on a flight for work didn't matter. Nothing else mattered enough to make me leave."

Stefano didn't know why he admitted to his brothers how little control he had had when he should have gotten into his car and driven straight to the airport, but he knew he had to tell the truth. To be precise about the facts. It was important.

"I was standing by my car, out in the street by the driver's-side door. If I had ignored that compulsion to stay, I would have gotten in, driven away and I would never have seen her." That needed to be said. His brothers had to stay alert. Be aware.

"There's a tradition in our family," Vittorio said. "When the first arrives, the others will follow."

"It didn't happen for our cousins in London," Ricco said. "None of them married or had children. Nor did the ones in Sicily."

Stefano kept going. He could give them this. A moment in his life he knew he would never forget. He would share what he considered a private, perfect, almost frightening moment. "I heard her voice first. She responded to something Joanna Masci said to her. That note in her voice turned the key, unlocking something deep inside of me. I *felt* it like a terrible wrenching inside. Everything in me reached for her. For that note she left hanging in the air. I heard the music in me answer."

He fell silent a moment, reliving that moment in time that had changed everything in his world. His heart had pounded in his chest. Hard. So hard it actually hurt. Physically hurt. He could go into a room full of enemies and his heart rate never once elevated, yet hearing that musical note in the air had acted like a key, unlocking a matching note in his body and throwing his iron composure.

"It wasn't snowing, but it was icy cold. The ground was wet and covered in puddles. Time seemed to slow down, but I was aware of everything, yet only her. I saw and recognized who and what she was by her shadow—by the tubes connecting her to everything. Every step she took, I could feel the channels opening everywhere until she took the one step that finally connected us."

His fingers closed, one by one, into a tight fist, as if he could hold her to him. He'd had a primitive desire to throw her over his shoulder and carry her to a dungeon, one with a lock so she could never escape. He couldn't give them that moment, that connection when they joined. That was for him alone. That was private. The jolt was intense. Sexual. His body had reacted, his cock hard and urgently full. Everything protective and primal in him had risen to meet her. To claim what he knew absolutely was his.

"She was freezing. I could feel how cold she was. How hungry."

His throat closed on him. His heart had stuttered in his chest. His woman. The woman who would end the gnawing loneliness. End the hunger for a family of his own. He was a force to be reckoned with. The world he lived in was dark and violent. Unrelenting and unforgiving. He protected the weak. He brought justice to those above justice. One word. One phone call. Life or death. He *protected* everyone. Yet his woman was freezing. Hungry. In the cold and wet of

Chicago. Alone. Unprotected. And she was scared. *In Ferraro territory.* When their shadows had reached for each other, he felt that as well. Her terrible fear.

He swore under his breath. Hating that moment. Feeling a failure. He would have to leave her there, out in the cold. Alone. Afraid. He'd felt helpless for the first time in his life. He'd started training, like those before him, at the age of two. He'd been trained to believe he was powerful. Strong. Intelligent. He moved where others couldn't, in a world of shadows. Silent. Deadly. Invincible. *His woman was cold and hungry.* What good was his training? What good was he?

"I did what I could, but she's in trouble."

"Giovanni won't let anything happen to her," Ricco soothed. "He'll watch over her until this is done. She's yours, Stefano, but she's ours as well. She belongs to all of us. You put teams on her. Nothing will happen to her. Let's just get this done and you can get back to her."

Stefano looked at his brothers. "I stood there, holding her against the wall, wrapping her up in my coat, the only thing I had to protect her with, to tell the world she was mine and I would hunt down anyone who harmed or attempted to harm her. I looked down at her and knew she is everything I'm not. She deserves a better life than the one I can give her."

That moment was etched in his mind forever. Burned there. She'd been frightened of him. He couldn't blame her, but still, he detested that look. At the same time, touching her skin, feeling the silk of her hair . . . Just that. It was all it took to wipe out every ugly thing in his life and give him something beautiful. He hadn't known beauty really existed until that moment. "She deserves better," he reiterated aloud.

The air stilled. No one breathed. Ricco exchanged a long look with Vittorio.

"What are you saying?" Vittorio asked, his voice gentle. "Stefano, you can't walk away from her. You can't do that."

"No. I can't." Pure regret. No remorse, but definitely regret. "I'm not that good or that strong of a man to let her go. She's mine. I take what's mine. She doesn't know it.

Doesn't want it. Doesn't want me or anything to do with me." A trace of amusement crept in. "She deserves better, but she'll be with me and no one else."

"We're hunters," Ricco said. "She doesn't stand a chance."

"No, she doesn't," Stefano agreed. "Let's get this done. You two be visible. The light's right outside. Ricco, go out first. I'll slide into the shadow of the doorway just behind you, and Vittorio can follow you out." He glanced at his watch. "If I get the signal to go, I'll do the job. Make certain you get your pictures taken and you're on the security footage of as many cameras as possible."

Ricco and Vittorio had boarded the plane in Chicago, playing their parts of bored playboys with too much money and time on their hands. They'd raced their cars through the streets to get to the airport to their private hangar, where their jet was already fueled and ready. A couple of paparazzi had followed them, snapping pictures, just as the brothers had intended.

Stefano arrived by helicopter and strode over to them, intercepting them before they could board the plane. They'd appeared to argue long enough to have several pictures of them taken, the big brother giving his younger brothers a lecture. He'd stalked away, shaking his head, back toward the helicopter. Except he hadn't been the one to go back to the helicopter. For one split second, Ricco and Vittorio had blocked views of Stefano and he'd entered the shadow and his brother Taviano had emerged, dressed exactly as Stefano was dressed. He shoved his dark glasses over his eyes and stalked back to the helicopter while Stefano used the shadows to board the plane.

Always, always, they had alibis. There was never a connection between them and the target. Nothing personal. Still, they lived in that world. Violence. Blood. Death. It was their world. Ricco and Vittorio were seen in public coming and going to the airport. They would be in the clubs all night, openly partying with a couple of movie stars and their friends. As far as anyone knew, no one else had flown with them and they were in Los Angeles to have fun.

Stefano had to shut out all thoughts of Francesca Capello and get the job done. Ricco stood, then Vittorio. Stefano last. Ricco put his hand out. Vittorio put his on top, and Stefano covered both hands with his. They never said anything. There was nothing to say. They just touched. Letting one another know without words they were a unit. A family. They had one another's backs. They loved.

Ricco went first, the door opening, throwing the shadows into stark relief. Stefano felt the pull of each of the shadow tubes. Openings he could slide through. The pull was strong on his body, dragging at him like powerful magnets, the sensation uncomfortable, but familiar. Stefano was one of the more powerful riders. Even small shadows drew him, pulling his body apart until he was streaming through light and dark to his destination.

He carried little equipment with him. Light. That was more essential than any weapon. *He* was the weapon. His body. His mind. Sometimes he thought his very soul. Weapons weren't as necessary as a light source. If there were no shadows, he could make his own.

He stepped into the opening of the largest shadow. He would move from one to the next, never seen, going to his destination. He knew he'd need most of the night for traveling, but he had the coordinates and he could find his way unerringly, even in cities he'd never been to.

It was always cool in the shadows. He moved fast, sliding, a rider of the shadows, slipping through the city unseen. In contrast, Ricco and Vittorio entered the latest hot spot, a club catering to the very wealthy. The music was loud and pounding. The lights dazzling. They wore their three-piece suits. The Ferraro family always, always, dressed for any occasion. They were famous for the look. The gray suits with the darker pinstripe, or the darker suit with the lighter pinstripe. Either a dark gray shirt or a lighter one with a tie just the opposite of the shirt.

On Ricco's arms were the Lacey twins. They snuggled close to him, their blond hair falling over his arms, their slender bodies pressed close to his sides. They stayed that way all night, the three of them blatantly dancing together, Ricco sandwiched between the two women. They moved against him seductively, suggestively. As the night wore on and the beat pounded, the liquor flowed and his hands were all over both of them.

All three of them knew the paparazzi had managed to sneak in. The twins liked the publicity and being seen with a wealthy Ferraro. They didn't mind if they were secretly photographed, not even later when the three retired to the twins' home and swam naked together in the covered pool or even later still, in the hot tub on the open deck, where a zoom lens could find them.

Ricco always practiced his art of erotic tying away from the camera. Still, the twins talked about how sexy and sensual it was to their friends, who then repeated everything to the paparazzi. Still, no photographer had ever actually gotten a picture of Ricco using the art of Shibari on a woman.

Vittorio was much more discreet. He danced with the Lacey twins' friend, another up-and-coming actress. She was quieter than the twins, but no less willing to be seen. If anything, she was even hungrier for publicity. There were no innocents in their business, and the brothers made certain of that. They didn't romance women. They had their fun, made certain the women they fucked had fun as well, but they didn't date. They didn't make promises. They never, never, took advantage of a woman who didn't know the score or the game.

There were rules. Lots of rules. They lived them to the letter, never deviating. The brothers were highly sexual and they had no compunction about finding women who were more than willing to see to those needs in return for the same, but there were never emotional entanglements. Any woman who looked as if she might be getting ideas, or real feelings toward them, was dropped instantly.

Stefano had more than his share of women. He'd been careful though, mindful of the fact that what was put on the Internet or in magazines never went away. Any indiscretion could be brought back at any moment. He didn't mind the press printing the truth—that the brothers went through women, that the women were wealthy celebrities or heiresses and that they all partied hard. The brothers and their sister provided alibis for one another. Always. It didn't matter what city, or which state— no job could ever be traced back to them, and though they didn't know it, the paparazzi aided them with those alibis.

Stefano found himself in a residential area, outside the home of his target. The neighborhood was a good one. The home was large, perhaps a good six thousand square feet. Well kept. The yard maintained. Edgar Sullivan resided there. In his community he was known as a hardworking man. An upstanding man. A pillar in his church. He had a wife and two daughters. Few people ever noticed that the women in his home had little to say. Rarely smiled. Jumped in fear if spoken to and looked to him before they answered the simplest questions.

Edgar ruled his family with an iron fist. He did the same with the prostitutes he frequently hired. He was warned repeatedly that the beatings and damage he was doing wouldn't be tolerated, but so far, the pimp had been unable to protect his women. At first the money Edgar had paid for the damages to the women had been enough to keep the pimp quiet, but after a while Edgar's urges couldn't be controlled at all, nor did he bother to try. The pimp had taken his money and Edgar expected him to continue to do so. Two women had been hospitalized. They knew better than to talk, but the pimp had had enough. There was no way for him to get to Sullivan, not without the law finding out. So he'd appealed to the Ferraro family for aid.

Anyone could make the appeal for a meeting. All meetings were conducted in person. Stefano's parents took those meetings. They chatted casually with a potential client. That was always necessary. Every person had a natural rhythm. Patterns of breathing. Of speaking. Heartbeats. Inflections in their voices. That casual conversation allowed the "greeters" to establish those patterns. From there they could almost always detect lies.

Essentially, "greeters" in the Ferraro family were people born as human lie detectors. That was their psychic gift. They listened to the petition for aid, but that was all. No promises. Just listening. If an undercover cop tried to infiltrate their organization, he couldn't fault the greeter for simply listening. Greeters never responded with any kind of commitment. They mostly remained silent through the entire interview. Once they got the casual conversation out of the way and established the pattern of truth, the greeters simply asked their potential clients to explain why they'd come. Former Shadow Riders often took jobs as greeters when they retired because all were born with the ability to detect lies.

Stefano wouldn't be standing outside of Edgar Sullivan's home now if the greeters hadn't passed on their client to the investigators. Stefano's family had two teams of investigators. His aunt and uncle formed one team, and his cousins, both men, formed the second team. It was the first team's job to find out every possible fact about the client. It was the second team's job to find out every fact about the crime. Both teams worked carefully and quietly. They wouldn't have the job unless, like the greeters, they were human lie detectors, and their voices could also influence others to talk, to open up and tell them anything they wanted to know. To be an investigator, they had to be a family member and also have both specific psychic gifts.

Stefano studied the shadows surrounding the Sullivan home. Lights were on in three rooms on the second floor. Stefano called up a blueprint of the house from his mind. He'd studied the house plans from the data the investigators had turned in. He read every scrap of information provided on both the client and the target.

Greeters, investigators and the shadow rider had to all agree before the job was taken. To do that, the shadow rider needed to know every fact about both parties, where they lived and who lived with them. Their routines, their friends. *Everything.* A shadow rider had to be able to slide through the portals, have a photographic memory and enough energy to disrupt electrical devices should there be need.

Stefano slid his burner phone out of his pocket. This was one of the very few times he would be vulnerable. He had to be out of the shadow's portal to make the call. That meant, if he didn't blend perfectly with the shadow, anyone could spot him. Like his brothers, he wore the signature three-piece suit—gray, pin-striped, the stripes giving the light-and-dark effect needed. At any given time, they were ready to enter a portal if necessary. The suit was synonymous with the Ferraro name, but it served a vital purpose.

He punched in the numbers and didn't give a greeting when the line was opened. "Do we have a go? Am in ready position." It was necessary to triple-check everything. The investigators continued to work even after they were certain. No one wanted a mistake. They also didn't do the work, if money was involved, until the client complied and paid.

The money would be deposited first into one of their offshore accounts. Once the money was there, it would be layered through several banking institutions the Ferraro family owned or had interest in, through several countries until the source was impossible to trace. The money came back to them through legitimate businesses the family owned. The family had managed their way for the last couple of centuries, the businesses growing along with their bank accounts.

Even now, with Stefano in place and his brothers partying it up, the transaction could be called off. He waited, uncaring of the outcome. It was a job, nothing more. He was good at what he did, but he could walk away easily if it came to that. The money had to be deposited before the job would be done. The investigators had to be completely satisfied that justice had to be served. No life could be taken lightly.

"It is a go."

There it was. He immediately slid back into the shadows. The phone would be broken and placed in a trash can at the other side of town, somewhere near the airport. He wore thin gray gloves, of course, never risking a print.

He studied the network of shadows and the tubes they provided. The pull was strong enough that his chest felt as if it were flying apart, his insides coming out. It was an uncomfortable sensation and one that he'd never gotten used to, no matter how many times he'd done this over the years.

Instinctively he chose the longer, narrower shadow, the one that led up onto the back porch and under the door. Inside, a faint light was on over the stove. He could use the shadows cast along the floor to find his next ride. The wrenching in his body was hard as the ride took him fast, nearly throwing him out of the portal and onto the kitchen floor. He stopped his forward momentum and took a moment to breathe and get his bearings. The narrow tunnels were always a difficult traveling experience because they acted like a slide, the body moving at such tremendous speeds. The strips of light and dark were fused closer together, providing a kind of rail that felt like greased lightning. He preferred the larger, darker shadows, and a slower, but more sustainable ride.

He stood very still just inside the tube, listening to the rhythm of the household. Every house sounded and felt different. Outside, chimes blew a soft melody into the night. A few insects made their presence known. Inside the house, it was eerily silent. The two daughters were teenagers and yet there was no television, no music. Just silence. He kept listening. Eventually, someone would make a noise. It was late, but he knew from the lights in the three rooms, that at least those rooms were occupied with someone awake.

A board creaked overhead. That would be in the smallest room upstairs. That one had a soft glowing light, as if a lamp rather than an overhead fixture illuminated the space. The footsteps were very light. The girls then. Not their bedroom, but the little room they used as a library.

He studied the shadows spreading out from the pale light source over the stove. Most were too short for what he needed, but two tubes went off in different directions.

Stefano chose the one that reached toward the darkened hallway. It ended just by the stairs in the family room. Another portal took him up the stairs and beneath the door of the library, where Edgar's daughters were.

He expected them to be quietly reading. They weren't. One lay on a short couch, her face distorted with swelling. The other girl leaned over her, pushing back her hair with gentle fingers and applying ice. Neither made a sound. Silent tears tracked down both faces, but not a single sob escaped. He stood just inside the portal, waiting to get the ice back in his veins. Deliberately he flexed his fingers, keeping from rolling them into a tight fist. He'd seen countless such things, most much worse. He wouldn't be standing in the house if there weren't a good reason. He could only put down his unexpected reaction to the fact that his woman's shadow had touched his and made him more susceptible to emotion. He couldn't have that—not while he worked.

He found the place in him that was dead—a place inside that could look at two young girls and feel nothing at all. He needed that, needed balance. He didn't try to comfort them, or soothe away those hurts. He wasn't there to do that. He was there to make certain it didn't ever happen again. Warm feelings weren't wanted or needed. Only ice. Only dead space that couldn't ever be filled because that was what allowed him to retreat to the other side of the door and find the slide to the room where he was certain Edgar Sullivan sat behind his desk, feeling powerful now that he'd beat up his thirteen-year-old daughter.

The slide took him under the office door. It was a plush room. The furniture was good leather. Sullivan sat drinking whiskey out of a cut-crystal glass. It wasn't good whiskey, Stefano noted, but then Sullivan probably didn't care about the actual taste. His hand, wrapped around the glass, dripped blood from scraped knuckles. He looked over papers and muttered to himself, clearly not happy with whatever report he was reading.

The shadow tubes radiated through the room in a starburst pattern. The light overhead, as well as the lamp on the desk, threw shadows all over the floors, and more climbed up the walls. Two went directly behind Sullivan. Stefano chose the larger of the two and rode it through the room, past the desk, between the chair and the wall until he stood behind the man. He stepped out of the portal and caught Edgar's head in his hands.

"Justice is served," he whispered softly and wrenched hard. He heard the crack, but still he waited, making certain.

He dropped the body back into the chair and slid back into the portal. In a matter of minutes he was riding the shadows back outside the house. Only then did he emerge from the slide in order to make a call.

"It's done." He ended the call and was once again inside the portal, riding toward the airport.

His brothers would be apprised of the status of the job. Stefano would sleep on the plane and they would continue with their outrageous behavior, following through until they could safely get back to the plane and all three could return home.

Franco Mancini waited for him. The door to the plane was open, Franco inside, lying on one of the beds. He sat up the moment Stefano entered, his eyes moving over his cousin to ensure he was unharmed.

"Quiet tonight," he informed Stefano. "I haven't heard from your brothers."

"Don't expect to. Vittorio might show up around four or five, but Ricco is with the Lacey twins again. He'll be wallowing in his rope art and sex." Stefano didn't bother to keep the worry out of his voice. Ricco walked the edge of control lately and nothing his brother had said to him seemed to rein him in.

Franco was silent a moment as Stefano removed his shoes and sank down into a plush seat. Franco poured him a drink and handed it to him. "Ricco is careful. Always. I know he seems reckless, Stefano, but he's never failed to do his job. He's quick and clean and never has a high afterward."

Stefano sighed, pressing the glass of Scotch to his forehead. It was true. Ricco, when sent on a job, performed like the well-developed weapon he was. He didn't hesitate, and he certainly didn't fuck around. He got the job done. It wasn't about Ricco's work. It was about the way he played. *That* bordered on out of control.

Stefano couldn't help but worry. He knew what it was like to live in a world of unrelenting violence with no way out. They'd been born shadow riders. They'd been trained for one thing from the time they were toddlers. There was nothing else for them, and there wouldn't be until they were too old to ride the shadows and perform their duties. They would be regulated to other jobs within the family. There was no way out for any of them.

"Stefano," Franco said, his tone clearly reluctant.

Stefano looked up quickly, his gaze moving over his cousin's face, recognizing that something was wrong and he wasn't going to like it. "Tell me."

"Emilio reported in." Franco deliberately poured himself a cup of coffee.

Stefano's heart nearly stopped. For a moment he could barely breathe. "You're stalling for time," Stefano accused. "Fucking just tell me." He could hear his heart pound. His mouth had gone dry. "Did something happen to Francesca?"

Franco winced. Stefano's tone cut like a whip. He nodded. "Emilio and Enzo took care of it, but she left our territory to go shopping with Joanna. They ran into a couple of punk-ass robbers and one held a knife to her throat. Emilio said he drew blood."

There was silence. The air vibrated with fury. Heated. Intense. "Are you fucking kidding me?" Stefano spat. "I had two teams on her. *Two.* Giovanni was supposed to be keeping an eye on her as well, and someone *cuts* her with a knife? What the hell? I thought I spelled out for them just who she is. What she is. Who she belongs to."

"They know, Stefano," Franco said, his voice low. "They protected her. She isn't really hurt."

"You just told me some fucking robber held my woman up at knifepoint and drew her blood." Stefano could taste his own fury. He had never been so enraged in his life. "Emilio had better have that fucker locked up and waiting for me."

"He does," Franco assured.

"Did Emilio take Francesca to a hospital?"

"It was a shallow cut."

"He doesn't know where that knife has been or even if the blade is clean, which it probably isn't. She could get an infection. How the hell did it happen on his watch?"

"Stefano, you told Emilio to hang back, not to get caught," Franco reminded. "The moment they realized she was in trouble, they shut that shit down."

"But not before she got cut. Where? Where did he cut her?"

Franco took a sip of the hot coffee, wishing he were anywhere but inside the aircraft. Danger shimmered in the air. It was stifling hot. Stefano could explode into violence in a heartbeat and when he did, it was always deadly.

"Her throat. But it was shallow, Stefano, barely there."

Stefano erupted into cursing. Franco poured more Scotch into his cousin's glass. Every member of the Ferraro family had their job to do. Always they lived for the good of the family. The shadow riders were absolutely necessary to the family's livelihood. They were rare, and when a couple could produce them, they were encouraged to have several children. Stefano never treated any family member as less than he was, but he was always in charge. *Always.*

The shadow riders kept the family's enemies from attacking them. No one outside the family knew just how Stefano and his brothers carried out their lethal work and because there were other branches of the family in other cities that also had a reputation for cleaning up messes, no one ever dared openly come after them.

In the underworld, where crime was a daily occurrence and enemies thrived on violence, no one ever dared to touch any member of the Ferraro family. Not gangs, not crime lords, not their bitterest enemy, the one they had a long-standing feud with dating back to the early 1900s in Sicily.

The Saldis had been the deadliest family in Sicily, and

they soon realized that people went to the Ferraro family for aid against them. They had demanded the Ferraros join forces with them, and when their invitation was refused, they sent their soldiers to wipe out every man, woman and child in the family. Only a few escaped and went underground. Those who had managed to escape had been mainly shadow riders, and they vowed such a thing would never happen to any family member again.

Stefano was a throwback to those first men and women fighting so hard to keep their family alive. Maybe all the shadow riders were like him, with a will of iron and the guts to fight against impossible odds. That made them both dangerous and extraordinary.

"Stefano, she's all right," Franco reiterated. "We'll get you back as soon as possible and you'll be able to see for yourself."

Stefano couldn't break the rules and call Emilio directly. He was supposed to be in Chicago, not Los Angeles. Even for his own peace of mind over Francesca, he wouldn't take a chance. The rules had kept them all alive and away from law enforcement. Those guidelines were in place for a reason.

Most people believed they were mafia, members of organized crime. Many, many times, they had been investigated, but of course nothing could ever be found. No matter how many times the businesses were looked at, the Ferraro books were in order. They had never had an indictment against them.

Three times, undercover cops had managed to infiltrate deep enough to gain an audience with the greeters. All three times, the greeters had known they were being lied to and played their part beautifully, acting as if they had no idea what was being asked of them, suddenly realizing and immediately acting shocked, horrified and outraged. Each time the undercover cop had been sent on his way.

"There's no point in trying to call Ricco and Vittorio back early," Stefano said, a resigned sigh slipping out. "Francesca had better be all right, Franco, or Emilio and Enzo will be answering to me."

Franco sent him a faint grin. "Emilio and Enzo already know they're going to be answering to you. They aren't looking forward to it, but they expect it."

"I'm not that bad," Stefano lied. His eyes met his cousin's and he found himself smiling ruefully. "Okay, maybe I am."

He was silent a moment. "Did Emilio say what she was shopping for?" He was inexplicably pleased that she was using his money. He hadn't thought she would. He'd worried she would hand it all to Dina and the homeless woman would kill herself with alcohol poisoning.

"I believe it was shoes," Franco said.

Stefano nodded. Francesca needed a good pair of shoes—several of them, but he couldn't exactly buy her a new wardrobe right away. He'd had a hard enough time forcing his coat and the money on her. He had to be patient. In the same way he prepared for a job, he had to formulate a plan of attack. He was in for the greatest fight of his life, and he had to win. There was no other option.

"I'm thankful to Dina. She had a coat last week, and you know how she is, Franco: she loses one every month. *Grazie Dio.* I love that Francesca gave Dina her coat." He took another sip of Scotch. He especially loved knowing that Francesca was wrapped in his coat.

CHAPTER FOUR

Stefano stood very still, looking into the window of Masci's. Francesca was at the counter, smiling at old man Lozzi. She looked beautiful—and alive. Real. Not the fantasy he'd feared he'd made up in his mind. The tension, coiled so tightly in his gut, eased just a little. He had needed to see for himself that she was unharmed. The glass was tinted and he couldn't see details, but she moved easily. She was friendly, but she didn't actually engage in informative chatter.

"Satisfied?" Giovanni asked.

"Not yet." Stefano turned to face his brother, his features set and hard. "Let's go home. I want to see those fuckers and find out what the hell they thought they were doing."

Giovanni slid back behind the wheel of their Aston Martin while Stefano climbed in on the passenger side. Both were used to high-performance luxury and neither noticed the smooth, purring ride as the car glided from the curb and into traffic.

"Emilio said it's the same three-man crew we've been hunting again. We only have two of them. The third is in the wind, or maybe he wasn't there that night."

Stefano didn't reply. Instead, he stared out the window, his gut churning. They could have killed her. The three muggers were notorious for their violence and it was escalating with every robbery they committed. Vittorio had "talked" with two of them once already when they'd mugged a woman in their territory. He'd gotten her money back from them and made them pay for her injuries. He'd also extracted a promise that no member of the Ferraro community would ever be targeted. That was their one chance. The only chance.

"Are we looking for the other one, Gee?" Stefano asked, still staring out the window at the passing buildings. He loved their small village within the city. He loved the people there. Some he'd known almost from the first breath he'd taken. Others had moved in later, but he considered them all his. Under his protection.

"We're looking, but so far, nothing. They've been living off the grid so there's no trail at all. The last place they stayed was an abandoned building about three miles outside of Little Italy. We think the third one drives for them and is named Scott Bowen. He wasn't in the abandoned building. He must have gotten the hell out when he realized it was our family that took his friends. He was either there the night they mugged Francesca or he heard word on the street. But whatever the reason, he's gone."

The gates opened and the car slid up the private drive to their sprawling home. The moment they exited the car, Henry, their valet, was there to take the car keys. Both men moved away from the house, selected a shadow and made the ride to the warehouse owned by their family in the very heart of the city, far from their territory. They didn't want a camera at a stoplight to accidentally catch their car moving through the city.

Stefano jerked open the door and strode through the cavernous space. The smell of blood and fear hit him first. That didn't surprise him. Emilio and Enzo weren't known for their kindness to anyone who beat up women. They hadn't wanted Vittorio to allow the two muggers to walk away when they'd first encountered them. Technically, the two men hadn't crossed into Ferraro territory, but even if they had no idea Francesca belonged to Stefano, they had to know Joanna did, or they were just plain stupid, coming that close to Ferraro territory.

Tom Billings and Fargo Johnson stared up at him through

swollen bloodshot eyes. Emilio had done a number on both of them. Terror entered their eyes when they saw who had walked in. Stefano stood in front of them, but didn't say a word. He merely reached for the file Enzo handed him. Seeing the thick papers, the two men looked at each other and instantly began fighting the ropes binding them. Stefano wasn't worried they'd get free. Emilio had mad skills when it came to tying knots. He didn't match Ricco's skill, but what he tied up stayed that way.

His cousins had been busy, detailing the muggers' long history of crimes. Stefano took his time reading. He didn't skim. When he was deciding someone's fate, it was only fair to explore every detail, even when the men had put a knife to his woman's throat. He couldn't let it be personal, but he found it was. No matter how hard he tried to think clearly, he knew he couldn't make the decision on what would happen to the two muggers.

"Send for Vittorio and Ricco," he told Giovanni. "Have them drop whatever they're doing and come immediately. Ask Taviano and Emmanuelle to come as well." Giovanni nodded and took the file Stefano handed him. "All of you read that. I'll stand down from this one and you four make the decision. If there's an even split, have Eloisa cast the deciding vote."

"Stefano . . ." Giovanni protested. "You have the right. She's your woman."

"No way am I touching this one. Not when I want to rip their dicks off and shove them down their throats."

Both muggers froze. Billings swallowed hard, shaking his head. "We didn't know who she was, Mr. Ferraro."

The knots in Stefano's belly only coiled tighter. His breath hissed out of him. There was no way to suppress the rage roaring through him. "It shouldn't matter who the fuck she is, you coward. You don't put a knife to *any* woman's throat. It was just your bad luck that you chose her, but had I heard you did this to any woman again, I would have come after you. Vittorio let you off with a warning and you should have left the city or at least gone to the other side of it and stayed as far from us as you could get."

He wanted to beat the holy hell out of both men, even though Emilio had already done it. There would have been great satisfaction in feeling his fists sinking into them, breaking bones and causing as much damage as possible, but that was against his rules. He lived in a violent world and he had to have a code. He had to live by that code, no matter how personal this was to him.

Not trusting himself, he stepped back, away from them. He would abide by the decision of his family. They had all the facts and as far as he could see, these men had spent years robbing and viciously beating others. Stefano knew that when a person was hungry or desperate, they might resort to theft, but these men had escalated what they did into savage beatings. Ninety percent of their victims had handed over wallets, money and jewelry and yet they still were beaten. Even had they not touched Francesca, Stefano would have decided to end them.

According to the files his investigators Romano and Renato Greco had compiled, the beatings had gotten steadily more vicious over the years and the last few months, the men had put several people in the hospital, two of them with severe knife wounds. Clearly, the violence was escalating and Stefano believed, sooner or later, they would kill. The thrill was getting harder to get, so they upped the ante. He was certain once they killed, they would continue to do so.

Ricco, Giovanni, Taviano and Emmanuelle walked over together and stood facing the two muggers after they'd consulted just inside the doors of the building. Vittorio came right up to stand beside Stefano. "This is my mistake, my mess. I let them off with a warning," he said softly.

Billings shook his head hard. "We'll stay away. Leave town. Whatever you want us to do."

Vittorio looked at him for a long while, the silence stretching out. "I should have ended you when I had the chance," he said, no inflection in his voice. "It's on me, the other victims. The ones you hurt. The ones in the hospital. It's on me that you put a blade to my brother's woman's throat. You cut into her skin and made her bleed. That's mine. I have to carry that burden for the rest of my life because I didn't do my job."

Tom Billings screamed, his voice high-pitched. Behind him, a shadow stretched out. Reached. Ricco, dressed as always in a dark pin-striped suit, just as they all were, emerged directly behind him, his hands on either side of his skull. Vittorio leaned forward and caught Fargo Johnson's head in an implacable grip. Both men jerked hard. They'd been instructed practically since birth in this quick, hard motion. They were experts. Few people could snap a neck easily, but they knew the exact motion, the exact amount of power needed, the perfect angle.

Both men stepped away from the two muggers. "Justice is served," Vittorio said.

Stefano took a deep breath and let it out. He had managed to maintain control even when it was the most personal job he had faced. Discipline had won out, although the anger still knotted his gut. Francesca had been cold and hungry when he'd first laid eyes on her. And terrified. Now a man had managed to slice into her throat and scare her, trying to rob her. The one person needing his protection the most and he'd let her down again.

"Hey, brother." Emmanuelle curled an arm around his waist, tucked herself in close against his side and hugged him tightly the way she had from the time she was a toddler. "I'm so excited for you. We all are." She didn't even glance at the two dead men slumped in the chairs.

Stefano didn't like her being there. He wrapped his arm around her and walked her back outside. From the beginning, when Emmanuelle had been born, he had known she would be trained. She was a shadow rider as well. The telltale feelers fed out of her shadow, seeking the shadows of others. He hadn't liked it then—and he'd been a young boy, nine years old, when she'd been born. He had tried protesting, as had his other brothers, hoping to spare her their life, but there were so few of the riders anymore that the family insisted she be trained.

Emmanuelle knew what he was doing, taking her out of that place of death, but she didn't protest. All of her brothers preferred to protect her. They had been raised to respect women. To treasure them. To protect them. They wanted her to have a life like all the other girls in the neighborhood, not one of violence and death. She had grown up with four big brothers always hovering close and she'd never protested or gotten angry with them. Instead, she'd developed a sense of humor and, much to their mortification, the ability to ignore them and do what she wanted anyway.

"I want to meet her."

"You will, *bella bambina*, as soon as I have managed to make her mine. She has no idea. I have to go carefully."

Her dark blue eyes moved over his face, the smile fading. "I want to help. I know this is going to be difficult for both of you, Stefano, but she will be my sister. She will make my brother very happy. She gives my other brothers and me hope. Surely, if she's new to our neighborhood, she needs a friend. I can do that."

Stefano thought it over. Francesca only knew Joanna. He nodded slowly. "Her friend, Joanna Masci, asked her to come here to work for her uncle. Francesca is in some kind of trouble."

Emmanuelle nodded. "Renato and Romano are working on finding out everything they can about her. Zia Rachele and Zio Alfeo are helping. I think they even have Rosina and Rigina helping. The entire Greco family."

His aunt and uncle and their children were all investigators— and good ones. Powerful ones. Rosina worked with Renato and Romano most of the time, using the computer as a rule, and Rigina helped her parents doing the same thing. If they were looking into Francesca's past, he had no doubt they would uncover her every secret. For a moment he actually thought to stop them. It was insane, but if she had something to hide, maybe it was best for him to find out before anyone else. She wouldn't like her privacy torn apart in front of his entire family.

"Stefano," Emmanuelle said softly. "We all want to help you. She's ours as well as yours. When she comes into *la famiglia*, she becomes our sister. A daughter to our parents. She has to fully embrace our life, be one of us. You know that. Let us all help you in whatever capacity we can. Give us that. You always take care of us. We've always counted on your strength and guidance. This time, let us be there for you."

He looked around him. His brothers faced him in a loose semicircle. Ricco, Vittorio, Giovanni and Taviano. His cousins, Emilio and Enzo, stood shoulder to shoulder with his brothers. *La sua famiglia*. His family. He put his hand over his heart, pressing his palm deep into his chest.

"Grazie." He meant it. Sincerely. His heart aching and full. He tightened his arm around his sister. "Perhaps you and the cousins could befriend Francesca and Joanna and do a few things with them. Put her at ease and make her feel as if she's putting down a few roots. My schedule's fairly heavy. If a couple of you could lighten my load"—he looked at his brothers—"I would greatly appreciate the time to try to work things out with her."

"Of course," Ricco answered immediately. "We'll divide your jobs between us for the next few weeks."

"And we'll keep our eyes on her," Emilio said. "This time, much closer. She already knows you put a couple of teams on her so there's no use in hiding."

"We could coach you," Emmanuelle ventured. "In what *not* to do."

He looked down at her upturned face. "I don't know if I want to ask you what the fuck that means."

"It means you can't act all scary, like you do. I'm used to it so you don't intimidate me . . ." She cleared her throat. *"Much.* But that's my point. You can't scare her off while we're all trying to work on her."

"You think I'm going to scare her off, then your job is to make her see me as a good guy, the white knight."

Laughter broke out, his brothers first. He was fairly certain Ricco started it. Emilio and Enzo joined in and lastly,

Emmanuelle. The warm, fuzzy feeling in his heart disappeared and he glared at them. "Seriously?"

"No one is going to look at you that way," Vittorio said. "You were born with that face and you came out of the womb as mean and bossy as a snake shedding his skin."

He couldn't deny the charge because it was probably true. "Fuck off. All of you." He turned to Emilio. "Call Zio Sal and tell him we need his cleaning service immediately. Tell him to bring clothes and shoes for Enzo and you. You know the drill—everything goes. Anything that can be traced back to you. Get rid of all of it. Give it to Zio Sal and let him and his boys do their thing. I want you showered and shaved, looking good and back out on the street where you're visible."

Emilio nodded. "Will do. You all need to be away from here."

His brothers and Emmanuelle turned toward the shadows to make their way back home. Stefano was anxious to go to Francesca, but it took a while to make his report to his parents—well, to his mother—his father never actually was there to hear a report, a necessary evil. He believed it was necessary just so Eloisa could look her child over and make certain no harm had come to him.

He drove from the main home where his parents resided to the hotel where he stayed and then walked from there to the store where Francesca worked. Each of his brothers and his sister had their own wing in the main house, but they all maintained a personal space outside of the Ferraro estate. He had a penthouse at the hotel they owned. The suite was enormous, taking up the entire top floor. He had a private elevator that went straight to his floor and another private entrance very few knew of.

He paused on the sidewalk, looking into the store. Francesca had her head down, but she nodded every now and then as she listened to the man standing at the cash register. Stefano recognized Tito Petrov. His father owned the local pizza parlor and Tito managed it and also cooked there. He was as good at making the pizzas as his father. He was also a bit of a ladies' man. He dated often and women seemed to fall hard for him. Stefano didn't like Tito's body language at all.

Ignoring Tito, who continued to flirt outrageously with her, Francesca smiled at the older couple behind him as she wrapped sandwiches for them. She knew they owned the small boutique three stores down. They had come in and introduced themselves her very first morning at work. Sweet. Genuine. Very Italian. They held hands when they could and smiled at each other often. She *loved* that. She considered Lucia and Amo Fausti the poster couple for romance, and considering she didn't believe in romance, she also thought maybe they brought a little hope with them.

She could never afford a single item they offered, all those beautiful designer dresses and silk scarves. She knew they traveled extensively to find the best designers. Joanna told her people traveled from all over the city to shop in the little boutique.

"How are you this afternoon?" Lucia asked her.

They came into Masci's every evening after work hours for their evening meal, Joanna had also informed her, but then, nearly everyone came into Masci's at one time or another. Masci's represented all twenty regions of Italy, importing cured meats, handmade cheeses, olive oil and even vinegar.

Francesca smiled at her as she took their money and put it into the cash register. "Fine, and you?"

She had walked into their boutique because the clothes in the window had really appealed to her. It was a beautiful space, open, marble, decorated mainly with huge leafy plants, lacy ferns and a few flowering plants. The clothes were from all over the world, designers from France, Italy, India and even the local area. They carried beautiful but very different items, all unique.

"It was a lovely day today," Lucia said. "Cold, but lovely."

"We're going to eat here tonight," Amo said. "It's nice to visit after working all day." He beamed at Francesca.

"I suppose it is."

"You could visit with me," Tito encouraged.

"Don't you have work to do?" Amo asked, winking at Francesca. He took his wife's hand and led her toward one of the small tables at the back of the shop.

"I'd have plenty of work to do, Amo, if you'd eat at my place instead of here," Tito called to the backs of the couple.

Amo laughed. "Prettier view in here."

"Can't argue with that," Tito said, once more leaning on the counter, smiling at Francesca, his voice low and flirty.

Stefano pushed open the door to the deli and instantly all conversation ceased. He had his gaze on Francesca, but he scanned the room as he entered. As usual, the place was packed. He recognized most of the customers and lifted a hand toward a couple of them as he made his way toward the counter. The few people waiting in line instantly shifted to make room for him.

Francesca looked up, and he saw her face go pale. She pressed her lips together, a hint of wariness creeping into her eyes. "You're back," she greeted. "Just a minute and I'll get your coat for you."

"Not looking for my coat, *dolce cuore*," he said, and then shifted his gaze to the man slowly straightening from where he'd been leaning against the counter. "Tito. How's your father? I haven't seen him for a while."

"He's good. Great." Tito looked from Stefano to Francesca. "She has your coat? I heard . . ."

"It's true," Stefano said, cutting him off before he could finish his sentence. The last thing he wanted was for Francesca to deny his claim on her in front of the neighborhood, especially Tito Petrov.

Pietro hurried out of his office. "Mr. Ferraro, good to see you. What can we do for you?"

"Drop the 'Mr. Ferraro,' and just call me Stefano."

"Yes. Of course. Stefano." Pietro nodded several times. He'd been invited more than once to be on a first-name basis with all of the brothers, but he never actually did it for long. "What can we do for you?" he repeated.

"Lend me Francesca. I'm starving and after seeing Tito, I'm hungry for one of his pies. I need a chance to talk to her, so I thought we could do both." He ignored Francesca's reaction. The quick, shocked deep breath. The shaking of her head. Stepping back from the counter. Away from him.

Pietro ignored it as well. "Of course. No problem. She worked extra hours yesterday."

"I'll get back to the restaurant and get busy on your pie," Tito said.

Stefano sent him a quick smile. "Thanks, Tito. I appreciate it. We'll be there in a few minutes. I have to talk to a couple of people first." He glanced at Francesca, who hadn't moved. "We won't need the coat. It's just down the block." Again, before she could protest, he walked away from the counter, to the back of the room where the Faustis were seated.

"Lucia, you're looking beautiful this evening." He leaned down and brushed a kiss at her temple. She immediately caught his head in her hands and kissed both sides of his jaw before letting him go. "Is Amo still treating you right? I'd run away with you if I thought I could get away with it."

She laughed softly. "Amo is the best, but if he ever messes up, Stefano, you are the front-runner."

His eyebrow shot up. "'The front-runner'?" he repeated. Switching his attention to Amo, he shook the man's hand. "How many men does she have waiting in line?"

"Too many to count," Amo said with a heavy sigh. "Such is the life when a man marries a beautiful woman. You would do well to remember that."

Lucia laughed again and leaned into her husband. "You two. You always make me feel so special."

"Because you are," Stefano said, meaning it.

"She's very beautiful," Amo said, indicating Francesca, keeping his voice low. "Very sweet to all the customers.

Works hard, that one. She doesn't talk much and she seems sad. Is she all right?"

"She will be."

"Anything we can do, Stefano. You're a good boy. You've always been good to us," Lucia said. "Ever since . . ." She choked, her eyes filling with tears, and she pressed a hand to her mouth, forcing a smile behind her palm.

"Don't, Lucia," Stefano said, crouching down beside their table, sweeping his arm around the older woman. "You're here with the love of your life . . ." He glanced at Amo. "Oh, and Amo, too."

She laughed. It was a little forced, but still, she managed to make the sound merry. Her husband reached across the table and took her hand in his. "This man is always trying to steal you from me, *bella*." He brought her hand to his mouth and kissed her knuckles. "This happens too often, woman."

"You should be used to it by now, Amo," Stefano said, rising, brushing another kiss on top of Lucia's head. "I think my woman is ready to go."

Clearly she wasn't, but Pietro had pushed her out from behind the counter. Francesca looked nervous and as if she might be working herself up to telling him to go to hell. He grabbed her hand as he came up beside her, tugging until she was next to him and he could wrap one arm around her waist, drawing her into his side.

"Later, Pietro," he said, and walked her right out the door while she was too shocked at finding her body locked tightly against his side.

"Later, Mr. Ferraro," Pietro answered, laughter in his voice.

Francesca placed a protesting palm flat against his chest and then pulled it off of him as if his heat had burned her. "I'm not having a pizza with you."

"You don't have to eat if you're not hungry," he said, covering the pavement in long strides, his arm sweeping her along, forcing her to keep up with him.

He kept her moving, not wanting to give her the chance

to protest. "Have you met Lucia and Amo Fausti? The couple sitting in the back? They own Lucia's Treasures. It's a little boutique a few stores down from the deli."

She snuck a little peek at him from under her ridiculously long lashes. She didn't have mascara on, and still her lashes were thick and long and curled upward on the end. He was fascinated even with that little detail. Her eyes were beautiful. The thought came to him unbidden that he wanted to be looking into her eyes when he took her, when he made her come apart in his arms. When they were locked together, and he was moving in her, bringing her what no other man would ever give her again.

"Yes, they're a lovely couple. You seem to be friends with them."

She sounded a little shocked that he could have friends. That made him want to smile, but he resisted, continuing to walk, nodding toward a couple of people who stepped out of their shops to greet him. He kept moving because he didn't want them to engage him in conversation and give her the opportunity to break away.

"They lost their only son. Cencio was murdered coming out of a theater across town with his fiancée. Lucia was so devastated she nearly died. Amo wasn't himself for a couple of years, either. I grew up with Cencio. He was a good man. Always laughing. Sweet, like his parents. We served together in Marine Recon. He was someone you could count on. We'd only been out two months before he was murdered."

Her face softened. The lashes swept down and back up, but the softness didn't leave her eyes. "I'm so sorry. That must have been terrible for all of you. He was their only child?"

Stefano shook his head. "They had a little girl. She died of cancer when she was three."

Francesca stopped right there in the middle of the sidewalk, her free hand covering her mouth. She looked as if she might cry. "Those poor people. To lose both children like that. I can't imagine anything worse."

He nodded, pulling her a little closer to him, keeping her

under his shoulder. "They're both very brave. Sometimes tragedy tears people apart, but they seemed to grow stronger together." He started them moving again. The entrance to the pizza parlor was only a few feet away.

"They're actually my favorite customers," she admitted. "Not that I've met all that many people yet, although the store is very busy all the time. Was the murderer ever caught?"

He glanced at her sharply. There was something in her voice that caught at him. She was looking at the ground, not at him and not trying to see where they were going. She sounded skeptical, as if she didn't believe Cencio's killer would ever be brought to justice. She also sounded very, very sad. That tore him up inside. He didn't want her ever to be sad.

He reached around her to open the door of the pizza parlor, automatically stepping back to allow her to precede him. At the last moment, he pulled her out of harm's way, and then pushed her behind him as a little boy with dark wavy hair barreled right into him with full force. His body rocked back, but he caught the child in his arms, preventing the boy from falling. He heard Francesca's breath catch in her throat as if she feared for the child.

He set the boy back on his feet and ruffled his hair. "Tonio, are you chasing after Signora Moretti again?"

The boy nodded, holding up a pink handbag.

"Good man. Get to it then, but don't run into the street. Come by my table when you get back."

Tonio grinned at him and took off running. Stefano held the door open for Francesca and waved her inside.

"He's a good boy, that one," he observed. "Signora Moretti will eventually come into the deli. She'll give you a very hard time. She'll insist on watching you make her sandwich and everything you do will be wrong because she'll change it as she goes along." There was humor in his voice. Affection. He couldn't help it. "Agnese Moretti is a holy terror. Never call her anything but Signora Moretti or you'll get your ears boxed." He rubbed his right ear, remembering the woman clobbering him when he'd called her by her first name.

"She *hit* you?" Francesca's blue eyes went wide with shock—and humor.

"Signore Ferraro, we have your table," the girl at the desk said, menus in her hand. She sounded breathless, gazing up at him with a dazed, flirty look.

He smiled at her. "*Grazie*, Berta." He put his hand on Francesca's lower back to guide her. To make certain everyone in the restaurant knew just who she belonged to. "How are your parents?" He had to acknowledge Berta before she tripped over her own feet. She wasn't watching where she was going, only watching him.

"They're both good, Signore Ferraro. Tito said to put you at this table." Still staring at him, she indicated a booth at the back, in the corner where the low lights cast shadows and allowed for privacy. His family always requested that booth, and he was grateful that Tito remembered. "The antipasto and breadsticks will be right up. Wine? Beer?" she asked.

Francesca slipped into the inside of the booth because he didn't give her much choice. He kept his attention on Berta even as his body crowded Francesca's until she gave in and slid onto the cool leather bench seat. Stefano slid in right beside her. Close. His thigh pressed tight against hers. He inhaled her scent. She was beautiful, there in the shadows where he lived his life. So beautiful and innocent looking. He was going to take that innocence away and the thought made him sad. He resisted reaching for her hand, but he knew he would have to touch her soon.

"What would you like, *bella*? Wine? Beer? Something else?"

Francesca hesitated but then relaxed, some of the tension draining out of her. "Water is fine."

"You don't drink wine?" He raised an eyebrow.

She nodded. "It's been a while since I've had any alcohol. I don't know how I'd react."

He liked her honesty. "I'll make certain you get home safe. One glass can't hurt." Before she could protest he turned to Berta. "Red wine. You know my preference. Bring the bottle and two glasses." When Berta left he turned his attention to Francesca. "My family owns a few vineyards and a winery in Italy. It's beginning to make a name, and fortunately I enjoy the wine our family produces. I hope you do as well."

She nodded, a little shyly. "Thank you. I'm sure I will. Tell me about Agnese Moretti. Did she really box your ears?"

He had never been more grateful for the older woman's difficult and very feisty personality. His story had piqued Francesca's interest enough that she was much more relaxed with him. She seemed to like the stories of the people around her. Good people. He liked his neighborhood and wanted her to see it through his eyes. It was where she would spend the majority of her life. Accepting their way. Accepting their rules. Living with a yoke of violence around their necks for the good of those around them. A part of him detested himself for doing that to her, but there was no way he could give her up.

"Oh, yes. She not only boxed my ears, but twice she grabbed me by the earlobe and marched me out of a room. Of course, I was a lot younger when the earlobe thing happened." Deliberately he rubbed his earlobe as if he could still feel the pinch.

Francesca laughed. She had a beautiful laugh. Melodic. Low. Almost as if the laugh was intimate, just between the two of them. His heart beat in tune to her low laughter. He wanted to hear it for the rest of his life. The sound drowned out the voices in his head that refused to die when those who owned them did.

"How old were you when she boxed your ears?"

"That was last year when I made the big mistake of getting 'fresh' with her by calling her by her first name. Apparently I'm not old enough yet to do that. She taught school and has never let me or any other student of hers forget it."

"She sounds like a character."

"She is," Stefano said. "She's wonderful. I can't tell you how many students she tutored outside the classroom to help them when they had difficulties with a subject. She never charged their parents. There were some kids who didn't have much and she would buy them the supplies they needed. Lunches. Jackets. She never let on that she did it, or made a big deal out of it, but they'd just find the supplies in their desk, or their jacket or lunch box."

"Wow." Francesca leaned her chin onto her hand, her gaze fixed on him. That sea-blue gaze that made him want to fall right into it. "She sounds incredible."

"She's a character. She forgets her purse anyplace she eats and her glasses in most stores. Tonio always rushes after her if she's anywhere around. If not Tonio, then one of the other children. He's the youngest and the most enthusiastic, which means he's a little tornado and you have to get out of his way when he's making his run."

Berta was back with the antipasto, small plates, warm, fresh breadsticks and the wine. She expertly juggled each dish and poured a small amount of wine in a glass for Stefano to taste.

He liked that Francesca watched him so closely, that she seemed fascinated by the conversation and by him. He nodded his approval of the wine, waited until Berta poured both glasses and left before he picked up Francesca's glass and handed it to her. Her fingers brushed his. Instantly a spark of electricity leapt from her to him. He felt their shadows connect. Merge. The pull was strong, just like the narrow slider tubes that nearly pulled apart his body when he stood in front of them—a powerful magnet drawing him close.

He heard her swift inhale. Her eyes darkened. Lashes lowered. Her breasts rose and fell. She pulled her hand away, bringing the wineglass to her mouth. She definitely felt the chemistry between them just as strongly as he did. It was explosive. His body reacted, going as hard as a rock, something that just didn't happen to a man with his kind of discipline. He knew if he leaned into her and took her mouth, he'd ignite a firestorm—they both would.

She was dangerous to both of them. He had to stay in

control around her and just being this close to her threatened that. He was the one shifting slightly to put distance between them, a mere inch, but even that little inch gave him a reprieve.

Tonio ran up, his thick, curly hair wild. Eyes shining. "I caught her, Signore Ferraro. Just as she was getting into her car."

"Good man, Tonio." He slipped his wallet out and handed the boy a bill. "I'm proud of you for looking after her. What do we do?"

Tonio puffed out his chest. "We always look after our women."

"That's right. Run along now and say hello to your parents for me."

The boy took the money and slipped it into his pocket. *"Grazie. Grazie."* He grinned at Stefano. "Is *she* one of our women?" He indicated Francesca.

Stefano nodded solemnly. "Tonio, this is Francesca. Francesca, Tonio. If you should ever need assistance, he is a good man and will come to your aid. Yes, Tonio, she's very special to me. She's one of ours." He glanced at his woman. She didn't know he was claiming her publicly, but that innocent question was welcome. Tonio would tell his parents exactly what Stefano had said to him. The boy always did.

Francesca looked pleased. He knew she would. She wouldn't be thinking about the underlying implication, only that the boy was cute.

"Pleased to meet you, Tonio," she said.

He nodded shyly. "Don't worry. I'll look out for you."

"Thank you. I appreciate that."

Tonio turned with a saucy grin and raced through the restaurant back to his parents' table. Stefano watched him go just to make certain he didn't knock over any of Tito's customers.

"He's adorable." Francesca dipped a breadstick into the marinara sauce and took a bite. Her eyes closed. "Wow. This is delicious."

"No one makes pizza, antipasto or marinara like Tito's family. They've been in the business for a couple of generations and they make the best. People come from all over to eat here."

"You sound proud."

"I am. They're a good family and they deserve success."

"You aren't anything like I thought you'd be," she ventured, and took another sip of wine.

"What did you think I'd be like?"

"I don't know. You seemed so scary when I first met you. I thought you were . . ." She trailed off and shook her head, color creeping under her skin.

"Tell me."

"I don't want you to be upset. It was silly of me. I was so nervous about the interview and it seemed as if everyone in the store was a little afraid of you when you came in. You also were abrupt and a little rude, dropping F-bombs all over the place."

He nodded. "I do that a lot, I'm afraid. More than once, Signora Moretti told me she was going to wash out my mouth, and that was this year."

She laughed. He loved the way she laughed. Just in the two days he'd been away from her, she seemed much more relaxed. "Her warning didn't do any good, did it?"

"No, I suppose it didn't," he admitted ruefully. "So tell me, Francesca, what did you think I was when we met?"

CHAPTER FIVE

Francesca studied Stefano's face. He was intimidating, no question about it. Even with the way he interacted with little Tonio, he had a look about him that demanded respect. More, he commanded the room. She was acutely aware that every single person in the restaurant had turned to watch them as they made their way to their booth. Even now, people were watching. They were trying to pretend that they weren't, but she knew better. It was fairly clear that Stefano Ferrero was a well-known man. Liked by some, feared by others.

Still, there was an underlying sadness about him that she caught glimpses of, and everything in her rose to soothe him. Needed to do that. She wasn't altogether certain how or why she came to be sitting beside him, but she was fascinated by his take on the people in the neighborhood. There was genuine affection in his voice when he spoke of them. She liked that he knew so much about them and seemed to care.

Up close, he was hot, hot, hot. A gorgeous man. She couldn't believe how handsome he was. Tough looking. Confident. Even a bit arrogant, but one could forgive that when his face was so perfect. The angles and planes, the strong jaw and straight nose. His mouth fascinated her and she had to work not to stare at it. Twice she found herself doing just that and wondering what it would be like to feel his mouth on hers. A really stupid fantasy to have about a man she thought was mafia two days earlier.

Francesca was a little ashamed of herself that she'd thought that of him, even when he'd had a foul mouth and was so abrupt. Clearly she'd read the silence in the deli as something it wasn't. It felt like fear, but looking back, she had been terrified of everything that day and probably had just projected what she was feeling onto the crowd in Masci's.

She couldn't decide if she liked his eyes the best, or his voice. His eyes were a beautiful blue, dark and mysterious, with long black lashes that matched his thick, wavy hair. His voice was soft, pitched low, a warm honey that moved over her, promising all sorts of sinful things.

"Francesca."

His voice startled her right out of her fantasy. She blinked rapidly and brought him into focus. She hadn't had time to go over the things about his body that appealed to her, but it was probably just as well. She lifted her gaze to his, and everything in her stilled. Stefano stared straight into her eyes, capturing her without even trying. He held her there—she was unable to look away. She was totally mesmerized by him.

Francesca felt his power. Felt a connection between them. Her heart stuttered and then began to pound. He leaned toward her, frowning. His finger slid along her skin, right at her throat, skimming lightly over the shallow laceration where the knife had burned as it went into her flesh. She shivered at the way the blue of his eyes darkened so intimately.

"This is obscene. Someone putting hands on you. A knife to your throat. I'm sorry this happened, Francesca. This is normally a safe neighborhood. We have small things, petty, teenagers drinking too much and getting a little out of hand, but this . . ." He broke off, shaking his head.

Without warning he leaned into her and brushed her throat with his mouth. Her heart stopped beating. She was certain it had. She froze, unable to move. Unable to think because her brain had short-circuited. His hair brushed her chin and along her shoulder. She'd never felt anything so sensual in her life.

Her breasts ached. *Needed.* Her nipples pushed into the lace of her bra and suddenly the little lace panties she wore were damp. Her sex clenched hard. Her breath caught in her throat and she couldn't move even to save herself—and she had a feeling she needed to save herself. She wanted desperately to run her fingers in his thick dark hair. She knew it was soft because the thick strands moved against her chin and throat. She blinked and he lifted his head.

"I'm sorry," he repeated. "You must have been so scared." His voice whispered over her like the intimate brush of fingers.

She touched her tongue to her lips, trying not to imagine his mouth on hers. "I'll admit, I was afraid, but mostly because I didn't want them to get blood on your coat."

His eyebrow shot up. "You what?"

Her mouth curved in a rueful smile, although her heart hammered hard in her chest. "I didn't want to get any blood on your coat. I was wearing it and when he cut me, all I could think about was that the blood might run down my neck into your coat."

His eyes went scary dark. His face stilled. His fingers curled around the nape of her neck and he pulled her head toward his. "Are you telling me that you were so afraid of me that when a mugger put a knife to your throat, the thing you feared most was getting blood on my fucking coat?"

His voice had gone scary soft to match the devil shining in his eyes. Her heart jumped and then thudded hard. She was acutely aware of his fingers curled around her neck—of every detail of him. His warmth. His broad shoulders. His enormous strength. The way the pads of his fingers felt possessive on her skin. His scent enveloped her, surrounded her, until there was only him and the other people in the restaurant faded away. He was too close to her to breathe, the shadows in the booth enfolding them in an unexpected intimacy.

"Dolce cuore." He breathed it.

She shouldn't like that he called her sweetheart. She shouldn't be sitting there with his hand curled around her neck. She was drowning, hypnotized by him. She'd never experienced such intense chemistry. She didn't even know physical attraction could be so strong. He was like a magnet and she couldn't seem to find the resistance necessary to break free.

"You're far more important than a fucking coat."

"It's your favorite," she whispered, shocking herself at what that admission implied. She'd been afraid of him, hadn't she? Not attracted. Not worried that he'd be upset over his coat and she didn't want that. Or that she'd come to love that coat and the way it made her feel.

"It's a coat, Francesca." His hand slid from her neck and he straightened, turning his head toward the interior of the restaurant.

She hadn't heard anything at all, yet he'd been aware of movement in the pizzeria. She blinked several times, trying to come out from under his spell, out from under the web of sexual attraction.

"Your pie," Tito said with a flourish, placing the pizza between them. "The house specialty. Enjoy." He winked at Francesca. "You'll think you're in heaven."

"*Grazie*, Tito," Stefano said, shifting his body subtly to put himself once more very close to Francesca, his posture possessive.

Even Francesca saw the blatant warning. She smiled at Tito. "Thanks, it looks fantastic."

Tito nodded, gave them both a small salute and slipped away, leaving her once more alone with Stefano.

Francesca knew she had to protest Stefano's proprietorial behavior. She wasn't in a position to have any kind of a relationship and in any case, she didn't do casual. Stefano was way out of her league. She couldn't imagine that a man like him would want to date someone like her. She shopped at the thrift store. He'd be appalled if he saw where she lived. She was appalled whenever she went to her little apartment, but still, it was hers. She knew she'd faint if she ever saw where he lived. His coat cost more than three months' rent, maybe four.

Stefano put a slice of pizza on her plate. "No one makes

pizza like Tito or his father. Benito Petrov is impressive. Big, like Tito, but that's where the similarity ends. Tito smiles all the time. Benito is very sober. Tito's sweet, and Benito is gruff."

"How did Tito get to be so different?"

"He takes after his mother. She was the sweetest woman alive. They lost her about seven years ago to breast cancer. Benito had a difficult time getting over it. That's when Tito stepped up and really took over the restaurant."

"What else is different about them?" Francesca was curious, but more, she loved to hear Stefano's voice. It was beautiful, perfectly pitched. Low. Sensual. She could listen to him talk all night.

"Benito is covered in tattoos, has one earring, is bald and looks like he would rip your throat out for a buck." He laughed softly. "He's a regular volunteer at the food bank and heads up the committee for fund-raising to help supplement it. He started a community garden with the idea that anyone could eat when they were hungry. He's been working on plans for a greenhouse so the food can be grown all year-round."

She forgot all about her protests and leaned on the heel of her hand, her eyes on his face. It was fascinating to see the way his expression softened when he talked about the neighborhood and its residents. "Where did they get the land for the gardens and greenhouse? I imagine that land here would be very expensive."

"Take a bite. You don't want to hurt Tito's feelings. The land was donated."

She knew his family had donated the land. She knew it instantly. She took a bite of the pizza and nearly moaned, it was so good.

He grinned knowingly at her, nodding. "Right? Superb."

"I had no idea anything could taste this good, let alone a pizza. I might be spending my paycheck here."

"On weekends, there's a line to get in. Petrov and Tito cater to the locals so there's an entrance around the side they open when the line's long. They slip the locals in. A few tables are held in reserve so they can seat them as soon as possible."

"This is a very tight-knit community, isn't it?"

He nodded. "Good people." He touched the scratch along her throat with a gentle finger. "I hate that this happened to you. I'm very sorry, Francesca."

She frowned at him. "Stefano." His name slipped out easier than it should have. She didn't care. She leaned close. "This wasn't your fault." That's why he had brought her to Tito's restaurant. He felt guilty. She felt such an overwhelming sense of physical attraction she'd nearly made the mistake of thinking it had to be mutual. He felt responsible. He watched out for the residents and someone had tried to mug her. "Please stop worrying about it. I'm perfectly fine."

"I had my cousins watching over you, but I told them to hang back so you wouldn't feel crowded. That was my mistake. Most residents are known. You're new. Criminals stay away, but . . ."

"Technically, we left the neighborhood," Francesca pointed out. Without thinking she laid her hand over Stefano's. "You had no responsibility in what happened to me."

The moment her palm curved over the back of his hand, she knew she had made a mistake. His heat seemed to fuse them together. Little sparks of electricity crackled along her nerve endings. She jerked her hand away, feeling as if she'd just gotten burned. Not burned. Branded. She'd laid her hand over his, yet she felt as if he'd captured her. Connected them. That connection seemed to grow stronger each time they physically touched.

"Any resident of our neighborhood should be safe anywhere they go in the city," he said, his voice suddenly scary. "They blew half of Cencio's face off. His own mother couldn't even see him in the coffin one last time." He sounded fierce. Guilty. As if somehow he was responsible for Cencio's death. He sounded grief-stricken.

That was the worst. That a man like Stefano, so arrogant,

so confident, strong and absolutely a rock could be so shaken. She couldn't help herself. She shook her head, her eyes meeting his. She had to take that pain from him, she didn't know why, but she had no choice. "I know what grief is, Stefano. To suffer the loss of a loved one through murder. To feel responsible when really, there was nothing I could have done. You can't look out for every single person in your neighborhood. It's impossible. You aren't responsible for me or the attack on me." Her voice was soft, persuasive.

She couldn't believe she'd given away what she had. She didn't talk about her past; she didn't dare. Still, she had to take the pain from his eyes. Her heart hurt just looking at the pain.

His eyes changed. Focused completely on her. Saw too much. Took her breath. Made her heart flutter and her stomach do a slow roll.

"Someone you loved was murdered?"

She nodded. "I shouldn't have said anything. I just don't want you to think that you have to protect the entire world because your friend died. You can't, Stefano."

"Not the entire world, Francesca." He picked up her hand and idly played with her fingers.

She should have pulled her hand away, but she couldn't make herself be that mean, not when she was trying to make him see reason. It was just that, with his fingers moving through hers, brushing along and between them, her body reacted, making her all too aware of secret places and a growing hunger—for him.

"Just my neighborhood. Just the people in my world. Someone has to look after them, and that's my job."

She wanted to cry for him. It was no wonder that that first time he'd walked into Masci's he'd seemed so alone. So remote. He had taken on an impossible task, even to the point of looking out for a total stranger. She shook her head and reached for the wineglass, needing to do something to counteract the empathy and awareness of him.

"Where is your family?" he asked.

She knew sooner or later he'd ask. It was a natural enough

question. "I don't have any family. My parents died in a car wreck when I was fourteen. I didn't have any aunts or uncles or grandparents. You have a big family, but it was just my sister, Cella, and me. She was older by nine years so she raised me."

There was a silence. He leaned back in the booth, his arm sliding along the back of the seat. "Are you telling me Cella was the one murdered?" There was an edge to his voice.

"I don't like to talk about it." She took another sip of wine. "I shouldn't have brought it up."

"You were trying to make me feel better. That just pisses me off. Someone fucking murders my best friend, Cencio, as he walks out of a theater, and someone murders your only sister."

The vibe around them got a little scary, as if his anger was so oppressive it could weigh down the entire room.

"Was it random? A stranger?"

Like Cencio? he was asking. She shook her head before she could stop herself. How had she allowed such personal information to slip out? They'd been having a good conversation, and just like that she'd ruined the mood. Stefano was intense. His anger was intense. He'd gone from being sweet and easygoing to vulnerable and then dangerous in the space of a couple of minutes.

"I'm sorry I spoiled the mood," she said, trying to back-pedal. "You were relaxing and I just . . ." She broke off when his fingers went to her neck, massaging the knots there, in an effort to ease the tension out of her.

"You didn't kill the mood, Francesca. You were trying to help me and I appreciate it. Very few people would have even seen that I'm still carrying that load around with me. I appreciate you sharing."

His voice was very low. Intimate. His eyes met hers and her stomach did another somersault. He was just plain beautiful.

"Signore Ferraro," a voice called from across the room.

She saw impatience cross his face, but it was swiftly masked. When Stefano turned to see the woman standing in the doorway, a good distance from them, he did so with a smile. The woman looked every day of eighty. She was short and a little bent, her skin thin and her face still beautiful in spite of the few wrinkles proclaiming she'd lived her life. She wore a long black dress and matching shawl and she wrung her hands together as she hurried through the restaurant toward them, weaving her way through the tables and ignoring Berta, who tried to stop her.

Stefano raised his hand to Berta and she skidded to a halt and then went back to her station. Stefano rose as the older woman made it to them. He towered over her, settling his arm around her shoulders with a gentleness that took Francesca's breath. No one would ever guess that he was the least bit impatient with the interruption. To Francesca's dismay the woman had tears in her eyes and her lips trembled.

"Signora Vitale, you're upset. Please sit for a moment and join us. Have a glass of wine." There was nothing but solicitation in Stefano's voice.

He held up his wineglass toward Berta, who clearly had been watching along with everyone else in the restaurant. She hurried toward them and placed another wineglass on the table as Stefano helped the older woman into the seat across from Francesca.

"Signora Vitale, may I present Francesca Capello? Francesca, this is Theresa Vitale, a dear friend of mine."

Francesca loved how gentle his hands were when they touched the older woman, pushing the glass of wine into her hand and keeping contact with her. More, his voice was soft with affection. She murmured a greeting, knowing the woman barely registered her presence. Signora Vitale's entire attention was centered on Stefano.

"Drink that and then tell me what has upset you."

Theresa took the wine in shaking hands and obediently took a sip. Francesca couldn't imagine anyone disobeying Stefano, not even a woman of Theresa's age. He might be gentle, but there was no mistaking that he was the absolute authority.

"Perhaps I should leave, give you privacy," Francesca ventured.

Stefano's fingers slid around her wrist, shackling her to him. "No. Stay. Please."

Her heart fluttered at the soft *please*. He had issued a command to her, but then he'd added that one little word that changed everything. She nodded, and he relaxed his hold on her. Instead of shackling her, the pad of his thumb brushed intimately along her inner wrist.

For the first time, Theresa looked at Francesca, dropped her gaze to Stefano's fingers around her wrist and then her eyes went wide as she looked at his face. "I'm interrupting something important." A fresh flood of tears came and she rocked herself back and forth.

"Francesca doesn't mind any more than I do, Theresa," he said gently, using her given name. "Do you, *bambina*?" he asked, his eyes on hers.

"Of course not," she immediately replied. "Please don't be distressed."

Theresa drank her wine and placed the empty glass directly in front of Stefano. Still keeping his hold on Francesca, he obliged Theresa by pouring her more.

"It's my grandson, Bruno," Theresa confessed, her voice very low. "He's in trouble again."

Stefano sighed and sank back against the booth, his thigh brushing Francesca's. He brought her hand to his mouth, nibbling on her fingertips absently, as if he had forgotten it was an actual flesh-and-blood hand. The feel of his mouth on her skin was even more intimate than when his thumb had brushed her inner wrist. The ache in her breasts increased and her body responded with more damp heat. His eyes were hooded, impossible to read, but Francesca had the feeling he was exasperated with the conversation, not at all aware of the explosive chemistry she was feeling.

"What kind of trouble this time?"

Theresa took another gulp of wine, looked left and right and then lowered her voice. "Drugs," she whispered. "I think he's selling them for someone and I think the police are watching him. He can't get arrested again. He just can't."

Stefano didn't move. He didn't speak. Around them, the air got heavier. Darker. Francesca felt the scary vibe he gave off. She knew immediately that Theresa's grandson was in far more trouble with Stefano than he would have been with the police. Theresa didn't seem to notice, but the rest of the people in the room did. Heads turned and conversation grew muted.

"What do you want me to do, Theresa?" he asked, the tone pitched very low. His voice was devoid of all feeling. His face was set in hard, implacable lines. Expressionless.

Francesca gently tried to pull her hand away, mostly because she was so aware of him, she couldn't think straight. His fingers tightened around hers and he bit down with his strong white perfect teeth. The little bite of pain sent a streak of fire straight to her sex. He pulled the finger into his mouth, his tongue curling around the bite, soothing the sting.

She froze. He wasn't looking at her. She wasn't even certain he knew she was there. His entire focus seemed to be on the older woman.

"You have to talk to him, Stefano. You have to talk to him," Theresa repeated. "If he gets caught, he'll go to prison this time. He's a good boy. He needed a father. My daughter, she was no good. You know that. Always the drugs with her. She just left him, and then my beautiful Alberto died and there is only me. I pray, but God is not listening to me. You have to, Stefano."

Francesca stopped trying to pull her hand away. Her heart hurt for Stefano. Everyone expected him to take care of their problems. It was clear this wasn't the first time Theresa had come to Stefano and Francesca was certain it wouldn't be the last. He carried a terrible weight on his shoulders.

"Bruno is twenty-four years old, Theresa. No one can stop him from doing what he wants. I've talked to him."

Theresa took a deep breath. "You haven't made yourself clear."

There was a long silence. The air was suddenly charged with tension. Most of that was coming from Stefano, but Theresa looked both scared and nervous.

"Are you certain you know what you're asking me, Theresa?" Stefano's voice dropped even lower, almost a whisper. Gentle. Still, it was somehow very menacing.

The old lady nodded. "He has to know there are consequences. It is the only way. Nothing has worked."

"There is no taking it back."

"I understand."

Francesca didn't. She was missing something big. Huge. Whatever Signora Vitale was asking for, Stefano was reluctant to do. She moved closer to him, wanting to comfort him. She didn't understand why, especially since his scary persona was back. As he sat there in his pin-striped suit with his expressionless mask and flat, cold eyes, she could understand why she'd first thought he was in the mafia. No Hollywood movie would ever find a better man to play the part.

Theresa held his eyes for a long time. Stefano lowered his long lashes as if weary beyond measure and then he lifted them. "*Bambina*, I'm sorry." He leaned into Francesca and brushed a kiss over her forehead. At the same time, still holding her hand, he slid his index finger out and drew a soothing line along the scratch at her throat. "I had planned to walk you home, make certain you were safe, but I'm going to have to take care of this."

"That's all right. I can get home by myself." Francesca could see the reluctance to leave her in his eyes. He really didn't want to go and that made some small part of her very satisfied, even though the bigger part of her knew she was being a little delusional in thinking his concern could be anything but fear for her safety.

He shook his head as he lifted his hand to Berta and she came running. "Put this on my tab," he said to the woman. He left two twenty-dollar bills on the table as he rose, a huge tip, and held out his hand to assist Theresa Vitale in rising. "My cousins will be waiting outside for you, Francesca. Please allow them to see you home."

She smiled at him. "It's unnecessary."

"I disagree."

His tone told her not to argue. His eyes and the hard look on his face told her the same. He was a scary man to defy, but she might have argued just on principle if she hadn't seen him so vulnerable over his friend's death. If she hadn't figured out that he needed to protect everyone around him.

"All right then," she conceded, not sounding very gracious. She'd enjoyed their talk together far more than she'd expected and she liked him much better than she had thought possible. Maybe too much. She'd certainly told him too much about herself. She was especially grateful that when she'd made that mistake, he hadn't pried further. "Oh no. Stefano, your coat."

He shrugged. "Did you get yourself a coat?"

She shook her head, not meeting his eyes. He wouldn't like that. He'd specifically told her to buy a coat. It was just that all the ones in the neighborhood were expensive. She wasn't going to use his money for a coat. "I'm saving for one."

"Francesca." There was warning in his voice. "Look at me."

"Go. You have things to do."

His fingers caught her chin and tipped her face up to his. "Nothing is more important to me. Get. A. *Fucking.* Coat."

It was difficult to look into his eyes and not give him anything he wanted, even when he swore the way he did. "Stefano."

"Francesca."

He actually growled her name. She didn't think a person could make that particular sound, but he managed it. Everyone in the restaurant stared at them. Waiting. Horrified at her defiance. She knew they couldn't possibly hear the exchange, but they could read body language and see that Stefano Ferraro was not happy with her.

He sighed. "Wear my coat home and be warm. I'll come by later this evening and see you."

Her heart plunged. He couldn't possibly come to her apartment building. The place would fall down if he walked into it. She didn't live in Ferraro territory. Joanna had explained the boundaries to her, and her apartment building definitely fell outside of it. Surely he didn't mean he would come to her apartment?

"Give me your cell. I'll put my numbers in."

This time her heart started pounding. She didn't have a cell, and she knew instinctively he wouldn't like that, either. It must have showed on his face because he swore savagely in Italian.

"Really? Damn it, Francesca. Do you know the first fucking thing about self-preservation?" His blue gaze glittered dangerously with pure menace.

Her stomach tightened. He was scary. Plain scary. Anger radiated off of him in waves. There he was. The man she'd first met. The man capable of just about anything—except his anger was over her safety and she understood him better.

"Some things have to be a priority, Stefano," she said in a low voice, determined not to match his anger because she was embarrassed over her circumstances. "Like food and shelter. Even if I could save the money for a cell phone, I'd have to have a monthly plan. That costs money. I'm just getting on my feet."

She tried to sound matter-of-fact. She didn't want him to think for one moment that she was complaining. For the first time in a long while she had hope. She had a job where she earned better money than she had thought she would. She liked the job and the neighborhood. She had a roof over her head. She didn't want him to feel responsible for her. She was responsible for herself.

He took a deep breath and, to her shock, nodded his understanding. His fingers left her chin. "I'll catch up with you later." Abruptly he turned and, slipping his hand under Theresa's elbow, led her out.

Francesca sank back down into the seat. She was exhausted. Totally. Going up against Stefano Ferraro was a bit like going up against a force of nature. She felt a little battered and bruised and yet he'd been very gentle when he touched her.

She picked up her wineglass and took another sip. It was

excellent wine. She couldn't remember if she'd told him so. She hadn't remembered to thank him for the meal—and it was a fantastic meal. If her stomach hadn't shrunk so much she would have eaten far more. As it was, she was taking the rest of the pizza home with her. No way was she wasting it.

"Hey, girl!" Joanna slid into her booth. "Wow. Can I just say *wow*?"

"Where did you come from?" Francesca asked. She looked past her friend but she was alone.

"Eating with Stefano Ferraro? You didn't tell me you had a date."

"It wasn't a date. He wanted to talk to me."

"About?" Joanna prompted, and helped herself to a slice of the pizza. "Was this his glass? Because I'm totally drinking out of it. If you know where his lips touched, just point out the spot and I'm all about setting my lips right over his. He's that hot."

Francesca burst out laughing. Joanna had brought back fun into her life. She'd forgotten what fun was.

"I stopped by the deli and Zio told me Stefano had kidnapped you. It's so *romantic*. I have to admit, I stalked the two of you, just to see how things were going. The Ferraros always sit back here and it's hard to see them in the booth. They kind of disappear into the shadows. You did, too, so even though I bribed Berta with three dollars—that's all I had—*and* she's my friend—I couldn't get seated close enough to the two of you to eavesdrop. So not fair." She picked up the wine bottle and read the label. "Oh. My. God. Of course he got you this. It's like the most expensive bottle I've ever heard of and there's not a drop left."

Francesca handed over her wineglass immediately. "I've had too much. It really is that good. But so is the pie."

"Tito and Benito are the *best*. You can totally have an orgasm eating their pizza. But if I'd been sitting that entire time with Stefano, I would have had, like, ten orgasms. He smolders with sex. He walks into a room and doesn't have to say or do anything."

"His voice can do it, too," Francesca confessed, and then covered her mouth. She'd had *way* too much wine to give that away.

Joanna laughed and then took a slow sip of the wine from Francesca's glass. Her eyes closed and she moaned. "I'm in heaven right now. This has been the *best* day."

"Really? Aside from your perving on Stefano Ferraro, what else happened?"

"I got a call from"—Joanna leaned close for dramatic effect—"*Emmanuelle Ferraro*. Can you believe that?"

"Stefano's sister?"

Joanna nodded solemnly. "She's the baby in the family. Can you imagine having five big brothers like hers? All of them are like Stefano. Definitely in charge. She never dates, but then I don't think there's a man on earth who would dare try it. They'd probably disappear, never to be found."

Francesca went still. "Joanna, seriously. You have to tell me the truth. Are the Ferraros a mafia family?" Because she actually *liked* Stefano. He'd given away so much about himself, and she liked what he'd given away.

Joanna glanced around the room. "It's not a good idea to talk about things like that, Francesca. Not ever. The Ferraros are different."

"Joanna," Francesca warned. "You're my friend. I'm not going to talk about it to anyone else. I'm talking to you."

Joanna sighed, took another sip of wine and then shrugged. "I don't honestly know. They could be. I know they've been investigated but nothing was ever proved against them. The family is very powerful internationally and they have like a bazillion cousins. Not just here, but all over the United States and Europe. No one has ever found anything on them, but people are afraid of them. Not us. Not here in their territory, but others. I don't know," she finished. "It's possible. Maybe even probable."

Francesca sighed. It wasn't an answer. It was speculation. She knew better than anyone how rumors got started and became truth in everyone's mind. She wasn't going to do that to anyone, believe gossip without proof. Still, she had to be wary.

"So tell me about Emmanuelle's phone call," she prompted.

"She said Giovanni told her about how I couldn't get into their club and she wanted to personally invite me to go with her and her cousins. She said I could bring anyone I wanted along. I thought I could ask Mario Bandoni—you know, you met him. He manages the shoe store. I already mentioned it to him and he seemed receptive." Her words tumbled over one another, and she leaned toward Francesca. "I've liked him forever. Even in elementary school. He was always so popular and I could never make myself make a play for him because I really, really liked him. I thought you could go and it wouldn't seem like I was asking him on a real date. Just casual, you know, a big crowd."

"Joanna, if you're going with Emmanuelle and her cousins, that's already a crowd." Francesca didn't want to let her down, but she couldn't go to a hot nightclub in her holey jeans.

"But not *my* crowd. I don't run in her circles, and neither does Mario. We're acquaintances, but not real friends. They aren't just rich, Francesca—they're ultrawealthy. I like them, but I'm not comfortable with them. I can't imagine that they're going to hang around with me in a nightclub. They'll be sitting in the VIP section and I'll be down on the floor, trying not to be tongue-tied with Mario."

"Honey," Francesca said softly. "You're never tongue-tied with men."

A thread of unease crept through her and she glanced up to look around the restaurant. Her gaze collided with a man's. He was across the room, standing by the hostess booth. A shiver went down her spine. He was medium height, but powerfully built. Wide shoulders, a thick chest. He had the body of a prizefighter. He wore his hair cropped close. From the distance she couldn't tell the color of his eyes, but his mouth was set in a forbidding scowl. He looked vaguely familiar.

Berta said something to him and he instantly turned his attention to her, smiling down at her. Francesca sighed and forced her gaze back to her friend. She was just being overly paranoid. She was hundreds of miles from California. No one knew where she was. She'd covered her tracks fairly well. She took a breath and turned her full attention back to Joanna, having missed her reply.

"What did you say?"

"I said, you've never seen me around a man I really, really like. I make a total fool of myself. Please, Francesca. Do this for me. I'll help find you something to wear. I can even help pay . . ."

"Don't," Francesca cautioned. "You've done enough for me. You want me to go, I'll find a way." Hopefully she could find something decent at the thrift shop. If not, she might have to dip into the money Stefano had left with her and that would be humiliating. She wanted to return the money along with the coat when she saw him next.

"Thank you, Francesca. This means the world to me," Joanna said happily.

"Are you ready? I have to retrieve Stefano's coat before your uncle closes up for the night."

Joanna laughed again. "You and that coat."

"Right? It's the bane of my existence."

Francesca followed Joanna from the pizza parlor. Joanna called a greeting to several people and waved toward the kitchen as they made their exit. The boxer—as Francesca thought of him—seemed to be waiting for a to-go order. She kept her eye on him just in case, but he didn't appear to pay any more attention to her.

Emilio and Enzo lounged by the door, and it was all she could do not to roll her eyes at them. They both grinned and put away their cell phones when she emerged.

"You cold?" Emilio asked.

She shook her head. Lying. The restaurant had been warm and the evening was very cool, but she knew if she admitted she was, Emilio would have whipped off his coat and then she'd be responsible for two of the darn things. Everyone seemed obsessed with her lack of a coat.

"Hey Emilio. Enzo," Joanna greeted. "Out for a stroll again tonight?"

"Got orders, Jo," Enzo said. "You two troublemakers decide you're going to rob the jewelry shop, we've got orders to stop you."

"So not fair! I've had my eye on a diamond bracelet," Joanna declared.

"Sorry, girl. You're going to have to give up that particular dream," he said.

The door opened behind them and Francesca glanced over her shoulder. The boxer had emerged carrying a small box. He looked toward them and then abruptly turned the other way and walked unhurriedly down the street. When she turned back, Emilio was watching her. He raised his gaze to follow the man's departure.

"Someone you know?" he asked. Low. Lethal.

He sounded just that little bit like Stefano. Definitely a relative. She shook her head. "I'm just a little jumpy." She touched her throat deliberately. The last thing she wanted was for Emilio to report an innocent man to Stefano. She didn't know what he might do, but she was leery. Until she knew what he was, criminal or just a very overprotective man, she was going to be very, very careful.

"We're walking with you, Francesca," Emilio said. "No one is going to touch you." She saw the weapon hidden in the shoulder holster beneath his jacket when he moved. Like his cousin, both men wore suits, although not pin-striped. They were attractive and dangerous looking. She had to admit she felt safe with them.

"Thanks. I didn't realize what a baby I've been until just now. I appreciate you taking the time."

"Sei famiglia," he said.

She didn't touch that. They stopped at the deli and retrieved Stefano's coat. Emilio, a gentleman like his cousin, held it out for her to slip into. She drew it around her, very close, loving the warmth. Loving that it still held Stefano's scent. Joanna remained at the deli with her uncle while the two men walked with her to her apartment.

Francesca liked that they walked to her building. She stopped outside of it. Until that moment, she hadn't been aware of just how different her building was from the ones they'd just passed. In the Ferraro neighborhood, all along the street where the businesses were, the buildings were immaculate, as were the sidewalks. Her apartment building was old and crumbling. Litter and debris were scattered everywhere along the walkway and, she knew, inside the building itself. Worse, it wasn't that difficult to spot a needle or two lying near the entrance to the alley that ran along the side of the building.

"This is good," she said firmly, halting abruptly. "I can take it from here."

"Got orders, Francesca," Enzo said.

They even talked like Stefano, in clipped, abrupt sentences when she knew they had the best education possible from private, very expensive schools as well as tutors in the home. Joanna had given her the magazines to read, the ones that had tons of information regarding the Ferraro family with their fast cars and faster women.

"Take a risk. Live dangerously. Ignore them," she advised.

Emilio reached above her head and pulled open the door. "That's not going to happen. You obviously don't know Stefano. He'd skin us alive if we took another chance with your safety. How come anyone can walk into this building?"

She sighed. "If you insist on coming upstairs with me, try not to sound like him. It's annoying."

Truthfully, she hated walking into her apartment building, especially walking past the owner's apartment. She was always afraid he'd open the door, and he was . . . disgusting. She didn't feel in the least bit safe, but it was a step above sleeping on the street, her only alternative. There was something very creepy about the apartments. Oily and disgusting. She was fairly certain drug deals took place regularly both inside and outside of the building. She'd already stepped on a needle that had been thrown on the stairs. Luckily she'd been in her new boots and not her holey shoes.

The place was poorly lit. The stairs were creaky and the carpet torn and shabby. The walls were dingy and smelled like smoke. Still, it was a roof. It was cheap. She needed both.

Her apartment was on the third floor. She unlocked it, and before she could say anything, Emilio gently set her aside and went in first. Enzo kept a hand on her shoulder to prevent her from moving as Emilio walked through her apartment. That had to be one of the most humiliating moments of her life. She didn't look at Emilio when he emerged. She knew what she'd see on his face.

He handed her the keys. "All clear. Lock the fucking door, Francesca, not that it will do you any good."

Yep. He sounded just like his cousin. And he was unhappy.

CHAPTER SIX

Stefano rode the shadows to Francesca's apartment building, his gut in knots, his rather famous temper held in check by a mere thread. He was furious. Beyond furious. Emilio had been tense, quiet, and very upset when he'd described the apartment Francesca resided in. He'd bit out the ugly description between clenched teeth, a muscle working hard in his jaw. There was a storm of fury gathered in his eyes.

The Ferraro neighborhood stopped just two small storefronts before her building. Their block ended and they paid little attention to the state of properties bordering them. They couldn't monitor the entire world, so they were careful not to interfere, other than to warn any criminal coming into their territory not to come back.

Why the hell had Joanna allowed her friend to get an apartment outside their territory? He wanted to pay her a visit, yank her ass out of her comfortable bed in her safe home and demand the reason. It was fucking bullshit to allow Francesca in harm's way while Joanna was taking advantage of the Ferraro protection.

Joanna knew where the borders were. Francesca didn't. Joanna knew that anyone living in their neighborhood was protected inside their borders and would be watched over and avenged if anything happened outside of them. Francesca was vulnerable where she was. Joanna knew that. The moment she heard Stefano claim Francesca as his, she should have insisted her friend move within the borders or at least come to him and tell him the situation. Anything could have happened to her.

Emilio had been very uneasy just entering the apartment building. Everyone in the Ferraro family was born with a psychic gift. Most weren't shadow riders, but they were sensitive to the world around them. If Emilio said something was wrong in that building, there was no question that he was right.

Stefano stepped from the tube and waited until the car glided up, hovering at the curb, Taviano behind the wheel. He could have caught the ride with his younger brother, but he had needed to be alone. He was far angrier at himself than he'd ever been in his life. His first duty was to Francesca. He should have ensured her safety before anything else—even a job. Without her, there would be no future generations.

The Ferraro family needed her to survive. *He* needed her. Now that he knew of her existence, it was all he could think about. His own woman. He'd never really believed he would find her. To have her just show up, walk right through his territory, her shadow reaching for his, connecting so strongly with his that the jolt had felt like a lightning bolt flashing through his entire body.

He took a deep breath and tried to let some of the anger go. He would need to keep his foul temper under control to get her to cooperate. If Emilio lost his temper looking at this place, Stefano was fairly certain he'd lose his mind. She wasn't staying—and there was going to be retribution.

There was no keypad on the outer wall beside the door. Anyone could enter, not just the residents. No safety features whatsoever. His gut tightened and his jaw clenched. With controlled violence, Stefano yanked open the door and stepped inside the building. He stopped just inside, taking a deep breath as he looked around him. The lighting was very dim, only a few of the overhead lightbulbs actually working. The elevator was to his left. It looked like a death trap. The stairway was to his right, and that didn't look much better. Again, the lighting was poor. Half of the stairs appeared to be in the dark.

Enzo slid out of the murky darkness, coming from around the corner. Renato and Romano Greco, in their distinctive dark suits, the dark purple ties indicating to their family they were investigators, possessing the ability to hear lies, lounged near the door to the first apartment. Giovanni approached from the far corner. He didn't look happy.

Renato gestured toward the door. "He's in there. Name's Bart Tidwell. He's got a rap sheet you wouldn't believe. Inherited the building from his daddy. The daddy was just as fucked up as he is."

"What kind of rap sheet?" Stefano asked, knowing just by his gut instinct he wasn't going to like it. He didn't need the look of utter distaste on either of his cousins' faces.

"B and E, multiple counts. Armed robbery. More importantly, he's a sex offender. Two counts of aggravated rape. Served time on one of them. Several arrests after that, but every time since then the charges have been dropped. Stefano, each time, the alleged rape occurred in his building," Romano warned. "He fancies himself a fighter, ex-boxer, and he likes to go to bars and beat the shit out of people. Again, the charges are always dropped."

"He have family? Someone who would put pressure on the witnesses or victim for him?" Stefano asked.

"We're still digging. The only person in his life that appears to be constant is his lawyer." He glanced at his watch. "Facts are still coming in. *Mamma e papa* are still working that angle. Stefano, the lawyer is Adamo Bergenmire. He's the head lawyer for the Saldi family."

There was a small silence. "Damn it," Enzo said softly. "We should have known that fucking family would be involved."

Stefano shrugged. "We've already got a feud going with them. We have had for centuries. What the hell difference will it make if we piss them off again? I'm happy to stick it to them any chance we get. It's not like the old days, Giovanni, when they could wipe out all of us in one shot. We got smart. They can't get to all of us and they know it. They order a hit and someone's going to be slitting their throats right in their bedrooms."

"We don't retaliate like they do, killing every man, woman and child," Renato said. "Don't have it in us and they know it."

Stefano nodded. "But we've retaliated enough that the bosses fear us. They aren't going to come after us because there's a connection between Tidwell and the Saldi family. Hell, they'll probably be happy to get rid of the pain in their ass. Let's pay him a little visit." Stefano glanced at Enzo. "You have men upstairs?"

"Do you need to ask? I called in half our crew to protect her. Ricco's watching her door personally. Had a couple of nonresidents on the floor, but they left when they saw us. We weren't trying to be invisible." He sounded as grim as Stefano felt.

Romano knocked on the owner's apartment door. Hard. Controlled anger in the sound. Within a minute the door was flung open, the occupant cursing at them. He was a big man, bald, with roped muscles and a scowl meant to intimidate. He wore jeans and a wifebeater. There was a beer in his hand.

Stefano stepped into him, delivering a short, hard punch into the belly, and the man folded. Stefano walked him backward into the apartment, his men coming in behind him. Enzo closed the door and stood against it while Romano prowled through the apartment to ensure they were alone.

The room was messy, beer bottles everywhere. It stank of a combination of cigarettes and weed.

"You're going to want to take a look at this, Stefano," Romano said, poking his head out of the room at the far end of the apartment.

Stefano skirted around Tidwell and glanced into the bedroom. There was a bank of screens set up along one wall. Each screen showed an occupant's bedroom. A recorder displayed a green light beneath each screen, clearly spying on the women dressing, undressing, bringing in men and performing various sexual acts meant to be strictly private. Rows of labeled home-recorded DVDs were on the shelves.

Stefano immediately suspected this was why the charges of rape had been dropped. Tidwell showed his victims tapes and threatened to put them on the Internet. The third screen from the left showed Francesca asleep on a sleeping bag in the corner of the room, her long hair spread across a pillow. There was no furniture in the room at all. His coat hung on a single hanger above her head. In the opposite corner was a small bag. He presumed her clothes were in it.

He ran his fingers along the DVDs, finding the latest ones, the recordings labeled *Francesca*. He shoved one in the player and watched as Francesca walked through her door. She turned and pressed the lock and looked around the empty room. She was in his coat. His stomach settled just a little, feeling as if she at least had that protection. Very carefully she shrugged out of his coat and hung it on the only hanger. She stood in front of it, smoothing out imaginary wrinkles, her hands lingering. He liked that. Too much. His gut tightened. She looked vulnerable. Sad. His heart clenched. She pulled her blouse over her head and very carefully folded it, standing in her bra and jeans. Rage ripped through him.

Bart Tidwell had watched his woman undress and shower. He'd violated her privacy. Invaded her home. Swearing, Stefano watched as she stepped into the shower to start the water. Her hands went to the back of her bra and he switched the video off. Gathering up everything that said *Francesca*, including the one still recording, he caught up one more that he was certain depicted a rape—just in case he had no choice but to prove to Francesca he was telling the truth when he took her the hell out of there. He had a feeling she'd resist, and he wasn't about to let her stay.

Stefano bit out several ugly words, ripped the cord from the wall and slammed the screen to the floor. It shattered with a loud crash. "I want all of these DVDs collected and destroyed. Every single one of them."

Enzo nodded. "What do you want done with him?"

"Who inherits the building if he disappears?"

Tidwell let out a mewing noise and frantically shook his head. Stefano glanced at him. The man was on his knees, his mouth bleeding, his nose broken and one cheek split open. Emilio had returned, and he was definitely nearly as angry as Stefano.

"No one," Romano reported. "It will be a nightmare for the tenants. Renato checked in. He has an aunt, but she's not listed as his heir, but my guess is when it's all straightened out, she'll be the one inheriting and she's married to a . . ."

"Saldi. Fucking building should be condemned," Emilio snarled. He took out a gun and pressed the barrel to Tidwell's head. "Pervert needs to die, Stefano. Give me the word."

"Not like that," Giovanni said. "You're as bad as my brother. Get Vinci. We'll need his expertise. Nothing like having a lawyer in the family. Stefano, let us take care of this piece of shit and you get your woman and get her the hell out of here."

"You take this building, Giovanni," Emilio said, "and we're going to be bleeding money into it for a long time. To include it, we'll have to expand our borders. We need a vote on that."

Stefano glared at him. "Fuck the vote. Some of these women have been through enough. He filmed his own rapes. Did you look at those titles? We can renovate the building and give them a decent place to live."

Tidwell tried to rise and Stefano turned and hit him. Stefano was enormously strong and the man went down as if he'd been hit with a baseball bat.

Emilio shrugged. "I guess I can't argue with that." He pulled his cell phone from his pocket. "I'll call Vinci and have him get over here to straighten this out."

Stefano pinned Tidwell with his eyes. Flat. Cold. Killer's eyes. "You want to sell this piece of real estate, don't you, Tidwell? It's nothing but an albatross around your neck."

"You don't know who you're fucking with." Tidwell spat on the floor at Stefano's feet, a mixture of blood and saliva.

Stefano raised his eyebrow. "You mean your connection to the Saldi family? We know. You get into a lot of trouble, Bart. A *lot*. You make Adamo work for his money, don't you? They have to continually send their top lawyer in to get your ass out of trouble. Then there's the muscle to scare the crap out of your victims and the witnesses. You're more trouble than you're worth."

"My aunt . . ."

"Thinks you're a piece of shit, and her husband *knows* you are. Selling this building would make them happy, don't you think?" Stefano's voice was softer than ever. He pushed at the soft leather between his fingers, bringing Tidwell's attention to his thin gloves.

Tidwell licked his lips and then shook his head. "No. No. I don't want . . ."

Emilio crouched low and shoved his gun under Tidwell's chin. "That's too bad. My cousin's woman is in this building and you were violating her privacy. He's not a patient or forgiving man the way I am."

"I didn't know. I didn't know who she was. I swear, I wasn't going to touch her. I've stopped doing that. Adamo said if I did it again . . . I'm cured."

"You want to sell, don't you, Tidwell?" Stefano asked again, ignoring his confession and declaration.

Tidwell looked around the apartment, his gaze going cunning. "Yes. Yes. Let me up. I'll sign any papers."

Stefano smiled. It wasn't a nice smile, but then he wasn't feeling nice. Tidwell thought himself a fighter. He was big, and most bar fights he got into were with others not his size. They didn't have his skill.

"Let him up," he ordered softly.

Emilio stepped back and Tidwell exploded into action, rushing Stefano, trying to wrap him up with both arms. Stefano stepped to the side and slammed his fist deep into Tidwell's ribs. He felt the satisfying give beneath the devastating punch. Tidwell grunted. Turned white.

Stefano had trained from the time he was two years old.

He'd never stopped training. His four brothers and sister had all been put through the same regimen as he had. They were pitted against the best opponents the family could find until they moved like lightning, smooth and fast, each punch or kick penetrating the body with such force, it shook up the insides, broke bones and damaged internal organs. They still trained every single day.

His cousins, although not riders, were all proficient as well. They worked together for the good of the family. It was drilled into them from birth. There was no other way of life but that constant training of the body, turning it into a weapon, and the education of the mind.

Stefano was fast, systematic and relentless. Tidwell didn't land a single punch. The beating was both brutal and savage. Deliberate. Inflicting as much pain as possible. Lamps were smashed, furniture overturned and beer bottles crushed as the boxer tried his best to get away from the punishing blows. Eventually, and way too soon as far as Stefano believed, Tidwell hit the floor hard. Stefano didn't end it there, but continued the vicious assault.

"You're going to kill him," Giovanni pointed out. "He needs to sign over the building. He's already unconscious."

Stefano stepped back immediately. In spite of his jacket, he hadn't worked up much of a sweat. "You know what to do when it's done, Giovanni," he said. "Make certain you drop a few hundred thousand into his account so it's all legit. We want the deal to be solid and to stand up under any scrutiny, especially if this fucker goes missing."

"Stefano," Giovanni cautioned. His tone was mild.

The two brothers locked gazes. Stared at each other while the temperature in the room seemed to go up and the air was so heavy with rage, it felt impossible to breathe.

"Damn it, Gee."

"I know. I feel the same way." Giovanni didn't look away.

Stefano sighed and shook his head. "Where do I put this rage?"

"Not here. You know that. Nothing close to us. Nothing

personal. He has to be seen. We can beat the shit out of him, but that's all. We protect the family. Always."

"Fucking call New York. I want Geno in on this one," Stefano capitulated softly. His cousin Geno from New York would have to handle the problem of Bart Tidwell. He yanked out his cell phone and dialed a number.

"Yeah, Saldi, Stefano Ferraro. I'm standing here in this piece of shit's apartment. I understand he belongs to you."

There was silence.

"Tidwell," Stefano confirmed. "He was after my woman. He's got hundreds of recordings the cops would like to get ahold of. Rapes he committed. Watching the women in his building. He's got it right in his bedroom. That's how stupid this dumb fuck is."

The explosion of foul words on the other end of the phone was loud enough for everyone in the room to hear.

"Out of courtesy, we're going to destroy that evidence," Stefano assured, his voice soothing. "We'll leave the fucker on your doorstep. He'll be a little worse for wear, but that might be beneficial. He might listen. If not, well, that's up to you."

More silence while Stefano listened.

"No, Saldi, that's not what's going to happen." Stefano's voice dropped even lower. "He fucking went after my woman. He's going to pay, and he's damn lucky I feel in the mood to extend courtesy to you. He's going to hand over the building and he's going to get the beating of his life. He can count himself lucky that's all that's happening. He comes near what's mine again, I'll rip his fucking heart out. Got that? Are we clear? I hope we are, because if you really want to go to war over this piece of shit, I'm willing. That's how pissed I am right now."

More silence while the voice on the other end soothed him. Assured him the deal was fine. Stefano snapped his cell phone shut—the cell phone that made his brothers and sister laugh at him. He had a bad habit of throwing the damn thing when-ever it pissed him off, which was often. They thought he should have a smartphone, the way they all did, but he liked slamming the damn thing closed when he was annoyed with whoever was on the other end. He looked at his brother. "I want Vinci to make certain the real estate deal is airtight. Tell Geno this weekend when we're at the club. If Tidwell's in Saldi's home, all the better."

"Sorry, Stefano. No." Emilio shook his head. "Not this one, cousin. This one's mine."

Stefano's gaze jumped to his cousin. "I had another job in mind for you, Emilio." They didn't like any other family member other than a rider to get blood on their hands if at all possible. Emilio had a kind heart, but he was a Ferraro through and through. He didn't like men who harmed women.

"What would that be?"

Stefano jerked his head toward the door. Reluctantly, Emilio followed him out into the hall. "Call Vittorio and tell him you'll meet him at Joanna's house. I want her woken up tonight. Have him drag her ass out of bed and down to you. The two of you get answers. Those answers had better make sense to me."

"Stefano," Emilio cautioned. "I know you have every right to be angry. No way did Joanna know that Francesca would be spied on by the owner of this dump."

"You and I both know Tidwell was setting up to fucking rape Francesca. Joanna sleeps good at night, and so does her family because of us. We give them that. The moment she knew Francesca was my woman she should have gotten her out of this shit hole. Tidwell *saw* Francesca undressing. Showering. He looked at her without her consent. He's a fucking dead man, but Joanna needs to answer to *la famiglia*. You tell Vittorio that I don't like the answers, it will be me conducting the next interview and I won't be polite."

"Stefano . . ." Emilio cautioned.

"You like Joanna. You're friends with her family. So am I, but Emilio, right now, I don't trust myself. By now, Vittorio knows what is happening here. He'll be as pissed as I am. I need you to do this right."

There was a long silence. Emilio sighed. "You're not sending me away because . . ."

"No. I need to make certain none of us do anything stupid tonight. If I was the one questioning her, I have no idea what I'd do. I need you to do this for me, Emilio."

"Go get your woman, Stefano," Emilio advised, capitulating. "Everyone's going to feel a whole hell of a lot better when she's safe."

"Vinci has to make certain the deal is done a couple of days earlier. Can he get the papers filed with the correct dates?"

"That's his department, and he's never let us down. He's really good at what he does, Stefano. You can't micromanage this. Just go get her," Giovanni advised. "I'm holding on by a thread, too. One of us has to be sane here, and I'm going to lose it if you don't get her out of this place."

Stefano took a deep breath and clapped his brother on the shoulder. *Famiglia*. This was how it had worked for centuries. They had developed into a single entity. One stepping up when another needed them. Stefano was always the leader, but his brothers were more than capable of leading. They were every bit as dedicated and trained as he was. He was grateful for Giovanni. Right then, his temper had no outlet and he was thinking with his emotions, not his brain. Ordinarily, if it was personal, he would never have touched the mark, but he couldn't stop himself from going after Tidwell. He'd never had such a loss of control. He needed to get Francesca out of there as much as his brother and other family members needed him to do so.

He turned on his heel and made for the stairs. Ricco waited at the top. Their men were shadow figures, spread throughout the building, keeping Francesca from harm. The stairs were dark in several places, dangerous for anyone, let alone single women. The rage smoldering in the pit of his stomach grew with every step he took.

He was angry with Joanna, who had to have known this apartment building was worse than substandard. Most of all, he was angry with himself for not checking on Francesca's living conditions before he went out of town. He had assumed she was staying with Joanna until she got on her feet. It was a very misguided presumption. A mistake. Stefano didn't like making mistakes.

He was a protective man. He had been born that way. Every rider was. The need to protect and control was bred into every single one of them. Those two traits were so ingrained in them, there was no getting either characteristic out. No getting around them.

"One incident I didn't like," Ricco said. "Earlier, Enzo reported that a man, not a resident of the building, had twice come up to this floor. He actually walked right up to Francesca's door, paused, looked around, and when he spotted Enzo, took off. A few minutes ago, he actually came back into the building. There aren't any security cameras and he wore a hoodie. No one got a good look at his face, but from Enzo's description, I'm guessing it was the same man."

Stefano took a deep breath. What the hell was going on? Everything around him was spinning out of control when he was all about control—when control was absolutely necessary. He was taking control back. Francesca was just going to have to deal with the truth about him and the life she would lead with him as her man.

"Anyone sees him again, scoop him up and take him to the warehouse. I'm getting her out of here tonight. I'll take her to my penthouse suite at the Ferraro." Their hotel was a study in sheer luxury. He had several homes, scattered around the country and overseas as well, but when he was in Chicago, which was most of the time, he stayed at the hotel in the penthouse.

Ricco nodded and trailed after his brother. Stefano knew his brother wasn't protecting him so much as protecting anyone who might try to stop him. The second flight of stairs was almost completely dark, lit only by one dull bulb, which gave off little light. The carpet was filthy and threadbare. Anyone could trip and fall with the holes in it. His temper rose another notch.

The long hallway was totally without light, other than what managed to spill in from the dirty windows at either end of the hall. Francesca's door was midway between the two windows. Stefano wondered if Tidwell had deliberately given her that apartment. Probably. He had to put the single women in apartments where cameras were already set up, although it was possible he had them in all the rooms.

He raised his hand, fingers in a tight fist and controlled his impulse to pound on the door, demanding entrance. Instead, he knocked quietly, his other hand automatically dropping to the doorknob. To his shock, the door inched open. He hadn't turned the knob. Just his gloved knuckles knocking so politely had been enough to spring the door open. What the hell was wrong with her? He glanced back at Ricco's face. It was set in stone, just the way, he was sure, his was.

Before he could jerk open the door and confront her, something made him crouch low and examine the lock. He could see the thin piece of tape placed over the mechanism— a simple but very effective method of preventing Francesca from locking the door.

"Fucker," he spat out, stepping back to show his brother.

"Let's get her the hell out of here, Stefano. Even if you have to carry her out like a caveman. Taviano's waiting in the car. Just get her and go before a bunch of us decide to burn this place to the ground with Tidwell in it."

Ricco's voice was strained. Stefano cursed again. The entire family was affected because he hadn't done his job. He hadn't taken charge of Francesca. He wanted time to court her. To give her that. To let her get to know him before he had to come clean about the shit life he was going to have to ask her to accept. He closed his eyes briefly. He knew it wasn't about asking her. He had to find a way to get her to accept not only him, but his life and his family, because there was no other choice. Worse, he wasn't just asking her to accept it for herself; she had to accept it for their children as well. He *detested* that.

He stood slowly and pushed open the door. His heart

stuttered in his chest. The door opened into a very small room—so small the closet in his master bedroom was larger. There wasn't a single stick of furniture. No chairs. No tables. Nothing at all. The room included a miniature kitchen with a single stained sink and tiny refrigerator. He detested that Francesca—or any woman—would have to stay alone in a place like this. Why hadn't he checked before he left for his job?

He walked into the next room to find her lying on a sleeping bag, her hair spread out over the pillow. The room was freezing. There was no heat coming from the old radiator and she shivered continuously in her sleep. She would have done better to have his coat covering the sleeping bag, but instead, it was hung carefully on a hanger a few feet from her head.

She looked very small under the thin sleeping bag. Her face was turned toward him and he thought she was the most beautiful thing he'd ever seen. Her lashes were exceptionally long and turned up on the ends. Black, like her hair. He crouched down beside her. Close.

"*Bambina*, wake up." He kept his voice low. Soothing. Not wanting to scare her. He should have taken better care of her. None of this was her fault. He had to remember that when he wanted to put his fist through a wall—or through Tidwell—and rage at the world in general.

Her body jerked. The lashes fluttered. Lifted. He found himself staring into sea-blue eyes. Almost turquoise. Beautiful. The sight hit him low, a wicked punch to his groin. He took a breath. Fear crept into the startled blue of her eyes.

"Stefano." Francesca breathed the name. The room was dark, but enough light came through the curtainless window to illuminate Stefano Ferraro's very masculine features. His brooding eyes were on her face and her stomach did a slow roll. Her heart pounded so hard it actually hurt.

She couldn't just lie there with him staring down at her with his incredible eyes. Eyes that saw everything. Eyes that saw her shabby room with no furniture. Saw that she had *nothing*. Color crept into her face. She swept back her hair and struggled into a sitting position, holding the sleeping bag over her chest. She wore an old threadbare T-shirt and lacy boy-short underwear, the only thing she had bought new.

"What are you doing in my bedroom?" She tried to make it a demand, but her voice wasn't working correctly. She winced at the word *bedroom*, wishing she had just said *apartment*. God. He was scary. He didn't move a muscle. He didn't blink. He was hot as Hades, and every single cell in her body responded to him. Was aware of him. Her breasts felt swollen and achy and she was very, very glad for the sleeping bag she had pulled up over her chest so he couldn't see her nipples getting hard.

No one had ever made her body come to life like he did. Just looking at him. Just smelling his cologne. It was humiliating. She knew she should be outraged that he was there in her apartment, but something was wrong. She could see it in his eyes. Her hand flew defensively to her throat.

"Joanna," she whispered. "Did something happen to her?" She would never forgive herself. Never. She shouldn't have come. She thought she'd covered her tracks, but money talked and if someone was still looking for her, they'd eventually find her—and anyone who helped her.

"She's fine, Francesca. You need to get up and come with me now."

She glanced beyond him to the door of her bedroom. Someone was in her front room. She couldn't make out who, but she saw a shadowy male figure.

Shoving back her hair with one hand, she held tightly to her sleeping bag with the other. "Just tell me, Stefano."

"You can't stay here."

Her heart stuttered at his expression. Grim. Implacable. His jaw tightened as though anticipating her argument—and she was going to argue.

"Well. No. This is where I live."

Something dangerous flickered in the depths of his eyes. He suddenly looked feral. Predatory. In that moment she could almost believe he was some sort of crime lord. He wasn't the kind of man to take no for an answer.

"*Bambina*, you've got two choices. You can walk out of here dressed, or I'm carrying you out just the way you are. You fucking decide, because I've had it with this hellhole."

She swallowed hard. He wasn't joking. She held up one hand to ward him off. "How did you get in here?"

"Are you fucking kidding me? Your fucking door wasn't even locked, Francesca."

He was *really* furious to throw so many F-bombs at her. "No. It was. I locked it." She narrowed her eyes at him. "I'm not stupid, Stefano. I locked the door. How did you get in here?"

"I raised my hand to knock and the door opened on its own. There's a piece of tape over the mechanism to prevent it from locking."

There was the ring of truth in his voice and she felt panic rising. Her gaze skittered across the room toward her bedroom door. That door didn't lock. Only the main apartment door locked. "Who would do that? That doesn't make sense." Fear made her heart pound and put a strange taste in her mouth. "Just tell me what's going on."

"I'll tell you after I get you out of here and to somewhere I know you're safe. Come on, *dolce cuore*, get up." His features softened.

She moistened her lips. His eyes were so beautiful they took her breath away. She would do anything to see that look on his face. Anything at all for him. With the exception of getting up and allowing him to see the shirt she wore. She couldn't just go with him without an explanation. That wasn't even reasonable. She found it far worse that he could see how little she had. The last thing she wanted was for him to pity her. Sheesh. This was so humiliating.

"I want you to leave. We can talk about this in the morning." She forced decisiveness into her voice. He couldn't really *force* her to go with him. No one would actually carry out such a ridiculous threat.

His entire expression changed. His extremely masculine features went from soft to stone in the space of a single heartbeat. She knew immediately she was in trouble. He reached for her, hauling her into his arms, sleeping bag and all.

"Ricco, get my coat and her things. We'll be at the penthouse." Stefano tossed her easily over his shoulder and stood up as if she didn't weigh more than a sack of rice.

She caught at his shirt, upside down, staring at his backside. Clutching his jacket, she struggled against the iron band across her thighs. He ignored her and strode right out of the bedroom, past Ricco, who, when she lifted her head, smirked at her. Clearly, Ricco was another brother. They all looked alike, smug and full of arrogance.

"Put me down right this minute," she demanded. Breathless. Her belly was over his shoulder and he felt a little like an oak tree with no give.

"Too late, Francesca. Be still."

He stalked down the hall, and she caught glimpses of men falling into step behind him. Good God. Maybe he was part of a human trafficking ring and he was kidnapping her. What was wrong with her? She screamed. Loud.

His hand came down hard on her butt. She felt the sting right through the sleeping bag, although it didn't really hurt, but it did shock her into silence.

"I told you I'd get you to safety and then tell you what's going on," he snapped, his voice grim. "Just be still. I don't give a damn if you want to scream, but it's rather pointless. Do you really think in this apartment building anyone is going to stick their neck into our business?"

He was moving fast now, taking the stairs effortlessly. She felt a little dizzy and she clutched at his jacket harder.

"You're scaring me, Stefano," she admitted, hating that her voice trembled, but she was frightened.

"I know, *bambina*, but you'll be fine. I've got you now and I'm going to keep you safe. Which you weren't in this rattrap. Just trust me for a few more minutes and then I'll explain everything. Can you give me that?"

She laid her head against his back, feeling his muscles ripple as he moved into the foyer of the apartment building.

It wasn't as if she had much choice. The door to the owner's apartment was open and as they passed, she glimpsed men inside. The place was a wreck. Then they were out in the open air. He reached out and yanked open the door to the backseat of a town car. He was very gentle as he deposited her on the backseat, still cocooned in the sleeping bag. He slid in beside her, reaching to buckle her in.

The driver turned and tossed a cocky grin over his shoulder at her. "I'm Taviano, Stefano's brother. Nice to meet you, Francesca."

CHAPTER SEVEN

"This is crazy. You're kidnapping me," Francesca managed to say, finally catching her breath. She wasn't certain if she couldn't breathe because Stefano had just showed her his ruthless side, or because he was the most attractive man she'd ever met in her life and her entire body responded in a very intimate way when he'd revealed that ruthless side. Why being thrown over his shoulder and carried through a building like a Viking captive should make her body damp and needy made no sense, but she couldn't deny that she felt intensely alive and wildly attracted to Stefano Ferraro.

She caught at the safety belt to jerk it off of her, but Stefano's hand closed over hers, preventing movement. "Calm the fuck down and stop fighting me. It won't do you any good, and I'm already pissed off. I don't like repeating myself, either."

Francesca subsided against the cool leather of the seats, shocked at his tone. At the sheer anger. Stefano was definitely skating close to an explosion. She didn't want to be anywhere around him when he detonated. "Wow. You wake me up in the middle of the night, without knocking on my door, I might add, and carry me out over your shoulder like I'm a sack of potatoes and you're the one angry."

A little snicker came from the driver and she glared at him in the mirror, but he didn't look at her, his gaze studiously on the road. Still, she knew he was laughing.

"I was gentle with you," Stefano reminded her. "So not like

a sack of potatoes. I explained about the door, not that it would have stopped me had it been locked. You don't belong in that building and you damn well know it."

She winced at his tone. "Not everyone can afford to live at the Ritz." She gave him tone right back.

"I live at the Ferraro, not the Ritz, which is where we're going now."

Her mouth fell open. The Ferraro was considered the height of luxury. No one could afford it but the rich and famous. "You are not taking me to that place. I mean it."

"Why not?"

Her mouth opened several times but no sound emerged for the longest time. "Are you serious? I'm dressed in a sleeping bag. You can't walk through those doors without looking glamorous. They'll throw me out."

For the first time, a faint glint of humor crept into the deep blue of his eyes. "*Piccola*, I own the hotel. I doubt anyone could do that without losing their job."

Total male amusement. She didn't think anything was funny about the situation. "No way. Drop me off at the nearest shelter." She stuck her chin in the air.

Stefano looked down at her, and the impact of meeting his penetrating blue eyes felt like an arrow piercing her chest straight to her heart. Her heart stuttered and her stomach did a slow roll. All trace of amusement was gone, leaving his jaw hard and his eyes burning with a fierce anger that threatened to scorch everyone in the car.

"You are telling me that you would rather go to a shelter than come to my hotel with me?" He bit out each word separately from behind perfect white clenched teeth. "Would you like to explain why?"

No, she wouldn't like to explain why. First, if she told him it was because he was wealthy, that would make her sound prejudiced, which if she were being entirely truthful, she was. Second, he was the hottest, sexiest man she'd ever come across in her entire life and already, in the close confines of the car, even upset at him, she couldn't stop her body's reaction to him.

"Do I have to have a reason?" She stuck her chin in the air.

Taviano snorted, and when she glared into the rearview mirror, he assumed an innocent mask.

"It wouldn't matter anyway, because your reason is as much bullshit as you staying in that firetrap of an apartment. The only reason the building hasn't been condemned is because Tidwell is related to the Saldis and they're notorious for bribing officials or threatening them."

"Like you're doing to me?" she challenged.

"I'm not bribing or threatening," Stefano denied flatly. "You just don't have a choice."

His voice was very low, velvet soft so that the tone played over her skin like fingers. She shivered and burrowed deeper into the threadbare sleeping bag.

"It's called kidnapping if I don't want to go with you."

"I don't give a damn what you call it, *dolce cuore*, just so long as you're safe."

That was hard to argue with, especially since she was a little bit freaked out and unsure of what just happened. She was beginning to panic. "Taviano, you tell him he can't do this."

"Nice of you to join us tonight," Taviano said, glancing back in the rearview mirror. "I must say, my brother has good taste." The teasing note in his voice calmed her. "Even my parents gave up trying to tell him what he could or couldn't do when he was around ten," Taviano added, with a quick grin thrown at her through the mirror.

There was no help there, but then she'd been pretty certain Stefano's own brother wasn't going to get her out of this mess. Clearly he found the situation amusing.

She glanced at Stefano and then away, unable to meet his eyes. "I don't have any clothes." The confession slipped out. Low. Under her breath. She kept her gaze firmly on the floor of the vehicle.

"Francesca, look at me."

Her heart jumped and then began to pound again at his authoritative tone. She couldn't imagine anyone disobeying him. Her gaze jumped to his before she could stop it. It was a mistake. His eyes were glittering with a kind of menace she couldn't conceive. That, and something that made her stomach coil and the burn at the junction of her legs grow hotter.

"You're safe. Just settle. I'm pissed as hell and you aren't doing yourself any favors by trying to defy me."

She sucked in her breath sharply. "*Defy* you?" She forgot all about being afraid or intimidated by him. "Like I'm some errant child you have to reprimand? You have got to be the most arrogant, annoying, bossy man I've ever encountered."

"That about sums him up," Taviano agreed, his grin widening. "We're here."

To her horror, he had really pulled up in front of the Ferraro Hotel. Taviano drove the car right up to the red carpet extending from the building, where several valets waited to jump into action the moment a car glided close.

"I'm not getting out," Francesca declared. "I'm dressed in a sleeping bag for God's sake. Really, Stefano, just take me to a shelter."

She should have known better than to expect Stefano to comply. Apparently he really didn't argue when he wanted his way—and he wanted his way. The valet opened the passenger door. Stefano slid out and reached for her.

"I'll scream."

"Go ahead, *bambina*. Make a scene. I don't mind. You're still going up to the penthouse with me." His tone was implacable.

"Stefano." She wasn't above pleading.

He ignored her, his hands gripping her right through the sleeping bag. He was enormously strong and there was no prying his fingers off of her. He dragged her out of the backseat, tossed her over his shoulder again and without saying a word to anyone, he walked right up to the double glass doors. The doors were already open for him, the doorman grinning and giving him a little salute.

Going into the Ferraro Hotel was the most embarrassing thing Francesca could possibly imagine. Clamping her mouth shut so she wouldn't scream in sheer frustration, she buried her face against his back, holding tightly to his shirt. She stayed very still, not wanting anyone to see her, but knowing everyone was looking. For one thing, Stefano Ferraro was hot and superrich and owned the entire hotel. Okay, maybe his family did, but still, who would expect him to be carrying a woman over his shoulder, upside down, cocooned in a sleeping bag? It was mortifying.

He went straight to a private elevator, keyed in a number and stepped inside. The doors glided closed. "Are you all right?"

"What do you think?" she snapped, pouring sarcasm into her voice. "You just carried me through the lobby of a luxury hotel in a sleeping bag."

His hand shifted from her thighs to her butt. She felt his palm right through the material of the sleeping bag. Her breath caught in her throat. She was furious. And scared. The way he had his fingers splayed wide over her bottom affected her more than she cared to admit. She was so aware of him it was a sin.

"I did give you a choice. I told you that you could get dressed and come with me or I was carrying you out." There was no remorse at all in his voice.

"*God.* Seriously, Stefano? That wasn't a choice." She wanted to pinch him really hard or sink her teeth into him, but he'd already smacked her on the butt once; she wasn't going for a second time. Mostly because she had a strange reaction to his hand connecting with her even through the thin layers of material. Heat had rushed through her, arcing straight to her sex. Every cell came alive. Between her legs she felt damp and needy. She had a difficult time pulling in air. All from that brief contact.

"I don't argue, Francesca. It's a waste of time. You were

in danger there. I told you when I had you safe, I'd tell you what was going on but you clearly decided to argue."

"Do you think you could put me down?" It was sheer hell to be hanging upside down and trying to sound as if she were reasonable when all she wanted to do was bash him one.

"Are you going to hop like a bunny?"

Amusement tinged his voice and brought color spreading over her body. Her face was already red from hanging upside down. She couldn't see what floor he was going to, but the elevator ride was smooth and long. That meant they went up a *lot* of floors. The one thing she held on to was that he had carried her publicly through the lobby. "People may have witnessed my most embarrassing moment, but they aren't going to forget it. If you plan on selling me to some human-trafficking ring, someone will remember."

"Good to know." Sarcasm dripped.

It wasn't as if she really thought he was going to sell her to the highest bidder, but he didn't have to sound so patronizing.

The elevator doors glided open and he stepped into a foyer. It was quite large and opulent. She caught a glimpse of a mahogany table with a huge vase that looked like cut crystal with an enormous fresh flower arrangement in it. The floor was polished and seemed to be marble. She closed her eyes, not wanting to see any more. This was a nightmare. When Stefano put her on his black leather couch, he did so very gently.

She swept back her hair with one hand, holding on to the sleeping bag with the other. Her hair was wild from sleeping without braiding it, but she'd just been too tired. Mostly, she was exhausted from thinking about Stefano, having ridiculous, impossible, erotic thoughts about him that sent blood rushing hotly through her veins straight to her core. Her dreams had been worse, images she had no experience or knowledge of, but all with him.

It was his fault she hadn't been able to fall asleep easily. His fault that her hair was a big mess, after sleeping on it and then being hung upside down. She glared at him, and if there was any justice in the world, he would have withered on the spot. Clearly there wasn't because he paced across the room, completely unaffected, like a caged tiger, poured himself a couple of fingers of liquor from a crystal decanter and threw it back as if it was water.

Francesca licked her lips. Something about the set of his shoulders, the line of his jaw and the fluid pacing took her breath. "Are you angry with me?"

His blue gaze jumped to her face. Slid over her and went back up to hold hers. Oh yeah. He was angry.

"What the hell were you thinking, living in a place like that?" His voice was low. Venomous. Packed with menace.

She winced and studied him from under her lashes, trying not to look as if she was staring. He was really, really good-looking, but she'd seen attractive men before and her body had never responded quite so eagerly. He was totally confident in himself, bordering on arrogance and that alone should have put her off of him. Not to mention he was filthy rich and she totally detested that sort of person— a man with so much money that he clearly felt the rules didn't apply to him. With all of that, she couldn't stop her body from going into full-blown meltdown.

"I don't see how that's your business." She wasn't going to tell him it was that horrible apartment or a cardboard box in an alley somewhere.

Stefano opened his jacket, took out several DVDs, prowled across the floor and held them out to her. She kept her gaze on his face. He was angry. *Really* angry. He smoldered with a kind of rage she couldn't begin to imagine. Very slowly she allowed her gaze to drop to the DVDs in his hand. They were homemade, recorded off a machine. She took them reluctantly and turned them over to look at the labels. Her name was scrawled across the front of two of them. The third had no name, and the fourth was labeled *Vicki Wants It*.

"What is this?"

"Your landlord is a fucking sex offender. He has cameras in the apartments and he spies on women undressing, showering and sleeping."

Francesca felt the blood drain from her face. She knew she'd had a completely visceral reaction to Bart Tidwell from the moment she'd met him. He made her feel sick, but he owned the building and she needed a roof over her head. "Are you sure?" Her voice was a thread of sound, a whisper.

"Would you like to see the file we have on him?" Stefano poured himself another drink, downed it and turned back to face her. His features were a mask of sheer anger. "He also creeps into apartments and rapes the women and then blackmails them. He's connected to a very powerful crime family, the Saldis, and they protect that piece of slime so witnesses never testify. He was marking you for his next target. I'm fairly certain he planned on visiting you tonight. There was tape over the lock on your door."

She shook her head, her heart stuttering hard in her chest. Her mouth went dry. "That's not possible." But it was, of course. She could tell just by his anger that it was true. He was furious.

"I didn't look at the recordings, but I suspect those are of you showering and stripping to get ready for bed."

She couldn't prevent the wince at the word "stripping" or the color creeping into her face all over again. "Oh. My. God." She forgot all about holding up the sleeping bag and covered her open mouth with her palm. Her hand shook.

She didn't have anywhere else to go. Worse, her only clothes were in that apartment and she wasn't certain she could ever bear walking in there again. "Are you sure?" She knew the answer, but she still had to ask.

His eyes locked with hers. There was compassion there. Too much. She preferred his anger. Her stomach rolled and she felt the burn of tears behind her eyes. Blinking rapidly to hold them at bay, she took a deep breath to try to calm her churning stomach.

"Do you want to see what's on those DVDs? The last one, the one that is labeled *Vicki Wants It*, I'm certain is a recording of your landlord raping that girl. There were more of these recordings than I cared to count in that piece of shit's bedroom."

She stared at him in horror, wishing she didn't believe him, but there was no doubt in her mind that he was telling her the truth. He'd saved her. This beautiful man, far too wealthy and arrogant for his own good, the one she'd been afraid was involved in organized crime, had *saved* her. She just persisted in thinking the absolute worst of him.

Francesca looked down at the floor. The shiny, beautiful marble floor. "Thank you, Stefano. I don't understand how this man could have gotten away with putting cameras in apartments, but I appreciate you making certain the recordings don't end up on the Internet." She couldn't think about the possibility that Tidwell might have crept into her apartment and raped her. "How did you find out about this?"

"My cousin," Stefano told her, studying her face. She looked so fragile, as if any minute she might burst into tears or just faint. He didn't know whether to hold her in his arms and comfort her or shake her until her teeth rattled.

"Emilio. He took you home, did a walk-through of your apartment and didn't like the fact that it wasn't safe. He came to me, and I decided to talk to the owner about making certain his tenants were safe. My cousins, Renato and Romano as well as Zia Rachele and Zio Alfeo immediately began gathering information on him. They're investigators. That's what they do and they don't make mistakes. When I went to Tidwell's apartment, we discovered the screens up. You were on one of them, sleeping. It was easy enough to see he was recording you while you slept. From the labels on the rest of the DVDs, it wasn't that difficult to guess what was on the other recordings he had of you."

Her long, feathery lashes fluttered again and she shook her head. She'd gone from blushing to pale in the space of a few moments. Every protective cell in his body responded to her. She suddenly looked terribly young and vulnerable to him.

His body reacted, something that never happened to him. He was all about control and any kind of sexual response to a woman was allowed only when he was in a bedroom, certainly not when he was discussing a sexual predator with a potential victim. Totally inappropriate, but nevertheless, all he could think about was kissing her.

"I'll have to thank Emilio." She spoke in a small voice, barely a whisper.

"Do you want a drink?"

She pushed back the heavy fall of hair. Under the lights, the thick mass gleamed like silk, and he wanted to bury his fingers in that richness. Her lashes lifted and she met his eyes. The impact hit him low, like a wicked punch, a shot to his groin that heated his blood and made him feel primitive and a little bit savage. He was Sicilian, hot-blooded, and for the first time in his life, he knew what that meant—and it had nothing to do with his rather foul temper.

"Yes, please."

She was completely panic-stricken and trying not to show it. He wanted to hold her. Comfort her. Take her to his bed and make her forget everything but him. He poured a small amount of brandy into a crystal glass and walked across the room to her. His shadow, cast by the overhead chandelier, reached for her. Simultaneously, her shadow threw out a feeler, and as if powerful magnets, the two tubes connected. The jolt was hard, pouring steel into his cock. He nearly burst right through his trousers.

Francesca's eyes widened. Clung to his. Her lips parted, and he saw the telling flush on her face. She was no longer holding the sleeping bag up and it had fallen to her waist. Beneath the thin tee, her breasts rose and fell, her nipples hard little peaks, pushing at the worn material. That same sexual jolt had hit her just as hard.

Stefano stalked across the room, put the glass of brandy down on the small table beside the couch and leaned into her, both fists planted on either side of her hips. Close. So close he could see that her skin looked flawless and her lashes were even longer than he'd thought. Her scent caught at him, enveloping him in orange and cinnamon.

"You scared the hell out of me," he hissed, his anger boiling to the surface all over again, this time mixing with a fireball of pure lust.

She had to shrink back, save herself, do something, anything at all to help him stay in control. She didn't move away from him. The air felt electric. Their shadows remained connected, heightening his awareness of her. Of every breath she took. The length of her lashes. Her parted lips, a soft bow of a mouth, the tip of her tongue, her high cheekbones and the vulnerable line of her jaw.

He wanted to taste her more than he wanted to breathe. He realized it wasn't a want so much as a need. He froze, his face inches from hers, imposing iron will on himself. Never, at any time in his life, had he lost control, not until the situation involved her. Francesca Capello. His brother had had to pull him back from killing the piece of crap Bart Tidwell. Here, he was, standing over the top of her, a woman who was clearly afraid of him, about to kiss her. His life was about control. Where the hell was all that famous control now?

Francesca's lips rubbed against each other, a slow, sexy, *enticing* movement that robbed him of his ability to breathe. He couldn't remember wanting a woman the way he wanted her. Her scent surrounded him until he was drowning in a field of cinnamon and orange. Every breath he drew into his lungs took her with it until he felt her inside him.

"Stefano."

He groaned at the sound of his name. Soft. Sensual. Filled with longing. She felt it, too, that terrible pull brought on by the connection of their shadows. Brought on by the chemistry raging between them. She didn't understand it and there was fear in her eyes. Fear and longing. Need almost as great as his. She shifted her body very subtly toward his, her face lifting a fraction.

"You scared the hell out of me," he repeated, much softer this time.

Her lashes fluttered. Long. Feathery. Gorgeous. "I'm sorry. I didn't know."

"You shouldn't have been there, Francesca." It took effort to stay unmoving, while he battled for control. This was going to be the greatest fight of his life. He couldn't afford to lose. He was fighting for his life. For the life of his family.

She moistened her lips so they glistened invitingly. Tempting him. Enticing him closer. Did she know what she was doing? He doubted it. There was too much innocence on her face. Too much fear in her eyes.

That fear and innocence gave him back his control. He straightened, taking himself out of danger. He stepped back, his body hard, full and painful. That part of him wasn't under control. He turned away from her and went back to the decanter, every step difficult.

"Why didn't you stay with Joanna?" He kept his back to her as he poured liquor into his glass. He didn't want her to see the rage swirling so close to the surface. Rage at her friend who would allow her to stay in such dangerous circumstances.

"She wanted me to, but I felt like she'd done too much for me already." The confession was low.

He turned his head and looked at her over his shoulder. Her chin was up. She wasn't defeated, just frightened. "So you deliberately put yourself in danger for the sake of your pride?"

She opened her mouth to protest but snapped it closed just as quickly. Genuine confusion slid over her face. "I don't know. I guess that's exactly what I did. I didn't realize that Tidwell was such a sleaze . . ." Her voice trailed off and she looked away from him, more color creeping under her skin. She looked down at her hands. "I did know he was a sleaze, but it never occurred to me that he would put cameras in the apartments."

"Or tape over your lock so he could come in whenever he

wanted and rape you?" There was no keeping the edge from his voice. He still wanted to shake her. "You didn't try the door to make certain it was latched. You knew you were in a dangerous situation and yet you didn't take precautions."

There was a long silence. It stretched out between them. He knew how to use silence. He lived in silence. He worked in silence. Silence gained him the upper hand because he exercised control. He tossed back the bourbon and let the fire settle in his belly, warming him when he hadn't realized he'd been so cold.

"I don't have any clothes." Her gaze came back to his. She'd told him the same thing in the car. Clearly she was concerned about it.

She looked . . . vulnerable. Forlorn. That look tugged at his heartstrings. He turned back toward her and leaned one hip lazily against the table.

"That's not a worry. We'll get you clothes. You had the money in the coat."

Color swept up her neck into her face. He hadn't realized a woman could blush so much.

"I didn't want to use your money. I didn't know when I could pay it back." She cleared her throat. "I didn't mean in general. I have clothes, just not here. Just not *on*." She put the tip of her thumb in her mouth and bit down, her gaze not meeting his, but settling on his jaw.

"I see how that could be considered a problem." Humor crept into his gut, easing some of the worst knots. "I'll be right back." He left her, knowing she couldn't very well hop into the elevator and make her escape.

In the master bedroom, he selected one of his favorite shirts. The material was soft and would drape on her body lovingly. Because of the difference in their sizes, she would be sufficiently covered, but she still couldn't run off when she fully realized she didn't have a place to go.

When he returned to the room, her gaze jumped to his and then shifted away as he handed her the shirt. She took it, and the movement caused the sleeping bag to drop lower, pooling around her waist. She wore a thin T-shirt. There was a hole up by her right shoulder, allowing him to catch a glimpse of her soft skin. That little hint sent another rush of hot blood coursing through his veins.

Her breasts rose and fell beneath the material. He could see the outline of her nipples, the way they pushed hard against the restraint. She was nearly as aroused as he was. For a moment, he couldn't breathe. Couldn't speak. He could only look at her and savor the moment, knowing she belonged to him.

"This will do until we get you some clothes."

"I can't stay here." She made the declaration, obviously having worked herself up in the short time he was gone.

"Just for tonight. I have several rooms, and you'll be safe. If you're worried, you can put a chair under the doorknob." Not that that would ever keep him out, but he wasn't going to tell her that—yet. "You can get a good night's sleep and we'll tackle the problems in the morning."

She took a deep breath and without realizing she was doing it, rubbed the fabric of his shirt against her cheek. He recognized it as a nervous gesture, but to him it was significant. She didn't realize it, but already she was turning to him for reassurance.

"I don't see how this situation can be resolved," Francesca said. "I can't go back there, but I can't afford anything else."

"A situation can always be resolved. You're *not* going back there and we'll figure it out in the morning. I'll give you a couple of minutes to change out of the sleeping bag and into my shirt."

He allowed a trace of amusement to enter his voice. She rewarded him with a faint smile.

"I don't know, Stefano. This sleeping bag is pretty chic. The latest rage."

"I'll admit, on you, it looks pretty good, but I don't think you can walk around—or run from me like you'd prefer."

Her smile widened. Reached her eyes. Lit them so they glittered like gems. "I think I'm so exhausted that I'll kick off my running shoes for the night." The smile faded. "Honestly, Stefano, thank you for rescuing me."

His gut clenched hotly. "You're very welcome. Do me a favor and next time give me the benefit of the doubt."

"So you think there will be a next time?"

"Without a doubt." His phone buzzed and he glanced at the screen to identify the caller. "If you'll excuse me for a moment . . ." He turned his back on Francesca and made for the doorway. "Tell me, Vittorio." He listened to the explanation Joanna had given to his brother and anger began to swirl like a dark, murderous shadow in his belly.

"That isn't good enough. You tell Joanna that excuse is bullshit. The minute she knew Francesca was living in that building and wouldn't listen to reason, she should have come to me. I don't give a flying fuck if I intimidate her. She could have gone to you or Giovanni," he hissed. "She could have had her uncle call us. What she did was totally unacceptable."

He glanced over his shoulder, feeling Francesca's eyes on him. She had crawled out of the sleeping bag and dragged her T-shirt over her head, tossing it aside on the couch. She pulled on his shirt hastily, giving him a glimpse of bare skin and full curves. Need slammed into him, in spite of the anger. It was urgent, hot and decidedly uncomfortable. He watched her slide the buttons closed, one by one. He didn't take his gaze from the sight and she didn't look away from him. Not once.

"I've got to go, Vittorio. Please make certain she understands that Francesca will never be allowed in that kind of danger again. I will hold her responsible, and she doesn't want that." He snapped the phone closed and shoved it in his pocket.

Francesca swallowed hard. "Are you angry with Joanna for some reason?"

"Yes." His voice was clipped. Abrupt. It was the best he could do because he still wanted to drag Joanna out of her safe bed and scare the holy hell out of her.

"Why?"

She walked closer to him on her bare feet. She had small feet and shapely legs. The tails of his shirt came just midway down her thighs. The shirt enveloped her, but she looked sexy and enticing, as if she was wrapped up like a present for his bedroom.

He allowed his gaze to drift possessively over her body before coming back to her face—that face that he found so beautiful. "Francesca, you live in Ferraro territory, and that makes you mine. You don't have to understand it, but just accept that what I'm telling you is the truth. My family looks out for the people here. We take their safety and well-being seriously. If anything had happened to you, there would have been far-reaching consequences."

She nodded slowly, the pad of her thumb slipping between her teeth. She bit down in agitation. His cock jerked in reaction.

"What has that got to do with Joanna?" She halted a few feet from him.

"Joanna has lived in our territory all of her life. She's been safe and she counts on feeling safe. She knew better than to allow you to live in that shit hole."

She winced at his language, making him aware of it. He wasn't a soft man. He never had been and he certainly didn't mince words.

"Joanna doesn't have a say in anything I do. She objected, but I didn't want to take her money. She lent me the money for the bus ticket out here. She's been nothing but kind to me. She didn't turn her back on me even when it meant she was jeopardizing herself. I couldn't take more from her."

There was a long silence and her gaze skittered away from his when she realized exactly what she'd revealed to him. So there was a problem, something big that made her other friends and possibly family turn their backs on her. Joanna hadn't. He could be grateful for that.

"What happened that others turned their backs on you?" He made a conscious effort to soften his tone.

Her chin went up. She squared her shoulders. "It's of no consequence. I asked you why you would hold Joanna responsible for my actions. She couldn't force me to do what she wanted."

"She should have come to me." His tone said it all and he knew she got the message. Joanna might not be able to force her to compliance, but he could. He kept his gaze on hers, not allowing her to look away from him again. Wanting her to see he meant business.

"You aren't responsible for me."

He shrugged. "You saying that doesn't make me feel any different."

"Stefano, I have to ask you this, and I don't want you to be angry with me. It's just that you're very scary at times and I don't understand what's going on here."

"What's going on here is that I'm attracted to you. Aside from that, you belong in my territory. That means I protect you whether or not you like it and whether or not you're always comfortable with how I go about protecting you."

"Are you mafia? A part of organized crime?"

He kept his eyes on hers, refusing to allow her to look away. If she had the audacity to ask such a question, she should have the courage to look him in the eye while she did it.

"Does it matter to you what I do?"

"Of course it does. I don't like the idea of anyone selling drugs or running guns, doing anything so deplorable, protecting me."

"I can assure you I don't sell drugs, nor does any member of my family. We don't run guns, either."

He saw the relief on her face. She pushed at her hair and sent him a tentative smile. "I think you're right about going to bed. It's been a long day and I need to sleep before I figure out what I'm going to do next."

He indicated for her to follow him. He hadn't lied to her. No member of his family would even consider selling drugs or running guns. That didn't mean they never worked with the scum who did do those things. He pushed open the door to one of his guest bedrooms. "This room has a private bath. I'm close if you need anything. Otherwise, sweet dreams, baby. Don't forget the chair under the doorknob."

CHAPTER EIGHT

Francesca drew the covers to her chin, snuggling down between the luxurious sheets. The mattress was pure heaven. The sheets felt even better. Sleeping in the street, in a shelter, or on the floor in a sleeping bag wasn't conducive to a great night's sleep. Worse, as a rule, she was afraid to close her eyes, but the bed was sheer bliss. The room was huge, much larger than the entire apartment she'd rented. She shivered, trying not to think about Bart Tidwell staring at her as she showered. It was such a violation.

She looked around the tastefully decorated room and wished she could stay. For the first time in three years she felt safe. She knew it was because of Stefano Ferraro. She had no idea why he made her feel safe, when she knew absolutely that he was a dangerous man, but he did. She wished she could stay right there in that wonderful room, in the even better bed, and just feel protected and cared for.

She crammed her fist into her mouth, closing her eyes, deeply embarrassed that she'd asked him if he was a member of organized crime. He'd been good to her—she couldn't deny that. He might have used crude language, but he'd been decent, and she'd rewarded him with false accusations. She'd lost faith in everybody. In everything. The justice system. Her former friends. Her former boss.

There had only been Joanna, and now she'd gotten her in trouble through her own stubbornness and pride. If she was being entirely honest, she didn't want to owe Joanna anything more because she couldn't bear to be hurt again. She didn't want to trust her more than she had to, and that was a very sorry thing to have to admit about herself. Joanna had proven to be a good friend. A better friend to her than she was to Joanna.

She felt herself drifting. Trying not to think about Stefano or his gorgeous, very hot, over-the-top masculine looks. She secretly liked that he was bossy. It made her feel as if he could really protect her from anything, although she knew better. Reality was far different from daydreams.

What woman in her right mind wouldn't fantasize about Stefano? She could give herself that. He was wealthy, handsome, confident, everything a woman could possibly want in a man. She knew he wasn't for her, so it wasn't a good idea to think about him while falling asleep, especially when she was in his home, in his bed.

She allowed her eyes to close and conjured up an image of her beloved sister, Cella. She was older by nine years and in Francesca's mind, absolutely stunningly beautiful. That had been the trouble. Cella was so beautiful she could stop traffic. It was impossible for anyone not to notice her. Noticing led to temptation. Temptation led to murder.

Cella's smile, as she stared back at Francesca, faltered. She opened her mouth to say something. To call out. To scream. She reached a hand toward Francesca, looking scared. Terrified. Pleading. Francesca reached for her, trying to connect, trying to hold on, to keep her sister with her. Blood spattered across Cella's face. Down her body. She was naked, her clothes ripped from her. There were bruises marring her skin, and five puncture wounds on her body. Each wound had blood dripping from it. One spouted like a fountain.

Francesca dropped to her knees beside her sister and covered the spray with both hands, pressing deep, sobbing, calling her sister's name, imploring her to stay. To not leave her alone. Her phone felt slippery as she called 911, and she dropped it twice, trying to punch in the numbers, Cella's blood all over it. Cella coughed, bringing up blood. It bubbled all around her mouth. Her eyes widened as she stared at Francesca. One hand reached for her. She coughed. Gurgled. Then her head turned and only her eyes stared. Lifeless. Gone.

Francesca screamed, "No! No, Cella, don't leave me. You can't leave me." Anguish was raw and terrible, ripping at her heart. Her screams tore at her throat. She lifted her horrified, grief-stricken gaze to stare up at the man framed in the doorway.

He sneered at her. "No one will believe you, Francesca. You'd better do what I say or you'll find yourself in trouble. You can end this anytime."

She launched herself at him, trying to take him to the ground, thinking she could hold him there until the police arrived. She was crying and her tears nearly blinded her. She couldn't see him clearly.

"Wake up, *bambina*," a male voice commanded. It was a command. Nothing less. "Open your eyes. Look at me."

She fought hard, trying to punch and kick. Her eyes *were* open. He was there. Watching her. He was always watching her. Laughing when the police dismissed her claims, ignored all of the evidence because it was *him*. He'd warned Cella. And then he'd killed her. Now he was warning her.

"Francesca. Open. Your. Eyes. Look at me."

Her wrists were pinned to the mattress on either side of her head. He was strong. Enormously strong. There was no way to break free. A sob escaped. Panic choked her. If she did, if she opened her eyes and it was him . . .

"*Dolce cuore.* You're killing me here. Look at me."

This time the voice was soft. Gentle. The tone found a path through the fear lodged so deep in her throat. In her belly. He held her wrists together with one hand, but he brought her body tight against his, holding her. His other hand pressed her face into his solid chest. She inhaled and brought a familiar scent into her lungs. Her body recognized it before she did. Stefano. She loved the spicy, masculine scent that seemed to seep into her body through her pores.

She pressed deeper into him, and he let go of her wrists to slide his arm around her back, locking her to him. "That's my girl. Relax. You're safe." His fingers delved deep into her hair, massaging her scalp. She'd never felt so safe and the panic began to slowly subside.

Francesca became aware that she was crying. She heard the soft sobs first. Muffled. A little wild. Stefano murmured to her in Italian. She understood a few of the words. Not many, because her parents had spoken the language in her home and she'd lost them. Once they were gone, Cella spoke mostly English. Sometimes it was . . . *Bella. Cara. Carissima.* She could have sworn he brushed kisses in her hair.

"*Bambina*, you have to stop crying. Take a breath and talk to me. It was a nightmare. You're here with me. Safe. Nothing can get to you here."

"He can," she said, the panic welling up again. Smothering her. "He'll hurt you. Joanna. He'll say terrible things and I'll lose my job. I have to . . ."

His hand found her chin, prying her face from his chest. He tipped her face up and brought his down. Close. "Look at me, *bella*. I am not a man others fuck with. Not ever. You're here. With me. That means you're safe." There was an edge to his voice.

She wanted to smile and the choking fear and panic slipped further away. She forced her lashes to cooperate. The moment she opened her eyes, he was there. Stefano. His face was close. That hard jaw. The masculine beauty. His eyes. The arrogant confidence and the aura of danger clinging to him. It was all there. She felt more protected than she'd felt for years. She wanted to stay right where she was, close to him. Feeling how solid he was. All muscle. He had a steel core. Truthfully, he was the first and only man she believed might be able to keep her safe.

It wasn't fair to him. To stay with him, knowing he felt he had to defend everyone around him, was wrong. She should find the strength to leave so she wouldn't endanger him, but there was nowhere to go. She had no money. She had nothing at all.

"I'm sorry," she whispered. Hating herself. Knowing she was going to give him that burden. That danger. Because she could no longer do this alone. She wasn't living. She was existing. Every second of every day, she was terrified. One could only live with terror for so long. Not just terror. Anger. Guilt.

Stefano Ferraro was an unexpected complication. Or savior. She had chemistry with him, intense and scary, but it was there and she'd never felt it before. Not like that. He'd said he was attracted to her. It was obvious that physically, he was. She knew if she let anything happen between them, he would be bossy and controlling. She didn't believe in relationships where one person was needy, and yet she was. She was exactly that person, but that wasn't the real her. It was circumstances.

"You're back with me." Relief tinged his voice. His arms slid around her again and he held her close, her ear over the steady beat of his heart. One hand stroked caresses in her hair. "Do you have nightmares often?"

She had to give him the truth if she was going to give him the worst of her. "Yes. All the time. I don't sleep more than a few hours a night because they come often. Every time I close my eyes."

She didn't lift her head. She couldn't tell him while she looked at him because the guilt would overwhelm her. She knew how a man like Stefano would react to her disclosure. He'd asked, but still, she knew he was off-the-charts protective. If he were really interested in her as a woman, he'd be even more so.

"I dream about Cella and the murder. Nearly every night. Again and again."

There was silence while his hand moved in her hair. She wanted to look up at him, but she couldn't bring herself to do it. Not yet. Not when she was throwing him into the pit where demons lived. She didn't know when it had happened. Maybe when he'd been so angry over the DVDs he'd handed her. The tone in his voice, his abhorrence that any man could act that way toward a woman, for one brief moment she'd let down her guard and he'd slipped in.

His coat. The bane of her life. The money. The way he'd talked to the little boy. Ruffled his hair. So sweet. The older woman, Theresa Vitale, who had cried and moved him to help her. The way he talked about the people in his neighborhood. There was genuine caring there. Unreal to her when she'd never seen it or known it until him. He'd found a crack in her armor and he'd slipped right in so that she trusted him when she barely knew him. When she didn't trust anyone.

"I'm sorry, *dolce cuore*. When did this happen?"

She couldn't believe he could sound so gentle. Stefano didn't strike her as a gentle man, yet he had been with Tonio, the little boy, and Theresa Vitale, the older woman. Even with Lucia and Amo Fausti. She moistened her lips and forced herself to look up, into his piercing blue eyes.

"A year ago. Almost eighteen months."

"Like yesterday," he murmured, still stroking her hair. "I'm so sorry."

She nodded, blinking back more tears. The aftermath of a nightmare always left her wrung out and exhausted emotionally, yet wide awake, afraid to go back to sleep.

"Did they catch him?"

She stiffened. She couldn't help herself. Her gaze started to slide from his but he caught her chin in an unbreakable grip.

"Answer me, Francesca. The truth."

"Someone confessed." That was strictly the truth. "He didn't go to prison because he was terminally ill. He died six months ago."

"But," he coaxed gently, "you don't believe he was guilty."

She took a breath, wishing she could pull her gaze from his, but it was like being held captive. She was chained to him, body and soul, and she had no idea how, in the faint light from the open window, that had happened. There were shadows all over the room. Her shadow merged with his on the wall. That was how she felt when she was close to him like this. Merged. Connected. One skin instead of two. Wrapped in chains, so that they both were irrevocably tied together.

"No. It wasn't him. I came in after and I saw him. I knew him. He spoke to me. Taunted me."

His blue eyes darkened to pure steel. "He threatened you?"

She nodded slowly. "I told the police, but they didn't believe me. He took away my job and my home and everything I had. Twice in the middle of the night he came with some others and tore up my apartment. Damaged the walls, ripped out the toilet, broke things, put horrible scratches in the floor . . ." She broke off, her hand going to her throat because she feared she'd choke to death on the large lump blocking her airway. "He could do that here," she added in a small, gasping voice.

"Take a breath, Francesca. Look around you. I own this hotel. There's security here. I'm here. He can't get to you and neither can his friends."

She drew in air and took the scent of him deep into her lungs. The nightmare was beginning to fade, and with clarity came horror at what she was doing. She wasn't the type of woman to manipulate anyone into doing something dangerous, such as standing in front of her—as she knew Stefano would—to protect her from the likes of the man who had murdered her sister. It was a despicable thing to do, and no matter how terrible her circumstances, she had no right to drag anyone else into her personal nightmare.

She tried to shift subtly, to pull back, give herself a chance to rethink what she was doing. His arm, locked across her back, held her in place.

"Stefano, he can get to anyone. He has money. Power. Politicians and cops in his pocket. He has lunch regularly with the governor of California and the local district attorney. He plays golf with the senator. He runs in your . . ." She broke off, her gaze sliding from his. "Circle," she finished lamely.

"His name."

She hesitated. This was what she wanted, but it wasn't right. She would be a terrible person for involving him more than she already had. "Stefano, I'm sorry. I really shouldn't even be talking about this, especially to you." She couldn't look at him. Shame burned through her. "I can't imagine your life, the way you have to live, always thinking you have to protect and take care of everyone around you. You make it easy to shift burdens your way. You don't protest. You don't ask for space. You just take control and no one has to worry but you."

His thumb and finger gripped her chin, lifting her face so she once again had no choice but to meet his eyes. "*Bambina*, I am that man. Don't make me out to be a saint, because I'm anything but. You aren't going to find me easy to live with, and I assure you, Francesca, we will be living together. I knew the moment I laid eyes on you what I wanted. You can turn over those burdens to me, and you won't ever have to worry. With that comes the price of belonging to me. Above all things, I want you safe. So tell me his name."

Her breath caught in her lungs at his declaration. The idea of belonging to him was both terrifying and exhilarating. She couldn't look away from his eyes. She'd only just met him yet she felt that she'd known him forever. She knew he was dangerous, possibly more dangerous than Barry Anthon, but still, that connection between them was so strong, she couldn't imagine not having him in her life in some capacity.

"I think I manipulated you to this point. I didn't start out that way, and then I did, and now I . . ." She broke off as his eyes glittered. "Stefano, you can be scary."

"Tell. Me. His. Name." He bit out each word separately. Enunciating them. Making them a command.

"Barry Anthon." She blurted out his name, and then was shocked that she had.

There was a small silence. She knew he recognized the name. How could he not? When she said he ran in the same circles, she meant it. Anthon even had his own racing team, just as the Ferraro family did.

The silence stretched, and her belly knotted. Her fingers closed into fists on his thin tee, bunching the material. Of course. She should have known. Why would he take her word over that of the police? Over Anthon's? She had been so fogged coming out of the nightmare and feeling so guilty for involving him that she hadn't stopped to think about whether or not he would believe her. How stupid. No one else had believed her. Not the landlords who threw her out of the apartments she'd rented and supposedly damaged. Not the boss she'd worked for since her teenage years. Not the police who arrested her for destroying property. Not the judges or even the lawyers who defended her. No one believed her about Cella's murder.

She strained away from him, against the hard bar of his arm, her hands going flat on his chest to push him away.

"Settle," he commanded softly, his eyes on her, but he was clearly somewhere else. "Barry Anthon the third, I presume. He has somewhat of a reputation with women."

So did the Ferraro brothers. She'd read all about them in the magazines Joanna had given her. She didn't say a word. He would have to release her sometime, and then she'd find a way to leave. She could stay in the street like Dina. The thought made her feel a little hysterical. She'd done that and it had been awful, worse than awful.

"I need to wash my face." She needed distance. She had to put everything into perspective, and she couldn't do that when he was so close to her.

His gaze searched hers for a long time. She felt as if he saw right inside of her, saw her deepest secrets, her shame for involving him, her fear that, like everyone else, he wouldn't believe that a man like Anthon had systematically set about destroying her entire life until she had nothing left. No home. No friends. No money. No way to get a job. She crushed down the sob welling up.

Stefano ran the pad of his thumb down her face, tracing her high cheekbone and making his way slowly to her lips. He rubbed his thumb along her bottom lip, his eyes darkening until her breath caught in her lungs and just stayed there. A strange throb began deep inside her, low and insistent.

"I'll make you hot chocolate. If I don't have any, I'll call down to the kitchen."

"It's too late for room service," she pointed out.

He shook his head. "What part of 'I own the hotel' don't you understand? I call down, they get me what I want, even if they have to send out for it."

"You're spoiled, Stefano."

"I suppose I am," he agreed. "Don't be long."

He slid off the bed, standing in one fluid motion that was all grace and power. He was dressed in a thin pair of sweat-pants she was certain he didn't wear to bed. He'd pulled on a tight T-shirt, and he looked every bit as good as he did in his three-piece suits, although the look was entirely casual.

Francesca watched him walk out of the room, mesmer-ized by the way he moved. She could watch him for hours. Listen to the sound of his voice. Even when he was totally angry and scaring the crap out of her, she liked the pitch, but when he was being gentle, his voice stroked like the softest of caresses over her skin. Stefano was larger than life and he dominated a room as well as everyone in it. When he walked out, he took the warmth with him.

She shivered and wrapped her arms around her middle, rocking gently to soothe herself. He was lethal to women in a way a man like Barry Anthon, for all his wealth, could never be. Stefano might snarl, he might even manhandle a woman, but he would never hurt her. Never. She knew instinctively, like that was written somewhere in stone.

She forced her stiff legs to straighten so she could scoot to the edge of the bed. After her nightmares, her body was always painful, as if she'd run a race uphill—or gotten in a physical fight and lost. She had done something so wrong, manipulating a good man into feeling responsible for her and then blurting out the name of one of his colleagues. How incredibly stupid was that? She was ashamed of herself and angry, too. She knew better. She was a better person than that. Cella had raised her, and she would have been ashamed of her.

Barefoot, she padded to the gleaming bathroom. It was large—larger than the kitchen and bedroom combined in her little apartment. The bathtub looked inviting, and she gazed at it longingly while she just stood there, trying to decide what to do. Stefano was probably calling Anthon right that moment. How could she have been so careless? Even Joanna didn't know all the details, but Francesca had been so selfish telling Stefano the truth, needing to feel safe, wanting to stay in Ferraro territory because she liked the neighborhood, and secretly she was so attracted to him. It would serve her right if he was talking to Barry right that moment.

"Francesca, get a move on."

He sounded impatient. Bossy. *So* like him. "Keep your panties on," she called back, smiling at the exasperated sound of his voice. The minute the admonishment slipped out, she clapped a hand over her mouth. She didn't need to make him angry by being her smart-mouthed self, or worse, have him think she was flirting. He might say he was attracted, and she definitely was, but he wasn't the type of man for a woman like her, under any circumstances, let alone the one she found herself in.

Right now, she was the damsel in distress and he was the white knight riding to the rescue. She'd even helped to manipulate him into thinking she was just that. Until she had revealed the name of her enemy. She'd vowed to rebuild her life and find a way to take Barry Anthon down. Her. Not someone else. Now that she was thinking clearly again, she wasn't going to shove her fight onto anyone else. It was too dangerous. In any case, the chances that Stefano Ferraro and Barry Anthon were friends were extremely high.

She pulled her hair back, braided it and, without a hair tie, just left it braided and hoped it stayed long enough to wash her face. The soap was a gel and smelled like heaven. Beside the gel was a moisturizer and she lathered it on.

When she walked out of the bedroom, Stefano was right there, draped lazily against the hall wall opposite her door. "Did you just tell me to keep my *panties* on?" His voice was pitched very low. Quiet.

Her heart stuttered. "I might have. That depends," she hedged.

"*Hmm.*" He straightened in one of his powerful, controlled, fluid movements that could rob a woman of breath for the next century, and held out his hand. "I think you're feeling better. You sassed me. People don't sass me, Francesca. Not. Ever."

"They don't?" She tried to look innocent, staring first up at his face and then at his hand. There was no reading his expression so she slipped her hand into his. Instantly his fingers closed around hers. Warm. Tight. Firm. He gave a little tug and started down the hall with her. "Not even your sister?"

"No. Not even my mother."

"Why not? I think sass is just what you need. I think, from observation, that you tend to get everything your way." Her heart beat too fast. She didn't know why he was teasing her, but it was better than having him throw her out on the street. Much better. Still, it wasn't true that he got everything his way. He hadn't wanted to leave the pizza parlor. He was enjoying having dinner with her, but he left for Theresa Vitale. She supposed he was dragged away often from things he wanted so he could help others.

"I need instant obedience," he said.

He smiled at her and her heart nearly stopped. She found it impossible to breathe. He had the sexiest smile she'd ever seen in her life. He could get just about anything from her with that smile. Staring at him, she nearly stopped moving because she couldn't remember how to walk. Her brain short-circuited. She concentrated on putting one foot in front of the other and followed him to the very spacious kitchen.

Francesca looked around her. "You live in a hotel. Why

do you need a kitchen like this?" She touched the stove with reverent fingers. "This is state-of-the-art. I could do things in this kitchen."

"You cook?" He let go of her hand and indicated the high-backed leather stool at the bar.

Francesca nodded as she climbed up onto the stool. "I love to cook. Growing up, Cella worked and I took care of the house. I spent a great deal of time watching cooking channels and trying out recipes until I understood the art of cooking—and it is an art if you love it, which I do. Even after I was old enough to work, I did the cooking."

"I've never cooked," he admitted. "Not anything that wasn't packaged, and that doesn't taste so good."

"Growing up, you didn't learn? Did you and your brothers think it was woman's work? Some of the best chefs in the world are men." She was a little disappointed that he might think that way. It didn't surprise her, though.

"My brothers and my sister were too busy learning other things that were deemed necessary by the family. We didn't have much of a childhood, and we certainly weren't encouraged to learn how to cook. Although, saying that, Taviano is an excellent chef, but he learned in Europe, certainly not from our mother."

"Other things?" Now she was curious. She couldn't tell from his strictly neutral tone whether or not he was altogether happy with his childhood.

He poured chocolate from a pan on the stove, added whipped cream from a can and put the steaming mug of chocolate in front of her. "We began training from the time we were toddlers. Languages, arts, martial arts, boxing, wrestling, jujitsu, all sorts of weapons, horseback riding, eventually driving skills and of course we were expected to excel in every subject in the private schools we attended. It was top of the class or in trouble."

She didn't know what to say to that. His revelation was unexpected. It didn't sound like much of a childhood to her, and she had to once again reassess what she thought. He might have all the money in the world, but her childhood had been just that—a childhood.

"You thought we spent all of our time playing polo and racing cars?"

"Chasing women," she corrected, trying to make a joke.

His gaze jumped to her face. She took a breath. Let it out. She had to ask. Her stomach muscles were tied up in knots and she knew she was a heartbeat away from panic. "Did you call him? Barry Anthon?" Her hands tightened around the warmth of the mug, lifting it, but not taking a drink. "Did you call him and tell him I was here?"

His gaze drifted over her face. "You don't think much of me, do you?"

She stilled; her heart jerked hard. She put the mug of chocolate down on the bar and forced herself to meet his eyes. "That's not true."

"Yes it is. You think I'm like Barry Anthon. That I have too much money and I don't know what hard work is. You didn't want to take my coat because of my money. You didn't want to allow me to help you at all."

His handsome features were stony, expressionless, his blue eyes glittering at her, but it was his tone that caught at her more than anything else. There was just the slightest hint of hurt there. If they hadn't been so weirdly connected, she knew she would have missed it, but the awareness of every little nuance was there, because she was so conscious of him.

"You're nothing at all like Barry Anthon," she said. "Stefano, if I thought for one moment you were like him, I wouldn't be here in this apartment with you. I'll admit to some prejudice when I first met you, but that changed very quickly."

"You don't relax around me."

"Well, that's because you're . . ." She trailed off with a little wave of her hand, color creeping into her face.

He tilted his head to one side, a slow smile softening the hard edge of his mouth, giving him that sexy tilt that sent heat scattering through her veins.

"I'm what?"

She pressed her lips together hard to keep from blurting out the truth. That he was gorgeous. Sexy. Dangerous. Hot. All those things. Everything she wasn't. He was so far out of her league it wasn't funny. He was nothing like Barry Anthon, but he ran in the same circles.

"It just stands to reason that you would want information about my situation, and as you know Barry, what better way to acquire it than by speaking to him personally?" It was prudent to change the subject.

"I definitely want the information about what happened, but you're right here with me. Why wouldn't I just ask you myself?"

She ducked her head. "Maybe you think I'd lie to you."

"Would you?"

She shook her head. "I might be tempted to leave things out. Or just refuse to tell you. It's all pretty far-fetched, and no one other than Joanna has believed me. They believe Barry."

"Barry wouldn't know the truth if it hit him in the face. He's been making shit up since the day he was born. He pays people to believe him, but that doesn't make it true, Francesca."

She lifted her chin, trying not to feel hope. "You should know, aside from being arrested for damaging property, I've also been in lockup for seventy-two hours in a hospital." She didn't take her eyes from his, waiting for condemnation. Everyone else thought she'd lost her mind, so why not him? Still, deep inside, where that strange connection was, she didn't think he would believe the worst said about her, either.

He kept his gaze steady on hers. Unflinching. Expressionless. Her heart pounded. She clutched the chocolate mug so hard her knuckles turned white. His gaze dropped to her hands and he reached, gently prying her fingers from the mug. His thumb slid over her knuckles.

"When Barry does something, he's thorough, but he's repetitive. Once something works for him, he keeps using it."

"You're saying he's done this before?" Hope blossomed. "What do you have on him?"

Her breath left her lungs in a rush. "Why do you think I've got something on him?"

"Because you're not dead. He would have killed you if he could have. If we look into the bank account of the man convicted of your sister's murder, there will be a lot of money his family inherits when he dies. This isn't the first time something like this has happened around Barry Anthon. Obviously, if you saw him at the murder scene and he's worked so hard to discredit you, he's afraid of you. He's got money and power. He's got cops and politicians in his pocket. He wouldn't be afraid unless whatever you have could ruin him and he can't risk killing you until he gets it back."

His thumb rubbed gently at her knuckles. It felt—exquisite. Each time the pad of his thumb slid between her knuckles, she felt his touch melt through bare skin and sink into her bloodstream. She shivered. She couldn't help it. Her body was tuned to his. Came alive for his. It didn't make sense, but then chemistry never did.

She took a breath. "I don't know you, Stefano."

"You know me."

He brought her hand to his mouth, his lips moving over her knuckles in the way his thumb had, only this was so much better. Way more intense. She felt an answer coiling hot at the junction of her legs.

"You don't have to tell me . . . yet. Drink your chocolate." He let go of her hand.

She curled her fingers around the mug again because when she wasn't touching him she felt cold, and it was such a relief that he believed her—that he knew the real Barry. Deceitful, *murderous* Barry.

"He's done this before? Destroying property and making it look like someone else did it?" *Murder?* She couldn't bring herself to ask that.

"All of it, right down to the jail time and the hospital,"

Stefano confirmed. "He likes to brag that no one can cross him. He threatened a couple of drivers. They ended up quitting. I didn't get the story until a couple of years later, but they wouldn't drive for anyone because they were so afraid of him. It ended their careers."

"Has he ever threatened you?" Francesca asked cautiously.

"Bambina."

One word. That said it all. His tone. Amused. Arrogant. Completely confident. She shivered again, but this time because she could see the danger in him. He wasn't a man other men crossed. If Barry was too afraid to threaten Stefano, what did that make Stefano? The thought flitted through her mind unbidden.

She took a sip of chocolate to buy herself time. It was delicious. There was no way it was from a package. "You made this."

Amusement crept into the deep blue of his eyes. "Yeah. I did."

"How did you learn to make such great chocolate?"

"I have a younger sister. She often had a difficult time sleeping so she'd come into my room, wake me up and I'd make her chocolate."

She thought it strange that his sister woke him up instead of her parents, but he didn't enlighten her further so she took another sip of the delicious brew.

"I've been thinking about your living arrangements. I've come up with a great solution. John Balboni and his wife, Suzette, own the hardware store. They've wanted to travel for a while, but she's nervous about leaving their home unattended and they got into a little trouble financially a couple of years ago. They have a little guest unit. I think it would be mutually beneficial if you could live in that unit. She'd be happy, they could use the money and she would feel they could comfortably leave home."

It sounded perfect but . . . there was Barry. If he found out where she was staying, he would come after her. He'd destroy any property. The horrible apartment building where she'd lived didn't much matter, but the Balbonis sounded like a nice couple who couldn't afford to have their guest unit destroyed.

He nodded as if reading her mind. "You see the problem. Barry is probably searching for you right now. How did you pay for your bus ticket?"

"When I got out of the hospital, I knew I had to get away from Barry's influence, so I stayed on the street and in shelters. I knew he had someone watching me. Street people stick together and they helped me evade the watcher. Joanna had sent me money and I used it to buy a bus ticket. I got rid of all my clothes, selling them, or trading in the thrift store so they couldn't recognize anything I wore. I boarded the bus and came here."

"But you know he'll find you." He made it a statement.

Francesca nodded. "Eventually. I was hoping I had the chance to get back on my feet before he did. He left me too afraid and too exhausted."

"So we'll have to change plans. This hotel is secure. You'll have to stay here. With me. He won't get his crew past security and there's no way he can destroy where you're staying."

Francesca held her breath. Her eyes met his. Temptation was a man who was so beautiful he looked like sin. "Stefano . . . Thank you, but I can't accept."

"I wasn't asking, *bella*. It's the only solution. It keeps you and everyone else safe. Besides. I've wanted to take on Barry Anthon for a long time. You'll stay here and we'll put a plan together to draw him out. Don't worry. I'll take care of you. He won't get close to you. With you under my protection, he's going to have to change his game. He's comfortable with that game, and he's going to start making mistakes."

"But I can't let you . . ."

"Did you not fucking hear me? You're staying here. With me."

He was back to swearing, impatience in his voice. She let

her breath out. She wasn't as afraid of Barry as she was of staying with Stefano. She might not just lose her body to him; she would definitely lose her heart. Still, even with knowing that, she couldn't resist temptation. Or safety. Or that bed. She nodded slowly.

CHAPTER NINE

Francesca stomped out of her bedroom, hair still damp, dressed in a soft skirt that fell to her ankles and a camisole that emphasized her generous breasts and narrow rib cage. She'd never worn anything like it in her life, but she'd definitely seen both items before—she'd admired them in the window of Lucia's Treasures. She had new underwear, a drawer full. Every pair of panties and each bra was exquisite—again, something so incredibly nice that she'd never worn before. She loved them, but they didn't belong to her.

She needed clothes because she had to go to work, but this was too much. How had Stefano managed to acquire clothes at three or four in the morning? And it had to have been after three or four. And how had they gotten into her room?

"These aren't mine," she greeted him, trying not to stare. Of course he looked gorgeous, already dressed in a pin-striped three-piece suit, his dark hair gleaming under the lights at the breakfast table. He glanced up from reading what clearly had to be some kind of report, his blue eyes meeting hers. Her heart stuttered in her chest and her reprimand died in her throat. No one should look that good in the morning.

Stefano smiled at her, his gaze drifting over her. "You look beautiful. Good morning. I ordered breakfast. I wasn't certain what you'd like so I took a chance on eggs and potatoes. They sent up fresh squeezed orange juice and coffee. There's tea if you prefer."

"Stefano, where are my clothes?"

He stood and reached for her. His long fingers settled around her elbow and he drew her to the chair opposite to where he'd been sitting. She sank into it more because her knees were suddenly weak than because she wanted to sit. She actually wanted to walk around, to continue feeling the swish of the soft material on her legs.

Once she was seated, he slipped into his chair opposite her and smiled—one of his amazing hot smiles, which sent her temperature soaring. She had to remind herself to stay on track because he tended to fry her brain.

"Sadly, there was a little accident with your clothes. Ricco said they didn't survive, so of course, since they were entrusted to our care, the family provided you with new ones. By the time you get off work, we will have jeans and tees for more casual wear. There wasn't enough time last night."

She took a sip of coffee because she desperately needed the caffeine to deal with his obvious bull. "My clothes met with an accident?"

He nodded. "Sadly."

She narrowed her eyes and gave him her best scowl. "Did your coat manage to make it back intact?"

He nodded. Sober. His handsome features suspiciously innocent. "Yes. I was relieved. My brother saved my coat, but couldn't quite grab your duffel bag. It floated right down the river."

"Oh. My. God. You are so full of it, Stefano." Francesca took a bite of scrambled eggs and shook her head.

"I have no idea what you mean. I'm merely repeating what Ricco told me. I can't imagine that he would lie."

She had to work at not laughing. "Right."

He lifted an eyebrow at her. "I trust you slept better last night after the hot chocolate. Emmanuelle swears it always works for her."

She nodded. "I did. But we're not finished with the clothes discussion. How did you manage to get everything in the middle of the night?"

He shrugged. "Amo Fausti, the owner of the boutique, is a good friend of mine. He opened the store immediately when I told him we'd accidentally lost your clothes."

"In the middle of the night? You just called him and he opened the store?" Coffee seemed more important than food. She clearly needed to stay sharp around him. He was totally unapologetic.

"He's a friend. You've already become one of his favorites, so he was happy to do so."

That pleased her because Lucia and Amo were definitely favorites of hers. "And the clothes got into my room, how?"

Again he shrugged. "I knew you would need them in the morning. I put them away myself."

While she was sleeping. She sighed. "As much as I love the clothes, I can't accept them."

He smirked. She would have resorted to violence but even his smirk was sexy and instead she just stared at him, astonished that a man could look as good as he did. It took a few moments for the Stefano spell to ease. She licked her lips and downed the orange juice. It was superb. Like his penthouse. Like the clothes. Like him.

"I suppose you could just wear my shirt to work. I like the idea of you wearing my shirt all day, but Pietro might object. On the other hand, you look . . . sexy in it, and that might draw in even more customers when word gets out. Although, if I'm being strictly honest, I'm not certain I want other men seeing you in just my shirt."

"I can see that sparring with you requires at least two cups of coffee."

"We're responsible for the loss of your clothes. Of course we'd replace them. Change the subject."

"Just like that."

"Bambina."

The way he said that one little word, as if it was an endearment, but reprimanded her, melted her insides. It was the tone of his voice. She liked that he called her *baby* or *sweetheart* and sometimes even *beautiful*. The way he focused so completely on her made her feel special. The appreciation in his eyes made her feel beautiful. She knew she wasn't going to win the argument. Her clothes were gone and he'd bought her new ones—new, exquisite clothing that she never could have afforded on her own. Never. Not in her lifetime.

"And the makeup and other things in my bathroom?"

"Everything was lost." He shrugged, dismissing the subject. "I'll take you to work this morning. If you leave the store, text me."

"Stefano, why in the world would I do that?" As if she could. She didn't have a cell phone. She'd already told him that. It wasn't like she had the money to rush out and get one, let alone pay for a plan.

His eyes darkened to a stormy blue. Pinned her. The air in the room thickened with heat. His heat. "Because I asked you to."

She supposed that was a good enough answer when she was sitting in his penthouse, eating his food, wearing clothes he bought and under his protection. "I can't." When his head jerked up and the room got even scarier, she held up her hand. "I said 'can't', not *won't*. Remember? I don't own a cell phone. I told you I didn't have one." She could see him struggle for control.

"That was before I knew about Barry." He leaned toward her. "Francesca. You have an enemy like Barry Anthon and you don't have a cell phone to call 911 if he catches up with you?" His voice was pitched low. Velvet soft. Totally menacing. "It should be your first priority."

Her heart pounded. "I couldn't afford one, let alone pay for a plan. In any case, the police don't believe me, Stefano. No one does. If he catches up with me . . ."

"I'll be standing in front of you. I told you, I'm coming up with a plan. Just give me a few days. In the meantime, I want to know that you're safe." He glanced at his watch. "I've got shit to do this morning, but Emilio will be watching over you. I'll send a cell to the store. Use it. My number will be programmed in, and I want to know where you are at all times. I'm not being controlling. I need to know you're safe."

"You're controlling," she corrected.

"True," he agreed, sounding completely unremorseful. "But I still need to know you're safe."

There wasn't any sense in arguing. Stefano was a law unto himself, and he would get her the phone and Emilio would be waiting right outside the store no matter what she said. She'd wanted his protection and now that she had it, she couldn't exactly throw a tantrum over how he chose to give it to her.

"Okay."

"Okay?"

She smiled at him. "I see no reason to argue when you're just going to get your way. The food is delicious. I didn't realize hotel food could be really good."

"Our hotel provides the best of everything. Our chefs are amazing. The pastry chefs are as well. Tonight, after work, you'll have to sample some of the desserts."

"I can see if I stick around here for too long I'll end up gaining weight. Pizza, pastries and amazing food."

"You could use a few pounds. I don't like that you weren't eating. Dina told me you didn't have anything to eat for a couple of days."

"Dina? You talked to Dina?"

"Why wouldn't I? She lives in our neighborhood. She's part of us. She prefers to live on the street so we make her as comfortable as possible. She has a small wooden lean-to we built for her in the alley behind the hardware store, which she can go into at night. When the nights are too cold, she comes to the main house and sleeps in the garage. There's radiant heating through the floor. She has a bathroom there and warm blankets. It's the most she'll let us do for her, other than new warm boots once a year and sometimes clothing. I don't know what happened to her coat. She had a nice one."

She leaned her chin on the heel of her hand and tried not to devour him with her eyes. She loved that he took care of the homeless woman in their neighborhood. She'd *so* misjudged him. "That's amazing."

"Not really. She's a human being with a few problems. Her entire family was killed in a car accident. Her husband, three boys and a daughter. She was the only survivor. No relatives. She just gave up. We've tried to get her help. She used to teach school. High school. She had all kinds of awards and her students loved her. After the accident she turned to alcohol to dull the pain. She left her home, just walked out of her house one day and drifted. She ended up here."

There was an underlying sadness that fascinated her in his tone. He genuinely cared about Dina, she realized, and that took her breath away. Stefano Ferraro was many things, and most of them were amazing, sexy and wonderful. She liked him. He might be bossy and arrogant and controlling, but that was only one small part of who he was.

"How do you know all that? Dina barely spoke to me."

"I prefer to know everything there is to know about those in our neighborhood. Especially a woman who is living alone on the streets. It's freezing here at times and I certainly didn't want anything to happen to her. It took some persuading for her to use the garage, but she knows where the key is and now she'll go there. We see to it that she's fed, but we have to be careful how we do that. She doesn't like too much attention."

She noticed he used the term *we* a lot. She presumed he referred to his family. "You're very close to your family, aren't you?"

"My siblings and cousins, yes. I suppose my aunts and uncles as well."

He didn't name his parents; in fact, he'd been very specific about those he was close to and he'd left them out. She wanted to ask but decided she'd better not.

"Were you close to your sister?" His voice was pitched low. Gentle.

"Cella? Yes. I adored her. She raised me after our parents died. She didn't have to—she was very young herself—but she insisted it wasn't a burden."

"Of course it wasn't. There's no way your sister saw you as a burden." His voice was soft. Persuasive. But certain. As if because family wasn't a burden to him he couldn't conceive that it would be to anyone else.

He mesmerized her. Everything about him. She forced herself to look away and finish her coffee. She'd managed to eat a little of the eggs and potatoes, but she'd gone without eating too often to have much room in her stomach to eat large portions.

"After work, I'll show you around the penthouse. It has quite a few rooms. I have a training room for martial arts, weapons and boxing. We also have a workout room with weights and various machines such as treadmills. You're welcome to use either one, but we need to finish up if we're going to get you to work on time."

"I'm finished."

"You didn't eat much."

She didn't reply. She was learning from his tactics. He didn't like to engage in arguments; well, two could play that game. She smiled at him and rose, placing her folded napkin beside her plate. "Breakfast was wonderful, thank you. I'll go brush my teeth and be right out. Thanks for the toothbrush. It's very much appreciated."

He rose with her and watched her go back to her bedroom. She knew that he did because she felt his gaze burning into her. He was so . . . potent. Virile. Masculine. He took up the entire room with his broad shoulders and his presence. She found she couldn't take a breath without drawing him into her lungs.

Francesca reminded herself that Stefano Ferraro was *way* out of her league in every way. He might be interested in her, she couldn't deny the chemistry was off the charts, but their union would never last. He'd grow bored with her very fast. He was a white knight riding to the rescue, and if she didn't need that anymore he would lose interest.

When she met him in the foyer, Stefano was wearing his coat. She had been certain he would have had it cleaned first.

He stood with another long cashmere coat in his hands, waiting for her.

"You bought that as well?"

"Come on, *bella*. I told you, I can't be late for this meeting." He stepped close behind her, dipping the coat so she could slide her arm in one sleeve and then the other. He turned her around the moment the coat settled on her shoulders and slid the buttons into place.

"I can do that."

"I know. I like to do it." He bent his head and brushed a kiss over her forehead. "The code for the private elevator allowing you into the penthouse will be in the phone I'm having sent to you. If you have a problem, text me right away. I'm already on the cell for you. You should have it within the hour."

There was no point in protesting. She was being steamrolled, but she'd asked for it. Stefano was a force. One just got swept along when he decided something. They stepped onto the elevator together, Stefano crowding her closer than she believed necessary, although maybe it was the confined space that made her so acutely aware of him.

Her heart beat too hard. Her breasts ached, nipples pushing at the soft lace of her bra. Her sex pulsed, a persistent throb beating in tune to her racing heart. His long fingers curved around the nape of her neck, his thumb sweeping along her jaw.

"You're so beautiful, Francesca," he said softly. "And chemistry is a fuckin' bitch. I promised myself I'd go slow with you, not scare you to death, but apparently that's not happening." He bent his head and took her mouth.

She shouldn't have done it. She should have more restraint, but she couldn't help herself; the moment his mouth brushed against hers, she parted her lips for him. Allowed his tongue to sweep inside and take her over. He kissed like he did everything else. With total confidence, with expertise. He started gentle and ended rough. The kiss was shocking in its intensity.

She felt possessed, taken, overwhelmed with sheer urgent

need. Every cell in her body responded. She swore he poured molten lava down her throat and into her veins, where it moved through her, burning his name into her along the way to pool low and hot between her legs.

She'd never been kissed like that. She didn't know anyone *could* kiss like that. Every nerve ending in her body sprang to life, on full alert. She couldn't stop her hands from running up his chest to circle his neck, or her fingers from finding his hair. She gave herself to him, holding nothing back. Her mouth moved under his, following his lead, kissing him back while her body pressed tightly against his.

The elevator *pinged* and he turned her, so his body hid her from view of those in the lobby. He lifted his head reluctantly, his blue eyes moving over her face. "You good, *dolce cuore*? Do you need a minute?" He kept his hands on her hips, holding her so she wouldn't fall flat on her face.

She touched her mouth with trembling fingers. "I don't know. You should be outlawed."

He smiled down at her, the smile slow and sexy, gorgeous as it lit his eyes. "You're good." He made it a statement. "Henry brought my car around. It's right in front." He took her hand and she went with him out of the elevator.

Instantly the atmosphere in the lobby changed. Heads turned. A few people whispered, but most were silent. Watching him. Watching them. She ducked her head and moved closer to him. Instantly, he swept her beneath his shoulder, locking her to his side protectively.

He didn't look left or right, but she knew he was aware of everything and everyone in the hotel lobby. Nothing escaped his notice. She knew why she felt so safe with him. He commanded everything and everyone around him with every step he took. He filled an entire lobby with his presence. No one would dare try to harm her when she was in his keeping. It felt good to actually feel safe after so long.

He handed her into the car, giving her the illusion of being a princess. She snapped the seat belt around her, admiring the interior of the Aston Martin. Francesca waited until Stefano was behind the wheel and the car was gliding down the street, faster than she thought he should have driven it. Evidently, Stefano and his family had a lot of cars for their use.

"I wanted to tell you thank you."

He glanced at her. Raised an eyebrow. She twisted her fingers together. It didn't matter that he looked like the hottest man on earth and maybe the richest, he deserved to know. "For rescuing me from that apartment and gathering up what would be horribly embarrassing recordings. And for giving me a place to stay that made me feel safe. I haven't felt that way in a very long time."

He reached out and caught her hand, curling his long fingers around it. "Then I'm grateful I was the one to give that to you." He frowned a little and brought her hand to his thigh, pinning it there. "Although you still had a nightmare."

"I have them all the time, but when I did, you made me hot chocolate and spent time talking to me, making me feel better. And you somehow—I still don't know how—managed to get me a closet full of beautiful clothes that actually fit. And the shoes are . . . awesome." She lifted one foot to admire the boot she was wearing.

She waited, holding her breath, watching his face carefully. His smile was slow in coming, but when it did, it was worth the wait. He brushed his thumb over her knuckles once and a million butterflies took wing in her stomach.

"We're here, *bambina*," he said as he parked the car. "Do you have money for lunch?"

"Pietro allows me to eat at the deli. I'm not going hungry, Stefano, but thanks for asking." She was embarrassed that he felt he had to ask, but happy that it mattered to him. After hearing him talk about Dina in such a caring tone, she knew every single person in his neighborhood mattered to him.

Francesca was shocked when Stefano slid out of the car, walked around the hood and opened the door for her. He held out his hand and she had no choice but to allow his fingers to close around her hand, or make a scene. She was acutely aware of people stopping on the sidewalks to stare.

Store owners stepped to the windows to peer out. She found herself blushing for no reason. It wasn't as if she was *living* living with him. She was staying at his penthouse, not sleeping in his bed. She knew if people thought that, they'd think she was after his money.

"I thought you had somewhere to go," she murmured, trying not to look at him.

He kept possession of her hand as he escorted her into Masci's. To her surprise, Pietro was behind the counter, pacing back and forth. He spun around when they walked through the door, his expression wary.

"Mr. Ferraro."

"It's Stefano, Pietro," Stefano said in a low voice.

He shouldn't have sounded menacing, but he did. The moment they entered the deli, Francesca knew something was wrong. Joanna sat at one of the tables. Her eyes were red-rimmed and her face splotchy, evidence that she'd been crying for some time. Francesca made a move toward her, but Stefano's fingers tightened around hers. He tugged and she found herself up against his body, her front to his side, his arm a bar, locking her in place.

"There was some unpleasantness regarding Francesca's place of living last night. She was in danger. I am not happy about that. I left her in your hands, Joanna." He glanced at her over his shoulder, but then his gaze came back to rest on her uncle. "Joanna knew where she was staying. I imagine you did not." He made it a statement but waited for Pietro to contradict him.

Pietro glared at Joanna and then shook his head adamantly. Joanna sniffed and then stifled a sob.

Francesca put one palm against Stefano's abs on the inside of his open coat and shoved. Hard. Nothing happened. He didn't budge, nor did he look down at her. "Stefano . . ."

He glared down at her. "Enough. This is between Pietro, Joanna and me." Once again he looked at her boss. "She's staying with me in the penthouse, but while she is working Emilio or Enzo will be close. I want her *safe*, Pietro." His voice dropped an octave. "Do you understand what I mean by 'safe'?"

Pietro nodded.

"At some point in the future I expect you'll receive a visit from a couple of men who will tell you all sorts of tales about Francesca. When you don't fire her, and you won't, they will return and threaten you. The moment these men contact you, no matter what they say, I expect you to immediately, and by 'immediately' I mean that instant, report to me. Personally, Pietro. Have I made myself clear?"

Pietro nodded so hard and so much that Francesca feared his neck would break.

"Good." Stefano dropped the iron bar of his arm, but turned his head and brushed another kiss along her temple. "Text me, Francesca. I won't be happy if you forget."

"We all endeavor to make you happy," she murmured softly, and smiled innocently up at him.

He shook his head, his blue eyes glittering with a promise of retaliation, and her stomach did a slow roll in anticipation. He turned his head toward Joanna. "I trust we will see you at the club Friday night, Joanna. Emmanuelle said you'd be there."

Joanna nodded. "I'm so sorry, Stefano."

He studied her pale, splotchy face. "You fucked up, Joanna. You also apologized for it and it's over. We're good."

Instantly a smile broke out, lighting Joanna's face. Francesca wasn't certain what she'd done to apologize for, but evidently when Stefano said it was over, Joanna must have known him well enough to believe whatever was between them was gone. Her smile said it all.

Stefano caught Francesca under the chin and turned her face to his. "I'll pick you up after work. If not me, one of my brothers or my sister or a cousin."

"I can walk."

Swift impatience crossed his face. His eyes darkened. "Don't piss me off, Francesca. Someone will be here."

She gave an exaggerated sigh. "Can you please try to tone down the bossy?"

His smile was slow in coming, but when it did, her stomach did a slow roll. "I'll try, just for you, but I wouldn't count on it, *dolce cuore*." He brushed his mouth over hers. A brief contact, but so hot, embers found their way to her belly. "Later, *bella*. Be good."

Stefano was gone, striding from the store with his fluid, easy way, which made him look like a cross between a fighter and a dancer. He flowed over the ground, his long coat billowing around his legs as he made his way to the car. Francesca watched as those on the sidewalk stopped to look at him or stepped aside to make room for him. He didn't ever have to pause. The crowd parted like the Red Sea for him. He waved to a couple of people, but he didn't stop. He slid into his car and even traffic seemed to obey, allowing him to pull in immediately.

Francesca turned to Pietro. "What was that all about? You aren't responsible for me, no matter what Stefano says. Seriously, Mr. Masci, I'm just grateful that you gave me this job."

"No, no, Francesca. You're a good worker. The best. I have no problem with you. Stefano Ferraro asked a favor of me, and I said I would do it for him and I let him down. I won't again."

She bit her lip, studying his face. "I don't want you to think you're in any way responsible for me. I'm a grown woman."

"No, no, Francesca, you don't understand what a great honor and privilege it is for one of the Ferraros to ask a favor of me. Since you've been working for me, they drop by, all of them, cousins, siblings, all of them. In my store. Daily. I've always done a good business, but it is up over 100 percent since you began and that's only a couple of days. It will grow even more."

Francesca wasn't certain what to say to that. She glanced over her shoulder at Joanna. "Let me put my coat away, hon, and I'll be right out. I've got a few minutes before I have to clock in and we can talk." She wanted to know what had Joanna so upset and Stefano declaring it was over the moment Joanna apologized to him.

As she hung up her coat, she glanced at herself in the mirror. Her lips still looked a little swollen from the very hot, very hard and aggressive kiss. She touched her mouth with trembling fingers. She'd almost gone up in flames, just spontaneously combusted right there in the elevator.

She didn't look the same in her first ever designer clothes and even more fabulous boots. She shouldn't be so happy over the shoes, but never in her life had she been able to afford such luxury. She *loved* them. The way they fit. The feel of the material of her skirt. Everything. It was impossible not to and she didn't bother trying.

"Don't get used to it, Francesca," she murmured aloud to herself.

Joanna had a cup of coffee waiting for her, and Francesca sank down in the chair beside her. "Honey, you've been crying. What's wrong?"

Joanna rubbed her temples. "I've been crying so much I gave myself a headache. I want to apologize to you, too, Francesca. I never should have told you about those apartments, let alone allowed you to live there."

The breath left Francesca's lungs in a long rush and deep inside everything stilled. "This crying jag is about me living in those apartments? You apologized to Stefano because he was angry with you over that?"

"Of course he was angry. He had every right to be angry with me. I'm angry with myself. Pietro is angry with me, too."

"How did you find out about it when it just happened?" Francesca asked, keeping her voice low and controlled. She pushed the coffee mug away from her with the tips of her fingers.

"Emilio, of course. He and Vittorio came to see me last night. They were both understandably . . . upset. They told me about that horrible man and what he did to women in his building." Joanna's eyes filled with tears all over again. "After everything you've been through, it's awful to think of you being exposed to that."

"Joanna, they had no right waking you up in the middle of the night and telling you all that," Francesca said carefully.

"You've been so kind to me. Without you, I'd still be on the street and in serious trouble. I appreciate every single thing you've done for me. This job, the money to get here. Just sticking with me, being my friend when so many ugly things have been said about me. The apartment isn't your fault. I chose to live there against your advice. You have no blame in what happened, and the Ferraros certainly had no right to involve you." Stefano was going to have to answer to her over that. Making poor Joanna cry and feel so much guilt that she apologized was just plain out of line.

"No. I'm your friend, Francesca. I knew you shouldn't stay there. There were rumors about the owner. I knew he was a sleaze. Every woman within a mile or two has heard he's been brought up on rape charges repeatedly and then the charges would be dropped." She looked around the empty store. They weren't open for another half an hour, but she still lowered her voice. "He's connected to the Saldi family. The Saldis are Sicilian and they go way back. They're reputed to be very violent, and he's related through marriage. His aunt married one of the Saldis. I've heard she's as bloodthirsty as they are, and the family protects him."

Francesca took a deep breath. Joanna had known about the owner and hadn't confided any of the information to her, only that it wasn't a good place to stay and bad things happened there. Francesca had lived on the street for a short while. She knew bad things, but she associated most of them with drugs. It hadn't occurred to her that the owner of the building had raped women. Still, to be fair, had she known, she might have stayed there anyway rather than risk the street while she worked to find the money to get a decent place.

"I should have told you," Joanna said. "If I had told you, maybe you would have stayed with me until you got on your feet."

Francesca had to concede that she might have, but she wouldn't make Joanna feel any guiltier than she already did by admitting it aloud. She shrugged. "It's over now. I'm staying with Stefano . . ." Joanna gasped and a huge smile brightened her face. "In his *guest* room, you crazy woman."

"How far from his bedroom is the guest room?" Joanna asked. "Because seriously, you might consider sleepwalking."

"I don't want to be one of ten thousand women who have been in his bed. I read all the magazines you gave me, and he's a hound dog. He was with a different woman in every picture at every event." Just admitting the truth out loud made her stomach churn.

"That's the point, Francesca. It was always a different one and no one ever went to his penthouse. Not ever. Believe me, like all the other women around here, I've been on Ferraro watch since I was thirteen. Stefano has never seriously dated anyone. If he was sleeping with them, he didn't do it in his own home."

"Oh, he definitely had sex with them," Francesca confirmed. "Because his kisses need to be outlawed. I didn't think anyone could kiss like that."

Joanna's eyes got wide and her mouth formed a perfect round *O*. "He *kissed* you? Oh. My. God. This is so cool, Francesca. My best friend with Stefano Ferraro."

"I am not *with* him. He's doing what he always does, taking care of everyone in his neighborhood. He's the white knight and I'm the damsel in distress. When I'm all fixed up, he'll move on."

Joanna burst out laughing. "You tell yourself that, girlfriend, if it makes you feel better. The rest of us know the truth." She glanced at her watch. "I have an hour to make myself presentable and go to work."

"And I'd better get moving, too, before your uncle fires me."

"There's zero chance of that happening," Joanna assured her and leapt up. She gave Francesca a quick hug and then blew kisses to her uncle before rushing out of the store.

Francesca put an apron over her clothes, for the first time worried about getting anything on them. She helped Pietro put fresh food in the refrigerated cases. She could see the crowd, already beginning to line up on the sidewalk, waiting for her boss to open the doors. The number of people coming to the store definitely seemed to grow from one day to the next over the days she'd worked there. She was happy for Pietro, but it also made her nervous now that she knew part of the reason for the booming business was her association with the Ferraro family.

She spotted both Emilio and Enzo in the crowd. Emilio leaned one hip lazily against the wall, while he flirted with a young woman who kept tossing her blond hair from one side to another and then winding it around her finger. Emilio had angled his body so that he could watch the street and yet keep an eye on Francesca. He winked at her as he continued to talk to the blonde. Francesca burst out laughing. She was becoming very fond of Emilio. He might be flirting, but his attention wasn't centered on the woman—he was totally alert to everything around him.

Enzo was in line, but standing at an angle that kept changing. He didn't look into the shop, but was studying the street, the buildings across the street and the crowd around him. She realized immediately that between the two men, the street, buildings and sidewalk were covered all the time. She found herself impressed with them because clearly no one else seemed to be aware of what they were doing.

A sudden chill ran down her spine and she straightened from where she'd been arranging inside the cases the special Italian meats imported from various regions in Italy. A sharp prickle of awareness had her gaze sliding away from Emilio and Enzo to search the crowd. She'd had feelings like this before and they were always dead-on, and never boded well.

Her mouth went dry. Surely Barry Anthon hadn't already found her. She hadn't even gotten established. There was no way to build a reputation enough that he couldn't tear it down. She took a deep, calming breath and forced herself to look through the crowd. Her gaze slid through the sea of faces until it rested on a man staring straight at her.

He wore aviator-type sunglasses and had a ball cap pulled low over his eyes. His jacket was old and stained and very rumpled, but bulky so it was nearly impossible to tell his weight. He wasn't six foot, because Enzo was close to him and she knew Enzo was at least that tall and the man was shorter. He looked vaguely familiar and she tried to place him. She'd seen him somewhere, but from a distance, just like now. He stared right at her, his mouth drawn into a thin frown of dislike. When he saw her staring back, he drew a line across his throat. He did it so fast and then turned and walked away, hands in his pockets, shoulders slumped, head down, that she almost wasn't certain he'd really made the gesture. He walked rapidly and disappeared from her sight within moments.

Francesca stared after him, her heart beating fast, lungs seizing. Barry had to have sent him with that message. They'd already found her. She was going to have to decide whether to run or stay. She had no money and nowhere to go if she ran. If she stayed, she would be putting her friends in jeopardy. She stared after the man for a long time, long enough that Pietro had opened the doors and people were already crowding in, forcing her to go on automatic pilot and work.

CHAPTER TEN

Francesca spent most of the morning and early afternoon looking over her shoulder and watching the traffic through the plate glass window. She was nervous and edgy, but kept her smile in place with the customers. Time went fast because it was very, very busy, so much so that they had to call in another worker in order to keep up. Pietro, normally in the back, stayed out front to work the cash register while Francesca and Aria, a young woman working part-time and going to school, took care of the customers.

Francesca ate lunch in the back room, rather than out front with the customers as she had done the day before. She was eating late, most of the day having slipped by with such a constant stream of steady customers. She was grateful to get off her feet in spite of the new, comfortable boots.

She thought a lot about her options—which weren't many. The truth was, she wanted to stay, but it wasn't fair to Pietro, who had been so kind giving her a job on Joanna's word. She knew what Barry Anthon would do first. His men would talk to Pietro and insist he fire her. They would tell him about her "mental illness," her police record of vandalism and destruction of property. If Pietro didn't listen and fire her, they would target his store.

The men would ruin Pietro's livelihood just to get to her. She couldn't allow that to happen. Stefano's hotel would be much more difficult to get to, although she was fairly certain even that wouldn't go unscathed. Barry's men had set fire to one of the apartments she resided in. She couldn't imagine having to face Stefano or his family if Anthon burned down their hotel. Barry Anthon's destruction was far-reaching. She closed her eyes and pushed her forehead into the heel of her hand. She was going to have to leave. It wasn't fair to put any of these people in Barry's path.

"Francesca? Are you all right?"

Startled, she jumped out of her seat, knocking the chair over, rocking the table so that the soothing cup of coffee she'd just poured splashed over the rim. Stefano's brother, Taviano, the one who had driven the car from her apartment to the hotel, stood watching her closely. He looked uncannily like his brother. He certainly was as still and as menacing, his blue eyes every bit as assessing and sharp as Stefano's.

"What's wrong?" he demanded. He even had the same abrupt, bossy tone.

Heart racing, she stepped back. Taviano took up the room just as Stefano did. "Nothing. You just surprised me."

Eyes on her, he reached down and picked up the over-turned chair, gently setting it upright. "I brought your phone." He held it out to her.

Francesca swallowed the sudden lump in her throat. Stefano. Looking out for her. Her fingers closed around the item. She felt as if she was grabbing a lifeline.

"You're very pale. Are you certain that you're all right? I can take you home if you need to go back to the hotel."

She turned away from him with a shake of her head and a quick smile, afraid he saw too much. "I'm perfectly fine. Thank you for bringing me the phone. Your brother is very generous." She hoped he was even more so. The moment the phone was in her hand, a new plan came to her.

"He'd like you to text him. Just so he knows you've got the phone. He said to remind you to text him if you leave the store."

Those eyes never stopped watching her. She drew in a

breath. "He did make that very clear. In fact, he was rather forceful about it."

That got her a smile. "I can imagine. If you need anything let one of us know. Our numbers are programmed into your phone. Emilio's and Enzo's as well."

"Thank you, this is very kind of your family."

He shrugged. "We take care of our own. Make no mistake, Francesca, you're one of us. If you have any kind of problem, you let us help."

She nodded, trying to look reassuring. "I will."

He started to turn away, but looked at her over his shoulder, a grin lighting up his face. "It's nice to see you dressed in something besides that sleeping bag. The look was good, but this one is much better."

"I suppose I'm not going to live that down."

"You suppose right," he said, and was gone, moving down the narrow hallway with the grace peculiar to the Ferraro family.

Francesca wiped up the spilled coffee and sank back down into the chair. The break room was small, much smaller than Pietro's office. She turned her chair so it was facing the door, rather than the window. She'd wanted to see out, careful to keep watch for Barry's man, but it wasn't a smart idea to have her back to the door. Anyone could sneak up on her.

She sat in silence for nearly her entire break, sipping her coffee and working up her courage. Finally, she sent Stefano the text. She needed a loan. She'd pay him back as soon as possible. The loan was significant. Three thousand dollars. Her stomach churned as she typed out the request. She hoped he wouldn't think she'd been stringing him along, biding her time, just waiting for an opportunity to get money from him. She bit down hard on her lip as she hit send before she changed her mind.

She could find more clothes at a thrift store, not take anything else from Stefano, but the money would get her out of the city and she could go somewhere completely different.

She knew how to get lost on the street. She'd done it before, losing Barry's man so he wouldn't know when she boarded a bus.

She couldn't go without money. She *had* to get a loan from Stefano. Once she was on her feet, she'd send him the money. She could work. She was a hard worker. She didn't know how Barry had found her so fast, but she would get better at hiding. She *had* to get better. He was already breathing down her neck and she hadn't been in the city that long.

Her phone rang. She stared down at it as if it were alive. She knew who it was. She flipped it open and put it to her ear.

"Don't you dare fucking leave that store, Francesca. I mean it. Whatever is going on you *tell* me. You don't plan to run off. I'll be there in a few minutes." He hung up abruptly, not giving her a chance to respond.

There was no greeting and no nice ending to the conversation. Stefano was not happy. She took a deep breath. He would be there soon, and he would talk her out of leaving. She knew he could persuade her because she didn't actually want to leave. She *had* to, to protect Pietro, Joanna, and even Stefano. He might look at it as running, but she knew first-hand that Barry Anthon was capable of murder and he wouldn't hesitate if anyone got in his way.

She couldn't go out the front door. Emilio and Enzo were out there. She whirled around and started down the hall, heading toward the rear of the building. She had to leave now, before she was ready. She could have asked for her pay. Pietro would have given her cash, but she didn't dare wait one more minute. She yanked open the door and nearly ran right into Enzo.

He grinned at her. "Going somewhere, Francesca?" He blocked the exit with his body. He was solid. Impossible to move. He leaned one hip lazily against the doorjamb. "I have to tell you, sweetheart, that man of yours is in rare form. He blew up my phone with orders and promises of all kinds of pain and torture if you manage to evade me. Which you wouldn't be so mean as to try to do, right? I mean, you know Stefano. He wouldn't be in the least understanding if you slipped past me."

Francesca stepped back, because she had no choice as Enzo stepped forward. She put a defensive hand to her throat. "I'm trying to do the right thing, Enzo. I'm *protecting* him. You have no idea of the enemies I have. I have to get out of here."

Enzo shook his head, a small smile playing on his mouth. "You're *protecting* Stefano Ferraro. My cousin." He grinned at her. "That is so rich. Protecting *him*."

"It's not a laughing matter."

The smile faded and he tipped his head to one side. "You're serious."

"Very. I know you love him. For his sake, you have to let me go. I'll get on a bus and disappear." She wasn't certain she had enough money to get her anywhere. She still hadn't gotten a real paycheck yet.

"Honey, Stefano Ferraro isn't a man who needs protection from anyone. People need protection from him. Trust your man to take care of you. Trust our family."

She sensed movement behind her, although she didn't hear anything. Enzo lifted his gaze beyond her shoulder and she turned her head to see Emilio coming up behind her. The two men caged her in.

"Want to tell me what the hell is going on? Stefano is losing his fuckin' mind," Emilio greeted.

"Francesca here is leaving to protect Stefano from some big bad enemy she has," Enzo supplied.

Emilio stopped in his tracks, his face showing shock. "What?"

"You heard me."

Francesca had had enough. "Move, Enzo. You can't stop me."

"Honey." Enzo grinned at her. "Physics apply here. You're not up to taking me on."

"Are you shitting me?" Emilio demanded. "You're protecting Stefano."

She sighed, trying to push down the relief. She didn't want to feel relief, but she did. She was terrified of leaving. She didn't want to go back to the streets, but more, she didn't want to be alone anymore. Barry Anthon had terrorized her for so long she had forgotten what good was until she'd been with Stefano. She'd forgotten what safe felt like until she'd been with him.

"Fine. I'll go back to work, finish my shift and face his majesty when I'm off work," she capitulated.

"I think you're officially off work for the day. He's blown up my cell, Enzo's cell and Pietro's phone. I wouldn't be surprised if every single one of his brothers as well as Emmanuelle show up."

"He wouldn't go that crazy."

"Honey," Enzo said. "He did."

That didn't bode well. She followed Emilio back into the store, Enzo trailing close behind. To her shock, she recognized two of Stefano's brothers lounging by the door, as if they were draped there very casually, but there was nothing casual in their expressions when their gazes settled on her face.

Enzo took her elbow and walked her around the counter straight to Stefano's brothers. "She was protecting him," he greeted with a small grin.

Francesca rolled her eyes. "It isn't that funny."

Taviano broke into a smile. Ricco didn't, but his eyebrow shot up.

"Seriously?" Taviano asked. "This is priceless. Can't wait for him to find out."

"I'd like to know what prompted your sudden desire to make a run for it," Ricco said, "but let's take this outside. We have an audience."

Francesca was acutely aware of the silence in the store. It was packed with customers, yet no one was making purchases or conversing with a neighbor. All eyes were on her and the Ferraro brothers.

Ricco yanked open the door, lifted his chin at Pietro, took her elbow and marched her out of the store. As he did so, Stefano's Aston Martin pulled smoothly to the curb. Without missing a beat, Ricco opened the door, put a hand to the top of her head when she hesitated, forced her into the car and shut the door.

Francesca took a deep breath and turned her head to face Stefano. The atmosphere in the confines of the car was searing. She could see why. He was seething. A tendril of unease snaked down her spine. "Stefano . . ."

"Put your seat belt on." He waited, blue eyes like flames, burning a hole through her.

She was insane. She knew she was, because Stefano Ferraro was furious. His fury burned all the oxygen out of the air, but she still felt absolutely safe. Happy. Relieved. Uncaring that he might roar at her, because she knew categorically that Stefano would never lay a hand on her in anger and that he wasn't about to let her go.

She snapped the belt into place. "I'm sorry you felt you had to leave work."

"It might be best if you didn't talk while I'm driving."

She was fine with that. She knew it was a small reprieve, but she didn't care. The interior of the car was warm, and Stefano's wide shoulders and rock-hard body gave her the illusion of complete well-being. For the first time since she'd seen Barry's man draw his finger across his throat, she breathed easier.

She sat in silence, admiring the way Stefano drove—with speed, but very controlled. He drove right up to the front doors of the hotel, got out, tossed his keys to the valet and reached in for her. His grip was strong, a vise around her upper arm.

"You forgot your coat," he observed, his voice clipped. Still angry.

"I'm beginning to think you might be a little obsessed with coats, Stefano," she said, trying to lighten the mood. "You should see someone for that."

He didn't smile or loosen his grip. He went through the

double glass doors, across the lobby and straight to his private elevator. The minute they stepped inside, he put a hand to her belly and pushed her against the wall, caught her wrists in his hands, pinning them against the wall on either side of her head and settled his mouth over hers.

Hot. Searching. Angry. Hungry. He poured those emotions into her, his body aggressive against hers. She took his scorching heat, not even pretending to resist. She hadn't known she'd ached for his mouth on hers ever since he'd kissed her that morning, but the moment it happened, need surged through her.

Hunger rose, sharp and terrible. Electrical sparks seemed to jump from his skin to hers. Her body reacted, going pliant, breasts aching, nipples peaking into twin, tight buds, her body slick and hot with welcome. She kissed him back, giving herself to him. Letting his mouth take command of her.

If he intended the kiss as a punishment, it quickly evolved into something altogether different. By the time the elevator reached the penthouse, her knees had gone weak and Stefano was forced to hold her up. Every single cell in her body was alive and reaching for him. He took his mouth from hers and she chased after it, lifting her face in an effort to prevent him from leaving her.

Stefano wrapped his arm around her, keeping her upright as he guided her off the elevator and into the foyer of the penthouse. "At least you know you belong to me," he snapped, anger still infusing his voice.

If he could kiss like that when he was angry, he was in for trouble, because she wouldn't mind making him *really* angry if that was what she received every time. She pressed her fingers to her mouth and went with him into the spacious great room. It was long and wide and had several couches and chairs. He took her straight to the one in front of the fireplace and put her into it.

"Stay put."

Francesca watched him through lowered lashes as he turned on the fire, using a remote control, stalked across the room, shrugging out of his long coat and tossing it over one of the chairs before turning back to glare at her. Not just glare. She shivered. He pinned her with his piercing eyes. Seeing her. Seeing the fear she tried to hide from him. His jaw tensed, a muscle ticking there. Danger clung to his wide shoulders and defined chest. He looked both powerful and intimidating. She knew he thought the fear in her was of him, because he made a visible effort to get his anger under control.

"Dolce cuore." His voice was soft. Caressing. "Don't look at me like that. I would never hurt you. Never. No matter how angry I get, you will never be a target."

She shook her head. "I know that, Stefano." She did know it. Stefano Ferraro was a man who protected women, especially one he considered his, even if it was temporary.

"Why are you afraid? What made you run?"

He didn't take his eyes from her face and she shivered again at the intensity there. She studied him. His expression gave nothing away, yet she felt as if she had hurt him. "I don't want anything to happen to you." The confession came out in a little rush, the words tumbling over one another, almost of their own volition. She wasn't certain she would have revealed so much to him if she'd thought about it, but the idea that she might have hurt Stefano with her actions was unacceptable to her.

He stood across the room from her for a long time, his blue gaze moving over her face. She twisted her fingers into the material of her skirt, bunching it into her fist. The atmosphere in the room changed, but she didn't know him well enough to read it.

"What do you think is going to happen to me, Francesca?"

She didn't understand how he could speak so low, so quietly and still convey so much intensity. She realized he was still angry, but the emotion was no longer focused completely on her. He held himself still, not making a move toward her. Her heart beat fast and hard, mostly because it felt a little like being in the same room with a lion. Any moment he could choose to bring down his prey, but he held himself aloof, waiting. Making her wait.

Francesca moistened her lips with the tip of her tongue. "Stefano, don't be angry. You would try to . . ."

He was across the room in four long strides, cutting her off, mostly because she couldn't breathe. He still reminded her of a lion, a large jungle cat, fluid and beautiful, graceful as it rushed its prey. He leaned down, his knuckles on either side of her hips. Close, so close she could feel his fingers through the thin material of her skirt.

"Stop. Talking. Bullshit."

His face was even closer than his hands, his mouth against hers. Every movement brushed her lips with his. His eyes bore into hers, stripping her bare, seeing her when she didn't think it was safe. She couldn't hide the fact that she wanted him, and there in his penthouse, with his anger pulsing in the air, that wasn't a good thing at all.

"Stefano." She thought to soothe him.

"We're past this. We talked about it and we both agreed. We're not going backward so tell me what the fuck happened to make you want to run from me."

It was a demand. Nothing less. Francesca took a deep breath, desperate for air, but drew him into her lungs instead. She felt his lips against hers, soft but firm. His lips might be the only soft part of him. Every other square inch seemed to be made from pure steel. She couldn't resist the temptation, not when he surrounded her with his scent. Not when his anger pulsed in the air, feeding the sexual tension until she was squirming with need. With a terrible hunger she barely understood.

Francesca slid her arms around Stefano's neck and pressed her mouth closer against his, moving her lips along his in little kisses, using the tip of her tongue to trace and shape the curve of his mouth. His breath stilled in his throat. His blue eyes darkened. His lashes fluttered. He had beautiful lashes, full and long and very black. His arm slid along her back and he dragged her to her feet, pulling her body into his, locking her there.

His mouth took over hers and it was nothing less than a takeover. His kiss was hard, and hot and delicious. She tasted his anger. It was there, adding even more heat. She gave herself up to his scorching temper and his intense hunger. To the dark passion that swept her up like a tidal wave.

She wanted this. She wanted him. She didn't care about consequences; she only knew that when she was with him, she felt alive. She felt as if she was home, where she belonged. More, her body felt sensual, and beautiful. That was Stefano. He made her feel those things when she never had.

Electricity arced between them, sizzled over her skin and sank into her bones. Her bloodstream turned molten, so hot she felt each separate connection running through her body. His mouth was possessive. Demanding. On fire. Taking rather than asking. That didn't matter, because she gave up everything to him.

His hands settled on her hips, almost as if he might set her aside. Francesca moved closer to him, needing to feel the strength in his body, the way his muscles rippled so elegantly beneath his clothes. She needed to touch him, his skin, to feel the heat scorching through her. Without thinking of the consequences, she jerked his shirt out of the waistband of his pants and slid her palms up his rib cage and over his chest.

His breath hitched in his throat. Hers caught in her lungs. A moan escaped her throat. A groan emerged from his lungs. His hand slid down her narrow waist to her hips, fingers bunching in her skirt while his mouth took hers again. She went up on her toes, reaching for more, drowning in his taste, in his dark passion. His hand slid over her bare thigh, up to her hip, and then down around to the inside. The feeling of the pads of his fingers was exquisite. All the while his mouth commanded hers. Taking her to places she hadn't known existed.

She needed to be closer, *much* closer. Skin to skin. On the far wall, over his arm, she saw their shadows merge, and felt the jolt of lightning, as if she'd been struck, as if somehow their two bodies became one inside the same skin. The blaze of fire sizzled down her spine, up through her belly to her breasts. Scorching hot. Making her hungrier for him. Addicted to his taste. His scent. The feel of his hard body against the softness of hers. She'd never been more aware of herself as a woman.

Abruptly, Stefano's hands locked around her upper arms like a vise and he put her away from him. Holding her still at arm's length, breathing heavily, shaking his head. She took a step toward him. Mesmerized by him. Completely under his spell.

"No, *bambina*. We can't do this."

"Yes, we can. I want this," she whispered, once again stepping toward him.

His arms locked, holding her away from him. "No."

One word. She saw his face. Uncompromising. Without expression. She was on fire, her body not her own, but his, and yet . . . he didn't want her. She was making a fool out of herself. Never in her life had she offered herself to another man. Humiliation burned through her.

Francesca turned away from him, pressing her fingers against her mouth to still the trembling. To seal the taste and feel of him to her. He didn't want her. She'd thrown herself at him and he'd rejected her. How could she have been so stupid? She didn't have a lot of experience, but she shouldn't have convinced herself he wanted her just because she wanted him. She'd never felt more mortified in her life. She wasn't certain how to salvage the situation, or even if she could.

"Don't." His voice was low.

She didn't turn around to face him; she didn't dare. Color had swept up her neck and into her face. She took a step toward the hall, away from him, thinking to flee to her room. She had nowhere else to go and she wanted to hide. To give herself time to pull herself back together, because he'd totally unraveled her. She would have allowed him to take her right there in his great room. On the couch. The floor. It wouldn't have mattered as long as she had him. But he didn't want her.

She'd never thrown herself at a man in her life. Never. She'd never been rejected and she didn't know how to act. What to do or say. She wasn't sophisticated. She didn't run in his circles, and she didn't know the first thing about casual kissing. To her, those kisses had been anything but casual, but what did she know?

"Francesca, don't." He repeated the command softly. Imperiously. "Look at me." Another command.

She refused to face him. She shook her head and took another step, the need to flee overcoming her pride. She whirled around, thinking to run to the elevator, but he was on her before she'd taken a single step. His hands caught at her hips and he kept moving, propelling her backward as he took her straight through the wide archway to the wall in the hallway. She would have fallen over, had he not been holding her up.

Heart pounding, back to the wall, caged in by his body, she could only stand there, wishing the floor would open up and swallow her. She refused to look at his face, into his eyes. She didn't want to do this with him, listen to him try to let her down easy. That was even more humiliating.

"I want to go," she murmured softly. "You can't keep me here."

"Look at me, Francesca." It was another one of his orders. Clear. Clipped. Expecting obedience.

Her breath hissed out. She braced herself to meet his eyes because she knew she had to comply with his command. He wouldn't let her go until she did. She didn't want to see pity there. Or compassion. She slowly forced her gaze up his chest to his strong jaw, that beautiful mouth, his aristocratic nose, and finally, finally, to his amazing blue eyes. At once she couldn't look away. Captured. Held prisoner there. Right in the depth of all that blue. Her breath caught in her throat. Not pity. Definitely not pity. Desire burned there. Hot and raw. Possession. Primal and a little savage.

"*Dolce cuore*, you're a runner. You've gotten in the habit of taking off when things get too hot. I'm not easy. I'll never be easy. I'll own you. You won't have one moment when I'm not aware of where you are and what you're doing. That's who I am. I'll always be that man. You have to be certain you're going to stick with me no matter what, because once I make you mine, once your body belongs to me, there's no taking it back. Not ever. You have to know what you're committing to."

She shook her head. "Don't say things like that, Stefano. I read the magazines and you had sex a thousand times with a thousand women. They can't all belong to you."

"It was sex, Francesca. I fucked them because I needed release and I like to fuck." He ignored her wince and continued. "I didn't bring them home. They weren't ever going to live with me. Or know me. Or know anything about me. I didn't claim them in front of my entire family or my neighborhood. None of those women belonged to me. I didn't want them for more than a few hours. We used each other—that was it."

Francesca bit down hard on the side of her lip, her heart pounding. She could barely believe what she was hearing. Somehow, she was different to him from all those other beautiful, sophisticated women? More to him than models? Heiresses? Actresses? The rich and beautiful?

"My life is fucked up, Francesca. It was from the moment I was born. I have no choice in what I do. I was born into a family business, trained for it, and have people depending on me. My life has never been my own. I've got all the money in the world, and nothing that I want. Until you. I want you. You're what I want for myself."

She curled her fingers tighter around his biceps, afraid if she didn't hold on she would fall. The things he said made her weak with desire. There was stark honesty in his voice—raw emotion on his face.

"I'm not a nice man, *bambina*. I'm never going to be that nice man. If you give yourself to me, you're entering into a world that will scare you. You'll have to trust me implicitly. Trust that always, always, before any other, I will have your back. I'll keep you safe. I'll make you happy and give you the world. It isn't going to be casual sex, Francesca. You give me your body and that's it. I won't let you take it back."

"You're scaring me." He was. The part about his life, entering his world and coming right out and saying his world would scare her, she was afraid of what that meant. He wasn't being dramatic, or embellishing; he was stating facts, she could tell.

"You should be scared. I want you to see me, Francesca. The real me. The man you will be spending your life with. No illusions. I'm ruthless and implacable. I get the job done with whatever means necessary. I keep what's mine. I want children. A family. A woman who will love those children and get up with them in the middle of the night and comfort them when they're upset. I want that woman for myself and for my children."

He had said he got up with his sister when she had nightmares and he was the one who made her hot chocolate and sat up with her. Not his mother. Stefano had done that.

"I'll try to curb the way I am and give you some room, but I know myself. You're already my world. I think about you day and night. I worry about you. You'll convince yourself that once the threat to you is over and Barry Anthon has been eliminated from your life, I'll lighten up. But I won't, *dolce cuore*, I won't. I'll always need to know you're safe and that when I say something to you, you'll listen."

She heard the regret, the sorrow in his voice. As if she couldn't ever love him because of who he had become. What he'd been born and bred for. Whatever his life was, whatever his family business was, he wasn't giving that up. Not for her. Not for anyone. He would expect her to live with whatever it was. He would expect her to live with the rules of his world, the ones he laid down.

I'm not easy. I'll never be easy. I'll own you. You won't have one moment when I'm not aware of where you are and

what you're doing. That's who I am. I'll always be that man.
His declaration echoed through her mind. On that thought
came the next—that she would always know she was safe,
that her children were safe. "Safe" meant the world when you
hadn't had it.

I'm not a nice man, bambina. *I'm never going to be that
nice man. If you give yourself to me, you're entering into a
world that will scare you.* He didn't think himself a nice
man, but in the next breath he told her just as honestly . . .
*Trust that always, always, before any other, I will have your
back. I'll keep you safe. I'll make you happy and give you
the world.* He didn't understand how beautiful he was to
her. How amazing that a man like him existed.

"You don't know anything about me. What I'm like.
What my character is. It's impossible to want to be with me,
to say I'm your world, when you don't even know me." It
killed her to state the truth, because she was giving him up.
And she wanted him. But it was the truth, and she wasn't
going to live a lie just so she could have him.

He laughed softly, shaking his head, his gaze drifting
possessively over her face. "Do you think after spending an
entire lifetime knowing bad, studying bad in every form, I
don't know good when I see it? I've spent thousands of hours
in the company of superficial. Of shallow. All about looks.
Money. Image. Grasping and greedy. That's the last thing
you are."

"You can't know that, Stefano," she whispered. Her heart
pounded so loud she feared he might hear it.

"Really? *Bambina.*" His fingers curled around the nape
of her neck. "You gave your coat to a stranger, a woman in
the street, when you needed it desperately. Joanna has money,
a family, a warm house to live in. She was with you. She didn't
offer her coat. Neither did anyone else walking down that
street seeing Dina shivering and cold. They saw a homeless
woman if they saw her at all. You saw a human being."

"But . . ."

"I gave you my coat, Francesca, with well over a thousand

dollars in the pocket. How many women or men for that matter would have left that money there?"

"I bought boots." Her voice was small and color crept up her neck. Her gaze slid from his; she was ashamed at having to admit she'd taken his money and still couldn't pay it back.

His thumb slid along her jaw and then traveled to her bottom lip. He traced the soft curve, sending little shivers down her spine.

"*Bella*, I sent my brother into the store to make certain you bought yourself shoes. That was important to me. And you took extra care of my coat. Hanging it in Pietro's office away from anyone else. You were freezing in that horrible apartment, yet instead of using the coat to keep warm, you hung it carefully."

"I thought about using it," she admitted. The floor was dirty and even after she'd scrubbed it, she didn't want his coat ever touching it.

"But you didn't, even though you should have. You didn't want anything to happen to it. It mattered to you."

It did matter more than she cared to admit to herself. She kept saying she wanted to return his coat to him. It seemed so much of a responsibility, but if she was being strictly honest with herself, she knew the truth was she wanted to wrap herself in his scent. He made her feel safe. Having his coat was a little like having a part of him. She moistened her lips, the tip of her tongue tasting the pad of his thumb. Her heart jerked and her sex clenched and went slicker, hotter. Needier.

"Stefano, if you knew the things they say about me . . ."

"The things Barry Anthon said about you? Made up about you? Manufactured evidence against you?" His voice went cold. Hard. Scary. "When you woke up from your nightmare and you told me about him . . ."

"Stop." Now her face was cherry red. She was *so* ashamed of deliberately dragging him into her mess. "You have no idea what I did. I *manipulated* you. I knew you were scary protective. Off-the-charts protective. I told you about Barry . . ."

"Because you were half awake and scared out of your mind. You think holding you in my arms I couldn't feel that? We're connected. I know you feel that, too. The moment you were awake enough, you backtracked."

She had. "Still, I did drag you into my nightmare. It doesn't count that I regretted it afterward. That is a terrible character flaw, to use someone because I felt so alone and tired and . . ." She broke off.

"Scared. You were scared and you needed someone."

"Not just anyone." She had to give him that much. Give him truth. "You made me feel safe for the first time in what seems forever, since my parents died, since my sister was murdered," Francesca confessed in a little whisper.

"I want you to feel safe when you're with me, *dolce cuore*. Most importantly, when you thought Anthon had found you, you decided to run to *protect* me. In my lifetime, I can't remember another human being protecting me. I was raised to be a shield standing between harm and everyone else. I learned that from age two. You have no idea what it meant to me, knowing that you were terrified, no money, nothing at all, yet you would leave in order to protect me."

She shook her head. "Stefano, you're making me sound far better than I am."

"I knew what kind of woman I wanted in my life, for the mother of my children, and when I saw all those things in you, I knew. I knew it was you. Not to mention, the chemistry between us is off the charts. I think I mentioned to you that I like to fuck. I do. A lot. I came off a job and needed a woman desperately. I couldn't get relief because suddenly no other woman would do but you. There's only you for me. You're the woman I want under my body. You're the woman I want to see coming apart when I take you. I want to be with you in every way a man can be with his woman."

"I don't know what I'm doing."

"A little trust, *bambina*." There was a hint of amusement in his voice. "I know what I'm doing, and I'll make certain it's always good for you."

"What about being good for you? That's important to me, Stefano," she confessed.

He went still, his blue eyes darkening, intense, moving over her face with that raw possession and something else she couldn't quite name. "There it is," he said softly. "The reason I want you with every fucking breath I take."

CHAPTER ELEVEN

Stefano's fingers tightened on the nape of Francesca's neck and he bent his head slowly toward hers. He needed her mouth. The taste of her. No matter what she said, no matter that he'd acted as if he was giving her a chance to get away from him, he knew better. He knew she was already lost. *His.* He'd never thought he'd really have a chance at finding a woman of his own, one he could love and center his world around, one who would accept him and his fucked-up life, but now that she'd stepped into his world, he knew he wasn't about to let her go.

She should have pulled away from him. He'd told her the truth about himself and hinted at his world. He'd let her know exactly what she had to look forward to with him. She should have tried again to make her escape, but instead, she lifted her face to his. Offered herself. Her eyelids drifted down, covering that sexy, slumberous look that sent scorching arrows igniting the blood in his veins.

He took her mouth. Ruthless. Merciless. A little savage even. Hungrier than he'd ever been in his life. Her lips were soft, parting for him instantly on his demand, and his tongue slipped into her mouth. Her sweet, sweet mouth. Instantly his blood rushed hotly through his veins to pool low. Brutal. He devoured her. Taking everything he could get from her and demanding more. He would never get enough of her, of the way she kissed him. Giving to him. Giving him everything. She didn't know what she was offering him. Trust. Absolute trust. Her body went boneless, melting into his, her mouth moving under the assault of his.

It didn't matter that he was wild. Rough. That he was allowing the kiss to spin out of control. She just gave and gave to him. That got to him as nothing else could have. She didn't think she had anything to offer him. He got that. She had no money, no family, nothing at all in her eyes. Yet she gave him everything because she gave him this magnificent gift—her and her trust, when she had no reason to trust anyone, least of all him.

He had never had a woman who didn't want something from him. He knew the score and he was all right with that. Francesca was . . . extraordinary. A gift. A miracle. She just gave herself to him. He was connected to her through their shadows and he knew how she felt. Frightened, bordering on terror. Still, he mattered to her. She saw him, not the Stefano the rest of the world saw, but the man inside who needed. Who didn't want to stand alone. She gave herself to that man. And God help him, he wasn't ever going to let her go, so he had to do this right. He had to give the best he could, certainly not ripping her clothes off and taking her the way his body demanded.

He drew back before it was too late, before he took her right there in the hallway on the floor. Before the roaring in his head became too loud and the need in his body took away every ounce of sense he had. Dimly, he heard the *ping* of the elevator and instantly, even with his body on fire and his cock so damned hard and full he was afraid he might burst, he turned, blocking Francesca's body with his own, dragging his gun from his shoulder holster and tracking the elevator doors through the archway.

Ricco stepped into the foyer, followed by his other brothers, all of them, and his New York cousins. They looked grim. Determined. The truth was, he wasn't surprised to see them. He knew why they were there. Francesca represented hope to them. Already, knowing that he was claiming her, she was family to them. They took family seriously. They wanted to know what had her spooked, why she would think she had to run. More, why she would think she had to protect Stefano. He also knew that if they believed he was in danger, they would pull out all stops to ensure his safety as well as Francesca's. Any other time he would have been glad to see them, but the timing was poor.

"My brothers, *bambina*," he said softly, turning back to her as he slid the gun back into his holster. "And two cousins from New York." His cousins were the family investigators out of New York. "They will be asking you a few questions. If you aren't comfortable answering, look to me. I'll handle it. Understand?" Because even with his family, he would stand in front of her. Always. She didn't know that yet, but she'd learn.

"I don't understand." Francesca's eyes went from dazed and dark with need to confusion and wide with shock as she stared at the gun. "What questions? And why are you carrying a gun? Is that legal?"

He threaded his fingers through hers, his thumb sliding gently over her knuckles in a little caress. He felt her answering shiver. He could still taste her in his mouth, that particular addicting blend of Francesca's passion and innocence. He tugged until her front was tight against his side and he stepped from the hallway into the great room to greet his brothers.

"You know the family, and this is Lanz and Deangelo Rossi, my cousins. This is my woman, Francesca."

She nodded but didn't smile, clearly very confused.

He didn't tell her why they were there, that in his family, an investigator from another branch would help out when they were directly involved. He didn't want to risk questions. She wasn't ready to learn the family secrets. He needed to hook her deep, make certain she loved him enough to stay. She wasn't there yet, and he wasn't about to chance fucking his one shot with her up. He wanted the spotlight off his cousins. "Where's Emmanuelle?"

"Someone had to be the sacrificial lamb," Taviano said.

"She drew the short straw." That meant she would keep Eloisa, his mother, busy while they held this meeting.

Stefano nodded. "Anyone want coffee? Wine? Something else to drink?" He led Francesca to the shorter love seat, allowing his brothers to take the larger couches or more comfortable, deep armchairs.

Vittorio was already at the bar, mixing drinks for his brothers and cousins. He served his cousins first and then flashed Francesca one of his winning smiles. "What can I get you?"

She looked up at Stefano. "Am I going to need a drink for this?"

"It might be best, *dolce cuore*," Stefano said. He ran his hand over the fall of soft hair tumbling around her face. "We have some questions that need answering."

Her face instantly shut down. She shook her head, her hand slipping from his. She dropped her hands to her lap, lacing her fingers together tightly. "Stefano . . ."

"It has to be done, Francesca. We need to know what we're facing. I've got my cousins looking into what happened and also into Anthon's past, but we need to hear the truth from you."

She shook her head again, glancing nervously at his cousins. They remained steadfastly silent. "How are you going to know whether or not I'm telling the truth? I told the police, the judge, my boss at the deli where I'd worked since I was sixteen, the landlords of two apartments, and in the end no one believed me except Joanna. Your brothers barely know me and your cousins don't know me at all. Why would they even consider I'd be telling the truth over him?" She made a move to stand, getting ready to flee. "I've done this too many times. I don't want to do it again."

He stood solidly in front of her, refusing to give ground, making it impossible for her to move. She subsided back onto the love seat and he sat beside her, his arm sliding along the back of the couch, fingers settling on her neck. "Red wine, or would you like something stronger? Vittorio makes a killer margarita."

She moistened her lips. He felt her body shiver and instinctively he moved closer to her until she was locked against him, thigh to thigh, her body beneath his shoulder.

"You have to trust me to take care of you through this," he said. "I know it's upsetting, but you have us now. You're not alone. Anthon may think that, and he'll make his move, but you won't be alone ever again, *bella*. You're mine. I take care of what is mine."

"Ours," Ricco corrected. *"Famiglia."*

The others nodded in a show of solidarity.

Francesca's hands trembled and Stefano put his over them, tugging until she let him pull one open palm onto his thigh. He covered her hand completely with his, pressing her palm into his muscles, holding it tight against him. She looked up at him for a long time, her gaze searching his. He knew what she saw. He wasn't a man to lie. He was hard. Cold even. Tenacious. Ruthless, and when he had an enemy, without mercy.

He knew if it was just him asking the questions, she would answer without hesitation, but her gaze continually strayed to his brothers. She was uncomfortable with them there.

"We're here to help you," Ricco reiterated. "You belong to Stefano, so that makes you belong to all of us—even our cousins. We're all family. That means something to us. Don't be afraid. We'll know the truth. Don't you, when you hear it? Haven't you always been able to tell when someone is lying to you?"

Francesca nodded. "Yes." Her voice was very low and filled with reluctance as she made the admission, as if they would think she was crazy.

"Our entire family has that ability," Ricco said. "Our cousins and our parents, an aunt and uncle as well. It's a gift we deliberately chose to develop in our family, for generations, not just us. We'll know the truth when you give it to us."

Francesca's palm pressed deeper into Stefano's thigh. She knew Ricco had given both reassurance as well as warning, but she nodded and Stefano felt some of the tension ease out of her.

"I'll have a glass of red wine. I didn't eat dinner, and I've noticed even a small amount of wine seems to affect me. I'm a lightweight, but I do enjoy the occasional glass with dinner."

"You don't eat enough," Stefano said, his voice gruff. A bit bossy and disapproving.

That earned him a flash of amusement from her vivid blue eyes, and then it was gone as she accepted the glass of wine from Vittorio. Stefano felt something move deep inside him at that intimate look. He knew it was meant for him alone. He'd never had that. Not once in his life. A woman who was exclusively his. Francesca wasn't aware of it, but she looked at him with far more trust in her eyes than he deserved. She looked at him as if the sun rose and set with him.

"I'm not exactly thin, Stefano." She ducked her head, looking at her wineglass rather than at him as if the discussion about her curves embarrassed her.

She had gone hungry for a long while. Truthfully she'd lost some weight, but he could tell that she thought she needed to. Women seemed to always think that way. He preferred curves to supermodel thin. He didn't understand why women were so hard on themselves. Francesca was beautiful and he didn't want a single pound to go away.

His brothers, drinks in hand, found chairs and settled, all eyes on his woman. He knew that made her uncomfortable so he kept his fingers around the nape of her neck and his other hand covering hers on his thigh.

"Tell us about Barry Anthon, Francesca," Ricco said. "From the beginning. How he came into your life and what happened from there."

Francesca glanced up at Stefano for reassurance and then carefully set the wineglass on the small end table, fearing she'd spill it on the gleaming marble floor. Her entire body trembled and she didn't seem to be able to do anything about it, even when she commanded herself to be still. She didn't want to talk about Barry Anthon, or relive the nightmare world she'd been dragged into two years earlier when Cella first met Barry.

She risked another look around at the faces of the Ferraro brothers. Vittorio and Taviano looked encouraging. Ricco looked downright scary. Giovanni nodded at her as if to tell her to get on with it. She felt Stefano's body sitting next to her, yet he seemed to take up the room, surrounding her, in front of her, at her back. He was everywhere. Dangerous. Determined. Giving her a feeling of security. How he managed that she didn't know. The fingers massaging her neck almost absently were mesmerizing. Without consciously thinking about it she eased back into them, seeking more. Seeking his touch while she gave them what they wanted.

"My sister, Cella, is—was—nine years older than me. When our parents were killed in an automobile accident she decided to raise me herself. She didn't have to do it—she wanted to. She never once made me feel like a burden to her, even though it was difficult. We didn't ever have a lot of money and we lived in a tiny apartment, but I was really happy."

No one rushed her to get to the place where she met Barry, and she appreciated their patience in allowing her to tell it in her own time and way.

"I was working at a deli and going to school. Cella worked at a beauty salon as a hairdresser. She did nails as well. Her shop was downtown, in a good location, which meant they had a lot of high-end clients. She made decent money and her clientele really built. Next to her salon was a very busy and popular coffee shop. One day she was rushing back to work, and another customer at the coffee shop ran right into her. His coffee spilled all over her. It was hot and she got burned. She dropped her purse, everything went flying and he knelt down and picked everything up for her, immediately took her to a boutique to buy her new clothes for her workday and asked her out. That man was Barry Anthon."

The brothers exchanged a long look and she hesitated, and then glanced up at Stefano. "What?"

"He does that. He sees someone beautiful that he wants and arranges an 'accident,' where he can play the mortified white knight, and asks the woman out, sweeps her off her feet and gets her hooked before his true colors come out."

"You know that about him?"

Ricco took a drink of amber liquid from the tumbler in his hand and nodded. "He uses it when he's at parties. I've witnessed it a time or two."

A little shudder went through Francesca. Unconsciously she pressed closer to Stefano. Instantly his hand went from her neck to her shoulders and he shifted her right against him before his fingers slid back beneath her hair to caress her nape.

"That's what he did. Cella would come home laughing and talking about him like he was Prince Charming. I was happy for her. She was certain she was falling in love. They dated often over the next six months, although little things she wasn't thrilled with began happening. First, he was introduced to me, and I didn't like him at all. Not. At. All." She enunciated each word. "He was too charming and he would touch me all the time. Stand too close. Breathe on the back of my neck. More than that . . ." She broke off, frowning. How could she tell them without sounding insane? She was already going to have to combat insanity charges when she told them the entire story.

"Francesca." Vittorio leaned toward her, evidently reading her reluctance. "*Cara*, we're all family here. Say whatever it is and let us decide. We hear truth. We told you that. We meant it, quite literally, so whatever you say can't be much more bizarre than that."

Absently, beneath Stefano's palm, her fingers bunched the material of his immaculate pin-striped trousers into her fist, holding on for support. "I know how this sounds, but sometimes, when I'm standing a certain way and the light is just right, my shadow will connect with someone else's shadow. We're not physically touching. Just our shadows, on the wall, or floor. Wherever." She bit at her lip and then took a slow sip of wine, taking her time putting the glass down.

She'd started. Now she had to finish. They were really going to think she was insane.

"*Bambina,*" Stefano murmured, his mouth against her temple, lips brushing her skin. Breath teasing her hair. "No one is going to think you're lying."

She sighed and forced her shoulders straight. "I don't know if that has anything to do with it, the part about shadows, but I just noticed that they were always touching when I would get this sensation. I could feel what the other person felt."

The brothers exchanged another long look and she hastened to try to make her explanation sound better. "I can't explain it, only that sometimes, I just know what a person feels. He would have slept with me, but he didn't feel anything for either of us. Not me. Not Cella. Not in the way Cella thought. It was more like a cat playing with a mouse. He was playing her for his own amusement. He planned on humiliating her. Dumping her. That kind of thing makes him feel powerful."

She waited for recriminations, but no one said anything. Ricco nodded at her assessment of Barry Anthon. That was the most she got from them. "I tried to tell her. It was the first time we ever had a big fight. She refused to believe me." That had really hurt. She couldn't understand why her sister wouldn't believe her. She didn't lie. She never lied. They were close. It didn't make sense to her.

"After the fight we had, Cella noticed little things that upset her. Barry never took her out in public. He would attend fund-raisers and go to huge events where the media was all over, and he would take an actress or some celebrity. He'd tell Cella he had to, because it was important to get the maximum amount of coverage for the event as possible, but even at ball games he'd be photographed with other women. He would make little remarks to her, sneering at her clothes or shoes, or laugh because she didn't know which fork to use at his club. She made excuses for him, saying that she probably was looking for something to be upset about because of the way I felt about him."

Ricco shook his head. "I've heard him do that, put his date down. Make fun of her. Say things to take away her self-esteem. He does it to just about all of the women he dates."

Giovanni nodded. "I heard him talk to a friend of his once, about how you put a woman in her place and she'd do anything to be with you because she knew you were better than she was and she was damned lucky to have you. He believes that shit."

"Fucking asshole," Taviano muttered under his breath, and abruptly jumped up and paced across the floor to the bar to pour himself another drink. "I despise that fucker."

She nearly smiled, more because she realized all the brothers were alike, even down to their colorful language. And they seemed to believe her. At least they knew Anthon and had observed his behavior so what she was telling them wasn't so far out of line they wouldn't hear her the way the police and judge had been with her.

"You aren't alone," she told Taviano. Because, in spite of the language, if there was a person on earth who could be described with that one word, it would be Barry Anthon.

"Keep going," Stefano instructed.

She took a deep breath, trying to keep the door in her mind from cracking open, the one where she relived finding her sister dying on the blood-slick floor of their apartment.

"She spent the night with Barry at his condo and she called me very late. She was upset because she said that he had talked to her about this multimillion-dollar fight that was huge, televised, a title fight that had been in the making for a couple of years. She wasn't into the fights at all and she was a little bored that he went on and on about it. That evening he bragged about how much money he made betting on the fight. He kept repeating how he knew how to pick them."

"The Henessy and Morrison fight," Giovanni guessed.

Francesca nodded. "Those were the names. He was called to the door and he went outside with a couple of his men, who seemed to be upset. He'd left the door to his office cracked open. Usually it was locked. That was the one room in his home she'd never been in, so she peeked in to see what it was like. Cella told me she wandered around a little bit and then as she was going to leave, she was behind his desk and she saw a book open with names and numbers, and she recognized the name of the fighter who lost—the one Barry said everyone expected to win. It looked to her as if he had paid the fighter to lose. In case, she took pictures of the pages with her phone and then a video of the entries, and there were hundreds of them."

"The book was just lying open on his desk?" Ricco asked, his voice disbelieving.

She bit her lip hard before she realized he wasn't disbelieving what she was telling him, more that Barry was an idiot for leaving such a thing out, maybe for even keeping records, although she suspected it was for blackmail purposes.

"Cella said that he was in his office working late. He was interrupted by a commotion at the door and several of his men took him out where she couldn't hear. She'd been in the kitchen cooking for him. He liked her to cook whenever she came over. Cella wasn't the best cook. She worked all the time, but because I usually did the cooking for us at the apartment, she took the opportunity at his condo. She went into the bedroom and called me and told me she wasn't going to spend the night. That she wanted me to call in a few minutes and say I was sick."

Her voice faltered and she put her hand to her throat defensively. Already a lump was forming. Tears burned behind her eyes. She took another deep breath to keep from going to pieces. "I should have gone straight home right then. I needed to study and I was already at the library. It was so silly really, how important I thought it was to do research for a paper I was writing." She shook her head and had to swallow several times. Her chest hurt, her lungs burning for air.

"Just tell us the rest, *dolce cuore*—say it fast and get it over with," Stefano murmured, his mouth once again against her temple.

"I called about ten minutes later and told her I was sick with the flu. She made lots of sympathetic noises and made her excuses to Barry. She didn't realize he had a camera in his office and everything she did was recorded. When he found the door open, he looked at the feed and apparently saw her looking at the book. He went after her." She tried desperately to separate herself from the rest of it, to be unemotional and recite the events as if they'd happened to someone else, but she couldn't. Her voice shook, betraying her. She sounded strangled, close to tears and no matter how many times she took a breath, she couldn't get enough air into her lungs.

"I came home late and the apartment was dark. The moment I tried to get in, I knew something was wrong because the door was cracked open. I could smell blood and I heard a mewing noise, like a wounded animal in terrible pain. The lamp was closest and I turned it on. Blood was everywhere. All over the walls, the furniture and the floor. Cella lay close to the couch, in a pool of dark red, her clothes red. Her hair was matted with blood. I ran to her, dropped to my knees beside her and tried to stem the blood and at the same time call 911."

"All right, *bambina*," Stefano said softly. "You're safe with us now. He isn't going to get away with this."

"He was there. Barry was there. He had blood all over him. He didn't try to deny that he killed her. He wanted me to know. He told me that she'd been stupid and that I'd better give him what he wanted. I could hear the sirens and he just walked out, as if it didn't matter who saw him. In the end it didn't. I told the police it was him, and they said he had an airtight alibi." Her voice shook, turned bitter.

The two cousins leaned forward, almost in unison, instantly drawing her attention. She had forgotten they were there. For some reason, she didn't mind Stefano's brothers hearing her story, but the cousins didn't seem as sympathetic. They were much more unemotional, although, she had to admit, not unkind.

The moment the cousins shifted forward in their chairs,

their gazes fixed steadily on her face, every one of Stefano's brothers reacted, hitching forward as well, but protectively. She felt that instant shield go around her. She looked around and saw that every shadow was connected. She was feeling the emotions the brothers were, and they were definitely protective of her. Stefano's hand on her shoulder was suddenly different as well. His fingers dug into her arm, and she knew he was fighting anger.

His brothers hadn't come here to hear her story; they had come to show solidarity. The knowledge hit her instantly and made her want to cry. They believed her on her word alone; it was the cousins she had to convince. She didn't know why Stefano and his family had rallied around her, or had chosen to side with her against Barry Anthon, but she was grateful they had. Surprisingly, it was Stefano's anger that settled her churning stomach. She didn't want him upset at his cousins when clearly he had asked them there to listen to her story.

"He didn't find her phone then," Lanz said, making it a statement.

She shook her head. "But at the time, I had no idea what he was talking about. I didn't for a while."

"Continue," Deangelo encouraged.

Her heart began to beat harder and a little faster. She turned her hand, the one on Stefano's thigh, threading her fingers through his, needing his reassurance. He instantly bent his head, his lips pressed to her ear, right through the thick mass of hair tumbling around her.

"Francesca, if you need a break or this is too upsetting, we can continue later. We don't have to do this now."

She wanted to take that out. The rest of her story was a roller coaster of emotions. She had managed to tamp down the horror of her sister's murder, the terror of the man she knew had savagely killed her. She was tempted to take the out he gave her, but looking around the room at his brothers waiting so patiently for her decision, knowing all of them would back her up, gave her the necessary courage to continue.

Francesca shook her head. "It's better to do this all at

once. If you want to know, I'll tell you now. Barry Anthon is a monster and he does all kinds of horrible things and gets away with it. You have to know what he's like, because if I stay here, and I think he's already found me, he'll come after anyone who helps me."

"I believe you're correct on that," Lanz said, sitting back in his chair.

At once she felt the difference in Stefano and his brothers. The tension in the room eased and several of them lifted their glasses to their mouths, where before they had just held them without moving. They *wanted* Lanz and Deangelo to believe her. That meant the two cousins had the same gift of hearing truth when others spoke. They believed her. She hoped they would continue to believe her because no one else had.

"An older man was arrested for the crime. He walked into the police department and turned himself in. He had the knife and his fingerprints were all over it. He said he'd been drinking and followed her home. He had brain cancer and sometimes he would fly into a rage. He was remorseful. Crying. He pleaded guilty and died before he ever served time. I believe he did it in order to get money for his family before he died. He couldn't even look me in the eye."

"His name," Deangelo said abruptly.

"Harold Benson. His daughter, Carla O'Brian, was with him. She works for Barry Anthon and has, apparently, for several years."

Deangelo nodded. "That's easy enough. It does seem like everything leads back to him. But there's more, isn't there?"

Francesca nodded, tightening her fingers around Stefano's. "Barry came by about a dozen times. He'd just show up in my house. It didn't seem to matter what locks I used—he'd be in there with a couple of his men. They pushed me around a lot and threatened to . . ." She swallowed and lowered her voice, unable to look at any of them, the humiliation and fear crowding too close. "Rape me," she finished. "They would shove me down and rip my clothes, always demanding I give them what Barry wanted. They never said what it was, but I knew they hadn't found her cell phone."

The tension in the room was back and with it, oppressive, scary heat. The room vibrated with rage. Not just Stefano's but all of his brothers' collectively. That was a lot of anger to fill even that large space. Only their two cousins seemed unaffected.

"But you didn't have it," Ricco prompted.

"I had no idea where it was. I couldn't have given it to them if I wanted to, which I didn't. I knew they'd kill me if I handed it over to them.

"I moved and they tore up my place one night. Acted like a party had been held there. It looked like it. Holes in the wall, burns in the carpets, mirrors broken. I was at the library, but my landlord didn't believe me. The more I went to the cops, the more insane I appeared to them. Two apartments later, the judge gave me jail time for vandalism and hefty fines. Along with that, I had to pay the damages for both apartments Barry and his men had destroyed. What little money I had was gone. Then my job. At that point, another arrest and a judge ordered me put in lockup for seventy-two hours in a hospital."

"That fucking bastard," Taviano burst out. "Was he there? In the courtroom?"

She nodded, the terrible knots in her belly unraveling at the reaction of the brothers and Stefano. They believed her. When no one else would, they believed her. Not her neighbors, not her boss, fellow students, teachers, all the people she'd known for most of her life. Not one had believed her. Until Joanna. Until the Ferraros.

Tears burned and she had to look away from the rage on their faces none of them bothered to hide. Rage on her behalf. For her. She didn't deserve it, not after thinking they were an organized-crime family. They were standing up for her. All of them. She turned toward Stefano and buried her face against his jacket. Immediately his arms enclosed her, hiding her tear-wet face from the others.

"Are we about done here?" he growled. His voice actually rumbled, a deep, disturbing and definite warning. It was an order more than a question.

"She hasn't told us what happened to the cell phone," Lanz pointed out, not in the least intimidated by Stefano, although Francesca thought he should have been.

She was intimidated. Stefano could sound very scary when he chose to. The moment the words were out of Lanz's mouth, the hostility in the room rose by volumes. Again, the Ferraro brothers' reaction was what enabled her to answer without falling apart.

"She must have packaged it up and mailed her phone to our post office box on her way home. I didn't check the box for a long time after because of everything that was going on. Most of our mail came to our house. We didn't use that box for anything but packages and that was because our parents had done it that way. We kept the box for sentimental reasons."

Deangelo nodded. "Some of the older generations still keep that tradition. I think it had something to do with bombs being sent when they were feuding."

Francesca sucked in her breath. Cella and she had joked about that, teasing their parents that they were in trouble with the Sicilian mobsters. Both sets of her grandparents had resided in Sicily, as had every generation preceding them. It was her father and mother who had immigrated to the United States.

"I found the phone and knew I couldn't keep it anywhere near me. By that time I was living on the street, but Barry's men were always watching me. So I sent the phone to the only person I knew I could trust. I put it inside our mother's jewelry box and wrapped that, put it in a box and sent it out of town. I knew if Barry killed me, at least there would be some evidence that I was telling the truth."

"Why didn't you take the phone to the police?" Lanz asked, his voice very, very gentle.

She swallowed the terrible lump that had been forming in

her throat, one she'd barely recognized was there. But Lanz and probably everyone else in the room had heard the way it strangled her voice. "They believed I was insane, or they were on his payroll. It didn't matter which it was. I knew they would find a way to throw out the evidence and he would get away with his crimes like always."

"We could take it to the police," Deangelo suggested.

She shook her head. "No. Now, it's the only reason I'm still alive. The moment that phone surfaces, he's going to have his men kill me. He can get away with murder. I doubt if a little thing like a police station would keep him from destroying any evidence against him."

"So you'd prefer him to walk?" Lanz persisted.

"No. I'd prefer him in hell," she answered adamantly, "but men with the kind of money and power Barry Anthon has are untouchable. I've tried to tell Stefano that he's dangerous and everyone around me will be in danger, but he isn't listening." She looked around the room. "All of you could get hurt. It really is best if I just leave . . ."

Stefano tipped up her face and slammed his mouth down over hers, effectively cutting off what she would have said to him. The moment he took possession and his tongue demanded entrance she was lost, the way she seemed to be always when he touched her. She *felt* him. His urgency. His hunger rising stark and brutal. Edging the kiss with danger. It was hot. Wet. Deliberately dominant.

She loved his kisses and gave herself up to him, pouring herself back into him, into his mouth, her arms creeping up to shyly circle his neck. She forgot about their audience. She even forgot who and what they were asking about because the world around her dropped away until there was only Stefano. His arms. His body. His awesome, perfect mouth. The taste of him she knew she'd never get enough of.

When he kissed her, her body heated, blood rushed hot, need pounded in her sex and thundered in her ears. There was no one like him and there never would be. Again, it was Stefano who slowly, reluctantly, broke the kiss. She was grateful he was reluctant, but she clung to him, wanting more. She stared up at him for a long time, lost in the vibrant blue of his eyes.

"You aren't going anywhere, Francesca," he stated, his voice low, but absolutely firm. "Not ever. You're going to stay with me. Do you understand?"

She was mesmerized, completely under his spell in that moment, and it was impossible to do anything but nod. She didn't understand at all. Not why or how Stefano would want her, but he did. There was no question about that now.

When she managed to look around her, Stefano's brothers were grinning at her, not in the least giving them privacy or pretending to look the other way. Even the cousins were smirking, the tension gone, replaced by their smiles.

Ricco's eyebrow shot up. "I'd say, little sister, you're staying right here with us, where you belong."

CHAPTER TWELVE

Francesca stared at herself in the mirror, feeling a little as if she was a princess in a fairy tale. She smoothed her hand down her dress—the dress Stefano had bought her for tonight. He was casual about it, coming to her room, knocking once and opening the door. He walked straight to her, a large box in his hand, bent his head and brushed a kiss across her mouth.

His touch was all too fleeting. Barely there. But it was a brand and it burned right through her. He pushed the box into her hands. "Gotta go, *bambina*, things to do, but Emmanuelle and my cousins will be here to escort you to the club. You stick close to them until I get there. Understand?" The pad of his finger traced her lips. "I don't want you dancing with other men. Stay with Emme."

Stefano never got close to her without touching her. His arm snaked around her waist to pull her tightly to his side. His lips brushed her temple or her mouth. He liked being close, but he hadn't made a move on her, not a real one. She found herself at night, lying in her bed, staring at the ceiling, heart pounding, waiting. Just waiting.

She'd seen him leave tonight. As always he wore an impeccable suit. This one was charcoal gray with ultrathin lighter stripes. It was one of his inevitable three-piece suits and he looked amazing in it. He was so sweet to her. Making certain she ate meals. Insisting she text him from the deli several times throughout the day. Always, if she stepped outside, one of his cousins was close.

Stefano made her feel as if she mattered. As if she was his entire focus, even when he was at work, or wherever it was he went. Her eyes went back to the mirror and she raised her hand to her throat. She never asked him what he did. She thought about it and prepared herself to ask him, but he always distracted her before she did. He was just so intimidating and darkly sensual, filling the room with his presence until she could barely think straight.

She inspected herself very carefully. The dress was beautiful—the most beautiful thing she'd ever seen, let alone worn. It was also the sexiest, most flattering dress she'd ever put on. The material clung to her like a second skin, leaving little to the imagination, and yet revealing only hints of actual skin. The dress followed every curve to her small waist before dropping away over her hips. It was short, but elegant. Sexy, but not cheap.

She stared at herself, unable to believe that it was actually Francesca Capello looking back at her in the mirror. She didn't look like that. Hot. Beautiful even, with her hair left loose to tumble around her face and down her back. She couldn't wear a bra with the dress, but it had a lining that gave some support because the material hugged her so tightly. In the box along with the dress was a tiny black lace thong. There was a bow on the back of the waistband, if you could call it a band; mostly it was tiny black strips of material. The thong rode low on her hips, barely there, so no lines showed beneath the clinging material of her dress.

She'd put on her makeup with an edge toward drama, but still barely there. She liked the color of her lipstick, a nice deep red that showed off her full lips and good skin tone. Her shoes were perfect black heels with complicated straps that edged up her ankles and looked superhot. The shoes had to have cost as much or more than the dress. She loved the entire look.

The elevator *pinged*, warning her, and she caught up her

clutch and hurried out to greet Joanna and Mario Bandoni, Joanna's date, as they stepped into the foyer. Joanna looked awesome in her hot red dress. Both she and Mario were staring around the huge room, taking in everything so she had a chance to walk right up to them. Francesca couldn't blame them. When Stefano was there in his apartment with her, she felt at home and safe, but the moment he was gone, she felt like a fraud, an intruder. She didn't belong in his extremely wealthy world. She was very uncomfortable there.

Joanna's eyes widened in shock when she caught sight of Francesca. Her mouth dropped open and she stared openly. Mario made a low sound of approval.

"You look . . . so good, Francesca," Joanna said. "Beautiful. Really beautiful. I'm not certain you should go out in that dress. Has Stefano seen you?"

Francesca laughed. Joanna and Mario had boosted her confidence level immensely just by their reactions. "Not yet, but Emmanuelle and the others should be here in a few minutes. Stefano and his brothers are already at the club. They had a meeting or something. His family is crazy large. Cousins have arrived from New York and they're showing them around. I've never seen so many cousins as Stefano has."

"Most of them are male," Mario pointed out. "He's got Rosina and Rigina, Romano and Renato's sisters. They're pretty nice, although I've never said more than hello to them."

"I nod," Joanna said. "Females can be really bitchy and I never wanted to be put in my place so I was careful around them."

"They put people in their place?" Francesca asked. She knew she *looked* good, but it was the dress. She didn't run in Stefano's circles. If his cousins decided to be mean to her, she'd much rather stay home. She really wanted to go out wearing the dress and shoes, but not if it meant feeling awful about herself when some woman made her feel like she didn't belong.

"No, they've never done that," Joanna hastened to say. "Get that look off your face, honey. You're with Stefano. No one would dare to be mean to you." She looked around the large room with its high ceilings and open floor plan. "Show us around. I've always wanted to see where Stefano lived. This is . . . *amazing.*"

Francesca's stomach knotted. This was Stefano's home. His private sanctuary. Instinctively she knew he wouldn't want anyone peeking into his private world. Joanna looked eager, nearly rubbing her hands together with glee. Mario was happy to go along with her, but Francesca just couldn't do it. Showing them Stefano's home felt too much like a betrayal.

She shook her head. "I can't do that. This isn't my home, Joanna." She kept her voice very firm.

Joanna pouted. "Seriously, Francesca? Come on," she wheedled. "I won't say anything. It's not like he'd know. I really want to see where he sleeps. At least show me his bedroom. I can imagine it's all sexy. Big bed. Satin sheets. Very hot."

Mario laughed. "You're giving me ideas, Joanna."

"Keep getting them, Mario," Joanna flirted.

Francesca wrapped her arms around her middle and held tight. There was no way she was going to show Joanna anything at all. She hated the idea of anyone fantasizing about Stefano's bed and sheets, let alone about him.

Stefano had shown her around the enormous suite—and it was enormous. He had his own workout room complete with every machine imaginable. There was another room that he used for training in several types of martial arts and boxing as well as street fighting. His brothers and sister and sometimes his cousins trained with him there. She'd peeked into the large rectangular room and had been in awe of the equipment there as well as the mats and floor. There were racks of swords and knives and other weapons, some wooden, some not, on the far wall.

Stefano's hand had been on the nape of her neck, or fingers threaded through hers, arm sometimes around her waist, as he'd taken her through his home. The tour had felt intimate, Stefano showing her his private world. She wasn't about to share that, not even with her best friend. She felt the need to guard him, to protect him. This was where he came to relax and no one was going to invade his privacy, not even her friend.

Francesca had seen him every night throughout the week and knew his life was difficult whether he was aware of it or not. The phone rang constantly with demands for his time. His cell went off as much or more than the house phone. No one left him in peace. More than once she'd been tempted to give his neck a massage while he impatiently—and dropping F-bombs liberally—listened to pleas for his help, most of which he answered positively.

"You can just forget all about seeing his bedroom, Joanna." She glanced up at the clock, hoping it was time to go, knowing she had to change the subject. Joanna often was like a wrecking ball when she wanted something. "You look good in that dress. Red is definitely your color. And, Mario, that suit is amazing."

Mario's hand went to his tie a little self-consciously. "I can't be the only one not looking sharp tonight. Look at my girl." He sounded proud, his eyes on Joanna.

Joanna forgot all about pouting and beamed as she slipped her hand onto his arm. "You look very handsome. Thanks for coming with me tonight. I think it will be fun."

The elevator *pinged* and the doors opened. Emmanuelle emerged and Francesca's breath caught in her throat. Emmanuelle was the most beautiful woman Francesca had ever laid eyes on. Although short, no supermodel could hold a candle to her. She was everything an Italian beauty was reputed to be and more.

She wore a short black dress that clung to every curve. The front was a camisole that dropped into a little flirty skirt. The laces going up the front were tight over her rib cage and up under her breasts, but there was a generous opening showing plenty of cleavage. She looked hot. Gorgeous. Trendy. Sophisticated. Instantly Francesca felt as if she needed to check her own clothes again.

"Francesca. You look . . . beautiful." Emmanuelle sounded sincere and her smile was warm, enveloping all of them. "Joanna, Mario, how nice to see you both again."

She walked with complete confidence in her four-inch heels, coming straight toward Francesca without slowing down. She hugged Francesca tightly and then kissed her on both cheeks.

"Forgive me for not being with you when my cousins came to talk to you. I would have been with my brothers to protect you, if only so you'd have another woman present, but I had to keep the parents occupied." She squeezed Francesca's arm. "I know it was difficult for you—the boys told me. I want you to know how much I respect and admire you. Thank you for worrying about my brother and for making him so happy."

Whoa. That was the last thing Francesca expected from Stefano's sister. She made it sound as if Francesca really did belong to Stefano. That it was a done deal and somehow she was totally accepted into their family. Things moved very fast around the Ferraro siblings. Francesca felt uneasy, a fraud even. She wasn't as certain as they were that her relationship with Stefano had progressed to the point of his entire family claiming her.

She wanted a family. She loved that the Ferraros were so tight-knit, but she barely knew them. She didn't even really know what Stefano did for a living. There was just a little bit of fear when she was around them all. Power clung to them. They wore their wealth so easily, like a second skin. More than that, they wore a cloak of pure danger. When any of the Ferraros walked into a room, there was a stunned silence—a collective gasp from any other occupants of the room.

"Are you ready for a night out?" Emmanuelle turned to include Joanna and Mario in her query.

Joanna was staring at Francesca, wide-eyed, a grin on her face. She turned toward Emmanuelle immediately. "I've been looking forward to this all week."

"Rigina and Rosina are downstairs in the limo." Emmanuelle laughed, her voice low and melodious. "I figured we'd better have a driver if we're all going to party tonight." She slipped her arm through Francesca's companionably. "Has Stefano seen that dress?"

Francesca smoothed one hand down the dress, wondering why both Joanna and Emmanuelle had asked that. She nodded, color stealing into her face at having to make the confession. "He brought the dress to me."

Emmanuelle's smile widened. "But he hasn't actually *seen* you in the dress, has he?" Her eyes met Joanna's and they both burst out laughing.

Francesca wasn't certain what the joke was. "Is something wrong with the way I look?" She couldn't keep the anxiety out of her voice. She wanted to look good for Stefano or she wouldn't have accepted the dress from him. It cost more than her weekly wages and it had been a little disconcerting to have him go out and buy her the club dress. She didn't know why that seemed worse than pretending to believe he or his brother was responsible for losing her clothes and replacing them with much more expensive ones.

"No, Francesca," Emmanuelle assured. "Nothing at all is wrong with the way you look. You're absolutely beautiful and my brother is going to think so, too. It's just that he can be . . . possessive of what is his."

Francesca felt a jab to her stomach, hard enough that she hunched a little. The thought of Stefano being possessive toward other women really bothered her. She knew he had a history with women—beautiful women—but he'd told her that she was special to him. She really wished her self-esteem hadn't taken such a beating and she didn't constantly feel inadequate, worrying about Stefano and the beautiful women who had been in his life prior to her.

A limo awaited them, right in front of the hotel, the long sleek lines making Joanna squeal in glee. Francesca felt it was a little on the ostentatious side. She would never get used to the casual display of wealth and privilege. She slid into the vehicle after Joanna and Mario and discovered that two other women already occupied the leather seats. They were drinking red wine from elegant glasses. Both smiled at her, their gazes running over her dress and shoes automatically, as if they did a sweep of everyone they saw.

"Rigina and Rosina Greco, my cousins," Emmanuelle introduced. "They are sisters of Renato and Romano. I think you've met their brothers."

If she had, Francesca knew she wouldn't be able to place them. She'd been introduced to too many people and some when she was being carried upside down in a sleeping bag through a murky apartment building. She smiled and nodded. The women looked like Ferraros. They carried themselves with that same enviable confidence.

"Wow, Francesca," Rigina said. "I love your dress. It's beautiful. It's a Sophia original, isn't it?"

Francesca had heard of the designer Sophia. She was renowned for her gowns and club wear. Her originals were fought over by her exclusive clientele. Francesca ran her hand down her dress, smoothing imaginary wrinkles, all the while her heart pounding. If this was really a Sophia original, it was worth three months or more of her salary. She should *never* have accepted it.

"It's gorgeous," Rosina added. "You look beautiful. I can't wait to get inside the club and have Stefano catch his first sight of you in that dress. He's going to go ballistic."

Francesca frowned. "Why do you all keep saying that? Stefano wanted me to wear this dress. The last thing I want to do is embarrass him because it doesn't look good on me. You have to tell me." Her worried gaze found Joanna, her one real friend. If the others were making subtle fun of her, she was certain Joanna wouldn't do that. She'd never allow her to go out in public and be humiliated.

Emmanuelle reached over and took her hand, squeezing it in reassurance. Joanna frowned and shook her head. Rosina looked upset.

"Francesca, you look absolutely beautiful in that dress," Joanna said staunchly. "Gorgeous. Right, Mario?"

Francesca thought Joanna incredibly generous to have

her boyfriend, the man she was really interested in, give Francesca compliments.

"I have to agree," Mario said. "Beautiful."

Emmanuelle nodded. "My brother has escorted countless women to clubs and he couldn't care less what they looked like. Elegant or slut clothes didn't much matter to him because if he was with a woman, it was for publicity purposes, like a charity event, or a hookup. He claims you for his own. For his woman. He's made it clear to the family and to those in our neighborhood. He'll make it clear to the world very soon. That's why we're all laughing a little. Stefano is not like most men. None of my brothers are. You're his and he'll watch over you and protect you every minute of every day. With you dressed like that, hotter than hell, he's going to lose his mind, and we're all going to enjoy watching it."

Francesca liked some of what she'd said, was confused by other things and really didn't like the reference to Stefano's other women. She was going to have to gain some confidence in herself fast if she was really going to try to have any kind of a relationship with Stefano Ferraro. He was in a world where confidence mattered. Was needed. She'd been beaten down so far by Barry Anthon, she could barely walk with her head up. Stefano deserved better than that.

Francesca wished she'd met Stefano before Cella had been murdered. She had been different then, carefree and happy. Confident in herself. He would have liked Cella. Francesca hoped he would have liked her, because that was the real Francesca, not this woman who had such low self-esteem, nightmares and was afraid of her own shadow.

She let the talk flow around her. Joanna and Mario accepted drinks happily, and she sipped on champagne. She loved to dance. Loved it. Dancing was one of her all-time favorite things to do. Her parents had put her in dance classes when she was very young; ballroom, Latin, swing she'd learned it all. Not to mention the pole dancing she'd done as exercise in college. Cella had insisted that was the one splurge they would have after their parents' deaths.

Francesca loved her sister for that sacrifice. It wasn't like she was ever going to be a professional dancer, but still, Cella deemed those lessons important and she worked extra hours to pay for them. As soon as Francesca was old enough, she worked, cleaning houses, working at the deli, anything at all in order to help Cella with the bills.

The limo pulled up to the front of the club. Francesca was a little shocked when she saw the line of people trying to get in. It seemed to go on forever. She knew she would never have had the patience to wait in a line that long, especially if, like Joanna had said, there was a possibility that she'd be turned away once she reached the front.

"This is crazy, Jo," she murmured.

Joanna squeezed her arm tightly as they all got out of the limo. "I can't believe this. I feel like a princess arriving at the ball. Everyone's staring, trying to catch a glimpse of us. They think we're celebrities, Francesca."

Emmanuelle suddenly moved, flowing across the short distance separating her from Francesca. She was elegant even in her body's movement, like a ballet dancer. As she got to Francesca, she took her arm, turning her around toward the club. Emmanuelle's body provided a shield as a dozen flashes went off.

"Keep walking. Stay between us all, in the middle," Emmanuelle ordered, her voice low.

Emmanuelle's hand was steady on Francesca's back, pushing her gently toward the entrance. As they moved past the front of the line to the entrance, the bouncers unhooked the velvet ropes to allow them in. Francesca noticed that Emilio and Enzo fell in behind them. She had no idea where they came from, but suddenly they were walking with the small group of women, as if they'd always been with them.

The moment the doors to the club opened, Francesca could hear the pounding beat of the music. It was loud, impossible not to want to dance to and very trendy. The DJ was extremely popular, one who commanded all sorts of money, and yet stayed there in Chicago rather than moving to New York, where he would be given star status. There were several bars, each glowing a different color. Muted blues, reds, purples and greens pulsed to the music from the lights secreted in the bars. The bartenders were moving fast, bottles spinning in the air as they quickly made drinks for the customers pressing around the curved bars.

Francesca could feel the beat of the music already heating up her blood. They moved through the lower section in a tight group, Emilio and Enzo ensuring the crowd parted for them as they wound their way through the floor. Up a few stairs was the VIP section, where tables and booths guaranteed privacy. Even farther up were the very secluded tables and booths. Those were reserved for family and friends.

Emmanuelle led the way with absolute confidence. She clearly was the queen of the club. Deference was paid to her everywhere one looked. Nods. Smiles. Waves. She kept moving even when a few scantily clad women called out her name and stepped toward her. She was gracious, always replying, but she made it clear she was heading toward her own table.

A waitress followed them, ready to take their drink orders. There would be no queuing up to the bar for them. Francesca surveyed the room below her. It was exciting, the music already finding her pulse and beating there, calling her. Joanna was already swaying to the persistent call of the drum.

Emmanuelle sank into one of the plush seats, indicating the chair beside her to Francesca. "I have to join my brothers for a meeting in a few minutes, but I've got time for a drink. We've got cousins from New York here. Four of them. I noticed them on the dance floor when we walked in. They've already got women hanging on them. See that blonde down there?" She indicated a woman in a very short leather dress with cutouts on either side. The openings ran from her hips to under her arms. Her platinum hair was short and spiked.

"I see her." Francesca frowned. The woman looked very familiar. "Where have I seen her before?"

"She's a starlet. Plays in a drama on television and thinks

every man in all the states wants to sleep with her. She's totally after my cousin."

"We call her the barracuda," Rosina supplied.

Joanna giggled as she craned her neck, trying to peer into the dark crowd of moving bodies. "She's got on five-inch heels. Wow. I don't know if I could actually dance in five-inch heels."

Francesca suddenly recognized her. Not from the television, but from a magazine Joanna had given her. "She was on page seventy-three. Hanging on Stefano's arm." She whispered it before she realized just what that admission gave away. Color moved up into her face.

The waitress was back, putting their drinks in front of them, confirming that the Ferraros didn't have to wait for anything, not even their drinks. Francesca reached for hers and took a long drink as the woman hurried away. The Moscow Mule went down smoothly. She needed the alcohol to fortify her.

Emmanuelle leaned forward and put her hand over Francesca's, stilling the fingers that had been drumming on the table. Francesca hadn't even been aware she was so restless. Nervous. Jealous. *Sheesh*. How embarrassing in front of his sister and cousins.

"Stefano may have sowed his wild oats, but he's done with that. I can guarantee that when my brother chooses a woman, he will be faithful to her. It's for life."

Francesca bit her lip to keep from laughing. There was nothing humorous about Emmanuelle's statement, and yet it was laughable. "You can't know that."

"We live by a code. It's a strict one, but we cling to honor. It's just who and what we are. That can't change."

Francesca refused to look at her. Instead, she looked around the enormous room, where many, many women danced suggestively with partners. "So how many women right here in this club do you suppose Stefano has been with?" Her chin went up and she finally forced her head to turn toward Emmanuelle, her gaze meeting Stefano's sister's vivid blue eyes. "Would you say about half? Or am I being conservative?"

Why had she come? She knew better. She didn't belong in this world of casual hookups. It wasn't her. She didn't understand it and she'd never be comfortable in it. She never would. It wasn't as if she was a prude. Whenever Stefano touched her or kissed her, her body went up in flames. She would fall, just like all the women before her, but she wouldn't chase him. Once he dumped her, she would disappear from his life. She had pride. She couldn't very well judge the other women, not when she was going to be just as bad.

Still, she was being a total bitch. It wasn't Emmanuelle's fault that Stefano was a hound dog. A gorgeous one, but still a hound dog. She shook her head. "I just feel out of place here, and I think I'm taking it out on Stefano."

"He can't change his past, Francesca," Emmanuelle stated quietly. "As much as he'd like to, he can't change a thing. He never expected to have you." Her eyes searched Francesca's face. "He does have you, doesn't he?"

For the first time Emmanuelle sounded vulnerable. Francesca's heart jerked in her chest. She couldn't look away from Emmanuelle's blue eyes. She had that same ability as Stefano—the one that could capture and hold. It occurred to Francesca that Stefano's sister was every bit as lethal as the male Ferraros.

"I don't even know what he does for a living. I don't know him at all. This is all moving so fast I honestly can't catch my breath." She tried a tentative smile. "Your brother tends to steamroll right over a girl. He's so wonderful. Beautiful. Everything that I'm not."

Emmanuelle scowled at her. "Why in the world would you say that, Francesca? You obviously don't see yourself the way the rest of the world does." She looked up suddenly, her face instantly going expressionless in the way Stefano's often did. She flashed a small, brief smile toward the trio of women who had mounted the stairs and invaded their private space.

"Doreen. Stella. Janice." She gave a little nod, princess to peasant. "I had no idea the three of you were in town."

Francesca twisted her fingers together in her lap. Rigina and Rosina both had gone silent. Joanna looked as if she might faint, and even Mario was staring with his mouth open. The three women were in a famous band. Hugely famous. They weren't the kind of women one would just see walking up to them in a nightclub. Joanna clearly was pinching herself, grinning from ear to ear and practically bouncing on her seat.

Francesca recognized each of the women, all of whom Stefano had dated briefly. There had been several articles on the scandal. *Will the band break up? Keeping it all in the family.* There were many, many more. Stefano had quite publicly dated each of the women amid a flurry of torrid headlines.

"Emmanuelle." Doreen nodded, her haughty look not quite as well done as Emmanuelle's. "Stefano's supposed to be here tonight, but we haven't seen him." The three women exchanged a long look and then laughed together. "We thought we'd show him a real good time," she added, almost purring.

Francesca winced. This was what she'd be putting up with every time she went anywhere in Stefano's circle. His women appeared to be legion and all of them were famous.

"Why fight over him and all three of us lose?" Janice added. "When we can share and all of us have him?"

"He's man enough to go around." Stella ran one finger down her clingy short dress. "We texted him last night that we'd be in town."

Francesca felt the burn of tears. She'd been with Stefano and his phone had gone off so many times. Not once had she paid attention. Not once had she suspected women had been texting or calling him.

Doreen's laughter was a mere tinkle that irritated Francesca. "We sent him a few pictures of what he could look forward to." Again the three women exchanged a long sultry look and then burst into laughter.

That meant Stefano had their pictures on his phone. Francesca could well imagine what those pictures were like. The room was suddenly far too hot. Her lungs felt raw, burning, unable to drag in enough air. Her stomach churned and she pressed her hands tight to it, afraid she might throw up right there in front of all three of them.

The smile had died on Joanna's face. She looked as if she'd been struck. She had fantasies about the Ferraro brothers and it didn't include finding out they weren't husband material.

Emmanuelle sighed. "When are the three of you going to get some pride? Stefano made it very clear that he was done with you last year. He doesn't date. He doesn't have relationships. That was made clear to you. Quit stalking him. That's what it's called when you won't leave him alone."

"How do you know we haven't seen him in a year?" Stella sneered. "He wouldn't want to tell his little sister what he's been getting all this time."

Francesca wanted to cover her ears. Could the evening get any worse? She didn't think so. She needed to get out of there. Now. She looked around, trying to find a way to escape. Why had she believed she had a chance with Stefano? Could she have been any more ridiculous? She'd wanted to cling to him because he made her feel safe. Beautiful. Sexy. Wanted. Lord, but he could make her feel wanted.

"That's so disgusting. He doesn't want you, any of you, and certainly not the three of you together." Emmanuelle poured contempt into her voice. She took a sip of her drink, looking more elegant than ever.

Suddenly the three women didn't look nearly as beautiful and sophisticated as Francesca had first thought. They looked . . . skanky.

"You have no idea of his *needs* in the bedroom," Doreen spat out, pure venom in her eyes. "You think you're so high and mighty, Emmanuelle—you always have. We know what Stefano likes and we give it to him."

Joanna's gasp was audible. Doreen swung on her. "That's right, Miss Mouse. Stefano is an *adult*, all male. Pure male.

You could never hope to understand a man like that. None of you could." She turned, whipping her hair around, and stormed down the steps, her two bandmates following.

Emmanuelle let out her breath in a little hiss of anger. "Well, that was unpleasant." She leaned toward Francesca again. "You can't believe the things they're saying about my brother. They just aren't true."

"Of course they're true," Francesca said. "I saw his picture with each of them. He was with them. He had sex with them. There's no taking that back, and last night when I was with Stefano, his phone kept going off. He would look at it, sometimes text and other times he'd shove it in his pocket. I thought he was getting requests for his help like he always does, but instead he was getting naked sex pictures." She was ashamed of the little sob in her voice. "I have to get out of here."

Emmanuelle put her hand on Francesca's arm, staying her mad dash for freedom. "Don't. At least talk to Stefano before you run. He deserves that much, doesn't he?"

Francesca took a deep breath, her every instinct telling her to run while she could. Once Stefano was close to her, every brain cell she had seemed to short-circuit. She shook her head and picked up her drink again.

"I've got to attend a quick meeting," Emmanuelle said with a little scowl. "I'll send Stefano to you as fast as I can. I tell them meetings need to be conducted *outside* the club," she added, trying to interject humor into the situation. "Inside is for fun. Drink and dance. You know, those *fun* things. I don't think my brothers understand the concept." Emmanuelle shook her head and drifted away.

Rigina threw her head back and laughed. "They think the only form of fun is a hot, willing babe."

Francesca couldn't stop her reaction to Rigina's casual—but obviously true—remark. She stiffened, her fingers curling around the glass she held.

"Francesca." Rosina's voice was gentle, with an undercurrent of anxiety. "My sister didn't mean anything by that. I hope you weren't offended."

Francesca threw her a casual smile that she knew didn't reach her eyes. She took a longer drink. The combination of the ingredients always warmed her stomach and made her blood sing. She let the feeling sweep through her, wanting to get away from Stefano's cousins and the implication in Rigina's statement. They could try to take away the sting all they wanted, but she'd read the tabloids. She'd seen all the pictures of his women. So many of them. Tall. Beautiful. The thought of Stefano with them made her feel sick. Now she'd met them, and that made her even sicker, thinking of the things the three women were implying.

She wasn't experienced or sophisticated. She didn't belong in his crowd. Or with his family. She turned to Joanna with a bright, false smile. "You ready to dance? The music's calling."

Joanna had barely touched her drink and looked up, clearly to protest, but she took one look at Francesca's face and immediately stood up. "Can't wait." She flashed her brilliant smile at Mario. "You coming or you want to drink a little first?"

"I came to dance, woman. I'm with you all the way," Mario said, endearing him to Francesca. He was *so* the right man for Joanna.

"Francesca . . ." Rigina protested.

Francesca drank the rest of the Moscow Mule, and this time her smile bordered on desperate, but she couldn't help it. "No worries, I'm great. I love to dance and the music is calling. If the waitress comes back will you order me another drink please?" Still smiling brightly she led the way down the steps to the crowded dance floor.

She didn't want to think about anything at all. She found the rhythm of the music and let it transport her like it always had, to another place. The alcohol pounded through her veins, heating her from the inside out. There was only her body and the music. Nothing else. No one else. No Stefano with his gorgeous body and smoldering sensuality that made her so incredibly hungry for him she couldn't think straight when she was around him.

Two songs later, she became of aware of a man joining them. He seemed to know both Joanna and Mario, slapping him on the back and greeting Joanna with a kiss. He looked toward Francesca expectantly.

"My friend Dominic," Mario said loudly, trying to be heard above the music. "Dominic, our friend Francesca."

Dominic grinned at her, his body moving in close, matching the rhythm of hers with ease. She recognized a trained dancer when she saw one, probably in Latin and ballroom as she'd been. He leaned toward her, one hand sliding onto her hip. Just barely there, but connecting them. "You know how to dance."

She was pleased that someone actually recognized that she could. She nodded, barely able to hear him over the pounding music. He immediately reached for her hand and took her through a series of salsa steps. The music was fast but the beat was perfect for a salsa. She matched him no problem and he instantly took her close to his body, moving her into more intricate and very sexy steps. She lost herself like she always did, the music flowing through her, her body giving itself up to the beat.

Dominic's lead was confident and strong, just the kind she preferred in a partner, and she moved with him, even when the music slowed and he drew her close into a tight frame. He was a couple of inches taller than she was and he bent his head close to speak directly in her ear.

"You're very good. I haven't had a dance partner like you ever. Where in the world did Mario and Joanna find you?"

She tried not to stiffen. She didn't like personal questions. "Joanna and I went to school together."

His hand slid down her waist to the curve of her hip. She felt that slide and it sent alarm bells ringing as he tightened his hold on her.

"My lucky night," he observed, his hand sliding lower until it rested right on the cheek of her butt.

She dropped her own hand and moved his. "You don't know me that well."

He laughed softly. "Not yet, but I intend to."

Emilio loomed over his shoulder, looking grim. Huge. Unhappy. He tapped Dominic on the shoulder and jerked his thumb off to the side. Dominic instantly looked angry, but he stepped away from Emilio.

Francesca turned into Emilio's arms, smiling up at him, relieved in spite of the fact that she knew why he was there. He moved his foot and stepped right onto hers. She bit back a sharp little cry of pain and made a face at him until he realized what he'd done and lifted his big foot away. He didn't dance, just swayed. It was a far cry from the man who had so perfectly matched steps with her.

"Is there a reason you interrupted my perfectly wonderful dance with that gentleman, or did you just want to step all over my feet?" She had to look up at him and raise her voice over the music. The rhythm was slower, and a little mellower, but it was still loud.

Emilio leaned down, very close, putting his mouth against her ear. He actually hissed his disapproval. "For fuck's sake, Francesca, are you trying to get someone killed? What are thinking, dancing with another man?"

Francesca matched his scowl. "What other man? I danced with one man and he was a superb dancer. You cut in and stepped on my toes. I don't want to hurt your feelings or anything, but I prefer his dancing style to yours."

Without warning, a hard hand shackled her wrist and Stefano yanked her away from Emilio and into his arms. "What did I tell you about other men touching you?" he snapped.

She glared at him, struggling to put an inch or two between their bodies, but it was impossible. The more she fought to get free, the tighter he held her.

"Stop fighting me or we're going to have a very public scene. There are paparazzi in here and I can guarantee we're already on their radar."

His anger was palatable. Intense. Surrounding her with heat and fire. Still, as upset with him as she was, her body reacted, flooding her with need. She kept her face down, refusing to look at him even when she subsided, forcing herself to relax into the warmth of his body.

"Now tell me what the fuck you thought you were doing."

Even with her giving him what he wanted and letting him hold her close, his anger hadn't lessened in the least. That spiked her own temper. "I wasn't arranging to have sex with three men, if that's what you thought. Your little harem is here, waiting for you."

"Damn it, Francesca, we talked about this. I can't change who I fucked. I told you that was in the past and you have to accept that, because as much as I would like to have been different, I'm not a magician. There isn't any taking it back."

"Is that what you like? What they said? All three of them at once?" She hissed the query through clenched teeth, her heart pounding out of control.

CHAPTER THIRTEEN

There was a long silence while the music hammered at them. Created a cocoon of pure heat. His anger swamped her, but it only served to make her hotter. Her body felt liquid, breasts aching for his touch, nipples hard, pushing against the material of the dress in an effort to get closer to him. The junction between her legs was on fire, her clit pulsing with the beat of the music and absolute hunger. She knew her thong was already damp with hunger for him. She hated that she couldn't control her needs with him. He was angry, and that just added fuel to the growing fire in her.

"Is that what you think of me? That I would need three women at once to satisfy me? Is that really what you think of me, Francesca?" His voice was low. Furious. A whip that struck at her with more force than a leather one would have.

She inhaled sharply and drew him deep into her lungs, her face remaining pressed tightly to his jacket, right over his heart.

His hand came up under her chin and pried her loose. "Fucking look at me, *dolce cuore*. Now. I'm not fucking around with you."

Two F-bombs in under a second. He was more than furious. She had no choice but to lift her chin, but she kept her eyes childishly shut tight, afraid if she looked at him, she'd be lost. She was more hurt than she'd realized, hating that the other women had had him before her.

"Look at me." With an effort he softened his voice, but

it was still every bit as commanding. Impossible to disobey. "Open your eyes and look at me."

She bit down hard on her lower lip and lifted her lashes until her gaze met his piercing blue one. His eyes had darkened into a vibrant, intense color that screamed danger. Once she locked gazes with him, she couldn't look away. Her heart pounded harder than ever. Her stomach did a slow somersault. Deep inside her core, her muscles spasmed and then clenched hard in reaction.

"Do you really think I play with three women at the same time, Francesca?"

There was a promise of retaliation in his voice. Instead of scaring her, as it should have, she felt shaky with need—with hunger that seemed to be growing out of control. Of course he was going to force her to answer. Slow color stained her cheeks.

"No." Her voice was low. Ashamed. "It was just that they were so smug. They said they sent you pictures last night . . ." She trailed off.

"I deleted them the moment they came in and I didn't bother to reply to them. I haven't seen any of the three of them since last year nor have I intended to do so. Had I known they intended to show up here tonight, I would have banned them from the club. They invited me to go to Texas to meet them and I said no."

His anger hadn't abated at all, she could tell by the lines around his mouth and the set to his jaw. Abruptly he caught her hand and took her through the crowd, almost dragging her, uncaring of her high heels. Fortunately, the crowd opened up for him, even there in the dark on the dance floor, allowing them through easily.

Stefano took her toward the back of the club, going between two of the bars to the shadowy alcove where a door led to offices. The alcove was very dark and she knew the shadows enclosed them in their own private world. She shivered, knowing she shouldn't be alone with him. Not now. Not when he was so angry and she was needy.

He walked her backward until she came up against the wall and she couldn't move another inch. His body crowded hers until there wasn't enough room to slide a piece of paper between them, until she felt the imprint of his heavy muscles on her breasts and hips.

He tipped her chin up, forcing her eyes to meet his. "I'm going to spell this out for you, Francesca, using plain fucking English so there aren't any misunderstandings. I'm not fucking around with you. I'm telling you straight up that I want a relationship with you, a permanent one. Exclusive. You and me. No one else. No other women for me. No other men for you. I want to settle down and have a family with you. I know you're still getting used to the idea and that's all right. I'll give you time. But that doesn't mean another man puts his fucking hands on you. He doesn't get to hold you in his arms and feel your body up against his. Not. Ever."

"I danced, Stefano. I like to dance. I don't understand why you would be angry. You were busy, and I danced with him. I wouldn't go out with him. I'm not attracted to him. I'm not a cheater. I knew we were both considering a relationship, although honestly, it's moved so fast for me it's hard to believe it's real."

He leaned down, his arms suddenly around her, yanking her hard against his body. "You aren't listening to me. I will not tolerate another man putting his hands on you any more than I would expect you to tolerate another woman putting her hands on me. It's dangerous, Francesca. Dangerous to whatever dumb fuck thinks he has the right to rub his body up against yours. I saw his hand on your ass. That ass belongs to me. No other man puts his hand there. When I saw that, I wanted to kill him. I *needed* to kill him. I live in a world of violence and now, so do you. You don't want to put me in that position any more than I would put you there. That's all I'm going to say on this. I don't argue. This is your one and only warning."

She blinked up at him. "You're serious."

"Dead serious."

She moved subtly, trying to pull away from him without seeming to do so. Subtle didn't work. His arms became steel bands, locking her to him, and he leaned his weight against her so that it was impossible to move. The air around them was heavy with his anger. A little shiver of fear went down her spine. Not just fear. Still, impossibly, she felt safe in his arms. She realized that along with that spurt of trepidation, there was a dark, sensual excitement she couldn't deny.

"You don't hurt women." She made it a statement because she had to believe it was true. She knew lies when she heard them; she also knew honesty. He spoke the truth about wanting to kill Dominic, but his anger was directed at her. Still, his hands on her didn't hurt, not in the least. He could be rough, but he wasn't violent with women.

"No. I don't." He left it at that.

Could she accept him just the way he was? Like this? Darkly sensual? A man used to violence? A man she really knew nothing at all about? She knew she was already lost, too far gone, so attracted to him physically, the chemistry so intense she could barely think with wanting him. Her sense of self-preservation was gone. She should have asked questions, demanded answers.

Francesca moistened her lips. "All right, Stefano."

"'All right'? What the fuck does that mean?"

"It means you can stop using such foul language and take a breath. I won't dance with another man. I won't let another man touch me. I wouldn't like it if you were dancing with another woman, so even though it was perfectly innocent I understand what you're saying. On the other hand, there isn't any need to be dramatic and talk about danger, violence or killing. You wouldn't really hurt another man just because he danced with me." She wasn't so certain that was true, but she wanted it to be.

He shook his head, some of the dark anger dissipating. "*Bambina*, you're such an innocent. He wasn't dancing with you. He was trying to get into your lacy little thong panties. His hand was on your ass."

"I moved his hand back to my waist *immediately*."

"Which is why the fucker is still alive. The only man who touches your ass or your panties is going to be me. *Ever*." His hand slid down her hip to her bare thigh, fingers caressing her skin. "This dress doesn't look the same on you as it did on that mannequin."

His fingers began making little circles up her thigh. Barely there. Burning. Branding her. It felt as if he touched her with fire. She shuddered, leaning her weight into the wall, hoping it would keep her upright.

"I suppose the mannequin was board straight, and you've got all these sexy curves." His other hand found her right breast, drifting over the soft curve until his fingertips were directly over her nipple. "I should have taken that into consideration."

The fingers inched up her thigh, right under the hem of her dress, moving upward with soft, deliberate strokes. She put her hand on his wrist to stop him, her gaze moving around the club. It was dark and Stefano had taken her well back into the shadows for their little talk, but still, in another minute she knew she'd be too far gone to care what he did to her. She wanted his hands on her. His mouth on her. She *had* to have his touch more than she needed to breathe.

With her breath burning in her lungs and need driving her, she ran one palm up his chest to his shoulder. It was a tight fit because he refused to move back, his much larger body directly in front of her. Should anyone come up on them, they wouldn't be able to see her the way he'd positioned himself. She realized that even when he was angry with her, he'd made certain to protect her.

"So you don't like the dress?" Her voice came out sultry. A whisper of pure sin.

A soft groan escaped. "*Dolce cuore*, you can't use that tone when we're out in public." His fingers dug into her inner thigh for a brief moment and then relaxed, gently caressing her skin over the sting. "I've never wanted a woman more in my entire life. There are half a dozen offices close by I could take you into and fuck you until neither one of us could move, but that's not what I want for your first time with me. I want to at least try to be gentle with you. Right now I'm not certain I could be. Help me out a little, okay, *bella*?"

His fingers, sliding over her bare inner thigh, drove her crazy. She needed him right now, and the offices sounded good to her. His knuckles brushed her sex and deep inside, muscles contracted deliciously. She gasped and he immediately bent his head, his teeth finding her earlobe and biting down.

"Stefano." His name came out as a moan.

"You're already wet for me," he whispered. "So ready. For me, *bambina*, that's mine. All for me."

She nodded helplessly, clutching at his wide shoulders to keep from falling at his feet. Her mind felt chaotic, her brain refusing to work. She couldn't think of anything else but Stefano. She wanted his hands on her. His mouth. She *needed* that. "Please," she pleaded softly, asking for something, but what she didn't know.

His expression changed immediately. Gentled. Softened. Even his eyes changed color, darkening intently. His voice stroked caresses over her skin, making her shiver. "Kiss me. Right now. I need your mouth."

She would have given him anything he asked for. She lifted her face up toward his, an offering, both hands at his shoulders, holding on for life. Stefano's mouth instantly took command of hers. Took all control like a runaway train. The moment his tongue swept inside, he spread flames through her. Exquisite, perfect fire. Heat rushed through her veins straight to her sex, fanning the fireball that had lodged there.

His arms went around her, dragging her away from the wall and into his body so that she had no doubt she was imprinted on his bones—and he on hers.

"I want you," he confessed, dragging his mouth from hers, resting his forehead against hers while they both tried to pull air into laboring lungs.

Her lashes swept down and faint color stole into her cheeks. "I want you, too," she whispered. "So much, Stefano."

"Say you're mine." There was steel in his voice.

She took a breath. Let it out. He was commanding more than that simple sentence. They both knew it. He was asking for commitment. Not just a night. A week. A month. He was asking her to say she belonged to him forever.

She heard the blood roaring in her ears. Her body was in flames. In terrible need. Wanting him. Could she give herself to him? She knew two things about him. He was a man with a strict code of honor, and he was a very dangerous man capable of swift violence.

"Give yourself to me," he whispered, his voice an intimate caress, sliding over her skin like the touch of fingers.

His mouth was so close. She could feel every breath he took.

"Trust me with your life, Francesca, and I swear you'll never have to worry about another thing. I can keep you safe. I will make you happy."

He was the devil tempting her. So gorgeous. An incredible man. She knew he paid attention to details, the smallest ones. It would be a trait in him she would both love and hate. He would always make her feel important, maybe the most important thing in his world, but he would also try to control every aspect of her life. Not, she knew, because he wanted to dictate to her, but because his need to keep her safe would make him crazy about her security.

"Say yes, Francesca. I didn't think it was possible to feel anything real for a woman. I just couldn't. I tried, but nothing was there. I knew I was capable of loving because I love my sister and brothers fiercely. With everything in me. But what a man feels for a woman, *the* woman, eluded me until you. Until I saw you."

He melted her resolve with every word he said. There was no shoring up her defenses, no getting away from the raw honesty in his voice.

"I know you don't believe in love at first sight because I always thought it was impossible. I tried to tell myself it wasn't real—it was just chemistry between us. And that chemistry is so explosive I knew I had a chance of being right, but then I watched you. I listened to you. I saw the way you were with others and I felt everything a man is supposed to feel for a woman and more. When I love, Francesca, it's with everything in me. I'm loyal and I'm a fighter, which means I'll fight with my last breath to make certain my woman is happy. I expect those in my life to be the same way."

Her hands, of their own accord, crept around his neck, fingers lacing. The heat of his skin was scorching, but that only added to the fire permanently burning deep inside her for him.

"I didn't care about any other woman, Francesca. Not a single one of them. I used them. They used me. I have a strong sex drive. I'm always hard. Always. I need a woman to give me relief, but I never wanted one for my own. Women were a tool, a body to bury myself in, nothing more. I didn't know how to have them mean more because I just couldn't feel anything at all for them, no matter how much I wanted to or tried. I know that makes me sound like a fucking bastard, but it's the truth and that's what I have to give you—the truth."

She felt perverse enough to love what he was saying to her, to love that those women sending him pictures didn't mean anything at all.

"I fucked a lot of women, Francesca."

She winced. She knew he had. She'd seen the evidence in the tabloids. Most of the articles weren't true, but the pictures didn't lie.

His arms tightened around her. "I can't lie about that. I can't take that back. I know what you see and read; the things these women might say to you will hurt and I hate that. I hate that I'm the cause of that. That what I did so carelessly in the past might be upsetting to you. I can only promise you the future."

"This is going so fast, Stefano."

His fingers massaged the nape of her neck. "For you, *bambina*, but not for me. Time seems to have slowed down until I want to curse with frustration. My grandfather was in love with my grandmother. They were inseparable. They detested being apart. I've seen real love. I've felt it when I was with them. They died three hours apart. My grandmother first and then my grandfather followed. Love exists, and that's what I'm offering you."

His mouth found hers again and she was instantly lost in him. So much heat. So much pleasure lashing through her, little strikes, like lightning flashing through her entire body. This time when he lifted his head, his teeth found her bottom lip, sinking in, tugging, driving her wild.

She heard herself cry out, almost a sob of pure hunger.

"Give yourself to me, Francesca." Pure command. Nothing less than a demand, and that told her something.

He *was* the devil, but she didn't care. On some level she even knew he was using her own body against her, pitting her innocence against his experience, but she didn't care about that, either. She wanted to leap into the fire with both feet, arms wide, eyes open. She knew his world might be something she would have a difficult time accepting, but he was worth it.

"Yes." It came out a soft whisper. Almost nonexistent. A strangled resolve. Maybe it was her mind's way of trying to save her. Self-preservation trying to stop her crazy jump off the cliff.

He went still. Absolutely still. His arms nearly crushed her. "Say it then. I need the words. Say you belong to me and that you're committing to me. Look at me, Francesca, and say it and know there's no taking it back."

She moistened her lips and lifted her lashes to look into his piercing blue eyes. There was such a mixture there. Possession. Desire. Triumph. Demand.

"There's no taking it back, Francesca," he warned.

She licked her lips again, right over the spot where his teeth had bitten. "I won't take it back, Stefano," she said softly. "I want to be yours."

"And you're committing to me? You'll wear my ring. You'll come into my family? Be a part of us," he prompted.

A ring? He hadn't said anything about a ring. That was going even further than she'd anticipated he'd want. A part of her was thrilled. The sane part was terrified. Already it felt too much like ownership. As if he had already branded her in her bones. In her soul.

"Don't." He tipped up her face, forcing her to stay in eye contact. "I get that you're afraid, *dolce cuore*. You have to trust me. Rely on me. That's what I need from you. I've got you, Francesca. All you have to do is let me have you."

She tried to think straight, but her body already belonged to him, her breasts aching for his touch, nipples pushing hard against the material of her dress. Between her legs, she felt empty and needy. Burning. Tension coiled so tightly she was afraid if she moved she might shatter. If she didn't have him she might not make it through the night.

"I can't think straight when you're so close to me." She could barely speak. His heavy erection pressed against her, high, along her waist and she felt every long, thick inch of him like a burning brand. "You're taking advantage."

"I'll take any advantage I can get. Right now, Francesca, I'm being gentle. Push me and I'll do more to get your yes. I'll have my fingers buried inside of you and if that doesn't work, it will be my mouth working between your legs. I'm shameless when it comes to you. This is a battle I can't afford to lose so yes, I'll use any means necessary to make certain your answer is what I want."

She licked over that throbbing spot on her lower lip again. "Is this what I would have to look forward to once we were together? You using sex to get your way?"

"Absolutely."

She wanted him so much. She could stall all she wanted, but in the end, she knew she would give in to him. "I said yes," she pointed out. "I may be scared, but I said yes."

He bent his head to brush kisses over her eyelids, almost as if he were closing her eyes so she wouldn't see the elation sweeping through him. But she did. She *felt* it.

"I'm going to kiss you one more time, Francesca, and

then we have to finish up so we can go home. It's too dangerous to be in public when I need to be inside of you."

The raw desire in his voice scraped at her, clawed at her belly, matching her own. She wanted to be home, too, as quickly as possible.

"Give me your mouth, *bella*."

She did so without hesitation, needing the fire pouring down her throat and into her body. Surrounding her heart. The familiar flames rushed over her breasts, connected her nipples straight to her clit, so that she pulsed and throbbed with desperation. His mouth was pure sensuality. Hot with passion. His taste was addicting and when he began to lift his head to pull away, she chased after him with her mouth.

He caught her chin firmly. "*Bambina*, not here. I don't have as much self-control as I'd like, not when it comes to you. I'm not about to fuck you against the wall where someone could just walk up on us, but we keep this up and it could happen."

It was nice knowing she wasn't alone in what she was feeling, but right at that moment, the idea of him "fucking" her against the wall was a blatant temptation.

He transferred his hold to her hand and stepped back to allow her to move away from the wall. "My cousins are here from New York. I'd like you to meet them."

She blinked up at him, feeling as if she was coming out of a fog, or an erotic dream, and couldn't quite shake it off. "I met them the other night, remember?" They made her nervous. She wasn't certain she wanted to see them again in her present state of absolute craving. They saw too much.

He smiled down at her. "More cousins. You met Lanz and Deangelo Rossi. They're brothers. They came with two other cousins, Salvatore and Lucca. Their last name is Ferraro as well. Salvatore and Lucca have one other brother, Geno. No sisters. Girls don't seem to run in our family much."

"Your family is so big, Stefano. I only had my sister. No aunts or uncles. No one else. You have enough cousins to make a small town."

He laughed softly, tugging her closer until her front was

locked to his side and she was under his arm. His cell phone chimed just as they stepped out of the shadows into the light behind the red bar. He stopped abruptly and pulled it from the inside of his jacket, refusing to give her any space, clamping her tightly to his side.

"You're a slave to that thing," she pointed out.

"True," he agreed and flipped it open. "Stefano."

He was as abrupt on the phone as he was in person, she decided, studying his face. He had a gorgeous face, one that belonged on the cover of a magazine. It was no wonder the paparazzi were obsessed with him. She was a little obsessed with him herself. Her heart was still pounding insanely at the giant step she'd just taken. She couldn't even blame it on alcohol. That was all her, unable to resist him.

She leaned back against Stefano, mostly because he gave her no choice with his arm locked around her, right under her breasts. He smelled wonderful, his scent enveloping her, surrounding her with . . . him. She was acutely aware of his heavy erection pressed tightly against her. He always seemed to be hard around her. She had to admit she liked that. She wanted him to want her.

She had tuned out his conversation, listening to the music instead, used to the constant demands made on his time. It took a few moments before his side of the conversation penetrated. This was no call about someone needing help. She inhaled sharply and turned her attention completely to Stefano.

"No, Saldi, I'm at the club with my brothers and cousins. We're celebrating tonight. Why the hell would you think I'd sneak into your fucking house and kill that piece of shit Tidwell right under your nose? I had no idea the bastard was staying in your home."

Silence and then more. "Are you fucking kidding me? I beat the shit out of him and sent him to you to do whatever you wanted with him. Taking his building was enough revenge for me."

Silence and then Stefano burst out with a string of profanities. "You're pissing me off, Saldi. I can't be in two places at one time. Come on down and see for yourself if you want, although the damn paparazzi has managed to sneak in and they're taking enough pictures for an entire magazine." Stefano's voice was clipped and angry.

Francesca tensed. Tidwell had owned her building and now he was dead. Someone had—what—murdered him? Was that what Saldi was saying to Stefano? She shivered. At once Stefano bent his head and nuzzled her neck. His teeth nipped and his tongue swirled heat over the little sting, making her intensely aware of him.

"I'll tone it down," he whispered to her and pressed a kiss against the sensitive spot right behind her ear.

His arm, a bar around her rib cage, didn't relax at all. He kept her tightly against him and resumed his conversation with one of the Saldis. Francesca had heard about them from several sources, but more, she'd read about them in news articles. They were definitely considered criminals. She knew that family was into organized crime, yet Stefano didn't sound in the least afraid. He swore at them and seemingly had no worries about retaliation.

"I don't give a damn, Giuseppi, what you think. What I think is that you'd better find someone else responsible for that piece of shit's cut throat. I'm not crying tears if that's what you're looking for. If it happened under your nose, look to your own people and tighten your fucking security." He snapped the phone shut with an angry click and shoved it in his pocket.

Her breath caught in her lungs. "Giuseppi Saldi is the head of the largest crime family right here in Chicago," she whispered, terrified for him. No one would talk to Giuseppi Saldi like that, not even the police. He was reputed to be extremely violent and often retaliated if he felt slighted.

"Yes." He nuzzled her neck again. "You smell so good."

"You weren't very nice when you talked to him, Stefano. What if he gets angry with you?" A shiver went down her spine. Stefano was reckless when he lost his temper.

He stopped moving to look down at her, his arms shifting

her so she was standing directly in front of him, her front tight against his. She had to tip her head back to look up at him.

"There you go, getting all protective on me. You're worried about me, aren't you?" His voice practically purred at her, a sensual mixture of possession, desire and something else—affection. "*Dio, bambina*, I love that."

"He's dangerous. Isn't that the second time you've sworn at him?"

"More like the hundredth. I don't like him and I doubt if he likes me much." He brushed his mouth over hers with exquisite gentleness. "Don't worry about him. He won't come after me. He wouldn't dare."

Her heart gave a painful jerk in her chest. "Why, Stefano? Why wouldn't he come after you?"

His hand shaped her face, his thumb tracing her high cheekbone, down to her mouth to linger over her bottom lip. "I told you, *dolce cuore*, no one fucks with me. I'm that kind of man. Stop worrying and come meet my cousins. You'll like them."

She hadn't been so sure of his other New York cousins, the ones that had definitely been interrogating her. She turned her head as Stefano once again shifted her beneath his shoulder, his arm locking around her to keep her close. She put one hand on his washboard abdomen as her gaze collided with Janice's. The woman had stopped moving right in the middle of the dance floor and was staring at her with absolute venom. Francesca shivered at the concentrated hatred in the woman's gaze. The dancers shifted and Janice was swallowed up by the gyrating crowd.

"What is it, Francesca?"

He was so tuned to her, but she wasn't about to admit his past women were giving her nasty looks and upsetting her. How jealous and lame would she appear? She was just jumpy. She was out in the open and it was impossible not to see the curious and speculative looks the crowd gave them.

"I've been hiding from Barry Anthon for so long that this makes me a little nervous. I feel very exposed," she improvised quickly.

He laughed softly, his arm tightening around her. "You are exposed in that little black dress. I can see that I can't just call a shopper for you, I'm going to have to *see* you in something before I approve it."

That distracted her immediately. She gave him her darkest scowl. "Seriously? You think you're going to actually get a say in what I wear?"

"Of course I'm going to get a say. I'm bossy and controlling, remember? I'm also jealous, a trait I had no idea I possessed until I laid eyes on you."

His voice held laughter so she wasn't certain if he was serious, although he looked serious. She was saved from having to reply because four men walked up to them, two dressed in dark pin-striped suits. She recognized Lanz and Deangelo immediately and knew instantly the other two were Stefano's cousins as well. All four men were extremely good-looking and fit, but the two new ones really stood out. Something about the way they moved made her think of Stefano. They could easily be brothers, not cousins.

Stefano stopped on the edge of the dance floor as the others came up to them. Francesca tried to step away from him, to put a little space between them, but he simply stepped behind her and wrapped his arms around her rib cage, right under her breasts. The feel of his arms pressing so tightly on the undersides of her breasts made her feel needy. Achy. He was too potent and she couldn't be so close, not with the spotlight so clearly on them. She couldn't even take a breath without breathing him in.

"You know Lanz and Deangelo, *bambina*, right? These are two more of my cousins from New York. Salvatore and Lucca, this is my Francesca."

Salvatore took her hand and brought it to his mouth. Before he could touch his lips to her knuckles, Stefano reached out and caught her wrist, pulling her hand away. Immediately his cousins burst into laughter.

"Damned swine," Stefano said, without the least rancor. "Francesca, it's best not to look directly at these New Yorkers.

They may be my cousins, but they're truly the devil's best friends. Stay very close to me so I can protect you."

She couldn't help but laugh as the cousins looked pleased with Stefano's assessment. Stefano waved his hand toward the VIP section and their table. Surrounded by the men, Francesca felt unbelievably protected as they moved up the stairs to their table. Stefano's brothers were already there, seated with Emmanuelle, and they actually rose when Francesca approached the table. She found herself blushing at the attention they were getting.

"Where's Joanna?" she asked Emmanuelle, a little worried that her friend might be upset that she'd disappeared.

"On the dance floor with Mario. They can't take their eyes off each other," Giovanni said. "I'm looking into that man. He'd better not break her heart."

Francesca liked that, even though he really did sound menacing and the quick nods the brothers gave one another made them seem just as threatening. Still, it was Joanna, and she was grateful the Ferraro brothers took her protection seriously.

"Rigina and Rosina are keeping an eye on things," Emmanuelle said. "Don't go all cavemen on poor Joanna. She's really into Mario, and he seems genuine enough."

Stefano held out the chair for Francesca and then, when she slipped into it, pulled the one beside it close, so their thighs were touching and he could easily wrap his arm around her shoulders. He caught her hand and pulled it to his thigh, pressing her palm deep into his heat.

The waitress was there instantly. Francesca knew she shouldn't—she needed to keep her wits about her—but she ordered another Moscow Mule with lime. The lime, vodka and ginger beer made a refreshing drink. It went down smoothly, sometimes too smoothly, but she didn't care. She relaxed into Stefano and let the talk flow around her, although the cousins, brothers and Emmanuelle made certain she was a part of the conversation.

There was a lot of laughter. The Ferraro family clearly was close and they liked one another enough to give one another a hard time. Salvatore and Lucca's brother, Geno, couldn't attend the family celebration but had sent his congratulations.

"What exactly is the family celebrating?" Francesca asked Stefano, leaning close to him, her head on his shoulder, her lips pressed against his ear to be heard above the noise of the club.

Stefano threw back his head and laughed. She *loved* the sound. Carefree. Masculine. Enjoying life. He didn't laugh a lot. "You, *bambina*, we're celebrating me finding you."

She was stunned by the sheer honesty in his voice. By the raw desire so plain in his vibrant blue eyes for anyone to see. By the possession stamped deep into his dark expression. He meant that. His cousins and family were celebrating Stefano finding Francesca. Claiming her. That knowledge went deep. She felt tears burn behind her eyes. Before anyone else could see them, she turned her face into his neck.

Immediately he wrapped his arms around her. "You're the best thing that's ever happened to me, Francesca. Of course I'm going to share the most important woman in my life with the people I love. My cousins from San Francisco couldn't make it, but they wanted to."

"We're careful not to all gather in one place," Taviano supplied. "San Francisco drew the short straw."

The short straw—she'd heard that term before when Emmanuelle hadn't come to support her during what she thought of as "the interrogation." "Why wouldn't you be able to gather in one place together?" She frowned at them as they all went silent.

Stefano shrugged casually, when she knew he was feeling anything but casual. She could feel the tension around the table.

"It stems from hundreds of years ago, a law handed down in our family generations ago. The Saldi family in Sicily murdered the Ferraro family, killing as many members, men, women and children, as they could. The decree that we don't all gather in one place was passed down by those surviving that massacre. It was a long time ago, just history really, but we still abide by that rule."

Stefano had sworn at Giuseppi Saldi, deliberately goading him. When the two families had feuded for over a hundred years or more, why would he feel he was safe talking to the head of a crime family like that unless the Ferraro family was also a crime family as she'd first suspected? A small, icy finger of unease snaked down her spine.

"We're celebrating tonight," Ricco said, raising his glass. "To our Francesca. May she be followed by the right ones in a very timely manner."

"Hear, hear," the others chorused and clinked glasses.

She had no idea what they were talking about, but they all seemed happy, so she sipped at her drink, smiling. Letting herself believe that she could have a big family. That a man would love her the way Stefano seemed to. She didn't deserve it. She hadn't earned it, but she was determined to do so.

The talk flowed around her for another hour. She wanted to dance. One more Moscow Mule and she wouldn't care whether it bothered Stefano or not. She leaned close to him. "I'll be right back, Stefano," she said. "I'm heading to the ladies' room and no, you can't go with me," she hastily added as he rose with her. To her horror they all stood. The entire table of men. To try to stop the furious blush rising, she tugged at her hand to escape him. "And I'll want to dance, so if you didn't bring your dancing shoes, be prepared for seeing me dancing with another man."

"That's not happening, *dolce cuore*, not unless you want to see bloodshed. Fortunately, I always bring my dancing shoes. And I will be escorting you, so don't argue with me anymore. I don't like it and it won't do you any good."

She blinked rapidly, annoyed. "You seriously can't say things like that to me. I mean it, Stefano. I'm sorry if I annoy you, but if I object to something, I'm going to voice it."

He wrapped his arm around her waist, pulling her in close, her front to his side as they made their way to the restrooms in the VIP section. "Voice it all you like, Francesca. I didn't mean you can't tell me when you disagree, but there isn't any purpose in arguing when it comes to your safety. You won't get your way."

CHAPTER FOURTEEN

Francesca made her way to the restrooms without looking at Stefano. It was easy enough because she was so close to him she could feel his heat right through his immaculate and extremely expensive pin-striped suit. He was annoying her with his bossy ways, but not enough for her to start a fight over it. She was far too mellow with her three Moscow Mules, the music, and the feel and smell of Stefano Ferraro.

"What's up with the suits?" she murmured, running her hand inside his jacket so she could feel the quality of his impressive dark shirt. "You and all your brothers wear them, your sister does and now your cousins. But not *all* your cousins. They all wear suits, just not pin-striped suits."

Stefano hesitated. Just slightly, but it was enough of a hesitation that she noticed it and she stopped, forcing him to stop right along with her. Only then did she realize that the party had accompanied them. They were surrounded by his brothers and cousins, including Emilio and Enzo. She was once again in the center, as if they were all guarding her.

"Stefano?" Her voice trembled a little. Suddenly, from feeling safe and protected, she feared maybe there was a reason they were all surrounding her. Was it because they'd confirmed that the man staring at her at the deli had been sent by Barry Anthon? She'd continued to work and he hadn't returned, nor had anyone else shown up.

"I'll explain about the suits at home, *bambina*." His voice was gentle, once again obviously reading her mood, but not the reason why.

She looked around the circle of tough, handsome faces and found herself pressing closer to Stefano. "Is something wrong? Did Barry . . ."

"*No.*" He was emphatic. "We're just watching over you your first time out in a public venue when the paparazzi are here. We try to keep them out, but cameras are everywhere."

For the first time, she detected a lie. They hadn't tried to keep the paparazzi out. Why would that be? And why would Stefano lie about that when he clearly hadn't lied about anything else? She didn't understand his world. It was filled with intrigue and danger. More, she feared it was filled with violence.

She studied his face, taking her time. Letting him see her trepidation. He was so beautiful to her. The planes and angles of his face, so absolutely masculine. He looked like a man, not a boy. There wasn't softness to his features, yet he still looked model perfect to her. The long sweep of his eyelashes and deep blue of his eyes, the shadow on his strong jaw, his straight aristocratic nose and especially his mouth, that sinful, amazing mouth that gave her so many fantasies— all together were perfection.

His fingers curled around the nape of her neck and he bent his head until his forehead touched hers and he was staring into her eyes. "You gave me you, Francesca. Give me your trust."

She went up on tiptoes and put her mouth to his ear, "You just told me a lie about the paparazzi, Stefano. You wanted them here."

She expected him to be upset that she caught his lie, but instead he looked inexplicably pleased and proud of her. "We'll sort out your questions in time. For now, *bella*, just trust me."

She took a breath. Inhaled him right through her nose, her mouth, her very pores until she was taking him deep into her body. He had wound himself so tightly around her bones and heart that she knew she would never get him out. She just nodded, because she was incapable of speech. Her heart beat a weirdly frantic tattoo and blood thundered in her ears so loud she couldn't hear anything but her own driving need. She touched her tongue to her bottom lip. His face was so close, the tip of her tongue touched his lip as well.

"*Bambina*, right now, go into the restroom while you still can. When you come out, we'll dance and then I'm going to take you home and fuck you all night." He whispered the promise against her lips and it felt like he was already doing just that.

Her sex clenched and went damp. Her nipples tightened. Her breathing went ragged. He lifted his forehead from hers and turned her toward the restroom. She wasn't entirely certain she could take those last few steps to the entrance on her wobbly legs, but she managed, slipping into a stall and closing her eyes, savoring the way Stefano could make her feel with just a few words.

Perversely, she even liked him bossy when he was telling her what to do sometimes. She liked that he was decisive, confident and willing to take charge. She supposed when she was thinking about other things besides sex that might make her a little crazy, but right now, that was part of the chemistry.

To her dismay, when she emerged to wash her hands, the three blondes were there. Janice, in her venomous glory, was leaning down to sniff a line of cocaine right off the sink. Francesca raised an eyebrow but said nothing, going to the opposite end of the sink to the last basin.

Doreen nudged Stella. "Little Miss Goody Two-Shoes is giving us the shocked eye."

Francesca swept her gaze over the three women coolly. "Not shocked, just a little horrified. That can't be too sanitary."

"Sanitary?" Janice straightened, rubbing her nose to get the white powder clinging there off. "You're going home with

Stefano Ferraro and you want to talk sanitary? Do you really think a little virginal thing like you is going to hold a man like that for more than one night? He likes spice, honey. He likes a woman to know what she's doing in his bed. You don't look like you know your way around a cock without a diagram."

The three women erupted into crude laughter. Francesca took the warm towel from the attendant, who met her eyes just for a moment, sympathy plain there. Maybe even a show of support. That quick, with just one brief moment taking her eyes off the other women, Doreen stepped behind her, her arms whipping around Francesca, holding her in place.

A toilet flushed in one of the stalls. Stella called out, stepping in close to Francesca. "Stay in the stall, bitch, unless you want to get hurt. You"—she indicated the attendant—"go find somewhere else to be."

Francesca forced herself to remain calm, when her temper was rising at an alarming rate. "Are you kidding me right now? You're grown women. You have careers. This is absolutely ridiculous. Doreen, let go of me."

"We're going to see how much Stefano likes his little virgin when he sees she's really a coke whore," Janice snarled, her eyes so narrow they appeared to be twin bright slits.

Doreen tried to push Francesca forward toward the sink and when Francesca resisted, Stella joined forces, shoving hard. Francesca was horrified. It had never occurred to her that three successful women, all grown and supposedly sophisticated and elegant, would resort to such childish and criminal assault. She realized they really meant it; they were going to push her face into the cocaine Janice had smeared on the sink. She slammed her heel hard into Doreen's shin, scraped down it so that she tore Doreen's stockings and stomped hard on her foot.

Doreen screamed out a string of ugly curses and flung Francesca forward into the sink. Francesca hit hard against the marble, but she spun around before Stella could push her face into the white powder. Janice shoved her open hand into Francesca's face in an attempt to coat Francesca's nose and mouth with the drug.

Suddenly Janice was dragged backward and Emmanuelle was there, moving so fast she seemed a blur of motion, barely discernible as she smoothly and efficiently dispatched all three women, using her hands and feet. One moment they were all standing and the next they were on the floor, faces swelling and bloody. All three cried, makeup running down their faces. Emmanuelle stood over them, contempt on her face, her body posture threatening. She looked every inch a Ferraro—a woman no one would ever want to mess with.

"Are you okay, Francesca?" In spite of her clear threat toward the three women trying to push themselves up onto their hands and knees, she appeared as calm and relaxed as ever.

"Yes. They didn't hurt me."

"Stay still," Emmanuelle hissed, nudging Janice with her foot. "You just tried to drug my future sister-in-law. She's Stefano's fiancée. What do you think he's going to do when he finds out what you've done?"

The faces turned up toward them went very pale. Doreen began to cry. The three of them made no move to get off the floor, obeying Emmanuelle's directive.

Francesca checked her face in the mirror to make certain there was no trace of the white powder. "I'm fine. We don't need to share this with Stefano."

"Yes, we do," Emmanuelle said firmly. "You can never keep anything from Stefano. *Never*, Francesca. Especially when you've received threats. The slightest threat needs to be shared with the family."

Francesca took a breath. Emmanuelle was saying much more than what appeared on the surface of her admonishment, but what it was, Francesca had no idea. Still, in spite of the fact that Emmanuelle was very small, even shorter than Francesca, she appeared a woman of sheer steel.

Slowly, Francesca nodded. "Let me tell him."

Emmanuelle gave her a look. "You'll give him a lame

version, and that's not going to fly, Francesca. What they tried to do to you was criminal. You could have been seriously hurt. All because they were jealous." She toed Janice with her Jimmy Choo sandal. "You're going to lose everything, you skank. Your money, your career, your friends, *everything*. He would never have dated you, any of you, not in a million years." She poured contempt into her voice. "Trying to harm Francesca because she's everything you're not is just plain stupid."

"Emmanuelle," Francesca intervened softly. Emmanuelle had the Ferraro trait of being intimidating. "Let's go."

Emmanuelle looked as if she wanted to start with physical violence all over again, but she stalked to the sink and washed her hands, smiling sweetly at the attendant and then pushing a large tip into her hands. She caught Francesca's arm and they left the restroom, the three women still on the floor, afraid to move, afraid of going against Emmanuelle's orders before she left the room.

Uneasiness crept into Francesca's mind. The three women were terrified of Emmanuelle—or at least of the threats she made.

"Stefano can't really wreck their careers, can he?" she asked, already afraid she knew the answer.

Emmanuelle just leveled a look at her. Francesca's heart lurched and then began to pound. The moment they had taken four steps out of the restroom and Stefano got a look at her, he claimed her, taking her hand and pulling her into the shelter of his body. His hand swept over her hair in a little caress.

"What happened?"

He chose to look to his sister for an explanation rather than to Francesca. Her temper flared. "Seriously, Stefano? Your skanky women tried to assault me—that's what happened."

She was rather shocked at the instant reaction. The crowd of his brothers and cousins went silent. Ricco in particular looked horrified. His gaze met Stefano's over her head.

All of them reflected the same emotions. *All* of them.

The brothers and cousins. Shock. Anger. The collective rage was so strong it was difficult to breathe with the violent tension filling the air. Stefano looked like thunder, a dark storm gathering in his vivid blue eyes. Stefano actually made to move past her, heading toward the restrooms, his face reflecting his rage.

"I'm all right." Francesca caught his arm, halting him, hastening to reiterate. "Emmanuelle came along and went all superwoman on them."

"What *exactly* did these women try to do to you?" He bit out each word between clenched white teeth, all the while smoldering with fury.

She swallowed down the truth and went for a less dramatic version. "They had the idea that if I had a little of their cocaine on my face you'd not find me so attractive."

Emmanuelle coughed delicately behind her hand. Francesca glared at Stefano's sister, giving her a wide-eyed plea after. Francesca couldn't believe how angry the Ferraro clan was over the incident, and she feared for the three women when they emerged from the restrooms. Emmanuelle had already beaten them up. Aside from pressing criminal charges, which Francesca wouldn't do—she was never going to the police again—there wasn't much else to be done.

"I said *exactly*." Stefano caught her chin and tilted her face up toward his, his blue gaze inspecting every inch of her, looking for damage. *"Exactly."*

There was no getting around Stefano in this mood, or the others for that matter. They had sucked all the breathable air available and left behind a heavy layer of oppressive anger. "The three of them, Janice, Doreen and Stella, seem very upset that you aren't continuing your relationship with them. They were in the restroom doing a little pick-me-up cocaine right off the bathroom sink, which has to be totally unsanitary . . ."

"Francesca. Dios, woman, you are making me crazy. Just tell me."

Someone snickered. She thought it was Vittorio and she

was grateful to him for lightening the mood because the air became a bit less oppressive and she felt like she could actually breathe.

"Their idea was to smash my face in the powder. Doreen grabbed me from behind and Stella helped her. Janice tried to rub the coke into my nose and mouth." She rushed the story, hoping by telling it really fast, no one would actually hear the panic in her voice—the panic she had refused to feel when the three women had attempted to assault her.

Stefano cursed loud and long, first in Italian—and he was very inventive—and then in English—and he was very expressive.

"I believe these women reside in New York," Salvatore stated, his voice implying all sorts of things that scared Francesca.

Her gaze jumped to his face. "Emmanuelle took care of it," she reminded softly. "She beat the crap out of them."

Stefano shook his head. "No one touches you, Francesca. Not ever. The three of them won't have a fucking thing left when we get through with them." His hands ran over her, as if inspecting for damage. "Fucking bitches. They knew the score. They wanted publicity, and they got it. They'll be getting more than they can ever handle now."

He looked at his cousin Enzo and nodded. Just once, but Francesca was certain Stefano was giving his cousin an order. Enzo walked a distance away, punched in a number and put his cell phone to his ear.

Stefano curled his palm around the nape of Francesca's neck. "I haven't been with any of them for over a year."

"But they kept trying," Francesca pointed out. "The first night I was in your apartment, they called you. Sent you pictures."

"Mostly Janice. She was the worst of them. I should have known it was a mistake to hook up with her."

Francesca winced and looked down at her hands. This was all too much for her. Life in the fast lane wasn't for her. She wasn't in their league with their fast hookups and casual sex.

She didn't work like that. The music pounded a beat in her head. The lights moved in a variety of colors throughout the room. Bodies swayed or danced to the beat while the sound of conversation and ice clinking in glasses felt like shards of glass pressing into her head. Why had she ever thought she had a chance with a man like Stefano Ferraro? It hurt to think of him with women like Doreen, Stella and Janice. It didn't lessen the hurt because the encounters were casual.

"*Il mio piccola bella amore*, I can't change the past as much as I'd like to," he said softly. "I can only tell you that you have my future. Only you."

He said it out loud. Right in front of his family. His blue eyes held hers captive and she couldn't help but read the sincerity there or hear the honesty in his voice.

"I'm sorry these women tried to hurt you, *dolce cuore*. I'll take care of it. You need a female bodyguard to accompany you into dressing rooms and restrooms, Francesca. I'll get on that immediately. Emilio and Enzo have a sister, Enrica . . ."

"No." She shook her head. "I'm not going to have a bodyguard. I won't, Stefano, and there's not a single thing you can say that will change my mind."

His eyebrow went up and his mouth settled into a hard line. "It's a matter of your safety, Francesca," he reminded quietly.

He didn't argue, she remembered. She sighed. "Let's just drop it, Stefano. The three of them are hiding out in the restroom and probably will remain there until we leave."

Stefano shook his head, looked to Emilio and Enzo, who was back. "The police have been called."

She went white. She knew she did. She felt the color draining from her face and she shook her head adamantly. "No. I don't want to make out a report or bring charges against them. I won't talk to the police, Stefano, not ever again."

Salvatore's white teeth flashed and he nodded approvingly. "Good girl. This is a family matter. We don't talk to the police—not ever."

She didn't understand what he meant by that, because already she could hear sirens above the music, which meant the police were right outside. Enzo must have called them on Stefano's orders.

"You aren't going to press charges, Francesca," Stefano said gently. "The police have been notified that the attendant in the ladies' room observed three women using and selling cocaine in large amounts. The police will find plenty of evidence to back this charge up. No one will mention an assault, especially not Janice, Stella or Doreen. They can kiss their careers good-bye."

Her hand went defensively to her throat as bouncers escorted six police officers along the edge of the dance floor back toward the ladies' room. Ricco, at Stefano's nod, followed Emilio and Enzo, she guessed to represent the Ferraro family as owners.

"Stefano, actresses and actors and singers tend to do better whether publicity is negative or positive."

"Not in this case. My family has an investment in several entertainment fields, including their record label. Every contract has a clause for certain types of behavior. It's never exercised, but it's there in case it's needed."

She frowned, realizing he was serious. He'd have the women arrested on drug charges. She knew they were guilty of using and if they had a large supply, they very well could be guilty of selling. "Shouldn't being arrested and having to defend themselves in court be enough karma for them?"

"No."

Every brother and cousin as well as Emmanuelle replied at the same time. She could see the paparazzi were already moving into position to get pictures of whatever scandal was happening at the club. The circle of men tightened around her and Emmanuelle as the police brought out the three singers and flashes went off like mad. Most of those dancing on the floor turned to watch the three women being escorted out.

Janice, Stella and Doreen looked terrible. Their makeup was smeared all over their faces and they looked as if they'd been partying for hours, vomiting and sleeping on the bathroom floor, plus they looked bruised, with swollen faces from Emmanuelle kicking their asses. The photographs that would appear in the magazines were not going to be flattering in the least.

Francesca couldn't help the little pang of pity. "Maybe we should . . ."

"Enough, *bambina*. They're getting what they asked for. They would have forced drugs on you and painted you in a light that was far from flattering."

"I've been painted in that light for a long time, Stefano."

He took her hand and tugged her close to him. "I believe I owe you a dance or two."

"Uh-oh, Stefano," Ricco said. "At your five o'clock."

Beside her, Francesca felt Emmanuelle stiffen. She reached out without thinking and took Stefano's sister's hand. She had no idea why. Emmanuelle oozed confidence and poise. Nothing seemed to shake her—until now. The tension surrounding the brothers and cousins shot right back up until it stretched to a breaking point. Carefully, mostly because Emmanuelle's fingers tightened around hers as if she was a lifeline, Francesca turned her head in the direction of five o'clock.

A tall, very handsome man emerged from the crowd, striding toward them. He had broad shoulders and very dark, nearly black hair spilling down his forehead into vivid green eyes. He wore a white shirt and expensive dark slacks. A second man kept pace with him, a little shorter and clearly arrogant. He moved with the fluid motion of a boxer and the crowd parted for him.

"Valentino Saldi and his cousin Dario Bosco," Vittorio identified. "Son of a bitch, what would they be doing here?"

Stefano shrugged. "Apparently Tidwell got his throat cut tonight right in the middle of Giuseppi's home. Giuseppi must not have believed me when I told him we were having a celebration tonight and I was nowhere near his house."

The brothers grinned at one another, exchanging smug

looks with their cousins. Francesca's heart gave another hard jerk. She was missing something important, but already the men had schooled their faces into their expressionless masks.

"Who the hell is Tidwell?" Salvatore asked.

"He was Francesca's landlord," Emmanuelle explained. "I told you about what a pervert he was, remember?"

"Pure slime. He was staying at Giuseppi Saldi's house. Giuseppi's nephew is married to Tidwell's aunt. They both were staying there for protection—can you believe it—from us," Stefano explained. "She claimed she was swimming in the pool and he was in a lounger right beside it. The pool is indoors and right smack in the center of Saldi's house. When the aunt emerged from the pool, there was her nephew dead, throat cut and no one heard or saw a thing. I guess they sent Valentino to the club to check our alibis."

"That's horrible," Francesca said. She couldn't really conjure up much distress, not when the man had raped women and had planned to rape her. Still, she felt sorry for his aunt.

Stefano swept his hand down Francesca's back in a caress meant to comfort. "If you prefer not to endure the stench of all things Saldi," he said to his cousins from New York, "you don't have to stick around for introductions."

"We'd prefer to stay," Salvatore declared.

Francesca expected Emmanuelle to drop her hand, but she didn't. If anything she moved a little closer to Francesca as if for protection. Francesca didn't get it, not with all her brothers and cousins towering over them, but she shifted her body subtly to bring herself just in front of Emmanuelle, partially blocking her from the newcomer's sight.

"Stefano," Valentino said, walking right up to the group, showing no fear or hesitation. "My uncle told me you were having a party, but he didn't say what you were celebrating tonight." His sharp gaze took in the strangers from New York as well as Francesca, before coming to rest on Emmanuelle. "I see you even let the little princess out tonight. I wouldn't have thought she was old enough for a nightclub."

"Bite me, Val," Emmanuelle snapped.

"Anytime, Emme." Valentino ignored the way her brothers shifted closer. "Just say when and where." Even in the dark it was easy to see the way his gaze drifted insolently from her head to her toes, taking in every detail. "I can see you're hurting for money, babe. You couldn't afford an entire dress tonight? Stefano, you should help the poor girl out."

"Are you always so rude?" Francesca demanded, mostly because Emmanuelle's fingers bit so deep into her hand she was afraid her bones would break. She would never have guessed that anyone could upset Emmanuelle with a few nasty comments.

Stefano instantly shifted his body, thrusting Francesca behind him. The brothers closed in from either side and behind her, forming a solid wall between the two women and Valentino Saldi.

"Why do you do that, Val?" Stefano asked. "Why pick on a woman? I don't get it, but then I never have."

Valentino shrugged. "Emme always rubs me the wrong way. I don't know why, but I'll apologize if that's what you want."

"Not me," Emmanuelle said. "It wouldn't be sincere anyway, so what's the point? Just go away. We're celebrating my brother's engagement."

The bottom fell out of Francesca's stomach. Right. To. The. Floor. She was suddenly on a runaway train with no way to jump off. Valentino's gaze jumped to her face. He looked genuinely shocked. "Engagement? Stefano?" He recovered quickly enough, smiling gallantly. "Congratulations, Stefano. I'm happy for you."

Strangely, in that moment, Valentino Saldi sounded sincere. His voice rang with honesty. There was no mistaking it.

"Francesca, Valentino Saldi and his cousin Dario Bosco," Stefano introduced with more than a little charm, but he didn't move, preventing the two men from getting close to her.

Dario nodded abruptly. Valentino's smile crept into his eyes. "I'm sorry I made you uncomfortable, Francesca, and that's a genuine apology. Stefano's a lucky man. Emmanuelle, one dance before I go." It wasn't a request. He sounded every bit as arrogant and bossy as Stefano.

Francesca was certain Emmanuelle would tell him to go to hell. Her brothers and cousins all bristled, making it clear from the swell of anger vibrating around them that they weren't happy with the order. Emmanuelle hesitated, but then her fingers loosened the death grip around Francesca's hand and she stepped out from behind her family.

Valentino held out his hand. Francesca inhaled sharply as Emmanuelle put her much smaller hand in his and allowed him to lead her onto the dance floor. Dario followed his cousin, keeping pace right behind him, clearly acting the part of a bodyguard.

"Why the hell does she do that?" Taviano demanded. "Every. Damn. Time. She lets that bastard order her around."

"She's defusing the situation," Vittorio said. "It works."

"It only works because he has our sister in his hands and we can't beat the holy hell out of him," Giovanni said.

Stefano tugged at Francesca's hand and she went with him onto the dance floor. The others followed, each catching up the hand of a woman as they passed her. Francesca felt sorry for the ladies dancing with the Ferraro family. The women were thrilled, but she knew the brothers and cousins had only taken to the dance floor to surround Emmanuelle and Valentino in a show of strength. Emmanuelle had her head resting against Valentino's broad chest, her eyes closed as they moved in perfect rhythm to the music.

Francesca *loved* dancing. She'd always felt the music intensely, heard every instrument individually and then together to form, with her body, a perfect harmony. Adding Stefano to the equation only amplified the feeling. She'd danced with partners, but none felt a perfect match in the way she felt with Stefano, as if the two of them shared the same blood running through their veins, shared their skin and bones. Desire rose, sharp and intense, until she drifted, caught in his spell—caught by the rising tide of lust and passion that surrounded her, that consumed her.

Francesca nuzzled Stefano's chest, breathing him in, that scent unique to him that filled her lungs and surrounded her heart. She wasn't certain how he'd managed to penetrate her armor and gain her trust, but he had. She had questions, but the answers didn't seem to matter when she was close to him. She had to believe that he was real, that he was innately good, because it was already too late for her. If he wasn't as he seemed, if what was building between them wasn't real for him, she wasn't certain how she would survive.

His hand slid down her back, following the curve of her spine along the seam of her dress. She was acutely aware of his body, pressed so tightly against hers. His erection was hard and unashamed, a long, thick reminder of his need to possess her, burning a brand against her ribs, nearly nestling between her breasts. She shivered as his hand caressed her through the thin material of her dress. She felt every tiny movement, his muscles rippling beneath his elegant clothes, his breath against her hair, when he turned his head, the way his lips brushed against her temple. His hand slipped lower, to her thigh and his fingers began to write his name on her bare skin, branding her—his.

She'd never felt so alive, every nerve ending in her body on fire. Her breasts ached, her nipples hard little peaks, rubbing against him as they moved in perfect synchronization. Her body coiled tighter and tighter until she wanted to weep with a need for release. A fire built, roaring now, between her legs. Her panties were damp and all she could think about was his fingers so close to where her clit throbbed and burned for his touch.

She heard a small, strangled moan escape. She needed relief desperately. She needed his mouth on hers. His hands on her. Fingers in her. And his cock, so hot, so thick and demanding—she needed that most of all.

"Stefano." She whispered his name, knowing she was pleading, but she didn't care.

"Me, too, *amore*. We'll get out of here as soon as possible."

She loved that she wasn't the only one. That he felt the

same desperation. She tilted her face upward to look at him, needing to see the raw desire stamped there. Needing to know his need was as great as her own. What she saw there made her breath catch in her throat. His hard features were stamped with absolute possession, with an urgency and passion she knew she couldn't yet compete with. That only brought on a fresh flood of liquid heat.

He took her mouth. Abruptly. Almost savagely. His tongue was demanding, not giving her a chance to catch up; he just swept her away on that tidal wave of sheer feeling. She couldn't think and didn't want to. There was only her body and his. Moving together with the music flowing through them, binding them together with fire, need and the symphony of sound.

He kissed her again and again until she thought she might faint with absolute hunger. She didn't know a man's mouth could be so ravenous. She didn't know his cock could be so hard or his arms so strong, his body like steel. She didn't know his taste would be so addicting or that he could wipe out every sane thought and replace it with sheer, absolute need.

Her blood thundered in her ears, the beat matching the drum in the song. The beat pulsed in her clit, the clenching in her sex following the persistent clenching of her inner muscles and the spasm that accompanied every touch of Stefano's fingers.

"I've got to have you, Francesca. Be inside you. Right. Fucking. Now." He breathed the words into her mouth. Darkly sensual. His eyes hooded. Hungry.

The terrible tension coiled tighter. "Let's leave. Just go," she whispered back. Embarrassed that her need of him was so strong she would have let him have her right there in that club, somewhere dark, against the wall, on the floor; it didn't matter as long as he was filling her, taking away the ache that had built into a terrible conflagration.

"We'll go, *dolce cuore*, in another minute. I've got to get myself under control."

She wasn't certain she wanted him under control, but she

liked that he needed to get himself that way. That meant he was every bit as affected as she was. They moved together on the dance floor, Stefano using the music to guide her closer to an exit.

She suddenly felt uneasy, coming out of the cocoon Stefano had woven around her. She blinked, keeping her cheek pressed to his chest, right over his heart, but she looked around the darkened room. Stefano's hand stroked the back of her thigh, high, under her dress, and she was acutely aware of the pads of his fingers against her bare skin. He traced letters, his name, there as well. This time his fingertips slid along the seam of her cheeks and thigh, right where they met, rubbing caresses, continuing to build that terrible, *needy* ache.

She moistened her lips, her gaze moving around the other dancers, aware suddenly that they weren't alone. She'd been so deep into the sexual web Stefano drew over her that she'd forgotten where they were—that they were surrounded. Those dancing close were his family members, keeping their backs to Stefano, but very close so that no one else could penetrate that circle.

Valentino Saldi had disappeared and Emmanuelle was dancing with a man she didn't know. Joanna and Mario were all over each other, Joanna looking flushed and happy some distance away. The strange uneasiness grew stronger in Francesca, in spite of the fact that no one seemed to be paying the least bit of attention to Stefano or her. She was grateful, because she was letting him touch her very inappropriately for their surroundings. She should have stopped him, but she felt as if she needed his touch on her bare skin just to survive.

She looked carefully around the crowd again, and her gaze met a man dancing very close to the exit Stefano guided her toward. A shiver went down her spine. He was dressed in very nice clothes, his hair falling around his face. He held a woman in his arms, but she could tell he barely noticed her. It was the same man she'd seen in Petrov's Pizzeria. It was the same man who had stood outside Masci's Deli and had drawn a finger across his throat in a gesture meant to frighten her. He was a distance away, but she felt his malevolence toward her. Suddenly she wasn't so certain Barry Anthon had sent him.

"What's wrong?" Stefano stopped on the dance floor, his hand going under her chin to lift her face so he could look at her.

Her gaze slid to his and then she turned her head to look back toward the man. The crowd of dancers had come between them and when they moved to the music, providing gaps, he wasn't there. She shivered again. If she told Stefano he'd turn the place upside down looking for the man.

Francesca pressed herself tighter against Stefano. "Take me out of here. I want to be alone with you." It was the truth. The stark honesty would be impossible to miss. The need and rising hunger in her was just as plain as the honesty but she didn't care if she was blatantly throwing herself at him. She needed Stefano Ferraro, even if she could only have him for a short time—before everything bad in her life caught up with her—and it would. She wanted as much time with Stefano as possible before that happened.

CHAPTER FIFTEEN

Stefano kept Francesca's body very close to his as they rode the elevator up to his apartment, so close she could feel the heat of his body scorching her right through her clothes. The pads of his fingers continued to trace his name along the back of her thigh, up close to the cheeks of her butt, his fingertips brushing along her bottom as well. She'd worn a thong and he had a lot of skin to explore. He did so almost absently, while she was a bundle of nerves, her heart beating wildly out of control.

His arm was a steel band just under her breasts, locking her in front of him. His erection was long and thick and jerked hard against her back as the elevator ascended. He didn't speak, but the hand tracing his name into her skin suddenly cupped her bottom, fingers pressing deep, almost to the point of pain, but it was an exquisite pain, sending darts of fire straight to her sex.

The elevator jerked to a stop and the doors opened. He caught her up without preamble, just swung her into his arms as if he couldn't take another moment without her. He strode into the apartment straight to the nearest surface, the long, narrow, gleaming sideboard that jutted out from the decorative post to serve as a partial room divider. Sweeping the sideboard clean of the books, he laid her down, his body coming over hers to pin her there.

Stefano's mouth found hers, and the kiss was unlike

anything she'd ever known. Devastatingly sweet turned instantly hot, hard and demanding. The kiss continued to evolve, going rough and insistent before his mouth left hers and began to trail a path of kisses, nips and licks down to her chin. Francesca's hands clutched either side of his skull, holding on in an effort to stay anchored and sane as he continued kissing his way down her throat.

He sucked gently at her skin and then laved the spot with his tongue before proceeding to the next spot as though he planned to cover every inch of her with teeth, lips and tongue. His hand slid up her inner thigh, the pads of his fingers like hot brands, tracing his name into her sensitive skin there. She squirmed, bucking her hips, needing more contact, feeling as though a fire burned out of control between her legs.

He caught at the front of her dress—the beautiful, exquisite designer dress he'd bought her—and ripped the thin material right down the front, so that her generous breasts spilled out. Instantly his mouth covered her right breast, pulling her nipple deep. The nearly painful pleasure had her arching her back, trying to come up off the narrow sideboard, a little cry of pure need escaping.

The hand at her thigh caught at her damp panties, tugged hard and tossed them away, onto the elegant floor of his apartment. Francesca could feel the hard, cool surface of the marble sideboard against her bare butt. His fingers went straight, unerringly, to her clit, and another strangled sound escaped, this one nearly a sob.

"Stefano." His name came out low, needy, more of a whispered pant than anything else. "That feels . . . extraordinary."

His mouth moved over the curve of her breast, suckling gently, and then he lifted his head, his fingers still working between her legs. His gaze was fierce, possessive, the blue so dark with hunger her womb spasmed.

"How many men have fucked you?"

Shocked, she let her eyes fly open and both hands went to his wrist, the one between her legs. She tried to pull his hand away, but he was far too strong. She couldn't sit up, couldn't move; he had her pinned there like a butterfly stretched out on a mat.

"Stefano."

"Answer me. How many?"

She blushed. An entire body blush. Her body had melted until she felt boneless, incapable of fighting the flood of need his fingers produced. He didn't look away from her, his blue eyes boring into her, mesmerizing, demanding her response.

"That's none of your business." Her voice was low, shaky even. He was scaring her just a little bit. She was alone with him and her body had long since betrayed her. She knew she would never get over wanting him. His mouth. His touch. She felt empty, and she needed him to fill her.

"Fucking answer me now, Francesca."

Even his voice was scary. She couldn't imagine anyone disobeying him. He didn't raise his voice; in fact, if anything he lowered it. She lay there, totally exposed, naked, his fingers inside of her, moving in a hard, stroking rhythm that sent her brain into total chaos.

She moistened her lips with the tip of her tongue and capitulated. "One. I've had one man. Once."

He stilled. Even his fingers. She writhed. Bucked her hips. Needing those strokes. She'd been close. So close and now it was all fading away. He was still in his suit, even his jacket, and she was naked, her bare butt on a marble sideboard. Her hips moved involuntarily, but he didn't take the hint.

"*One? Once?* Did the fucker even get you off?" He sounded angry. As if her admission had enraged him.

Now even the fact that his finger was still pressed over her clit and another one had worked its way inside her, stretching her, causing a slow burn, couldn't keep that feeling of terrible need going. She pulled desperately at his wrist, trying to remove his hand so she could sit up.

"Stefano, let me up."

"Not a fucking chance in hell, Francesca. Now answer

me. Did he make you come? Was it at least good for you? Did he take his time?"

"Why are you asking me?" This was so humiliating. He was pure stone, with the exception of his eyes. She hadn't known blue could turn into a flame. That desire could be so intense it was stamped into every line of his face.

"Bambina." He made an effort to gentle his voice. "My cock is as hard as a fucking steel spike. In case you haven't noticed, I'm on the very edge of my control. I don't want to hurt you and I need to know just how much you can take. I'm feeling rough, brutal even. I want to fuck you so hard you feel my cock all the way in your belly. In your throat. So please answer me, *dolce cuore*."

One possessive hand swept down her body, from her neck to the vee at the junction of her legs. The finger pressing down on her clit moved. Circled. Sent waves of lightning streaking through her. Just like that she couldn't see straight. Couldn't move. She belonged to him. Would always belong to him.

Francesca shook her head. "No, it wasn't good." The admission came out a whisper. "You've made me feel more just now than I ever felt with him."

There was a silence as his blue gaze moved over her body. "You're mine, Francesca." He made the statement quietly.

Her heart pounded. It was the way he said it. The way his blue gaze branded her, every inch of her.

"Your body is mine. No one touches you. No one else ever puts their hands or their mouth on you. I'm not easy, *dolce cuore*, but I'm yours. I swear that to you. I'm yours, and I'm going to make you feel so good." He didn't wait for a reply, bending to take her mouth.

Her heart stuttered as his declaration and kiss swept every bit of sanity out of her head. He kissed his way to the swell of her breast, sucking and nipping with his teeth until the little stings and soothing caresses had her gasping for breath and moaning low in her throat. His mouth and teeth trailed fire right down the center of her body, to her belly button, where he paused to swirl and dip his tongue, and then his mouth continued the journey, to claim every inch of her body. He sucked hard in spots, bit down until she jumped or cried out with the shocking bite of pain and then the soothing caress of his tongue. Just like that, he took her back to that place, surrounded by him, willing to be his, needing him.

He dragged her body closer to the edge, forcing her legs over his shoulders as he continued the assault on her senses, his tongue sweeping across her clit so that she nearly jumped right out of her skin. She heard her low, keening cry filling the room as his tongue began a dance over her most sensitive spot, flicking hard and then softly stroking until she thought she'd go insane with need. He began to suckle, a strong, hard pull, while his tongue continued to flick and tease until she was thrashing wildly.

Nothing had prepared her for his assault on her nerve endings. Not that first fumbling boy who had come too fast and left her hurting and embarrassed, vowing never to try sex again. Not her own fingers when she was desperate for something she didn't understand, chasing a feeling that would never come.

Stefano was relentless, not giving her time to think or breathe. He just took over her body, his finger sliding into her wet tightness, curving, finding that perfect spot deep inside she hadn't even known existed. The gathering tension coiled so tightly she knew a tsunami was coming.

"Touch your nipples, Francesca," he ordered. "Pinch and pull, hard. Like I did. Don't be afraid of being rough. You like that. Every time I bit down, I could feel how wet you got for me. So hot. So slick. I want to watch you."

She'd never done anything like that, but she didn't think to disobey him. Her hands slid up her body to cup the weight of her breasts in her palms and then she flicked her nipples experimentally. She wanted his mouth back. He was poised, right there. She could feel his breath on her clit, his lips so close. His eyes, those twin blue flames, burned into her, watching her, waiting for her to do as he told her. She knew if she didn't, he wouldn't give her what she wanted.

Her fingers pinched her nipples. Tugged. Rolled.

"Harder, *bella*." His lips, when he spoke, teased her clit.

A moan escaped. His demands only made her body climb higher with need. She did as he said, tugging harder. Pinching and pulling. Streaks of fire raced straight to her center so that her inner muscles spasmed, contracted, so close, the terrible pressure building even more. His shoulders held her legs spread wide, while his mouth worked at her and his finger continued to push that need to the breaking point.

She writhed and tried to push against him. She needed a moment. Just one moment to catch her breath, to get back her sanity, to try to still her wild mind enough to think, but he pressed one hand flat on her belly, fingers splayed wide, easily controlling her, holding her in place so that she had no choice but to plead for release. She begged him as he took her close several times, but stopped or slowed before she could tip over the edge.

He plunged a second finger into her without any warning, simultaneously giving her an order. "Now, baby, come for me now." She did, screaming, as her body shattered, fragmented, her back arching, her hips bucking, a sob welling up as the tsunami roared through her.

Stefano's blue eyes were dark with satisfaction, arrogance stamped into every sensual line. He slowly straightened, taking her legs with him as he did so. He ran his hands over her body, from her breasts, down her narrow rib cage to her belly and then along her thighs. Francesca couldn't move, her body so boneless she thought she might have melted into the marble she lay on.

He reached down and caught both her wrists in one hand, pulling his tie from around his neck with the other. He wrapped the soft tie quickly around her wrists and then pulled her arms above her head, securing the loop he'd made into a hook built into the wall at the end of the sideboard. He accomplished the entire thing with dizzying speed. She actually didn't comprehend what he'd done until he stepped back from the table, slowly shrugging out of his jacket, his eyes never leaving her face. He smiled, a feral, predatory smile as he slowly unbuttoned his shirt while the fact dawned on her that she was his captive.

Francesca tugged at her hands, still dazed, watching him as his hand slowly undid his belt buckle and unzipped the fly of his trousers. "Stefano?" Her voice was weak with excitement and trembling with fear.

"You're all mine, *amore*, and you're going to have no doubts about that by the end of this night."

She had no doubts already and watching him remove his trousers to reveal his heavy erection only added to the scorching heat building so fast inside her. He was impressive and beautiful to her. She'd never thought a man could look so hot as he stepped in close again.

"You on birth control, Francesca?" he asked. His hand slid down her belly to the junction of her legs. His hands stayed right there, waiting for her answer.

She couldn't find her voice, so she just nodded.

"I'm clean, *dolce cuore*. I've never fucked a woman without being gloved. Not ever." He had her spread wide still, his body forcing her legs apart while his hand circled the girth of his cock. "You come when I tell you, Francesca. You understand me, *bambina*. When *I* say. I'm going to make this good for you, but you listen to me and do what I say."

She shivered at the sheer arrogance, at the intense hunger in his hooded gaze. He bent to flick her nipple with his tongue and then he used his teeth, biting down while he rubbed the head of his cock over her clit, back and forth. She nearly exploded again, the bite of pain adding to the pleasure storming through her.

Francesca hadn't thought it would be possible to be so needy again so fast, but within moments she was squirming, trying to impale herself on that teasing spike that rubbed so seductively over her very sensitive bud.

"Look at me, Francesca. Keep your eyes open and keep looking at me while I take you."

The hard authority in his voice sent more liquid heat to bathe her entrance. He mesmerized her, captured her with his sheer personality. She couldn't have looked away even if the room filled with people. She was well and truly his.

Stefano slid his cock inch by inch, as slowly as he possibly could, into Francesca's scorching sheath, drawing out the moment as long as possible, savoring the feeling of her oh so fucking tight channel reluctantly giving way for him. He could feel every heartbeat right through his cock. He'd never been so hard in his life. So near the loss of control when control was everything to him.

It might make him the biggest bastard in the world, but he liked that she was his to teach all the things he liked, the things he needed. He was a jealous son of a bitch, although that trait was brand-new, just emerging since he'd found her, but the thought of another man with his cock inside her made him killing crazy. He could understand why he'd been taught discipline at an early age. One couldn't hunt down some boy who had stolen his woman's virginity from him and kill him, although he acknowledged the urge to do so was there. He didn't ask his name because he didn't fully trust himself to act in a civilized manner. He didn't feel civilized when he was around Francesca. He felt primitive, a savage brute who would keep his woman away from other men by any means available to him.

He loved watching her eyes widen with shock as he pushed through those tight, scorching-hot petals. So tight she was strangling the life out of him, but he was going to die a happy man. It was a form of ecstasy, the pleasure and pain mixing until he wasn't certain where one began and the other left off, but there was no way he'd ever stop. No. Fucking. Way.

Finally, he managed to bottom out, forcing her body to take all of him. He was long and thick and she was so tight that for a moment he had to fight for control to keep from spilling his seed right there and then. Fucking perfect.

He stared down at her, his cock swelling impossibly more at the sight. She was spread out like a feast, his marks all over her. Bite marks branding her as his, purple circles coming up where he'd suckled her delicate skin, forming a pretty necklace that declared to the world she belonged to a very possessive man.

Watching her eyes, he pulled back slowly, savoring the feeling of her tight muscles dragging over his throbbing cock as he withdrew. Blood pounded through the thick, heavy spike in time to his heartbeat, proclaiming his hungry, urgent need. Her eyes widened. Her mouth formed a perfect little *O*. He loved how she looked, her breasts jutting upward, nipples tight, arms stretched over her head, hands bound together, his marks all over her little curvy, smoking-hot body. His. All. His.

He tried for control. For careful. Mindful of her innocence. Mindful that she was new at this. But heaven help him, she started moaning. Whimpering. Mewling like a little kitten. Her body writhed and bucked and deep inside he felt the tremors, the way her tight muscles milked and gripped. It would have been too much for a saint and he was the devil himself, so there was no way to stop him from driving deep. Francesca let out a small scream that vibrated right through his cock, destroying his self-control completely.

He slammed home. Brutally. Rough as sin. Fire streaked through him. White lightning. She cried out as his fingers dug deep into her hips and yanked her into him as he hammered into her. Over and over. Not letting up. Taking her. Pounding without mercy for either of them.

His hands cupped her ass, that beautiful delectable, *edible* ass he loved to watch as she walked. He'd dreamed of her ass, had multiple fantasies about it. He dug his fingers into her and held her pinned, completely immobile while he lost himself in her. He'd never fucked so hard in his life. She screamed when he bore down hard over her clit. Thankfully that hadn't been a scream of pain. He wasn't certain he could have slowed down or stopped.

Francesca stared at him with dazed, shocked eyes. Obeying him. Remembering on her own to let him see what he was doing to her. How she was reacting. He was out of control, but thank fuck she gave him her eyes so he could ensure she was enjoying what he was doing to her. Her breasts jolted invitingly with every brutal thrust. Her breath came in ragged, gasping pants, adding to the music of her whimpers, screams and the sound of his name, so breathy he wanted to double his efforts to hear more. He'd never seen anything so fucking hot in his life.

Stefano couldn't pretend he hadn't been with a lot of women before Francesca. He'd felt momentary pleasure—a *lot* of pleasure. The truth was, he had an intense job, and fucking was release to him. It was good and he liked it, but being with Francesca wiped out every other time before her. He knew he would never forget this moment as long as he lived. The way she looked. The way he felt. His cock was in fucking heaven, the pleasure ripping through his body, until every nerve ending he had was a part of the fireball streaking through him.

He used his hands to control her hips, to place her in the best position, tilting her until he heard her gasp as his cock sawed over her clit and hit that sweet spot deep inside her over and over. The pounding beat thundered in his ears, roared through his body as he felt her shudder from the pleasure he created with his cock hitting that perfect spot. He wanted to feel her come apart from the inside.

He watched her face. Her eyes. Her head thrashed and she moaned continuously, her breath hissing out of her. She was close. So close. He wanted it all from her. Her orgasm, so strong she convulsed, her submission, so total she knew she belonged to him. He wanted her to know *he* gave that to her, an all-consuming rush of fucking heaven.

"Keep looking at me, *dolce cuore*—don't look away. Stay with me."

Her lashes had begun to drift down, her head turning to one side. At his command, she struggled to obey.

"Francesca, come now for me. I want to feel it. Let go for me." He wasn't asking. He poured steel into his voice as he hammered deep.

He rammed into her over and over, harder than ever, each thrust jolting her body. He was merciless, relentless, pounding his cock right into her G-spot. "Now, baby," he reiterated. "Let go."

Francesca's gaze clung to his, and he knew the exact moment she gave herself to him. The submission. The trust. She let go and gave herself into his keeping. She screamed, loud and long, a wail that filled the room as her sweet, scorching-hot sheath clamped down on his cock like a fucking vise, taking him with her. Her body shook, breasts dancing, hips bucking, legs stiffening as she mewed, her inner muscles convulsing over and over, as her climax ripped through her. Jet after jet of hot seed pumped into her, filling her, prolonging and adding to the strength of her orgasm.

He stayed locked to her, feeling her body convulse around his, over and over, the aftershocks nearly as strong as the continuous climax. He had no idea until then that perfection could actually be achieved, but that moment was utter perfection. Looking at her. The dazed look in her eyes. Her flushed body covered with his marks and brands. He fucking loved that. His body joined with hers so that they shared the same skin. Her sheath, so scorching hot surrounding him, still milking his cock while his seed boiled inside of her.

He wished he had recorded it, so he could replay his claiming her over and over. If he could have, he would have ordered his name tattooed across her breasts. He'd have it branded on her ass. He wanted every other man in the world to see her like this, under him, in complete and total submission. He'd been a selfish bastard taking her like that, but he wanted her to know who he was, the kind of man she'd be living with. He'd been half terrified that she wouldn't be able to take him, but she'd loved every single thing he'd done to her. Yeah. She was exactly what he needed in his bed.

His woman. A woman he never believed he'd ever have. Not. Fucking. Ever. He hadn't believed he would have anything or anyone that was totally his alone. He'd lived his entire life knowing his life wasn't his own and never would be. He'd been born a shadow rider and that meant he had responsibilities not only to his family, but to others. He couldn't walk away from those responsibilities, not ever.

"You're so fucking beautiful, Francesca," he said. "I'm not nearly finished with you. I'm going to take you in so many ways tonight you'll be so sore you won't be able to move tomorrow." He wanted to come all over her beautiful breasts and rub his seed into her skin. Into her pores. Without unlocking himself from her body, he reached up and carefully unhooked his tie and gently pulled her arms down. The movement caused another powerful aftershock so that her sheath clamped down again, massaging life back into his cock.

She let out a small whimper and he immediately ran one hand down her body, from her throat to her belly in a soothing caress. "Relax, *amore*, let me get this." He unwrapped her wrists and kneaded her arms, making certain the blood flow hadn't been interrupted.

"Do you do that a lot?" The question was hesitant. Her voice trembled.

His gaze jumped to hers, trying to assess exactly what she meant. Exactly what was bothering her. "Do what?"

She gestured with her chin toward his tie. "That."

"I would have used my belt, but the tie was softer."

She took a breath, her face flushing. "Do you tie up all your women, Stefano?"

"I've never tied up another woman. Never. Why would I bother? They didn't belong to me, *bambina*. You belong to me. Only you."

Relief crept into her eyes. It wasn't that he'd tied her hands that bothered her, only the thought that he might have done the same to another woman. He fucking loved that. Reluctantly he allowed his cock to slip out of her. For one brief moment he'd been sated. That was already gone. Just seeing her body spread out before him like a feast was enough to get him started again. Catching her ankles, he slowly lowered her legs from his shoulders to the sideboard and then he reached for her.

He swept her into his arms, cradling her close to his body. "Put your arms around my neck."

"My clothes . . ." She looked around her a little helplessly.

"Sorry, *bella*." He couldn't quite help the laughter in his voice. "I destroyed them." He strode through the large apartment to the master bedroom.

Her fingers clutched his shoulder. "My room is the other way."

"This is your room. You belong with me." There was no room for argument. She was sleeping in his bed and would for the rest of her life. "And you'll sleep naked or in some hot little number that I'll rip off you in three seconds flat. I want to feel your soft skin next to me, and know that all I have to do is roll over and push my cock deep inside you anytime I feel like it."

He took her right through his bedroom to the master bath and set her feet on the tiles. With one arm locking her to him, he ran warm water over a washcloth and then crouched in front of her. "Widen for me, Francesca."

She blushed. It was cute as hell, especially given the way he'd fucked her. He tapped her inner thigh when she didn't obey him. She dropped a hand to his shoulder to steady herself but obediently spread her legs for him.

"I'd prefer to do that myself."

She had a little snippy bite to her voice that made him smile. "You're mine, *bambina*—that makes this my privilege." He carefully washed her thighs and then pressed the cloth against her slick heat. "Did I hurt you?"

She shook her head. "You know you didn't. It was . . . amazing."

When he finished he leaned into her and pressed a kiss in the dark curls. "Go lie on the bed, Francesca. On your stomach."

Her small white teeth sank into her lower lip. "Stefano . . ." She broke off when he gave her a hard look.

"I'm not fucking around tonight, *dolce cuore*. I waited too long for you. Go lie on the bed."

She took a breath as he stood, deliberately towering over her, crowding her space. "Do you have any idea how scary you can be?"

He tipped her face up to his and leaned down to brush a kiss across her mouth. "Sadly, Francesca, you'll get over that all too soon." He turned her around, gave her a swat on her bare ass, at the same time giving her a small push toward the bedroom.

Francesca yelped and threw him a smoldering look over her shoulder, one hand rubbing at his handprint on her bottom as she made her way back into the bedroom. He threw back his head and laughed. She was *everything*. To the outside world, he had it all. But his brothers, his sister . . . He shook his head, his smile fading. His cousins in New York, the ones in San Francisco and those overseas, shadow riders, all of them had no life and no hope of one. Not one that belonged to them. Until Francesca.

Word had spread fast through the family that Stefano had found a woman and that not only was she capable of producing shadow riders, but he had fallen for her. They actually had real chemistry. It wouldn't be a marriage of convenience, but a true love match if he could manage to make her fall for him. If he could keep her. For him, Stefano knew there wasn't an *if*. He *would* keep her because now, for him, there wasn't a choice. He couldn't give her up. He wouldn't have done so before he fucked her, but now, after having his cock inside of her, after feeling her tight, scorching body surrounding his, he'd move heaven and earth to make her happy. To keep her.

She represented hope for his cousins, for his brothers and

sister. If Stefano could find Francesca, they had a chance. He glanced through the open doorway and his heart nearly stopped. His woman had done as he'd asked. She lay in the middle of the bed, facedown, nothing covering her bare body, just stretched out on top of the sheets, her face buried in the crook of her arm.

His heart swelled with pride. She was shy with him. A little scared. She had courage and had shown him more than once that she could stand up to him, but she'd *chosen* to obey his orders. She'd given him her trust again. He stood there a long time, one hip against the doorjamb, his gaze devouring her while emotions he'd never felt before threatened to overwhelm him.

He took his time cleaning his cock and thighs before going to her. She didn't move when he put a knee to the bed and then straddled her thighs. "You asleep, Francesca?"

"Not yet. Just drifting."

The drowsy note in her voice had his cock coming to attention. "Keep drifting." He bent to press a kiss between her shoulder blades and then he reached down to run his fingers down her left arm. "Give me your hand, *dolce cuore*." He shackled her wrist with his fingers and she turned it over.

Stefano pulled the ring out of the box sitting on the end table beside his bed and slipped it onto her finger. It looked good there. Perfect. A claim to the world that she belonged to him. If the world couldn't see the necklace of love bites, or the brands he'd put on her skin with his teeth, then his ring would have to do.

She pulled her hand to her face the moment he released her. He felt the sharp inhale as she took in the exquisite diamond surrounded by glittering smaller ones, smaller, but no less beautiful. "Stefano, I can't wear this."

"You'll wear it." He began to massage her shoulders and back, using firm, hard strokes to ease the tension out of her muscles.

"It's too expensive. What if I lose it?"

He liked that. She wasn't afraid of wearing it to proclaim to the world she was his, only that she might lose it.

"Then I'll buy you another one. You're mine and it matters to me that everyone knows you belong to me. I don't want other women like Janice or Doreen to make you doubt what I feel for you. When you're not right beside me, I want you to have absolute confidence that you're all I'm thinking about. You're the one woman I care about."

Her face was turned to one side, but he saw the small smile forming on her soft lips. He slid off of her, his hands catching her around her waist, pulling her up onto her knees and then pressing her chest to the mattress with one hand, leaving her ass in the air. He knelt behind her, his hands rubbing her bare cheeks. He was extremely fond of her ass, that firm, rounded, almost heart-shaped butt with a small dimple that he couldn't help leaning into to bite.

She cried out, but she didn't move from the position he'd placed her in, and when he pushed his fingers into her, he found her slick with her special brand of honey. "I love that you're ready for me, Francesca," he confessed.

"I think I'll always be ready for you, Stefano," she admitted. "Just the sound of your voice makes me wet."

She couldn't say things like that to him without his cock getting so hard it hurt like a bear. He pressed the broad, weeping head of his cock to her hot entrance and waited a heartbeat. Two. Savoring the moment. Loving the look of her. "I want my seed all over you and in you," he declared fiercely. "I want to cover your back, your ass and your breasts, Francesca, and then rub it in. I want to fuck your mouth and come down your throat. I want you every single way I can have you. Does that scare you?"

There was a pause. A silence while his heart slammed hard in his chest and his cock throbbed with the need to be inside her.

"Only because I don't know what I'm doing yet and I don't ever want to disappoint you," she replied softly.

He slammed into her. Deep. Watched his cock disappear into her and it was hot just holding himself there, very still, while his cock pulsed deep inside her. Taking her this way allowed him to go even deeper. She pushed back. Wiggled. Reminding him she wanted more. He laughed softly and swatted her heart-shaped ass just to see his handprint there, another brand. "Eager little thing. You can just wait. I'll give you whatever you're going to get when I'm ready."

"Macho much?" she muttered.

He flexed his fingers on her hips. He loved when she defied him. Or talked back. He loved when she submitted her will to his. He loved her sexy body and the fire she surrounded him with. He really, really loved how fucking tight and scorching hot she was. He eased back, deciding to take his time and make this last. Then he heard her sharp gasp, the ragged little protest as she tried to chase him with her hips and he took her in another brutal, merciless assault. He hadn't meant to, but her little sexy moans and whimpers, the pleas and soft little sobs, robbed him of control every time.

Stefano pounded into her, letting the thunder roar in his ears, hearing the music of her cries, feeling the absolute paradise of her sheath and he just gave himself up to that ecstasy. He took her up over and over, forcing her to shatter around him three times before he finally emptied himself in her. Before he collapsed on top of her, driving her down to the mattress with his heavy weight.

It took a long time before he could catch his breath enough to ease off of her. She moaned but didn't move. He cleaned her up and then himself before falling into bed beside her.

"I swear, *bella*, a couple of more times and I'll be able to find my gentle and take you slow and sweet the way I should have done the first time," he promised, curling his body around hers. He pinned her by draping one thigh over both her legs and then cupped her breast in his hand, his thumb lazily strumming her nipple. He pushed his semihard cock into the sweet crease between her cheeks, so that it nestled there, all warm and happy.

"A couple of more times and I won't be able to get up and go to work tomorrow," she pointed out with a small, whispery laugh that played along his nerve endings. She pushed her buttocks back into the cradle of his hips, driving his cock deeper into her.

He fucking loved that. "I meant to talk to you about that, *dolce cuore*—there's no need to work anymore. It might be a good thing if you let me tell Pietro that you aren't coming back."

She leaned down and sank her teeth into his arm. Hard. *"Dannazione donna!* Seriously?"

"I'm working, and don't you dare talk to Pietro. I mean it, Stefano. You do that, and I won't be sleeping in this bed or this apartment. You don't get to dictate to me."

She didn't lift her head from the pillow again; her tone was mild, but she meant it. That didn't sit well with him.

"First, Francesca, don't ever threaten to leave me. You won't make it out the door. I want you very, very clear on that. Second, something matters to you, it matters to me, so just say so without the drama. The bite, okay, I get that, but not the threat. Are we clear?"

"Yes, honey, we're clear," she said softly. "Now I really have to sleep."

"I was going to let you sleep," he pointed out, "but now you fucking made my cock hard again with that bite. You have to take care of that before you can sleep."

"You'll have to do that work."

"Fine by me. I wanted to fuck your breasts and cover you in me. That okay with you?"

"Everything you do is okay with me," she said, and rolled over onto her back. "I might be a little afraid sometimes, Stefano, but I'm always willing to try."

"*Dio, bambina*, you make me almost humble. I'm too fucking arrogant to actually be humble, but it's there."

He was rewarded with her laughter. He straddled her body, rubbing his balls along her belly. She felt so little under him. So soft. He cupped her breasts in his hands before leaning down to give them attention. "I'm going to see if I can make you come without doing anything but using my hands and mouth on your breasts and then I'll fuck you right here. I won't be cleaning you up, Francesca. You're going to go to sleep with me all over you."

"Why do I find that so hot? You're making me wet all over again," she accused. "Can you really do that?"

He proceeded to show her he could.

CHAPTER SIXTEEN

Fortunately, or unfortunately—staring at herself in the mirror, Francesca couldn't decide which—she had had the weekend off. She couldn't get up and go to work after she'd practically thrown a tantrum fighting for the right to do so. That meant Stefano stayed in his apartment with her and they'd barely made it out of bed. When they did, that didn't seem to matter to him. He took her in the kitchen on the table. On the counter. On the floor in the hall. Up against the wall in the living room. On furniture. In the shower.

Stefano was creative and he'd seemed determined to know every inch of her body and claim it for his own. She was fine with that at the time. Now, looking at the marks on her, the ones she'd loved him putting there, she thought maybe she was a little crazy. The necklace of purplish bites on her neck had barely faded and she doubted if she could find anything to cover them when she went to work.

She swore she could still feel him deep inside her. She was fairly certain she had skid marks on her butt and floor burns on her back. She touched one of the bite marks on her left breast. Just that, the sweep of the pads of her fingers, made her shiver. That was how sensitive she was. That was how awake he made her body.

There was no noise—Stefano never made any when he walked—but he was there, behind her in the mirror, one arm snaking around her waist and pulling her back into him and locking her there. He'd just taken her in the shower, after she'd sucked him off in bed. Her body still was having aftershocks, which she hadn't thought possible just a few days ago. He nuzzled her neck.

"I love how you smell," he murmured, his tongue and teeth already wreaking havoc.

She watched the way her nipples came to twin hard peaks and felt her body melt right into his, pressing back into his bare skin. He was always hot and hard. Perfect. She reached back and circled his neck with one hand, the action lifting her breasts as if an offering. Instantly he cupped them in his hands, and she felt his teeth sink into that sweet spot between her neck and shoulders. That bite of pain coupled with the brush of his thumbs on her nipples sent a spasm through her sex.

"You're so fucking beautiful, Francesca." His eyes met hers in the mirror. "You sure you don't want me to talk to Pietro? I'm all for staying in another few days."

"I'd love to," she answered honestly. "But I can barely walk. I'm sore, Stefano. Seriously sore and I can't seem to resist you. I'm also not going to be a kept woman. I need to earn my own money."

His head came up, body going still. His arm tightened into an iron band. "You're sore? Why didn't you say something to me?"

She turned in his arms and wrapped both hands around the nape of his neck. She knew him now. He was totally protective. He would *detest* that she was sore and he hadn't noticed or thought of it. Well, he'd thought of it; he'd run her a hot bath countless times, but she always ended up straddling his lap and they'd make a mess of the bathroom floor, water everywhere from their splashing in the tub. She shouldn't have said anything to him.

"Honey, I *loved* what we were doing. I wasn't going to miss one moment of it. I'm not *that* sore." That was a lie. She winced because he knew it. His expression told her he did. That and the sudden swat on her bare butt. He smacked her hard. "Ow. Seriously?" She tried to pull away from him but his arm didn't budge. He didn't even act like she'd moved.

"Don't fucking lie to me. Not. Ever. I don't like that I hurt you, Francesca. I like rough sex. I like knowing you're mine and I can put my mark on you and you love it. But not at the cost of hurting you. That's not okay." He suddenly caught both her wrists, pulled them to him so he could inspect them. He'd tied her up more than once. She knew it was more for fun than anything else, but he liked it. He liked having her at his mercy and she'd enjoyed those times with him especially.

"No bruises," she pointed out hastily. "Stefano, I wouldn't have wanted to miss one moment with you. It was the most beautiful weekend I've ever had in my life. I do have to get dressed for work though, and so do you."

He sighed, bending his head to press kisses into the pulse beating in her inner wrist. "You don't have to work. That doesn't make you a kept woman. When we have children, I want you to be with them, not working in some fucking deli so you can call yourself independent. You're never going to be independent. I'm your man, *bambina*, and that means you lean the fuck on me."

"We don't have children yet, Stefano. And stop saying *fuck*. I mean it. You need to clean up your language. Sometimes you use that word twice in the same sentence. When we have children, I don't want that to be the first word out of their mouths."

He stared down into her eyes, holding her there like he could, just with his gaze, mesmerizing her. Keeping her captive, under his spell. A slow smile transformed the hard edges of his handsome face. He was so beautiful to her. A gorgeous man and she was falling more and more in love with him.

He'd spent the entire weekend worshiping her body. Claiming her so possessively. Insisting on feeding her. Washing her. Brushing her hair. He treated her like a princess when he wasn't pounding into her. She liked the pounding most of all. And when he slowed it down and took her breath away, he brought tears to her eyes.

"I can do that for you," he agreed. "But you do something

for me. Start thinking of us together. What I have is yours. What you have is mine."

She swallowed hard. Shook her head. Felt tears burn behind her eyes and blinked rapidly in an effort to keep them at bay. "I don't have anything to give you, Stefano. I'm not bringing anything to the relationship but trouble. Barry Anthon is trouble. You know that. Any way you look at it, he's trouble. You have so much money, and you're so— extraordinary. You are. I'm . . ."

He took her mouth, cutting her off. His hands slid down her back, following the curve of her spine to her butt, his hands drifting lower to grip and pull her in tightly so that his cock was pressed hard against her. "Are you wet for me, *dolce cuore*?"

"I am," she whispered. "Of course I am. How could I be anything else when you touch me, Stefano?"

"That's what you bring to me, Francesca. That's what you give to me. You. Your trust. Your body. I want to do all sorts of things to you. Things that scare the hell out of you, things you're still a little too innocent for, but you trust me and let me do them anyway. You give me that, and it's the greatest gift a man can get. When you go down on me, you enjoy it. You think about giving me pleasure, not what you're getting out of it. You think a man doesn't love that? Need it? To know that you love giving me that is everything. I have it all with you."

"Stefano, I hesitate to tell you this, because you might be just a teensy bit arrogant, but *any* woman would do that with you. How could they not?"

He shook his head. "I've had more women than I ever want to admit to you, but I didn't want to do jack to them. Just get off. That was it. I wanted to fuck their brains out and get them the hell away from me. I didn't feel anything but that rush, *dolce cuore*, that release. With you . . ." He broke off, shaking his head. "I think about you every minute of the fucking day. I wake up in a sweat, wanting you, my body so fucking hard it's painful. I jacked off thinking about you wearing my coat a hundred times. It's pathetic how obsessed I am with you."

Her heart pounded. So did her clit. Deep inside she felt a desperate spasm. Her hand dropped to his cock. "I think now would be a good time to lift me up and let me wrap my legs around your waist. I don't care if I'm a little late for work. Pietro won't fire me, will he?" She leaned into him, her teeth closing over his earlobe. "And just for the record, you said 'fuck' three times just now."

There was pure seduction in her sultry voice and in her stroking fingers. She was getting darned good at learning what he liked. She paid attention because he was right; his pleasure did matter to her. She wanted to see that pleasure on his face, feel it in his body, in the spill of his seed when he took her. She loved the expression he got when he was inside her, when her body gripped and milked his. Just that could get her off. That was how much she liked it.

"I'll get you off with my fingers, Francesca, but not my cock. You're sore and I'm not going to make it worse."

She blinked up at him, shocked. "You're turning me down?" She had never considered that he would, not for one moment. It hurt, even though intellectually, she knew how protective he was. He was as hard as a rock, but still, he'd turned her down the first time she'd initiated sex with him. That felt . . . *horrible*.

He swept her up into his arms, in that way he had, fast and irrevocably, *decisively*. Before she could protest, he dropped her on the bed, and was down on top of her, blanketing her body, his face buried between her legs, his cock poised over her mouth, an offering. Already his tongue and fingers were in play, working at her, driving her up so fast she couldn't quite catch her breath so she stroked his cock and then began to lick him as if he were an ice-cream cone.

Her mind had gone instantly into chaos, the roaring in her ears driving out everything but him. His body, so hot and hard, pinning her down. The way the head of his cock teased along the seam of her lips, so that she could taste the addicting little drops that made her hungry for more. His mouth bringing fire, his tongue stabbing deep, flattening against her clit while he stroked and made her burn.

She all but swallowed him down. She *loved* the shudder that ran through his body, the way his hips jerked involuntarily. *She* did that. Francesca Capello. The power was incredible. Knowing she pleased him, that she could bring him to the very edge of control, was a heady, wonderful feeling. It added to the pleasure his mouth and teeth and fingers brought her.

The more his cock swelled and surged, the more his tongue plunged and the fire leapt and burned. She drew him down, trying to take all of him—an impossible task, but one she worked on diligently, happily. She used her tongue and hollowed her cheeks, suckling strongly. Her hand slid over him easily, pumping, because she'd gotten him so wet with her mouth.

He lifted his head and growled. *Growled*. She loved that. "Harder, Francesca." It was a demand, nothing less.

She complied, clamping her mouth tight around him, gripping him with her fist tighter than she thought possible. He was like iron. Hot. Velvet soft. Perfect steel. She was close. So close. She wanted him with her because she knew when she exploded, she would have to stop and that would leave him frustrated.

His hips moved to a faster rhythm, driving deeper than she had ever previously taken him. She had nowhere to go. She thought she was in control, but realized he was. She was under him, his weight pinning her down, his hips suddenly in charge, not her hand. That only added to her excitement. She did trust him. She knew, even when he plunged deep and held himself there, she didn't panic when she couldn't breathe. Stefano would never, ever harm her.

She almost cried out when his cock withdrew. Remembering at the last moment to take a breath, she suckled hard, drawing him back, reveling in his possession. Then fire was streaking through her. It happened so fast, so hard, it took her off guard. At the same time his cock swelled, heated, pumped into her, down her throat, forcing her to swallow. That triggered an even bigger quake, her entire body rippling and shuddering with pleasure.

He lifted his face from between her legs, but kept his softening cock inside her mouth. "Gently, *dolce cuore*, but take care of me."

She loved when he did that, too, those little instructions on what his preferences were, what he enjoyed. She detested feeling as if she wasn't seeing to his every need or desire. He saw to hers and she wanted to do the same for him so when he told her exactly what he wanted or needed, it gave her even more confidence. For Francesca, knowing she gave him that was as necessary to her as breathing. She took her time, mindful of how sensitive he was, feeling every reaction, the way his breath hissed out of his lungs, the shudder of his body, the involuntary buck his hips gave.

"*Dio*, Francesca, you're incredible. I could spend the day with my cock in your mouth and never get enough."

She laughed softly as he withdrew. "I might like that. Now I need to brush my teeth and get ready for work. That was spectacular."

He rolled off of her, every line in his face stamped with a sensual dark passion as he watched her walk naked into the master bath. He'd just given her an amazing, powerful climax, but knowing he was watching made her hot all over again. He was turning her into a sex fiend.

"Word of our engagement is out," he announced, casually. Too casually.

She paused in the act of spreading toothpaste on her brush, turning to look through the doorway at him. "It is? How do you know?"

"Francesca. Seriously? You're mine. I want the entire world to know. I had our publicity person put out a press release."

She smiled at him, shaking her head. "You don't do anything the slow way, do you?" She turned back to brush her teeth.

"Not when it comes to you. The point I'm making is that anything a Ferraro does is news. It's a huge thing to have one of us engaged. When I say 'huge,' I mean it will be reported, not only in this country, but in other countries as well. Our bank is international and one of the largest."

Francesca's heart dropped. Somersaulted. Beat too fast. She took her time, finishing her teeth and then rinsing her mouth multiple times before she turned back to him. "What exactly does that mean?"

"It means, *bambina*, reporters are going to be crawling all over this hotel. No member of our neighborhood would ever give you up, so you should be safe at work, but don't walk the streets where you could be spotted. I'll take you down the private elevator to an entrance that only my family uses and no one has knowledge of. Emilio and Enzo will be waiting with a car. You do whatever they say when they say it."

She walked barefoot over to the closet. Somehow her clothes had been transferred to the master bedroom sometime while she was at the club. She hadn't asked him about that, and now it seemed silly to do so. It had been presumptuous of him, but she was finding that Stefano was a very decisive and confident man. She liked having his eyes on her when she drew the sexy little boy shorts up her legs and settled them over her butt.

"Come here."

Francesca shivered at the command in his voice. Low. Sexy. So arrogant. She loved that, too. Holding her bra in her hand, she crossed the room to stand in front of him. He wiggled his finger in a little circle and obediently she turned her back to him.

His hands slid over the curves of her butt. "I left my mark on your ass. I can see it right through the lace. That's so fucking sexy, Francesca, I want to take another bite out of you." His hands stroked caresses over her bottom and then he touched several spots on her buttocks with his fingertips. When he pressed she knew exactly where each mark was. "I like my brand on you far too much, *bella*."

She shivered, her nipples peaking as she slid the satin-soft bra around to cup her breasts. The lace caressed her skin. She loved his brand on her far too much as well, but telling him that would only encourage him. "I think you're a little primitive."

"I'm okay with that." He caught her hand as she turned to get her clothes. "Where the hell is your engagement ring?"

"I can't wear it to work." She was horrified. "It's worth a car or something."

He was up in an instant, flowing out of the bed, every muscle coiled and ready to strike. He looked dangerous. Intimidating. He towered over her, and the very air pulsed around her with his anger. "Get. That. Ring. On. *Now.*"

Okay, bad move taking off the ring. She didn't even pretend to hesitate. She knew he would never strike her, but she also knew when he had that much anger over something, it meant a lot to him. She took the ring out of her drawer and shoved it back on her finger.

"Don't you ever fucking take that off again. You got me, Francesca? Are we clear on that? You tell me we're clear. I want to hear the words."

"We're clear, Stefano."

She heard the tremor in her voice and was instantly angry with herself. She didn't want him to ever think she was a pushover and wouldn't stand up to him. She put the ring on because it meant enough to him to be angry over it, not because she was afraid of him. Well. Not much. Well. Okay, maybe she was a little, or a lot, but in her defense, he could be very scary.

His hand snaked out, fingers curling around the nape of her neck and he yanked her to him, his mouth fastening on hers. It wasn't a nice kiss at all. Brutal. Merciless. Savage even. He was claiming her all over again and she knew it. Reveled in it. Drowned in it. She loved his mouth and the way he could use it. She was fairly certain no one else in the world could kiss like him. She didn't care if he devoured her. She wanted him to. She loved it when he got all macho and manly on her. Fear receded quickly when his mouth was on hers because inevitably, no matter how the kiss started, it always ended with her feeling as if he loved her. Wanted her. Even needed her.

When he lifted his mouth from hers, he pushed his forehead tight against hers. "You have to know how important you are to me, Francesca. My ring on your finger, everyone knowing we're engaged, these are ways to protect you. No one can fuck with you and live. It just wouldn't happen and anyone who knows me knows that. I need to know you're safe at all times."

"Emilio and Enzo will look after me," she soothed, moving away from him to pick up her clothes. She had to get dressed and get to work before Pietro decided she was fired, Stefano Ferraro's fiancée or not. "I won't take off my engagement ring, I promise. But it does bother me that Emilio and Enzo are with me instead of with you. I know they always looked after you."

"I can take care of myself, but you don't have to worry. I have more than two cousins who work as bodyguards. Tomas and Cosimo Abatangelo will be working with me. Ordinarily, they keep their eye on Emmanuelle. She's always giving them the slip and making them angry, but because of that, they're very, very observant."

"Why does Emmanuelle need a bodyguard?" She pulled on a pair of jeans. They fit like a glove and yet were very comfortable.

Stefano frowned at her as he began to dress as well. "*Dolce cuore*, wear that really beautiful skirt for me. The one with all the ruffles that falls to your ankles. I've wanted to see it on you from the moment I purchased it."

She paused in the act of zipping up the jeans. Her eyes met his. His gaze had darkened. Was sexy. Sensual. Hooded. Speculative. He was up to something. She glanced toward the closet where the skirt hung. She knew exactly which one he was talking about. She loved that skirt, but it seemed a little too nice to wear to work. Still, if it meant that much to him, and she could see by his expression it did, then she didn't mind in the least accommodating him.

She slid the jeans back down over her hips, watching his face. Watching the approval. The satisfaction. The sudden blaze of heat in his eyes.

"You won't need those sexy panties with that skirt, Francesca." His voice was pitched low, almost a growl. So sexy she felt the damp heat instantly.

"I'm going to work, Stefano." She tried to be firm. She couldn't just give him every little thing his heart desired, could she? He'd walk all over her.

"I was hoping to stop by work to see you, but I'll have less than an hour. No panties saves time."

She shivered. Her breasts ached. The heat between her legs burst into a full-out burn. Leaving her panties in place, she crossed to the closet and pulled down the skirt. "You could call me on that phone you gave me and give me the heads-up. I'll go to the restroom and remove my panties and be all ready for you. That way, I won't be dripping all day in anticipation."

"I like the idea of you dripping in anticipation all day. I could lick all that honey off your thighs when I come to see you."

She pressed her thighs together, trying not to squirm. "I'm wearing my panties, Stefano, so call when you want them off." She pulled on a matching blouse, one that didn't quite hide the necklace he'd given her. She touched one of the dark smudges with her fingertip. "I look like I'm in high school."

He laughed. "I'll be calling and texting, *bambina*, so keep your phone close and fucking answer it."

"What part of 'I'm working' don't you understand?"

"What part of 'fucking answer your phone when I call' don't you understand?" he countered. "I don't like you working, but I'm giving you what you want, so you give me this."

"You are exasperating," she informed him, pulling on knee-high boots. They were navy blue with three leather ruffles down the backs. They matched the skirt perfectly. "I'm leaving, but I'll keep my phone close."

"Wait for Emilio and Enzo. They'll come up and get you and take you to the other elevator." He caught her chin in his palm and kissed her. Hard. Perfect. "I'm calling them up to meet you now."

Francesca felt a little dazed when he released her. She nodded and forced herself to walk out of the bedroom. She got halfway down the hall when he called her. She turned back and he was leaning against the doorjamb, watching her. Naked. He looked gorgeous. Tough. Dangerous. Completely hot. And he was all hers. She quirked an eye at him, wishing she had his confidence. It didn't bother him in the least to be naked. She knew if the elevator doors opened and a crowd emerged, he wouldn't care.

"What time is your first break?"

"Around ten."

"Go straight to the restroom and lock the door."

Her entire body tightened. It was the way he said it. The look in his eyes. She couldn't imagine anyone sexier. She couldn't find her voice, her mouth had gone dry and the air seemed to have left her lungs. She just nodded and turned back toward the great room, to wait for Emilio and Enzo.

She was grateful for the bodyguards as the car she was in drove past the entrance of the hotel. Paparazzi were everywhere, a three-deep crowd laying siege in an effort to get pictures of her or Stefano, preferably both of them. In spite of the tinted windows she ducked down automatically.

"Is his life always like this?" she asked Emilio. She was becoming rather fond of both Emilio and Enzo. She knew they were devoted to Stefano and she liked them all the more for that.

"Yes," Emilio answered. "Don't worry, Francesca. We won't let them near you. Just stay away from the windows and if we warn you, leave the counter and go straight to the back. Pietro knows to protect you. He'll come out and handle customers. No one is going to talk about you or let on in any way that you're working there."

She shook her head. "The paparazzi pay good money to people for information. Don't count on it, Emilio."

Enzo snorted. "Seriously, Francesca? Do you really believe anyone would dare cross Stefano Ferraro? *Hell* no. No one in the neighborhood would be that stupid."

She frowned. It was back to the "mafia"-type warning. What did it matter if Stefano was upset with someone if they got paid an exorbitant fee for selling information? What would he do to them? Surely no one was that afraid. She shivered, remembering how he could look. One moment he was soft inside, looking at her with such a sweet look and the next, he was cold and distant, without expression. Scary.

The car pulled up behind Masci's Deli. She reached for the door handle but Emilio stopped her. "Wait until we clear the area. We'll give you the okay to get out, but you don't move until then."

She subsided against the seat with a little sigh. Becoming engaged to Stefano had changed her world all over again. She'd gone from homeless to being engaged to a very wealthy man in a very short time, and she felt like her mind couldn't quite catch up. She was very glad to get inside the deli, where only Pietro was waiting. Together they put everything in the cases and set up for the early-morning crowd.

She loved that it was so busy, keeping her from thinking too much, but by the time the first wave had come and gone, she found she was having to struggle to keep her mind from straying to Stefano and what he had planned for her ten o'clock break.

Joanna came in around nine, and since there were only a couple of people left to serve, Pietro told her to grab a coffee and visit for ten minutes. She did, slipping into the chair across from Joanna, feeling only a little bit of guilt that her boss was allowing her extra break time, but not too much because she wanted to show off her ring.

Joanna squealed loudly and appropriately. "I can't believe this. My best friend is going to marry Stefano Ferraro. That rock on your finger is worth a small house—you know that, don't you? It's beautiful. You're beautiful. I'm so happy for you, Francesca."

Francesca looked down at her ring. "It is beautiful, isn't it?" She found herself smiling at Joanna, so happy she wanted to cry. "How did things go with Mario?"

Joanna wrapped her arms around her middle. "Oh. My. God. He's *so* good in bed. Honest to God, Francesca, I'm having a mini-orgasm just remembering. He's the best dancer, and after you left, Emmanuelle and her cousins didn't desert us or make us feel as if we didn't belong. They were so nice. They picked up the tab for all the drinks and invited us back with them again. It was an amazing night. I would have been walking on air for months just from that alone, but then Mario took me to his apartment and I stayed there with him all weekend. He treated me like a princess. I could totally fall in love with him."

Francesca studied her face. Joanna had dated all the time and she hooked up with men often, but Francesca had never seen her like this. Her face was glowing and she couldn't stop smiling.

"So do you have another date with him lined up?"

Joanna nodded. "He made a point of saying he wanted us to be exclusive. He said he'd been waiting for an opportunity with me and he wasn't about to pass it up. He also said he wasn't about to let any other man edge him out, now that he had me."

Francesca was happy for her. "That's so awesome. I love that for you."

Joanna smirked. "Me, too. He's just everything I thought he would be and more." Her head went up and she widened her eyes. "I forgot. Were you listening to the news at all this morning? The three women arrested at the club, those singers who were so rude when they came to the table?"

"Stella, Janice and Doreen. The Crystals."

"Yep. That band. They pleaded guilty. Just like that. And there were multiple charges. No one does that. I've never heard of anyone so stinking rich with money to pay a really great attorney pleading guilty to that kind of charge. They aren't going into rehab—they're getting jail time. Why would they do that? And why in the world did their attorney allow them to? It doesn't make any sense at all."

"I didn't know they'd even go before a judge that fast other than to maybe set bail," Francesca murmured, unease creeping into her mind in spite of the happiness that had permeated her world all morning. Her fingers found her engagement ring and she absently played with it, trying not to think about what might cause three vindictive and very entitled women with the money to pay for a great attorney to plead guilty and allow a judge to sentence them without a trial.

"They're actually going to prison. Not jail. Prison," Joanna continued. "You just don't *ever* want to mess with the Ferraros. Anyone stupid enough to cross them has really bad karma."

Francesca didn't know what to say to that. "My former landlord was murdered," she blurted. "He was inside Giuseppi Saldi's home when he was murdered."

"I read about that. It was on the news as well. That was just weird, too."

Francesca nodded. "His aunt was actually swimming in the pool and when she got out, he was dead on the lounger, his throat cut."

"See? He messed with you and you're going to be a Ferraro and now he's dead. Do you think the Saldis killed him because they didn't want a war with Stefano's family?"

Francesca inhaled sharply. "I don't think it had anything at all to do with Stefano. He and his entire family were at the club, celebrating."

"Your engagement? I didn't even know it was an engagement party," Joanna said, sulking.

Francesca burst out laughing. "Neither did I."

Joanna stared at her a moment, wide-eyed and then she pretended to swoon. "That's the most romantic thing I've ever heard of."

Francesca rolled her eyes and went back to work as another wave of customers entered the store. She couldn't help but watch the clock as she waited on the various people. They were all very sweet to her and seemed to want to chat a little before handing over their money or credit cards, but she didn't mind in the least, other than she needed to keep the line moving.

Her heart beat very fast when Pietro came from the back room to take her place so she could have her break. She pulled off her apron and hurried to the restroom. The moment she had the door closed and locked, she removed her panties, bunching them into her hand. An arm came around behind her and took them away. She nearly screamed with shock, but his scent told her exactly who was there.

The room was fairly large but completely open. There was nowhere to hide. A sink, a toilet and a mirror were really all that was in the room, and yet Stefano had to have been somewhere. Maybe she'd been so eager she hadn't seen him when she hurried in. She started to turn.

"Stay still."

A clear order. She shivered, and remained facing away from him, growing damp and needy without anything else but the sound of his voice. She watched in the mirror as he bunched her panties into the palm of his hand and shoved them into the pocket of his suit.

He reached around her and began to undo the little pearl buttons of her blouse. The edges gaped open to reveal her breasts nestled in the lacy, satin-soft bra. Leaving her bra in place, he reached in and pulled out her breasts so they jutted up and out over the material, her blouse framing them. Francesca's breath caught in her throat as he reached down and took her hands in his, sliding them up her rib cage to press her fingers to her nipples.

"Work them for me, *dolce cuore*. You know how I like it. Rough. I want to see you panting. Needy. I love to see your hands on your body."

She licked at her lips, her breath already ragged. She

wasn't certain how he could do that, make everything feel so sexy, reduce her to a needy, melting woman wanting to beg him to hurry and take her. The fire built between her legs, scorching hot, and to her shock, she could actually feel the liquid need on her inner thighs as she complied with his order, tugging and rolling her nipples, watching him watch her in the mirror.

His hands went to either side of her hips, fisting the material of her skirt. Very slowly he began to pull it up, gathering it into his hands as the hem rose first over her boots and then her thighs and finally to her waist. He tied the skirt at her back, a quick twist and then a knot to keep it in place, his gaze never leaving hers.

"Harder, *bella*, pretend your hands are mine." His foot kicked her left leg wider and then her right. "I could hardly think straight this morning. Trying to work, go over reports, when all I wanted to do was get back to you. I thought about fucking you right on my desk at work. Or have you under it, sucking me off while I conducted business." His hand moved over her rounded cheeks, lingering on the marks he'd left there earlier. One hand pressed her head toward the floor.

She started to reach down and he stopped her. "I'll hold you. Trust me, Francesca. You keep working those nipples." His arm locked around her waist and then his hand was at her entrance, scooping out the honey and licking it off his fingers. "You taste so fucking good. Do you think I would have the control to talk on the phone, or have someone in the room while you were there, under my desk, my cock down your throat? Could I keep it together?"

"I hope not," she panted. "I hope I'd be making you feel so good you couldn't."

He'd already opened his trousers. When had he done that? She hadn't noticed because she was too busy trying to keep from melting into a hot little heap on the floor at his feet. He pressed the broad head of his cock into her entrance and her breath caught in her throat.

It felt like a red-hot brand. Too thick to fit. Stretching her.

She pushed back against him, needing him inside. She held her breath. Her heart pounded. A sob escaped. "Stefano."

"There it is," he said softly. "Tell me what you want."

"You. Right. Now."

"Me what. Be specific."

She blushed, but it didn't matter. "You inside me."

"More specific."

Her breath hissed out on a thin wail. "Stefano. Please. Your cock inside me right now. Before I go up in flames."

"Since you asked so nicely. Of course next time, *bambina*, I'm going to make you beg me to fuck you. You'll have to say *fuck* just like a bad girl."

She couldn't form a coherent thought. If that's what it took to get him moving, she would have gladly asked him using his favorite word. He thrust hard. Deep. Buried himself to the balls. She felt them slapping against her. She let go of one breast and jammed her fist in her mouth to keep from screaming. Fire raced through her. Then he was moving, slamming into her over and over, a jackhammer, thick and long, driving through the tight folds of her body, until she came apart over and over.

She didn't think he'd ever stop, sending one orgasm crashing into the next so that her body tightened around his and milked, strangling his cock. He swore in Italian, his voice as strangled as hers as she finally took him over the very edge of his control.

She closed her eyes, savoring the strong quakes, the contractions and convulsion of her sex around his. She had no idea how many times he'd forced her body to climax because eventually she couldn't tell where one started and the next began. But they were in the restroom long enough for Pietro to pound on the door and ask her how long a break she was taking.

She began laughing as Stefano helped her to stand. "I think you just might have that kind of control, honey. The kind where I could wrap my mouth around you, take you down my throat and work you while you conducted business. We might have to put it to the test sometime. Maybe even make a wager." She said it just to be wicked, but his eyes flashed at her as he reached around her to get a towel wet with warm water. He handed it to her and took another for himself.

"I like the idea. We'll set a date for you to come to my office."

That was *so* not happening, although she had to admit, as long as she was hidden and no one could see her, the idea was a little exciting. Once she was clean, Stefano untied her skirt so it would drop down and cover her. He leaned down and took her mouth gently.

"I'll see you at home, *amore*." He smiled. "I love saying that. Now that you're there, I have a home. You go out first. Don't say anything to Pietro. He doesn't know I stopped in and I don't have time to talk."

She nodded and allowed him to push her out the door. She turned and hurried down the hall. Just before she hit the main store, she remembered Stefano had her panties. She jogged back and opened the door. He was gone. She frowned, looking around her. The only thing she saw were the shadows of the buildings outside through the window racing across the floor. She sighed and shook her head as she went back to work.

CHAPTER SEVENTEEN

The paparazzi were relentless over the next few days. Francesca found that she didn't mind at all having Emilio and Enzo between her and everyone else. The reporters were everywhere: camped out at the hotel, trying to get a glimpse of her, and walking up and down the streets, entering shops to do their best to persuade the locals to help them get a picture of her or information on her. She was very, very grateful for the Ferraros' relationship with the people in their neighborhood because no one gave her up.

She enjoyed work, especially lunch or breaks because she never knew when Stefano would call or text her to meet him in the employee restroom. He was an exciting, creative man, very sexual, and he made her feel as if she were the most beautiful woman in the world. She found herself laughing more. Relaxed. Happy. She was *happy*.

His brothers and sister dropped by his apartment often. They trained together in the large training hall Stefano had. She liked to watch them as they sparred, feet and hands a blur as they tried to best one another. They were all very fast and smooth, so much so that she couldn't actually say with any certainty which brother or even Emmanuelle was better than the others.

She loved the camaraderie, how close they all were. It was very evident to her that the brothers watched over Emmanuelle, although they considered her an equal. She also realized that they didn't talk about their parents. She knew Stefano's parents worked for the family business, whatever that was, and that both were alive, but they were never really mentioned. It was odd when the siblings were so close.

Stefano was a man who liked to touch. When they were together, inside the apartment or outside, he had his hands on her. If they were alone he was initiating sex. She didn't mind that in the least. Sex with Stefano was always incredible. She could almost forget Barry Anthon and the threat he presented. Almost. Still, she was uneasy, a little persistent feeling nagging at her that her world was too perfect, that she'd found happiness and he was going to come and rip it away.

"Francesca." Pietro's voice penetrated. "Stop daydreaming. It's embarrassing." He threw back his head and laughed at his own joke.

She jerked around, leaning against the counter, watching him laugh at her along with favorite customers, Lucia and Amo Fausti. She loved their boutique and the clothes they sold as well as the other treasures they had acquired from all over the world. Of course, she couldn't afford anything and she'd learned not to admire too closely because somehow word would get back to Stefano and she'd have whatever she liked sitting on their bed when she got home from work.

"Ha. Ha. Very funny. I'm going to ruin your coffee, Amo," she threatened. "I'll accidentally put sugar in it."

Amo shuddered. "That would be mean, Frankie, and you don't have a mean bone in your body. You're like my beautiful Lucia."

That was the highest compliment Amo could have given her. He adored his wife, and Francesca wanted to throw her arms around him at such huge praise. He was the only person who ever called her Frankie and she liked it coming from him. "Thank you, Amo. As Lucia is amazing, I'm going to just bask in that for a while."

"While you're basking, could you finish their sandwiches and get Mr. Ferraro something to eat or drink?" Pietro asked.

Ricco leaned against the counter, looking hot, his arm around Lucia, nudging Amo with his elbow. "I don't mind waiting, Pietro. I've got my favorite girl right here. Lucia and I are contemplating running off together. We're discussing where we might go."

"You'd need a big head start," Amo said. "I've got a shotgun and I'd be coming after you. Can't live without my woman." He reached around Ricco and tugged Lucia under his arm. "I'd have to do you in, boy, and persuade her she can't live without me."

Ricco rubbed his forehead with his thumb. "I don't know, Amo. Lucia is extraordinary. Everyone knows that. Shotgun aside, I might have to fight you for her."

Lucia blushed like a schoolgirl. "You boys are terrible. What brings you downtown, Ricco? I don't see you very often."

"Keeping an eye on our girl," Ricco said with a little shrug. Even that brief lifting of his shoulders seemed a powerful, fluid movement.

Francesca studied him while she made sandwiches for the Faustis. He was very handsome, gave off the aura of power and danger, a heady combination guaranteed to attract any woman, yet like his other brothers and sister, he wasn't in a committed relationship. She knew Stefano worried about him. Of all the siblings, Ricco seemed to live on the edge the most. He drove that little bit too fast, lived his life a little recklessly, but he was always the first to back Stefano no matter what. She liked him, but then she liked all of Stefano's siblings.

"Ricco, Emilio and Enzo are close," she pointed out softly. "I appreciate you watching over me, but I'm fine."

"Damn reporters are crawling out of the woodwork." He watched her as she handed the sandwiches to Lucia and took money from Amo. When the couple retreated to the tables toward the back of the room, Ricco straightened and indicated that Francesca come around the counter and sit at a table with him. He chose one away from the few customers eating in the deli.

Francesca sank into the chair he held for her and waited until he brought coffee Pietro had made for them. "What is it? Is something wrong with Stefano?" She hadn't gotten that from him, but now that he made an effort to get her alone, she was frightened. Ricco wouldn't have come if it weren't important.

"Stefano's fine, *cara*. I would have said something immediately if he wasn't. Things are heating up a little right now, and I wanted to make certain we're taking extra precautions to protect you."

Her stomach lurched and she pressed a hand there. "It's Barry, isn't it? You've heard from him."

He shook his head. "Not yet, but we will. Stories are being written, Francesca. That's what happens when you become engaged to someone like my brother. These fuckers dig deep and write any shit they can find."

She went perfectly still, her heart pounding, the blood draining from her face, leaving her unnaturally pale. Of course they would find all sorts of terrible things about her. She'd been in a psychiatric ward for seventy-two hours. She'd been arrested twice. There were mug shots. Worse, they would dig up her sister's murder and it would once again be splashed everywhere, all over the newspapers and in the tatty little magazines that seemed determined to ruin everyone's life. Ricco wouldn't be there unless something like that was already in print. She was afraid she might be sick.

"Francesca, look at me." His voice was very quiet, but still carried absolute command the way Stefano's did.

She swallowed hard and lifted her lashes, forcing herself to meet his eyes. "Why didn't Stefano come to tell me?"

"He couldn't get away. He was in a conference with the New York branch. An emergency that's come up and he has to take care of it. You're good, *cara*. No worries."

She shook her head. "You wouldn't be here unless whatever they printed was awful. I don't know if I'm strong enough to go through that again." Barry would make certain his people would feed that frenzy. He'd make her out to be an unstable criminal. She knew he would. He controlled the media when he wanted.

"You're stronger than you think, and you're not alone this time. You have the entire family backing you, and then there's my brother. He's fiercely protective of you. And, Francesca?" He reached across the table and put his hand over hers, stilling her nervous drumming. "So am I. So are my brothers and Emmanuelle. People are going to read that shit and even here, in our own neighborhood, a few idiots might believe what they read, but most will follow our lead. You keep your head up and just smile or shake your head as if you can't be bothered to address all that nonsense."

She took a breath and tried to still the screams in her head. She hadn't had nightmares since she'd been sleeping with Stefano, but she was afraid they would start all over again. She felt as if she'd woken up from a beautiful dream to find herself in a horror film. Looking around the deli, she realized these people—Pietro, the Faustis, all the other customers she'd come to care about—were going to read those horrible things about her. They wouldn't want to believe it all, but there would be enough truth woven in with the lies to make them look at her differently.

"Don't answer questions. We're going to have either Emilio or Enzo inside the store while you work. The other will be outside in front so you're warned if any of the paparazzi come near the store. If that happens, you go to the back and let Pietro handle everything."

She put both hands in her lap, curling her fingers into fists. She really, really liked Ricco, but right then she needed Stefano. Her first reaction was to run as fast and as far as possible from the situation. Her picture would be plastered everywhere. She couldn't outrun that.

"Francesca, stop looking as if the world is coming to an end."

"It *is*," she hissed, leaning toward him. "You have no idea what it's like to have people believe horrible lies about you. To have to live on the street with no job, no money, not knowing when you'll have another meal. They took everything from me, including the people I thought were my friends. They took away my belief in the justice system, but most of all, my feeling of safety. I forgot, until Stefano, what it was like to feel safe. You and I both know, it's human nature to believe the worst."

She didn't realize she was crying until Ricco shifted closer to her, threw his arm around her shoulders and used a handkerchief to mop up her tears.

"Stop." He all but snarled the command. "You're a Ferraro. You never, *ever* fucking let them see they got to you. Even here, Francesca, you keep your head up. You remember who you are. If you can't do it for yourself, you do it for him. For Stefano. I know you love him. Don't wince. Don't act like you don't know. You might not want to admit it to yourself or to him yet, but it's there. I can see it on your face and hear it in your voice. We have gifts and we use them. Of course I would check to make certain you weren't going to fuck him over. He's so gone on you it would kill him."

The sincerity in Ricco's voice straightened her spine. The sheer honesty. He believed Stefano loved her. Needed her even. And he was right—as much as she was afraid to admit it to herself or to Stefano, she was totally falling in love with him.

"Stefano has a certain reputation, Francesca, and he needs to be respected. That's part of how he can do what he does. You're his woman. You can't allow anyone to tear him down. If they manage to tear you down, they are doing the same to him. You're a couple. That means whatever happens to you, happens to him." He released her and straightened, his eyes on the large storefront window as he lifted his mug of coffee and took a long, slow drink.

She knew he was giving her a chance to pull herself together. She forced herself to sit just as straight and to take a drink of coffee as well. She would never let Stefano down. For him, she could weather any storm. If he could take the horrible things they said about her, then she could. She knew the nightmares would start again, but they would be in the privacy of her home, not in public.

The door to the deli was pushed open by a young man in

his early twenties with long, straggly hair and dark glasses that covered half his face. He paused in the doorway when he saw Ricco, stiffening and then taking a deep breath before entering. He looked the worse for wear. His face was swollen and covered in bruises. He walked carefully, as if injured. He carried his arms in close to his body to protect his rib cage.

"Bruno," Ricco greeted, sitting back in his chair. Relaxed. Casual. "Nice to see you on your feet. Heard you had a little accident. You feeling better?"

Immediately the atmosphere in the deli changed subtly. There was an undercurrent of danger, yet Francesca couldn't see or hear any reason why it should feel that way.

The boy bobbed his head repeatedly and sidled closer to the counter.

"Your grandmother in good health?" Ricco persisted.

Francesca instantly remembered the name Bruno. She'd been sitting in the pizzeria with Stefano when a woman, Signora Theresa Vitale, had come up to the table and pleaded with Stefano for help with her wayward grandson, Bruno. This had to be that Bruno. Clearly he was in trouble of some kind. He'd been in a fight and looked as if he'd lost.

Bruno bobbed his head again. "Yeah. Yes, Mr. Ferraro," he corrected himself when Ricco continued to stare at him. "She's good."

"You good? You staying out of trouble, because you know, life can get really difficult when you're stupid and you forget who your family is. *Famiglia* is everything. I wouldn't want you to forget that. Not for a moment. It could get . . . rough."

The boy actually paled. He kept bobbing his head, until Francesca feared he might actually break his neck. Ricco was clearly issuing a warning and Bruno was taking it that way. She found herself shivering.

"Bruno"—Ricco said his name quietly—"I want to hear your answer. Out. Loud. You won't forget what *famiglia* is, right? You know you need a job, you need anything at all, your family is where you go. Not to outsiders. Your grandmother took you in, raised you right, sacrificed for you. She deserves the utmost respect at all times from you. Am I right, or what?"

The boy swallowed hard. "You're right, Mr. Ferraro. I'm going to work next week. Still a little sore from the . . ." He broke off when Ricco raised an eyebrow, looked around the room and then said, "Accident. But I can start work Monday and I'll be bringing home my pay to help out Nonna."

Ricco sent him a small smile. "Good. You need anything, you call. Stefano gave you the number, right?"

Bruno winced at Stefano's name, but continued bobbing his head. "Yeah. I mean, yes, Mr. Ferraro."

Ricco dismissed him by turning to Francesca and leaning close to her. The boy stood awkwardly for a moment before giving his order to Pietro.

"He's afraid of you," Francesca observed.

Ricco shrugged. "Don't know why. I'm just sitting here with my brother's woman, giving her a little advice."

"Thank you for that, Ricco. I appreciate it. You made me see things in a different light. I probably would have been stupid and made a run for it."

His eyes darkened and another shiver went through her. Ricco Ferraro was every bit as scary as his brother, maybe more. There were demons in his eyes that Stefano didn't have. She had the feeling something terrible had happened to him, something he'd buried deep, but that still drove him hard. "Don't ever do that, Francesca," he warned. "Stefano would come after you and he wouldn't be alone. All of us would help him find you. You're ours, part of our family and just like I was trying to say to Bruno, that means something. You don't walk away from that because it gets hard."

She nodded, took a breath and took the plunge. "You can talk to me, Ricco. I know you aren't going to talk to your siblings, but I want you to know, you can talk to me. Whatever happened, however terrible, I would understand."

He shut down. Instantly. She knew she was right about Ricco and his past, but he wasn't going to share. Instead, he gave her the famous Ferraro smile, the one reserved for cameras, interviews and strangers. "Thanks, *cara*, but I'm just fine." He stood up abruptly and pushed back his chair. "I appreciate the offer though."

She forced a small nod and stood up, too. It was time to go back to work. The next wave of customers would be arriving very soon. The afternoon shift was always the most difficult to keep up with. The deli would be totally packed with lines outside and every table inside filled. She liked that shift because time flew by and it was a challenge to keep up with all the orders, but it was also exhausting.

Francesca was able to chat with the first wave of customers, laughing a little with them, watching closely to see if she could spot anyone who had already read the stories about her, but so far, Pietro's customers didn't seem to read many of the gossip magazines. By later afternoon, she was beginning to relax. The crush was nearly over and nothing had been said, no whispers had invaded the shop, no strange, telling glances. She was beginning to think she would escape completely today and have time to prepare a defense.

Enzo suddenly burst through the shop door and pointed at her. "Get in the back, Francesca. *Now.*"

Pietro caught her by the shoulders, turning her body and all but throwing her away from the counter. There was no mistaking the urgency in Enzo's voice or Pietro's hands. Tugging at her apron, she glanced out the large windows at the front of the store. In the street she could see a frenzy of paparazzi descending on the deli. Someone had finally sold her out. She turned and hurried down the hall to the employee break room. There was a screen where she could see what was happening. Standing just inside the door, she stared at the chaos already reigning in the front of the store.

Paparazzi pushed their way in and were asking everyone questions. Emilio came up behind her. "Stay right here. I'm going to help Enzo throw their asses out. Don't you move."

"I won't." She had no intention of being that stupid. She'd dealt with all this before and it had been one of the worst times of her life.

Her phone vibrated and she pulled it out, still staring at the screen. Emilio had waded into the crowd, trying to keep the customers defending Pietro and her from getting into fistfights with the photographers desperate to get photographs that would make them money.

"Bambina." Stefano's voice was a lifeline. "Emilio said you're under siege." So calm. His voice strong. A low, sexy tone that soothed even as it took charge.

"You could say that. I don't think Pietro will want me working here anymore. What a mess."

"It isn't that he won't want you there, Francesca—it's a matter of your safety. He's already grown fond of you and he doesn't want anything to happen to you."

"I hope I'm not hearing smug satisfaction in your voice. I happen to know you don't want me working. You didn't somehow manage to engineer the raid on the store, did you?" She tried to make a joke of it when she really wanted to cry.

"Dolce cuore, I would never send a hoard of paparazzi after you even to get my way, and I'm pretty ruthless." His voice turned grim. "However, I will find out who did. And did you use the word *smug*? I can't imagine anyone ever thinking I'm smug."

She laughed softly and winced a little when Emilio, Enzo and Tito from the pizzeria forcibly ejected a burly man. As he staggered backward on the sidewalk, Agnese Moretti knocked him in the head and about the shoulders with her purse. She appeared to be giving him a lecture as she attacked him.

A hand fell on her shoulder hard, fingers digging deep and she was yanked backward, right out of the employee break room. She emitted a startled, frightened yelp before the hand went from her shoulder to clamp hard over her mouth.

"Shut the fuck up, you bitch. You're coming with me." A knife cut into her skin just below her throat, right over the spot where the necklace Stefano had given her had nearly faded away.

She had no choice but to move backward, off balance as the intruder dragged her down the short hallway to the back exit. She kept her phone clutched in her hand, hoping Stefano could hear every word.

"Who are you? What do you want?" She asked him the questions more for Stefano's sake than her own. She didn't care who he was or what he wanted. The knife blade cut into her again, a second shallow laceration. She felt blood trickle down her skin to the curve of her breasts.

"I'm the man clever enough to get you right out from under the noses of the fucking Ferraros. A few paparazzi figure out where you are and your idiot bodyguards rush to get them out of the store and leave you unprotected."

"Tell me what you want." He'd dragged her out into the alley now. Francesca shivered and then let out a little scream when he sliced into her skin again. "Stop cutting me with the knife. Tell me what you want."

"I want to know where my friends are—that's what I want, you bitch. You go running to your boyfriend, whining about a little scratch they put on your neck, and they disappear. Where the fuck are they?"

He shook her, and this time the cut was deeper and a little lower, right on the upper curve of her left breast. She could tell it was shallow and probably an accident but it burned like hell.

"I don't know who you're talking about." But she had a sinking feeling she did.

"They mugged you, and Emilio and Enzo took them away. No one's seen them since and the Ferraros are looking for me." He slid open the door to an old van and tried to shove her inside. In order to push her, he had to remove the knife.

Francesca was not getting into the van. She was certain he'd kill her just to make a point to Stefano. She turned on him, swinging her fist. He grunted, took two steps back and kicked her in the stomach. Francesca folded in half and found herself sitting on the ground. She tried to roll over, to get to her feet before he could come at her again, but he was enraged and he reached down to grab her hair in his fist.

"I'll fucking cut your throat," he snarled, and the knife

came right at her exposed throat as he jerked her head backward.

Stefano loomed up behind him, a dark, shadowy figure she almost couldn't make out. He seemed to emerge from thin air, from the darkest of the shadows, coming up right behind her assailant and catching his head in the vee of his arm, one hand to the back of the skull, forcing the head forward.

The man dropped the knife from nerveless fingers and sagged in Stefano's arms. Stefano dropped him like a piece of garbage on the ground, not even bothering to kick the knife out of reach. He caught Francesca in his arms just as his brothers and Emmanuelle emerged from the shadows.

"She's bleeding," Emmanuelle announced unnecessarily. "How bad, Stefano? Does she need an ambulance? A doctor?"

Francesca shook her head. "I'm fine. Really. Just scared."

Emmanuelle ignored her proclamation, clearly looking to Stefano to give her the word one way or the other. The brothers formed a protective ring around her while Stefano inspected her for damage.

"She has several cuts, shallow, shouldn't need stitches, but I saw him kick her. She'll have a bad bruise."

"Who is he?" Francesca asked.

"Later, *amore*," he said, his voice clipped. "We have to do damage control."

"Get her home," Ricco advised. "We'll do cleanup and call you when it's done."

Francesca didn't like the sound of that, all too aware that the man had said his friends had been the ones to try to rob her and they'd disappeared. The last she'd seen of them, Emilio and Enzo were putting them into a car and taking them off somewhere.

"Stefano," she tried again.

He simply pulled her into his arms, swinging her up to cradle her close, snapping orders. A car pulled up, a man driving she'd seen, but didn't recognize. Clearly he was family to the Ferraros; another cousin she was certain. He had to be one of the bodyguards who had taken Emilio's place.

Stefano carried her to the car, Ricco stepped forward and opened the door to the backseat and Stefano slid inside, keeping Francesca in his arms. The door slammed shut and the car was in motion. Stefano dropped his chin on top of her head. "That scared the hell out of me. Hearing him threatening you. Your scream. I think it took thirty years off my life."

She closed her eyes and sagged against his chest. "He seemed to think you had something to do with the disappearance of his friends. You didn't, did you, Stefano?" She didn't open her eyes, but she listened, because it was very important to her to hear his voice, to hear the truth or a lie.

"I know they are no longer alive," he admitted carefully. "But I didn't kill them."

That was strictly the truth, but even that admission was enough to start her heart pounding. She tried to push the thought away that Stefano and his family were part of organized crime, but no matter what she did, she couldn't get around it. There were too many coincidences as far as she was concerned. She tried to get off his lap, but Stefano's arms tightened around her.

"Settle, *dolce cuore*. We'll talk about this once we're home."

"Stefano . . ." What was she going to say? She couldn't leave him. The thought of being without him made her ill. She wouldn't survive it. Somehow, and she wasn't even certain when it had happened, she'd fallen hard and fast. She was in so deep, even knowing he was a criminal, she might not be strong enough to walk away from him.

He nuzzled her neck. "Let's get you home, clean you up and I'll make dinner for us while you rest. After, when you're feeling better, we'll clear everything up."

She heard the ring of truth in that as well. He wasn't avoiding talking to her. He just wanted her warm, safe and comfortable. That helped to ease her mind. Surely if he was a criminal he would be far more hesitant to talk about the muggers and why he knew they were dead.

"What's going to happen to that man? The one who attacked me?"

Silence filled the car. The air went very heavy with his anger. Heat vibrated in the air, and all over again, dread filled her. Stefano didn't answer and she didn't ask again. The car pulled up to the private entrance around the side of the hotel, the one that looked like an employees-only door, but only family had the code. The bodyguard got out first, took a careful look around, opened the door and signaled to Stefano.

Stefano refused to put her down, even in the private elevator or when they reached the apartment. He carried her on through to the master bedroom and put her on the bed before collecting warm washcloths and a first-aid kit. Francesca detested how safe she felt with him. The soft, loving look on his face. His touch as he cleaned the shallow lacerations. There was no doubt in her mind that he cared about her. She was important to him—maybe too important.

"Are you going to kill him, Stefano?" Francesca had to ask. She already knew the answer, but she had to ask. She had looked at his face, right there, when he'd had his arm around her assailant's neck and she knew he was capable of killing that man. His eyes had been flat and cold. Like ice.

"He's going to die, but I won't be the one to kill him." There was no inflection in his voice. None. "I'm not ever going to lie to you, Francesca. You're going to be my wife. I won't do that to you, but if you're going to ask me questions, you be absolutely certain you want and can live with the answers."

"What if I can't live with the answers?" she asked in a small voice. She heard the tremble. She was scared. Not of Stefano, but of what he was. Of what he might tell her and she'd lose him. She couldn't lose him.

"Then don't ask until you can." His hands dropped to her blouse. He pulled it over her head and tossed it away from him. It was covered in blood and he obviously didn't feel the need to try to save it. Her bra was next and then he was examining the angry cut across the swell of her left breast.

"Fucker," he whispered, and leaned down to brush the

lightest of kisses across the laceration. "I don't get how a man can do this kind of thing to a woman or to children. What's wrong with them, Francesca?"

She couldn't stop herself from cradling his head to her. He sounded tired. Sad. "This isn't just about me, Stefano. Tell me what's wrong."

"It's work, *bambina*—sometimes I see and hear terrible things I just can't comprehend. It's work though."

"I get that. You don't have to be specific, but you need to talk to me about this. Maybe you should go relax and I'll fix you dinner."

He lifted his head, his blue eyes meeting hers. "You would do that for me after being attacked, wouldn't you? You'd think about me, not yourself." There was wonder in his voice. Admiration. Respect. Mostly, she heard what sounded suspiciously like love. Her heart fluttered because yes, he looked tired and upset and she rarely saw him that way. She doubted if anyone ever did.

"I received a report today about a young girl. A teenager, seventeen years old. She lost her mother two years ago and was given to her stepuncles to take care of her. Unfortunately, all three uncles are involved in a very violent gang. Her mother had married their brother and they lived far away from the gang, but no one took that into consideration when they placed the girl with her uncles. She didn't know them, she didn't love them and now she's in a terrible situation."

"At seventeen, can't she ask to be removed?" Francesca felt her way carefully.

Stefano stroked his fingers over her breasts, down her belly to her jeans. He carefully tugged until she stood in between his thighs. He unzipped the denim and pulled them from her hips, taking her lacy panties with them.

"A social worker tried. The girl was being abused in every way. Sexually. Physically. Emotionally. She wasn't removed from the home and the gang threatened the social worker and her family. She'd promised the teenager she would get her out, and then she couldn't follow through, not without risking the lives of her husband and children."

"The police . . ."

"Can't stop the gang members from getting to the social worker and her family. So she petitioned for help from our family." He guided her back onto the bed. "Lie down, *dolce cuore*. I want to check out your stomach. I need to make certain there isn't any internal damage."

"Will you be able to help her?" Francesca stretched out. She had been naked around him for a week now, yet she still felt shy.

"I hope so. We'll see. I just don't understand that mentality. I can see belonging to a gang. I can't see abusing a woman that way. Especially when she's your family. I just can't seem to wrap my head around that."

His fingers probed all over her stomach. She winced a couple of times, but surprisingly, it didn't hurt very deeply.

"You'll have a bruise or two, but thankfully, he didn't manage to cause any real damage. I'm going to run you a hot bath and you can soak while I fix you dinner."

She caught his hand. "Let's both take a bath, Stefano, and then we can share the cooking. You said you aren't that good, but, honey, I am. I like to cook. You have a great kitchen. You've had a difficult day, too. I'd rather share the bath and dinner."

He stood over her a long time. So long she thought he might not respond. The expression on his face was difficult to read. Finally, he brushed at her hair with gentle fingers and shook his head.

"I'm so in love with you, Francesca. You give me so many miracles and you don't have a clue that you do. No one takes care of me. No one. Not when I was a boy and certainly not now. I think you're the most beautiful woman I've ever seen. I love the sound of your laughter, and your smile lights up a room. I watch you with the people in the neighborhood and you're so great with everyone. They all gravitate toward you, and you treat each of them with genuine interest and caring. I think that's enough reason to love you, but then you do this." He shook his head.

Francesca wasn't certain how to respond. He seemed shaken and she didn't really understand what she'd done. "Honey, you're every bit as important to me as I am to you. I *want* to take care of you. No, that isn't right. I *need* to take care of you. You matter, Stefano." She sat up and held out her hand to him.

He stared at her hand for a long time. "You asked me a couple of scary questions, Francesca. I gave you a couple of scary answers. You didn't flinch, but I saw it in your eyes that you thought you might not be able to live with those answers. I'm not altogether certain I could give you up now, but I'd try if you need to leave me. I can't walk away from what I do—it's too important. But you should have a choice, so I'm going to attempt to be a better man and give that to you. A onetime offer."

She could see that it killed him to make the offer. *Killed* him. She kept her hand outstretched toward him. "I couldn't leave you even if I wanted to. I don't know how I would survive without you."

He stared at her for another heartbeat and then he ignored her hand and took her right back down to the bed. It was a long time before they got their bath or food.

CHAPTER EIGHTEEN

Francesca woke with her heart pounding and her mouth dry, the taste of blood in her mouth. Her tongue found the small tear in her lip where she'd bit it to keep from screaming and screaming like she wanted to. Instantly she felt his arms. His thigh between hers. His body wrapped around hers, keeping her safe. Stefano. She drew in breath and took his scent into her lungs.

"Bambina."

His voice was soft. Warm. So gentle it turned her heart over. One of her favorite things to do with him was just lie in bed and listen to him talk, especially about the neighborhood and the people in it. The affection in his voice was always stark and real. She especially loved these moments— in the dark, surrounded by his protective body and his voice sliding over her like the touch of his fingers. Caressing. Soothing. Driving away the remnants of her nightmares.

Stefano was always gentle with her in the middle of the night when she woke, his mouth soft against her skin, his driving needs held in check while he comforted her.

"What was it?"

"He's coming for me." Her heart still pounded. Her stomach felt queasy. She knew there was no way Barry Anthon would have missed the news that Francesca Capello was engaged to marry Stefano Ferraro. The announcement was in all the news. In magazines. Television. Stefano's publicist handled everything and made certain information on the engagement was spread far and wide.

"That's the idea, *dolce cuore*. We want him to come after us. We want him out of your life once and for all. That means drawing him out. Letting him make a mistake."

"You can't underestimate him, Stefano," she warned, a cold shiver creeping down her spine.

He stroked her rib cage with the pads of his fingers. Traced his name, brushing the letters until they looped on the underside of her breasts. He painted little sparks of electricity all over her breasts with soft, unhurried touches. His hand moved back to her rib cage and he tugged until she rolled onto her back. He kissed the marks at her throat and over her breast, featherlight kisses to remove every trace of the sting of a knife.

Francesca's heart jerked hard in her chest at the sight of his face so close to her. God, but he was gorgeous. Impossible to resist. "I've fallen so hard for you, Stefano," she whispered. "Please be real. Please don't hurt me. I don't think I'd survive it." The admission slipped out before she could stop it.

She knew what she was revealing to him. Those fragile feelings she couldn't help. Stefano was larger than life. A throwback to an era gone by when men were fiercely protective of women and children. Where having a code meant something. Giving his word and keeping it was a matter of honor.

His blue eyes burned over her like twin flames, taking her breath. So intense. Desire flaring. Hunger and possession stamped into the sensual lines of his face. "It doesn't get any more real than what I feel for you, Francesca," he said softly. His hand moved from her throat to the junction of her legs, his touch gentle, unhurried, unlike his usual rough, wild possession. "What we have together. It fills me up, *bella*, until I'm almost bursting. I've always been empty, and now you make me full. There's no going back for me."

Stefano shifted his body, rolling over the top of her so that his thick, heavy erection was nestled in the cradle of her hips.

One knee nudged her legs apart. One hand caught her left leg, bent it and drew it around him, opening her up to him. Every silent command was gentle. Insistent, but gentle.

Her heart turned over and then began hammering, each beat thundering in her ears, rushing through her veins and pounding in her clit. She ran her hands up his chest. She loved the way his muscles were so defined, the way they rippled suggestively beneath his skin when he moved. Like a tiger. She shivered. Just touching him sent heat curling through her body and damp liquid made her slick with welcome.

"There's no going back for you, Francesca. Whatever happens, we'll face it together." He bent his head and kissed her chin. Nibbled his way under her chin to her throat. He punctuated each kiss with a bite. Each bite made her hips buck with need. This was a slow burn, not the out-of-control wildfire he created. The burn took her over, cell by cell, settling in before she was fully aware of what was happening.

"I reserve the right to protect you, Stefano."

His gaze moved over her face, melting her with those twin blue flames. "I love how you truly believe I need protecting and that you're so willing to try." He bent his head to her breast, his dark hair brushing over her bare skin. "Every moment I'm with you, *bambina*, I fall harder. It's difficult for me to believe you're real. You aren't the only one a little terrified."

His mouth made her squirm. Catch her breath. He knew exactly what he was doing to her, just how to bring that slow smolder to a hot burn. His hands moved over her skin. Possessive. Loving. Tender. So tender it brought tears to her eyes. His admission rang with truth and that brought a lump to her throat. Her Stefano.

He kissed his way down her body, keeping that slow, unhurried pace, but it was more intense than she thought possible. It felt as if he was worshiping her. Showing her with his mouth and hands how much he loved her.

Stefano took his time, savoring the taste and texture of Francesca. It was impossible to put into words what he felt for her. He'd had no idea he *could* feel for a woman what he did each time he touched her. Hell. That wasn't exactly the truth. It happened each time he thought of her, which was every minute of every day. She was fast becoming his obsession.

He couldn't wait to be in her. Home. That was what she was to him. A woman who saw him. He kissed his way up the inside of her thigh, feeling her shiver. He loved her reaction every time he touched her. The silk of skin. The heat. He knew he shouldn't be happy for all the women he'd had before her. He couldn't remember them and they paled into insignificance, but he was grateful for the experience, to be able to give his woman so much pleasure.

Her soft little moans sounded like music to him. He waited for the breathy hitch in her voice before he dipped his head again and nuzzled that sweet, sweet treasure between her legs. Her hips bucked and he pinned her down, forcing her thighs farther apart as he inhaled her scent.

She was a siren calling to him. His gaze slid up her body, drinking her in, devouring her. Could a woman be any more beautiful, laid out for him, her body flushed, breasts swaying with every undulation and shift she made. Her hair was everywhere, just like he loved it, that cloud of dark silk felt like heaven against his skin. He dreamed of her hair sliding over him as he fucked her slowly. Fast. Any damn way he wanted.

"Who do you belong to, *bambina*?" He licked at her, licked at the orange-and-cinnamon-scented drops of honey spilling out of her. All for him. Every single bit, just for him. She didn't know yet. She was still leery of the relationship, not trusting anything that happened so fast. Knowing his family was far more than he was telling her. Still, she was there. With him. Committing to him in spite of her fear.

He needed her to commit all the way. To be so far into him, she couldn't walk away. He wanted their shadows merged—a dangerous thing to do if she wasn't fully his. It was a risk he knew could lose him everything. He'd end up a shadow himself, no longer a rider, something he was born to do. Every day they were together like this, so intimate, their shadows connected, beginning the seal between them.

"Answer me, Francesca." He used his black velvet voice. The one no one ever dared disobey. The one commanding truth. "Who do you belong to?" He plunged his tongue deep, because he couldn't resist her scent one more moment. His hands shaped her hips, her thighs. Slid over the dark curls at the vee of her legs. Possessively. He knew exactly who she belonged to.

"Stefano."

She said his name on a gasp, her hands finding his hair, gripping, pulling. He loved the bite of pain. His cock loved it, too.

"I belong to you."

Four beautiful words. He added a finger to her tight sheath and her muscles contracted around it, bathed him in hot liquid. He marveled that she could take him. She always felt far too tight, yet she was perfect for him.

"That's right, Francesca. You're mine." Because he couldn't live without her. He couldn't ever again come back to one of his houses without her in it.

He moved up her body, keeping her thighs wide, bending one leg at the knee to curve it around his body, wanting her to lock him up tight. He did the same to the other leg so that her body cradled his and her legs circled his thighs, ankles crossed to hold him to her.

He brushed at her hair, and took her mouth again. He'd never be able to resist her mouth. He loved everything about it. How soft. Like velvet. Full lips. Her smile took his breath every time. She had the cutest little dimple, barely there, that came and went when she smiled. Her taste was exquisite. Addicting. He kissed his way down her chin and took a small bite. Felt her body shudder beneath his in reaction.

Her neck was next. He loved the way she arched, giving him access, even when he bit her that little bit too hard. It was impossible not to sink his teeth into her. She was just too—perfect. Just too his. Everything he could imagine he would want in a woman and so much more.

Her hands stroked his back, fingernails bit deep into his shoulders. His cock jerked, his balls tightened. She was perfect. Fucking perfect. He worshiped her breasts, taking his time, even when she tried to impale herself on him. He loved that. Loved the way she needed him. Her eyes had that glazed look he was hungry to see. The look that said she was so far gone he could do anything to her and she'd let him, because she was every bit as wild for him as he was for her.

He guided her legs higher, so that they wrapped around his waist, exposing that soft center of hers. A flower. He lodged the head of his cock there, feeling the burn. So slick with welcome. He loved that too. How wet she got for him. How responsive she was to him. She was everything. When a man had nothing for his entire damn life, there was no mistaking the real thing when she walked unexpectedly into his world.

He pushed slowly into her. Inch by scorching-hot inch. Watching as she took him in. Watching as her body swallowed his. It was beautiful. Fucking perfection. His gaze on hers, he threaded his fingers through hers and pressed their joined hands into the mattress.

He'd never felt anything so intense as he did right in that moment. The clasp of her sheath strangling his cock, a vise made of breathing silk, the tunnel so hot and tight it took his breath. He moved slowly. He didn't want to. He wanted to fuck her hard, but right then, he couldn't. He was helpless, caught in her spell. Mesmerized by her beauty—by the beauty of her body and what it could do to his. Mesmerized by her heart, the heart that belonged to him.

He found himself hypnotized by the small noises Francesca made in her throat that always drove him wild. The way her eyes darkened as lust overtook her. He was acutely aware of every detail, every movement. The way she tilted her pelvis to take him deeper. The way she lifted to meet him, matching his rhythm exactly. Accepting whatever pace he set. Hard. Slow. Gentle. Fast. She gave herself completely into his keeping.

"That's right, *dolce cuore*," he whispered, feeling it build in her, coiling and burning. She was close. The hitch in her breathing, the raw carnal need etched into her face. So beautiful. All his. "Give it to me now." He pushed command into his voice, wanting to feel the pulse of her body, that tight grip milking at him. The scorching friction and searing heat she surrounded him with. He wasn't yet ready to let her take him over the edge. He wanted more. Much, much more.

She gasped as the climax took her, her gaze never wavering from his. Her eyes went wide with a kind of dazed shock and her body shuddered and rippled with a powerful orgasm. He kept moving in her, picking up the pace, pounding through her climax, prolonging it.

He couldn't help himself. He drove deeper, lifting her hips to him, fingers digging into her perfect little heart-shaped bottom. Fucking her hard. Really hard. She belonged to him. Every inch of her. Her orgasms belonged to him. Her silken sheath, so tight he thought he might not live through every time she surrounded him—that belonged to him. He buried himself in her over and over. Taking her. Owning her. Savoring her. Her scent. The feel of her. *Dio*. Her taste, so exquisite he was addicted and woke every fucking morning with her on his tongue.

He wrapped her hair around his fist, just because he fucking owned her hair, too. She let him, even when he jerked, pulling hard, turning her head to force her to keep watching his face. He reveled in the sight of her under him, pinned there, unable to move, her legs wrapped around his waist, locking them together while he rode her hard.

He belonged there inside of her. She was . . . *la sua casa*—his home. Home wasn't a place with four walls. Home was a scorching-hot, tight sheath made of silk. Home was blue eyes he could drown in. Home was soft skin and an eager mouth, hands that stroked and caressed, nails that bit deep in passion. *She* was home. Francesca.

He was close—so close to the end of his control. He felt the heat skittering down his spine. Up his thighs. His balls tightening. She was beautiful, her entire body flushed, her mouth open, panting, singing a ragged chant, a breathy call of his name. "Mine." He nearly spat the word. Telling her. Wanting that word branded into her bones. Wanting his name carved deep in her soul. She. Was. *His*. His everything.

Her muscles tightened, clamping down again, that scorching vise he would never get used to, the one that felt so fucking good. Paradise. Exquisite pain and pleasure coming together in perfect harmony. Forcing his explosion so that his entire body seemed to come apart. Milking him dry.

"Francesca." He breathed her name in reverence. His woman. He hoped she felt what he was trying to show her with his body. Love wasn't the right word, not when it was everything. Not when it was so intense.

She stroked his hair, her eyes drowsy. Sated. Staring into her eyes shook him because he found himself drowning in her blue gaze, experiencing the most powerful emotion he'd ever felt. She shook the foundations of his world.

He allowed himself to collapse over her, burying his face against her neck. He nuzzled her there. Kissed her. Bit down as gently as he could, feeling her body shudder and quake around his as he glided into her over and over. Slow again. Bringing them both down from that exhilarating rush.

When he finally found the strength to withdraw, he rolled her onto her side, back to him, curling his body around her.

"I have to clean up."

"No." He made it an order. "Tonight you sleep with me inside you." He had a primitive desire to own her body all night. He waited for her to protest. What woman wouldn't protest? His seed would run down her thighs. Make a sticky mess. She had every right to protest. He closed his eyes and pressed his forehead into the back of her head, into the luxurious mass of dark hair. Waiting.

Francesca laughed softly, and the sound teased every one of his senses. Made him indescribably happy. He lifted his head because he had to see her. One hand moved the cloak of hair, exposing the tilt of her mouth. That sweet, sweet curve.

"You're kind of a caveman, sometimes, Stefano. But it's sexy. Really, really sexy."

The breathless quality to her voice brushed like fingers over his belly, making his cock grow semihard when he'd just been feeling sated. She could make him insatiable. She already had. He was used to having a strong sex drive, mostly when he came out of the shadow portals, the adrenaline rushing through his veins, but now, he thought about sex about every third second. Sex with his woman. Francesca.

"Glad you think so, *amore*. You need to go back to sleep. You have work in the morning. Unless . . . " He paused hopefully. When she didn't take the bait, he sighed. "You could quit."

"I'm not going to be a kept woman, Stefano."

He was silent. He wanted to keep her. It was necessary to him. "You do know I'm filthy rich, right? My family has money. I have money. I would much rather spend it on you than on anything or anyone else." He spoke low, trying to keep his tone even. He knew money was going to be a sore subject with her. She'd been homeless. And she had a streak of pride a mile wide.

"You bought me an entire wardrobe, honey," she said.

Her voice was quiet. Almost gentle. He could tell she was trying to tiptoe around his pride. It wasn't that though. "It's about me needing to do things for you, Francesca. It makes me happy. You have no idea how happy. I've never had this before."

It was difficult to make the admission, not with his emotions choking him. He was grateful he was behind her, his body locked around hers. He tightened his arm around her chest, and pushed his hips deeper into her. She was so soft. Incredibly soft. And warm. Her perfect little ass pushed back against him, and he closed his eyes against the streak of white lightning shooting through his cock to his belly.

"I'll keep my job for the time being, Stefano. It helps me

learn about all the people in the neighborhood. You grew up with them. I would like to get to know them. I can tell they matter to you—you help them out a lot. If I'm going to be your wife, then they should be able to come to me so I can take some of the burden off you."

His heart jerked hard in his chest. The pressure was strong, an actual pain. She *was* going to be his wife. He would accept nothing less, but to have her want to get to know the people in his world just so she could help him reduced him to putty. She didn't know it—and thank God she didn't—but she had him in the palm of her hand. She had all the power in their relationship. She probably always would.

"You're killing me, woman. Go to sleep." Because he couldn't take much more.

"Not yet."

"Bambina," he said softly, sweeping the hair from her neck to over her shoulder. He pressed his lips against her bare nape. "Go to sleep. If you don't, I'll know I didn't do my job, wearing you out." He murmured the words against her soft skin, his teeth scraping back and forth gently, the desire to take a bite out of her strong in him. "That will mean I'll start all over again, which I don't mind, but I'll get you sore. So close your beautiful eyes for me and go to sleep."

She sighed. "I wish I could, but I keep thinking about the poor girl, Stefano. The one you told me about."

He closed his eyes. He had no right blurting out details of his assignments no matter how disturbing or upsetting. "Francesca, I should never have told you about her. I don't know why I did. You don't need to hear things like that. Not ever." He stroked her hair. He loved touching her. He fucking needed to touch her.

"Of course I do," Francesca protested, snuggling deeper into her pillow.

He loved the way her bare skin slid over his. Like silk. Or satin. So sinful he wanted her all over again. His cock just kept throbbing. Demanding. He pressed deeper against her ass, finding the crease there. He used one hand to circle his shaft, closing his eyes against the pleasure sweeping through him.

"Anything that upsets you, I want to share. I want you to be able to talk to me about your work. I might not be able to do anything but listen, but at least I can do that. The thing is, if you're reading reports on this girl, that means you're considering some way to help her."

He met her statement with silence. She turned her head to look over her shoulder at him. *Dio*. So fucking beautiful. Her eyes. The way she looked at him as if he were the only man in the world. He buried his face in her hair, escaping that wide blue gaze.

"You're too damn smart for your own good, Francesca. We're getting into things I can't talk about until my ring is on your finger."

She blinked at him and then turned back to lay her head on her pillow, her fingers curling into a fist beside her chin. "Your ring is on my finger," she pointed out, her voice low.

He reached across her body to lift her left hand, his thumb sliding over the engagement ring. He loved seeing it on her finger. Feeling it there. "You have to have my wedding band here as well. That's how this works in my family, *amore*."

Francesca was silent for a long time, and his heart pounded. She couldn't slip away. She just couldn't. Not now. He wouldn't allow it. He stayed quiet, afraid to say anything. Afraid not to.

"Stefano, I know your business isn't legal. I suspected all along, but you told me your family doesn't sell drugs or run guns and I believe you. I can't imagine you involved in prostitution or, worse, human trafficking."

His heart continued to pound. Blood thundered in his ears. Was she making a leap of faith or about to tell him to fuck off? He held himself very still, waiting for her to shatter him.

"Your family isn't like the Saldi family, in the news suspected of all kinds of heinous crimes. Still, in spite of your banks, hotels, nightclubs and even the casinos, I'm fairly certain your family has an illegal side to some of the things you do."

Not his *entire* family. Just the ones that would matter to her. He wanted to kiss her, cover her mouth with his. Stop her. In that moment he knew she could shatter him. Break him into a million pieces and he'd never recover. Not in this lifetime. He realized all the lore in his family was truth. Ferraro men, when they found the right woman, loved her with everything in them and they did it only once. Francesca was his once.

"To be with you, I can accept a lot of things, Stefano, but not silence. Not being kept in the dark. I know that there isn't always justice in the world. Believe me, I am living proof of that. It isn't like I'm ever going to go running to the police believing they'll help me. I did that too many times."

She made a move, as if she might put distance between them. He wasn't having that. He refused. He tightened his arm under her breasts and tucked her into his side, pushing his cock into the cleft of her rounded cheeks, deep, claiming that part of her for his own as well. Making a statement. She subsided, but that didn't stop the tension from coiling tighter in his gut.

"This girl. The one you read about. I don't know why people come to you for help, but if you can get her out of that situation, I'm behind you 100 percent."

She turned her head again to look at him over her shoulder. Her blue eyes were dark. Beautiful. Filled with possession and pride. For him. Fuck. She was killing him, taking him over, one slice of his soul at a time. His cock hardened until he thought he might shatter. Or maybe his heart was going to fragment into a million pieces.

"And, Stefano, I don't care how you have to do it, legal or otherwise. Just help her if you can." A soft dictate. An acceptance.

His heart nearly exploded. He reached down and caught her hips, tugging her into position, one hand sliding between her legs. She was filled with him. Slick with him. Slick with the both of them. He lifted one of her legs and just slid home.

Buried himself deep. Stayed planted as deep as humanly possible while he held her to him. While he buried his face in the ultimate luxury of her thick dark hair. He didn't move, just stayed locked to her. Buried in her, right where he wanted to live. Home.

"Stefano?" Her voice caressed his skin. Melted into his bones. "Honey, you have to move. You can't tease me like this."

He found himself smiling like an idiot. If his brothers saw him now they'd call him whipped, and he wouldn't care. She was exhausted, had to get up early and she had that little demand in her voice that was sexy as hell. So hot, his woman. So fucking hot. He complied and gave her exactly what she wanted. He'd give her the world every time.

Francesca woke to the first streaks of light invading the bedroom. She knew instantly she was alone and for a moment her heart thudded in protest. She buried her face in the pillow. The scent of Stefano still lingered in the room. In her. On her. She stretched and muscles protested deliciously. She liked that. She liked belonging to him. Knowing his mark was on her and that every time she took a step, she'd feel him inside her.

She sat up, pulling the sheet with her when she realized she didn't have a stitch on. Blinking, she pushed at the hair tumbling around her face and down her back. The room was immaculate. Stefano had picked up their scattered clothes. She found herself laughing as she made her way to the master bathroom. She was happy. She hadn't expected to ever be happy again. Not after losing her parents. Not after losing her sister. Not after Barry Anthon had begun his campaign to take everything from her.

The water was hot, just the way she liked it. It poured over her, soothing the soreness in her muscles. Stefano always, always ensured she found nothing but absolute pleasure in his arms, but he wasn't a gentle lover. He could be sometimes, but it was rare. Gentle usually turned into rough. Hard. She loved rough and hard with him; anything at all he wanted to do, she was totally into. He liked to put his brand on her. She loved those marks of possession, but her body sometimes protested. Hot water took care of that, leaving her with a straight happiness vibe.

She dressed carefully in one of the many skirts Stefano had bought her. He had great taste in clothing. She was fairly certain she'd seen this particular skirt in the window of Lucia's Treasures. It was a beautiful royal blue, the material exquisite. Flowy. A handkerchief hemline. The skirt rode low on the hips and the matching top, out of the same material, was a corset with a zigzag of royal blue cord through eyelets lacing up the front. She loved the way it narrowed at her rib cage and emphasized her small waist.

She had curves—hips and breasts and, as far as she was concerned, too big of a butt—but the cut of the skirt and matching blouse was flattering. She loved the way the material felt as it swished around her legs and fell over her hips in a sexy sway. She added soft suede boots and dried her hair in a loose cloud of dark waves. At the deli she'd have to pull it back to work around the food, but she wanted to look nice when she kissed Stefano good-bye. Her sweater was lacy, an intricate pattern, soft and warm, with tiny buttons going up the front.

Giving herself one last look in the mirror, Francesca stepped out into the hall and started toward the living room. Immediately she heard a woman's voice. Low. Furious. Filled with contempt and repressed anger. Not a hot anger, but cold, like a vicious snake, coiled and ready to strike.

"Do you have *any* idea who this woman is? You should have had her investigated before you ever allowed the media to get ahold of pictures of you with her. My God, Stefano, she's been in a mental facility. She'll drag our good name through the mud, and you'll let her."

Francesca stopped moving instantly, one hand going protectively to her throat, her legs like rubber. That cold voice was talking about her. There was no mistaking that at all. She'd been locked up for seventy-two hours.

"They do say that the mentally unbalanced are a good lay," the voice continued, the contempt deepening. "But I *forbid* this. Our name means something, and just because you can't keep your dick in your pants . . ."

"Eloisa, that's enough."

Francesca flinched at the tone of Stefano's voice. He was angry. Not his usual enraged but under-control anger; this was a smoldering, scary, very low voice that indicated he was extremely dangerous.

"I'm your mother . . ."

"Don't." His voice was a whip, lashing out with a viciousness Francesca hadn't known him capable of. "You lost the right to call yourself my mother a long time ago. You never played that role, and now isn't the time to start. You don't know the first thing about my relationship with Francesca."

He called his mother by her first name? Eloisa? Clearly there was a huge rift between mother and son. Stefano was a man who believed in protecting women. It was ingrained in him. At his very core. It shocked her that something had gone so wrong in their relationship that Stefano was disrespectful to his mother. She'd had a few clues. He hadn't included her or his father in the meeting with his cousins when they'd asked her about Barry.

"I know that you're running out of time and you saw a woman who was compatible with you and what you are. You know in another couple of years you'll have to make a match of convenience, so you took the first thing that came your way because you just *have* to be in control." Eloisa's voice dripped with sarcasm. It also rang with honesty.

Francesca threw one hand out toward the wall to steady herself. What did that mean? A marriage of convenience? Why would Stefano *have* to marry anyone? That didn't make sense. He could have his choice of any woman. He was gorgeous, had tons of money, as well as a million other reasons why a woman would want him. What did Eloisa mean? *Compatible with you and what you are?* What was Stefano that any woman wouldn't be compatible with him?

"What I choose to do or with whom I do it isn't your concern."

Knots coiled tight in Francesca's belly. Stefano wasn't denying anything his mother had said. He was protesting her right to say it to him.

"This family is my business. I've given my *entire* life for it, and I won't let your sex drive or your need to prove to me or your father that you're the one in control, not us, ruin everything."

"I've given my life to this family," Stefano said, his voice dropping even lower.

His tone made Francesca shiver. She could actually feel the heat of his temper filling the room and drifting down the hall toward her. She wouldn't have been surprised to see the walls bulge outward in an effort to contain his temper. She never, ever wanted him that angry with her.

"My sex drive is none of your business and it never will be. I am the one in control of the family, not you and don't ever be stupid enough to test me on that, Eloisa. You didn't listen to me when I told you what would happen if you sent Ettore into the tubes. I told you he was too young and far too sensitive for this kind of work, but you just had to pull rank on me because you didn't want the family to know you didn't know the first thing about your children and they were all there. The others told you. Ricco, Giovanni, Vittorio, hell, even Taviano and Emmanuelle. All of us. But you just had to prove your point. My baby brother. I was the one who held him in my arms. I was the one who got up at night to feed and change him. Not you. I picked him up when he cried and rocked him back to sleep."

"He was weak," Eloisa said in a small voice. "He needed to be a man. I tried to make him a man. You coddled him too much. You always did."

"He was different, Eloisa, but you refused to see that

because, God forbid, you and your husband couldn't possibly produce a less-than-perfect child. Now Ettore's just dead."

Francesca's heart broke for Stefano. There was genuine sorrow in his voice. The sorrow a parent would feel for the loss of a child. She took a step toward the living room, needing to comfort him.

"I've known Barry Anthon's parents for some time, Stefano. He comes from good people," Eloisa continued, as if they hadn't just been discussing the loss of her son. "This deranged woman you call your fiancée accused Barry of murdering her sister—did you know that? It's absolutely absurd. She's got a police record. She's a criminal as well as a mental patient. Give her money to go away. She's not the only rider in the world. They're out there. You just have to look around a little bit. *Dio*, Stefano, at least admit you wouldn't have looked at her twice if she weren't a rider. Be honest with yourself and with me."

"That may be true, Eloisa," Stefano said. "But I did look at her."

Francesca closed her eyes. She'd heard enough, far more than she wanted to hear. Stefano's reason for seeking her out hadn't been compassion because she didn't have a coat. It hadn't been because he was attracted to her. Whatever being a "rider" meant was his true reason for going after her. For asking her to marry him.

She closed her eyes against the tears burning in her throat and behind her eyes. She just had to get out of there with a little dignity and then she could sort things out.

Francesca took a breath, striding down the hall. "Honey, I've got to go. I'm late. I'll text you when I get to work." She burst out of the hall and was nearly all the way to the elevator before she allowed herself to "see" Stefano had company. "Oh. I'm sorry to interrupt you." She flashed a fake smile at Eloisa and took the four steps to the elevator and summoned it with a stab of her finger.

"Francesca," Stefano called out, and took a step toward her. Fortunately the doors opened and she stepped into the lift and hurriedly closed the doors on his face. He knew. He knew she'd heard everything. It was written on his face. She didn't care. She practically ran out of the hotel. To her dismay Emilio and Enzo were waiting for her. Emilio opened the door of the car and she slipped inside, praying Stefano wouldn't call him until after he'd gotten her to work. Her fiancé still had his mother to deal with, and she hoped that took a very long time.

CHAPTER NINETEEN

Francesca resolved not to do anything rash. Stefano had been good to her. There was always honesty in his touch. In his voice. She stuck her thumbnail between her teeth and chewed at it, trying to get past the hurt. She had never felt good enough for Stefano. That wasn't on him—it was on her. Tears burned so close, but she didn't dare shed them. Any moment Emilio's or Enzo's phone would ring and Stefano would order them to turn around and bring her back. A little hysterically she made up her mind to jump out of the car if that happened. She wasn't going back . . . not until she'd had time to think this through.

She could go to Joanna's for the night. Just sit quietly where Stefano's overwhelming, intimidating presence wouldn't color her judgment. Her finger dropped down to the ring he'd given her. So beautiful, like him.

The car pulled up to the curb and she was out before either of her bodyguards could exit. She didn't look at either of them, but rushed into the safety of the deli. Pietro waited behind the counter. He looked up when she entered, a strange look on his face. He was already filling the cases.

"I'm sorry I'm late," she apologized hastily, rounding the counter, more to keep Emilio and Enzo from being able to herd her back out to the car. She glanced out the window. Sure enough, Emilio was on his cell, his eyes on her through the glass. Her heart began to pound. She clenched her teeth. She wasn't going to be pushed around.

"You have the day off today, Francesca," Pietro announced unexpectedly. "I won't need you."

She froze, her hand going to her throat in a defensive gesture. Barry Anthon had made his move. "Pietro," she began. "Whatever he told you, it's just not true. You've gotten to know me . . ." She wouldn't beg. She just didn't expect Joanna's uncle to take Barry at his word without at least giving her a chance to defend herself.

"Girl, what are you talking about? Your man called, and he needs you today. I have no problem calling in Aria or anyone else if Stefano needs you. You work hard, Francesca. I didn't expect you to stay on after you got engaged and I really appreciate that you did, so a day or two off here or there isn't a problem."

Stefano had called him. The relief that it hadn't been Barry was enormous, but she still wasn't going to let Stefano push her around. The door opened and Emilio and Enzo entered, both standing just inside, arms crossed over their chests.

"Let's go, Francesca," Emilio said. "Stefano wants you home."

Her chin went up. How *dared* he order her home. "I don't particularly care what Stefano wants right now, Emilio. I'm working." She turned to Pietro. "If you don't want me working right now, that's fine. I've got other things to do." She had no idea what those other things were, but she'd think of something.

"Francesca." Emilio straightened, looking every inch a true Ferraro. He might not have the same last name, but he could be intimidating when he chose. There was a warning in his voice.

"No." She was adamant. "I'm not going back there. Pietro? Do you need me today or not?"

Pietro hesitated, glancing uneasily at Emilio and Enzo. She immediately wished she hadn't put him in such a position. She put a conciliatory hand on his arm. "I forgot you said you already called Aria. That's great. I had some things I wanted to do anyway. It will give me time to get them done."

Pietro looked relieved and he patted her. "Talk to Stefano first, Francesca. Whatever is happening between you, trust him to clear it up."

Trust. It really boiled down to trust. That—and her insecurities. Still, she wanted to take some time to think things all the way through. That shouldn't be asking too much, even from a very decisive man like Stefano.

She nodded at Pietro, gave him a cheerful little wave and marched right between Emilio and Enzo. Enzo got the door for her and she turned away from the car, toward Lucia's Treasures. She really liked Lucia and Amo. She loved the clothing they sold. It was far beyond her pocketbook, but looking was always fun.

Enzo stepped in front of her and Emilio came up behind her, boxing her in, close to the side of the building.

"Francesca, get in the car," Emilio said.

"It's not going to happen." She found herself seething, grateful for a target. "Stefano Ferraro doesn't tell me what to do. He doesn't own me."

Enzo shook his head. "Babe, don't fight battles you can't win. Pick them with him. Whatever happened this morning to upset you both needs to be worked out."

She glared at him. "First of all, it's no one's business what happened this morning. Second, I have every right to work things out in my own way. And I'm going to do just that." She took a step to get around him and he blocked her with his much larger body, cutting her off so she was pushed almost entirely up against the wall. "Step back. You can't force me to go with you."

Enzo glanced at Emilio and then to the street. Francesca followed his gaze and her heart sank. Of course they were just buying time, arguing with her, and she fell right into their trap. Stefano stalked toward them, looking every inch a dangerous, prowling predator. He walked right up to Francesca, up close, crowding her body, one arm wrapping possessively around her waist and pulling her in tight to his side. Locking her with enormous strength to him so there wasn't a doubt in her mind that if she struggled, he'd subdue her immediately and easily.

"Thanks Emilio, Enzo." Stefano nodded to them and turned her away from the car and began walking in the direction she'd chosen to go, taking her with him. "You didn't stick around to let me explain. Were you running from me?"

She couldn't tell if there was a note of hurt in his voice or not. His tone troubled her, and she glanced up at his face. His mask was in place. The scary one.

"No. I was trying to sort things out in my head."

He stopped abruptly and caught her chin in his hand. "You want to sort out a problem with me, *dolce cuore*, you do it *with* me."

"I had to go to work," she muttered, because he might have a point.

"Bullshit, Francesca. You heard the crap my fucking mother spouted, you were hurt and didn't understand half of what she said and you ran like a rabbit."

She glared at him. "I did not. I was hurt, yes. And you're right. I had no idea what she was talking about when she said I was a 'rider' and that you took the first one to come along. Or that you'd have to settle for a marriage of convenience if you didn't marry me. None of that made sense." The only thing that she'd really understood was that Stefano had lost a sibling—one he loved—and he blamed his mother.

"Tell me about your brother," she prompted.

He took a breath, his face darkening. His jaw set. His eyes were alive with pain, but his features remained an expressionless mask. He began walking again, Francesca tucked tightly to his side. For a long while she was certain he wouldn't respond. They'd walked an entire block, past Lucia's Treasures and Petrov's Pizzeria, and then halfway down another block before he cleared his throat.

Stefano's arm tightened until she almost couldn't breathe, but she didn't protest. Instead, she rested her palm on his very ripped stomach. Beneath his three-piece pin-striped suit, she felt his muscles ripple. Emilio and Enzo trailed them, close enough to help if trouble presented itself, and a discreet enough distance away that Stefano and Francesca could talk in private. They also were able to discourage others from going up to Stefano and Francesca just by shaking their heads. She was vaguely aware of them and what they were doing, but mostly, she concentrated on Stefano, willing him to talk to her.

"Ettore was born eleven months after Emmanuelle. In our family it is necessary to have several children. My mother wasn't—isn't—the mothering type. She didn't want children, and she certainly didn't want to be married to a man she didn't love. Their marriage was arranged. My father is a man who is very difficult to explain. He has a very large ego. He's goodlooking and he knows it. Eventually he began to have affairs. He was discreet, but he had them. He paid no attention to any of us. I think having children cramped his style. If a woman got too clingy, my mother would have a chat with her. Their strange lifestyle didn't leave a lot of room for any of us."

She didn't make the mistake of giving him sympathy. She couldn't imagine growing up that way. Her parents had loved her sister and her. When they died, Cella had stepped up and given her that same unconditional love.

"I saw what my cousins had. Aunts and uncles loving one another and their children. They tried to make it better for me—for us—but they couldn't be in our home 24-7. So I decided that I'd make a home for us."

She knew he had. It showed in the way his brothers and sister reacted to him. Loved him and one another. They were a tight-knit family with Stefano at the helm.

"Ettore had respiratory problems from the moment he was born. He was small and his lungs weren't developed. He was in the hospital for two weeks. My parents went to see him twice. Aunt Rachele and Aunt Perla—you haven't met them yet, only their children—took me every single day to see him. The nurses let me put my hands in the gloves and touch him. Eventually I could hold him." He swallowed hard and looked away from her.

Francesca pressed her hand tighter against his abdomen, matching her steps to his because he'd begun to walk faster. She could see they were headed for a small park in the middle of the neighborhood.

"He just never got strong. My parents were extra hard on him. I told you, we were required to train from age two. They refused to give him more time. Neither spent any time with him, and if they came into contact with him, they were irritated by him. He learned very fast to keep out of their way and my brothers and Emmanuelle took to deflecting their attention immediately if they spotted him."

"I don't understand." Francesca couldn't help but break her silence. "Why would they be irritated by a child?" There was genuine confusion in her voice because it didn't make sense to her. The boy obviously needed love and attention, not annoyance or anger.

"He wasn't perfect, Francesca. In my home, growing up, nothing but perfection was allowed. Our training. Our education. Our ability to speak languages. We had to be not good at everything, but *great*. Ettore tried, but he couldn't keep up. We all tried to help him, tutor him, work with him on physical training, but he was always behind. And the martial arts and boxing took a toll on his body."

"How? Wouldn't that strengthen him?"

He shook his head. "He didn't heal from the inevitable bruises and injuries we got. He was slow at other things, too, things that were necessary in our work. I tried to talk to the parents about him, but they wouldn't listen to me. He was far too sensitive for our kind of work."

She still didn't know what his kind of work was, but if helping out a seventeen-year-old girl who was being horribly abused was anything to go by, she was fairly certain she knew Stefano meant even reading the reports on such things hurt Ettore's heart.

"That's so terrible, Stefano. He should have been protected." She wanted to wrap her arms around him and hold him tight. She knew what it was like to experience loss.

Stefano obviously loved his brother very much. More like a parent with a child than a sibling.

"He should have been, but when he was sixteen, the parents insisted he become active. We got into a terrible fight, but they pulled rank on me. Ettore died. I went to get his body and I carried him home myself. I never allowed them to make a decision regarding any of my siblings after that." There was steel in his voice.

The parents. That was how he referred to the man and woman who had given him life. Stefano loved family. Her fingers curled in his vest, and she turned her head to press a kiss into his side, regardless of the fact that they had a lot more things to work out. Her heart ached for him. She had to blink away tears of sympathy and swallow the terrible lump that had formed in her throat.

He looked down at her bent head. "*Amore mio*, you are far too soft to be without my protection. When you're upset or hurt, or you don't understand, trust me. Talk to me. We're going to be together a lifetime, and I don't ever want you to be afraid or hurt and not come to me. You'll hear a lot of ugly things."

They had entered the park and he guided her toward a bench. The rain had left everything looking brand-new and shiny. He halted, stepping in front of her, tipping her face up to his. "We live our lives in the spotlight quite a bit of the time and it's necessary. People can be very ugly. You have to trust me to look after you and protect you. You have to let us." His thumb slid over her lower lip and then brushed back and forth over her chin.

"I didn't run away, Stefano," she denied softly. "I just needed time to process."

He nodded as if in understanding. "You can't possibly process without having the facts, Francesca." His fingers curled around the nape of her neck, his thumb sweeping her cheek as if he couldn't get enough of her skin.

"It was a shock to hear the things she said."

"I'm certain that's true, *bambina*—she is very judgmental

and demanding. Above all, she wants the Ferraro name pure."

Her heart clenched hard in her chest. So hard it was painful. She had enough scandal tied to her name to sink an entire continent of Ferraros.

Stefano cupped her face gently in his palms, bending so that his forehead touched hers, breathing her in. Breathing for both of them. "We manage to create enough scandal ourselves without our women worrying that they might not be good enough. I love you. I love everything about you. You make me happy. It isn't because you're a rider—it's because you're you."

She swallowed hard. There it was. The "rider" business. Something about what his mother said was the truth, although she heard the ring of honesty in his voice.

"Did I notice you because you're a rider?" he continued. "Of course I did, *dolce cuore*—how could I not when so few come our way? But once we connected, once I was that close to you, I knew."

She stepped closer to him, her hands going inside his jacket and under his vest to clutch his shirt. She wanted to touch bare skin, to be absorbed by him. Melt right into him. Since that wasn't an option, she settled for curling her fingers into his shirt and feeling the heat coming off of him. There was a lot of heat.

"Are you going to explain to me what a rider is?"

Stefano lifted his head, his hands sliding from her face reluctantly. He turned her toward the bench, and Francesca sank down onto the wrought iron. It was cold until he sat beside her and pulled her into his arms. He liked being close to her. He insisted on touching her when he was close. She liked that. A. Lot.

"Once I tell you that, there's no going back from it. Eloisa was . . . indiscreet. You should never have heard that term."

"You have a lot of secrets," Francesca observed.

He was silent, something scary working in the depths of his eyes. "Does that scare you?"

"Everything about you scares me, Stefano, but that doesn't

seem to matter. I'm still here. I would have worked this out on my own."

"You work things out with me," Stefano said firmly. "It has to be that way," he added hastily when she stirred in protest. "Once you know all the secrets, they have to remain secrets. There's no talking to Joanna or anyone else other than immediate family. We're close for a reason. We depend on one another. We have to. Can you accept that, Francesca?"

"I want a family, Stefano, and I like how yours is so close, so yes, that's an easy one to accept."

The tension hadn't left his body. She could feel it there, coiled and ready to strike to protect him. But from what? Her? Stefano suddenly shifted, one arm going under her knees, the other around her back. He lifted her easily and sat her on his lap, his arms circling her. She recognized the move as aggressive—claiming—rather than sweet. Her heart began to pound.

"In our family it is necessary for someone like me to produce children if at all possible. Those children have to be created with another person like me."

"A rider." She supplied the term he was so reluctant to use.

He nodded. "Yes. Another rider. When I said *children* plural, I mean we would have to try for a large family." He sighed. "I don't know who I'm kidding. I *want* a large family, and I want my wife staying home and taking care of them. I want her to get up with me in the middle of the night and change their diapers and feed them. I want her to shower our children with love every minute of the day. I want her to be strong enough to stand up to me and balance my need to keep them all safe."

She understood the tension in him. He'd never had that—not what he wanted for his children. Francesca slid her hand up his chest to stroke the tension from his hard jaw. "Honey, I grew up in a house filled with love. I want nothing less for our children. I don't want someone else raising them. I want family picnics and laughter and trips to the beach that cover all of us in sand that we drag back to our car."

"You'll stay home with them?"

She laughed softly. "And be a kept woman? Seriously, Stefano."

"You'll be my wife. The mother of my children. That means you'll be the heart in our home. Not kept, Francesca, important. The most important of all. I grew up being both mother and father to my siblings. I saw what I wanted for them and for my own children when I visited my aunts and uncles. There was love in their homes. Our children will have to train as I did, but that should be balanced out with love and acceptance. With the ability to recognize each child as an individual with different needs."

She fell in love just a little bit more. How could she not? She heard the longing and need in his voice. He was baring his soul to her. Laying himself on the line. Whatever a "rider" was, it was unimportant next to what he was revealing to her. That was work; this was about his heart and soul. He was giving her that. Stripping himself bare so she knew exactly what he wanted and needed in his life.

"I have to know if that appeals to you, Francesca. I don't want to lose you. I want to give you the world, anything you want. At the same time, you need to know the things most important to me. Our family. You. Me. Our children and my siblings. You'll be the heart for them as well. Can you do that? Am I asking too much of you?"

She heard uncertainty for the first time in his voice. Her man. Strong. Invincible. Arrogant even. Yet he was uncertain when it came to her. He was asking for a home filled with love for his children. For him. For his sister and brothers. Asking if she would be right at the center of that. She knew that position would also put her in charge of the neighborhood, the people he obviously loved and considered under his protection. He would give her those people as well.

"I love you, Stefano. I want to be the mother of your children. I wouldn't know any other way of parenting than to show them as much love as possible. I'll certainly insist on raising them with you. I've worked since I was thirteen years old. I'm not certain I would know how to stay home, but I imagine having multiple children is work in itself. So, yes, I love your idea of a home and family and I am certainly on board with it. However"—she turned his face toward hers and looked him in the eye—"there will be no more telling my boss I'm not working, or telling Emilio and Enzo to bring me home."

He leaned that two inches separating them and brushed kisses from her cheekbone to her chin. "Can't promise that, *amore*. You run away from me like that and I lose my mind. I forget everything but the need to get you back."

She burst out laughing, she couldn't help it. She didn't want to encourage him, but he was just too funny. "You're impossible."

"But very much in love with you, Francesca," he said, framing her face with his hands, looking into her eyes. "I'm so in love with you I can't even breathe without you. I know absolutely, I was born to be your man. Our shadows connected and that truth was there for both of us to see."

It was a beautiful declaration and her eyes burned with reaction. Stark. Raw. He meant every word. She even knew what he meant by their shadows connecting. She'd felt that jolt of urgent chemistry and the rightness of Stefano Ferraro. She often felt emotion when her shadow connected with someone else's, but she'd never felt such a physical and emotional connection as she had when her shadow touched his.

Although he was incredibly possessive and always stating in no uncertain terms that she belonged to him, he hadn't said she was born to be his woman. He had said he was born to be her man. For some reason those words touched her as nothing else could have. She took a breath and let it out. She wanted everything he was offering, no matter how controlling and obsessive he was. No matter how secret their family life would have to be or what a "rider" was.

"I can live with all of it, Stefano, because I suspect I just might have been born for you."

He dropped his chin to the top of her head and just held her in his arms for a long while. She watched the people moving around the park. A few joggers. A couple strolling hand and hand. It was cold and when she shivered, Stefano put her on her feet.

"Let's go home, *bella*. We can spend the day together. Maybe ask the siblings over for dinner tonight. But I just want a restful day. Eloisa always wears me out." He stood up, locked his arm around her waist and began walking back toward the entrance. Emilio followed them. Enzo was nowhere to be found.

Francesca gave an exaggerated sigh. "I don't know about that woman as a mother-in-law, Stefano. She doesn't like me. At. All. In fact, she said she was friends with Barry Anthon's parents." She tried to hide the anxiety in her voice, but she was fairly certain he heard it anyway.

"Don't worry about Eloisa," he assured. "First of all, she isn't anyone's friend outside the family. She's close to her sisters and brothers, but no one else. She doesn't let anyone in. She might know Barry's mother, but she doesn't like her. Margaret Anthon is a society queen. Eloisa, for all her faults, can't take that kind of snobbery. Margaret doesn't touch a single charity unless there's something big in it for her."

"That's a little sad. About your mother, I mean," Francesca pointed out. "That she doesn't have friends. What about Emmanuelle? Surely she's friends with her daughter?"

He shook his head. The car waited at the entrance to the park, Enzo in the driver's seat. Stefano opened the back passenger door for her. Francesca slid onto the cool leather seat, scooting over to make room for her fiancé. Emilio slipped into the front seat.

Stefano shook his head. "Not Emmanuelle. If anything she was nearly as bad with Emme as she was with Ettore. She was incredibly hard on both of them. We all tried to shield them, but during training, we had no real say at all. Emme doesn't ever talk about it, but she keeps her distance from Eloisa and Phillip the way we all do."

There was pain in his voice, and Francesca immediately threaded her fingers through his and brought his hand to her mouth, kissing his knuckles. "Honey, you did your best. Emmanuelle's happy. She loves you and her brothers and cousins. I think she's amazing. You did a good job with her."

"She is pretty amazing," Stefano agreed, pulling her hand to his thigh and holding it there over his solid muscle. "I'm very proud of her. She doesn't have a mean bone in her body, but she can be steel when she needs to be."

"She can fight, too," Francesca said. "You'll have to teach me. She wiped up the floor with the three bimbos."

He raised his eyebrow.

She scowled at him. "Don't pretend you don't remember your three exes. Janice. Doreen. Stella. The horrible threesome with a penchant for doing coke in a bathroom."

"Ah. Them."

"They pled guilty to possession with intent to sell. They have access to high-priced lawyers and yet they took a plea deal. That didn't make sense. They have a good career going . . ."

He shook his head. "They'd been doing more partying than recording, and their last tour was a disaster. Stella was so drunk she fell off the stage, and Janice OD'd right after. The PR people had a nightmare trying to cover that up. Their excesses made them a terrible liability for their label. This last stunt put them over the edge and the label dropped them. Their career is gone."

"Did you have something to do with them losing their label?"

He shrugged. "No one fucks with my woman."

She narrowed her eyes at him. "They were arrested and received a hefty sentence."

He shrugged again and she sighed. She couldn't actually feel sorry for the three women, especially since they'd tried to shove cocaine in her face.

"Emmanuelle beat the crap out of them and didn't even break a fingernail, and she did it when she was in high heels."

He burst out laughing. "You sound admiring. I'll teach you a few moves, *bambina*, but you'll have bodyguards from now on, even when you go to a restroom. I have a female cousin or two trained in security."

"Of course you do." She rolled her eyes. "Emilio and Enzo have a sister, do they?"

He nodded. "Enrica. I've already asked her to come on board."

"Did you think you might want to consult with me first?"

"I told you, I don't argue. You like that shit and I'm just not going there with you when something needs to be done, like hiring a female bodyguard to watch you everywhere."

"So Emilio and Enzo can go back to looking out for you?" Her tone was just a little shy of challenging him, but she had faith in Emilio and Enzo and wanted them looking out for Stefano, not her.

Stefano laughed again, the notes warm and alluring. The sound washed over her like the sun, bright and warm. She didn't hear him laugh nearly enough and it was disarming. At the hotel, Emilio opened the door for them and Stefano slid out, retaining possession of her hand so that she followed him out of the vehicle and was drawn close. She realized Stefano always did that. He liked her close. She found herself smiling in spite of the fact that he hadn't answered.

In the privacy of the elevator, she leaned into him. "Will your mother call Barry Anthon and tell him where I am? Or ask him questions about me?"

His eyebrow shot up. "You're my fiancée. You have my ring on your finger and I told her in no uncertain terms that we would be married as soon as possible. She understands that, whether or not she agrees or likes it. That makes you family."

"I'm confused, Stefano. She really didn't like me. Won't she try to find a way to stop us from being married? Barry would be her perfect solution."

The doors opened and they stepped into the apartment. "It doesn't work that way, Francesca. Not in our family. Family is family. You protect your family. Close ranks around them. My mother is all about family to the extent of everything else. She would never betray you to Barry Anthon or anyone else. It just isn't done."

She tried to grasp what that meant. The enormity of it. His mother had been so adamant. Clearly, mother and son had major issues. Still, he was absolutely certain she wouldn't call Barry or his mother. "I don't . . ." She trailed off, shaking her head.

Stefano stopped abruptly and tipped her chin up to his. "She would protect you. Physically protect you. Step in front of you if a bullet headed your way. As long as my claim is on you, any one of my family would do so."

She would have done that for Cella, or for one of Cella's children. She didn't want to think that Cella would never have a child for her to protect.

"You have all of us. And Emmanuelle. She'll have children. They all belong to you now, Francesca. Can't you feel that when you're with them?"

"This is all so new to me, Stefano." She'd been beaten down so far by Barry Anthon and his men that she had lost herself. Her strength. Her belief in anyone. His family was so opposite of everything she'd come to believe it was difficult to comprehend that they could be real. "Sometimes I feel like I'm in the middle of a fairy tale and any minute I'm going to wake up and you'll be gone."

He kissed her gently. A brief brush of his mouth over hers. "That's never going to happen, *amore mio.*"

She loved the feel of his lips. Soft but firm. Demanding and commanding. Warm and then hot. She could kiss him forever.

"Stop or we'll be right back in bed."

She couldn't help but laugh softly. "Is that a bad thing?"

He shook his head. "Never, but I was a little rough last night. And the night before and all the nights before that. I think your body needs a little time. Besides, I want to spend time with you outside of bed, and you need to eat. You skipped breakfast." That was an accusation.

She shrugged. "I work at a deli. I can always eat there."

"I'm changing. Since we're staying in, I'll go for comfortable. And don't think I didn't notice that you said you *can* always eat there, not that you *do*."

She laughed and wandered into the kitchen. She liked to cook and she could just as easily fix eggs as call down an order to the hotel kitchen. She had two omelets nearly made when he entered the room in a pair of soft blue jeans and a T-shirt that stretched tightly over his chest. She drew in her breath, allowing her gaze to drift possessively.

"What are you doing?"

"Taking in the awesome sight that is mine." She pushed the omelets onto a plate and carried them to the small, much more intimate table than the one in his dining room. She'd already set it with utensils and napkins.

They ate breakfast together and she found herself enjoying every moment with him. It was easy being with Stefano. Out of the public eye, he was different. He lost his aloof, arrogant demeanor and appeared softer and relaxed. He smiled often and laughed occasionally. He always made her feel as if she was his entire focus. They played chess—he won three games. He worked with her in his training room, teaching her to break out of a choke hold and get away when a very strong man grabbed her wrist. They practiced for an hour, and then he made love to her right there on the floor.

They spent time just talking and then listening to music, dancing together in the living room. His siblings came over and they trained with her watching, shocked at the violence and speed as well as how good they all were. She found their martial arts training to be fascinating and beautiful to watch. She liked that Emmanuelle kept up with her brothers.

They ate together before his family left, and that was fun. Emmanuelle and Ricco helped her make pasta and salad. It was fun and easy, much more so than Francesca ever thought it would be. There was a lot of laughter and teasing, mostly between the siblings, but they weren't shy about including her.

After his family left, Stefano made love to her twice

more, both times very gently, once on the floor by the fireplace and the second time on the couch in the living room. In the end, she found herself draped over him, skirt and blouse back on, but her panties and bra nowhere to be found.

She started to move, to look for her underwear, but Stefano pulled her down on top of him, so that she sprawled on his chest and he rolled slightly, tucking them both against the back of the long, wide couch. He caught up the remote and turned on the television. She wasn't much of a television watcher, but she decided that didn't matter. Lying on top of Stefano, surrounded by his unique masculine scent and his incredible, very hard muscles, his fingers playing in her hair, she decided, was the best.

Francesca closed her eyes and let herself drift. Her ear was over his heart. He was warm and his hands in her hair felt soothing. She may have fallen asleep for a time, but she woke when she heard the newscaster's voice on the television set. No, it hadn't been the voice that woke her. Stefano's muscles had contracted, rippled beneath her in reaction, just for a moment, but she was so in tune with him she felt the difference, the alertness immediately.

"In local news, a group of schoolchildren out on a field trip stumbled across a gruesome scene. The body of thirty-four-year-old Scott Bowen washed up onshore. His neck was broken. According to the chief medical examiner, Dr. Aaron Pines, Bowen could have broken his neck when falling into the river." The voice droned on but Francesca was focused on the photograph flashed on the screen. She recognized him immediately. He was the man who had put a knife to her throat. She would have known him anywhere.

"Stefano?" Her hand crept defensively to her throat. She didn't know what she was asking. The two muggers had disappeared, he'd said so, and the last she'd seen of them, Emilio and Enzo were putting them into a car. They'd done the same with Bowen. Now he was dead, his neck broken. She couldn't help herself; she shifted her body weight, intending to slide off of Stefano.

His arms tightened. "Don't. Don't be afraid of me, Francesca. Not ever."

"Did you kill him? Did Emilio or Enzo?"

"No." He was silent a moment, stroking soothing caresses down her spine. "Let me tell you a little about Bowen and his friends before you go shedding any tears for him. They've robbed countless people and each robbery has become more violent than the last. They've put several people in the hospital, people who cooperated with them. It was only a matter of time before they killed someone. No one has been able to stop them, not the police, not even us, and we talked to them. They just kept getting worse."

"So you knew about them before they tried to rob me." She lifted her head to look into his eyes. There was no guilt. No remorse. No expression of any kind. Just cool honesty.

"Yes. But, Francesca, sooner or later, we would have had to deal with them. Someone needed to stop them. They put their hands on you. They put a knife to your throat. That made it sooner."

Her heart skipped a beat and then began to pound wildly. She turned his declaration over in her mind. He *had* done something to Bowen. To Bowen's friends.

"Bottom line, *dolce cuore*, that's who I am. When the cops can't do something to protect citizens, it's my turn. You have to decide if you can live with who I am. The real me." His arm was an iron band around her waist, but his hand was gentle as he continued to stroke caresses along her spine.

She heard the note in his voice. Uncertain. He wouldn't change for her. He couldn't. And he was asking her to accept him. Every part of him. She closed her eyes and pressed deeper into his chest. On some level she'd known all along, but still the admission caught her off guard. Could she live with that? With a man who took the law into his own hands? He was always loving with his family, with her, with his neighbors. Over-the-top protective. A little scary. Arrogant. He wanted a home, a wife and children, and she knew absolutely she'd be the center of his universe. She didn't doubt that for a minute.

"You asked me to help a seventeen-year-old girl last night. You knew what that would mean. You knew what you were asking me to do."

She started to protest, but then remained silent. She did. She knew. She'd been a victim of a man, the same man who had murdered her sister. She had no doubt that Barry Anthon would have murdered her if Cella hadn't dropped her cell phone in the mail before she'd returned home. She wanted justice for Cella and the cops would never give that to her. Only a man like Stefano Ferraro.

She took a deep breath and turned her head to press a kiss into his throat, closing her eyes. She'd already committed to him. In her heart, in her soul. Almost from the first moment she'd met him, she'd been mesmerized by him. Once she got to see him, once he'd let her into his world, she'd fallen hard and fast. She'd just known.

There was that first moment she'd been aware of their shadows touching. It sounded crazy but, from the time she'd been a child, if her shadow touched someone else's shadow, she "felt" them. With Stefano that knowledge had been deep and instantaneous. The chemistry had been off the charts. Most of all, she'd known he was a good man in spite of all the evidence to the contrary. She'd fallen and there was no going back.

"I'm in love with you, Stefano," she said softly, "so I live with whatever it is you have to do."

That declaration earned her his body again. This time he started out slow and ended up fast and rough. It was perfection.

CHAPTER TWENTY

The next two weeks passed in a flurry of activity. Francesca felt as if she'd been swept into a wild wind. Somehow, Stefano had gotten it into his head that her acceptance of him meant they were getting married immediately. To him, "immediately" meant as soon as the paperwork was done. She had no idea how it all happened, only that each day she went to work, somewhere in the middle of the afternoon and sometimes even the morning, Pietro would get a call and she'd find herself in the car with Emilio, Enzo and their sister, Enrica, going to some crazy fitting or consultation.

Emmanuelle and her cousins, along with Eloisa, seemed to be planning the event of the century, something Francesca wasn't at all comfortable with. She tried to talk to Stefano, but he shook his head and just kissed her senseless. Finally, realizing she wasn't going to be able to keep her job and not have poor Pietro calling in substitutes every morning, she gave in to the inevitable, giving her notice, telling herself Stefano hadn't really won that round, even though she knew he had.

In the evening, after a particularly grueling day looking at flowers and talking about colors and ice sculptures, she was grateful to just work in their kitchen, preparing the shrimp pasta Stefano requested. She hadn't seen him for most of the day. He'd been at work and when he came in, he looked tired and unsettled—something she was beginning to recognize when he didn't like a particular report on something. He sat down at the table, taking the chair close to hers, something he always did because his knee could touch her thigh and she was in easy reach.

"You do realize that we're being snowballed into a church wedding and they're planning to have it in another couple of weeks," she began. "Your sister and Eloisa have gotten this thing together so fast my head is spinning."

"Leave it, *dolce cuore*—there's no way in hell to stop them. Just let them do their thing. We'll show up, get married, party and everyone will be happy. They don't mind doing the work—in fact they want to do it, so if we don't care, let them."

She hadn't thought of it like that. Still. "I thought we'd just go to the courthouse or something."

He kissed her knuckles and then picked up his fork to eat the shrimp pasta. "Not a chance. Not in our family. Why are you nervous, Francesca? I'll be waiting for you at the end of the aisle."

She ducked her head, unable to meet his eyes, torn between smiling at his arrogance, and crying because he had no way of understanding. He had an *enormous* family. There would be no one sitting on her side of the church. "I'll be walking up the aisle by myself and will probably fall on my face, especially if Emmanuelle has her way and I have to walk in four-inch heels."

His head came up alertly. His gaze slid over her face like the stroke of fingers. Loving. Gentle. Tender even. "Long dress, *bambina*, that means you can wear any fucking thing you want on your feet. Or go barefoot. As for walking you down the aisle, Emilio asked for that privilege. You don't want him, any of my cousins will be happy to oblige. Enzo and Emilio arm-wrestled or something and the winner asked me. If you prefer Pietro or someone else, just say so."

The idea that Emilio and Enzo had arm-wrestled for the duty of walking her down the aisle made her suddenly want to weep. She had grown very fond of them both. To cover up the emotion threatening to choke her, she changed to the subject that worried her the most.

"What happened at work? There are shadows in your eyes, Stefano." She willed him to answer. She'd already accepted what he did to protect others and she didn't want him to shut her out.

Stefano sighed and reached back to rub at his neck. "The girl I told you about a couple of weeks ago."

"The teenager?" Francesca put her fork down and picked up her napkin, suddenly afraid. *Please, please don't let him say she was dead.*

He nodded. "Her name is Nicoletta Gomez. The investigations were completed and it's far worse than I originally thought. I'm going to have to leave tomorrow, Francesca. If I wait too much longer, she might not survive the next attack."

"Then go. Of course you have to go." She stood up and moved behind his chair, sinking her fingers into his tight neck muscles in an effort to ease the tension out of him. "I want you to go."

"*Dio, bella*, that feels good. But you should know . . ." He trailed off when the elevator door *pinged* in warning.

Ricco and Taviano entered a couple of moments later. Ricco sniffed the air and went straight to the kitchen, dished himself and Taviano a large bowl of pasta and dragged chairs closer to the table. "Dig in before the others come. We might have a chance at seconds." He grinned at her. "Hey, Francesca, looking good for a bridezilla. I figured your head would be spinning around at this point."

She continued kneading the tight muscles of Stefano's neck and shoulders. "I feel like a bridezilla. I really understand the concept of eloping, but Stefano doesn't get it."

"I always thought the woman wanted the big white wedding and the man was all for eloping," Taviano said, shoveling a heaping forkful of pasta into his mouth.

The elevator *pinged* again, and this time it was Giovanni, Emmanuelle and Vittorio. Francesca had come to realize that where one sibling was, more were close by. She was glad she'd made a healthy amount of pasta, although there weren't going to be any leftovers for lunch the next day.

Once they were all seated around the table and eating, pouring glasses of wine, she looked closely at their faces. "So what's wrong?"

Giovanni raised an eyebrow. "Why would you think something was wrong? Other than Emmanuelle's really bad taste in lunch dates."

"I didn't have lunch with him and certainly didn't go on a date," Emmanuelle snapped, glaring at her brother. "I ran into him and it was polite to speak, that's all. Stop with the teasing. He annoys the crap out of me."

Francesca knew instantly they were talking about Valentino Saldi. The brothers disliked him on principle, and Emmanuelle disliked him because he was always sarcastic with her. She really hated being called *princess* and Valentino apparently did it at every opportunity. Emmanuelle sounded annoyed, but a faint blush stole up her cheeks and when her eyes met Francesca's there was pleading there.

"Stop teasing Emme. It isn't distracting me. I know you all didn't show up here for the pasta, so something else is up," Francesca said. "Just tell me."

There was a small silence. Her fingers curled into Stefano's shoulders, holding on for the inevitable blow, because just by the silence, she knew it was coming.

"Barry Anthon is in town and he's on his way here," Ricco announced, his voice calm and matter-of-fact.

Francesca's heart stuttered. Instantly her stomach churned. She pressed one hand to her stomach and the other to her mouth, afraid she'd be sick right there with Stefano's family all sitting around the table, pretending they weren't watching her closely. For a moment her vision actually began to fade and her legs went weak.

Ricco was up instantly, nearly knocking over his chair, his fingers strong on the back of her neck, pushing her head down. "Just breathe. Don't panic on us. Don't give the bastard that."

Stefano's chair scraped and he crouched down beside her, holding her long hair out of her eyes while he examined her pale face. "He can't hurt you, *bambina*, not ever again. Whatever he says, and he'll be very, very careful, knowing you're my fiancée. He knows I'm not the kind of man to allow him to make implications or innuendos about my woman. He'll be on his best behavior. So will we. We're going to be all smiles and politeness."

She forced air through her lungs, ashamed of her weakness. Stefano's brothers and sister had dropped what they were doing to support her. "I'm all right now. I'm sorry. I just . . . He's . . ." She sighed as she straightened slowly.

Ricco and Stefano both kept a hand on her as she stood. Of all the brothers, Ricco was the one she felt kept himself locked away, his eyes permanently shadowed, as if something terrible had happened to him, but he refused to share, to lighten his burden. He was very much like Stefano in that he was scary, maybe even more so. A dark, dangerous man seeking an adrenaline rush all the time. He was the most unpredictable and yet, he was careful of her. Gentle even. All of the Ferraros were so nice to her.

"He murdered her. All those stab wounds. The blood. I see it nearly every time I close my eyes. He would hurt any one of you just because he thinks he can. He's made himself untouchable. I don't know if I can sit across from his smiling face and not pick up a knife and stab him just as many times." She made the confession in a rush, needing them to understand she wasn't afraid *of* Barry so much as for all of them—or of what she might do.

"But you won't," Stefano said. "Because you believe me when I tell you we're handling this. Barry Anthon will pay the price for murdering your sister and destroying the life you had."

"I can give you Cella's phone," she offered. "I don't know why I didn't before."

Taviano laughed. "Little sister, that's rich. You don't need to give it to us. We've already seen it."

"That's impossible. It's in a safety deposit box under Joanna's name. You'd need the key."

"She keeps it in her top left-hand drawer," Vittorio said.

"I made a copy when I had my little chat with her, and then Salvatore went to the bank and retrieved it. Don't worry. It's back in the box. He returned it once they made a recording. We needed the evidence for the investigation."

Francesca didn't know whether to be annoyed or impressed. "What investigation?"

"We always make certain of all facts, little sister," Ricco said, sitting back down to eat more of the pasta. "We don't make mistakes."

"Thorough," Giovanni added. "It can take a while, but we know we're right before we make a move."

Francesca threaded her fingers through Stefano's. "That's why you waited on the girl, isn't it? You had to make certain."

Stefano nodded. "Our solutions tend to be permanent. We can't afford mistakes."

She liked that. The fact that they took their time to make absolutely sure, even if they wanted to move on something—as Stefano clearly did with Nicoletta Gomez—made her certain she was right to trust Stefano.

"I was about to tell you that I have to go out of town tomorrow. Giovanni and Taviano will go with me. It will appear that only the two of them will board the plane and I've stayed here with you. Emmanuelle, Ricco and Vittorio will be with you at all times. Barry Anthon won't get close to you, but if you need me here, Francesca, now that you know Anthon is close, I'll delay the trip."

"No. Of course not. I've seen Emme in action, and if I decide to go crazy and go after Barry, I have no doubt she can stop me."

"You're sure."

She looked him in the eye. "You get her out of that situation. More than anything else, I want that. I was afraid for the people around me, Stefano. Barry destroyed my life and he beat me down. I came to Chicago with the idea of building myself back up. I planned to find a way to go after him. Believe me, I wouldn't have allowed him to get away with my sister's murder. He's going to pay."

Stefano brought her hand to his mouth and gently scraped his teeth back and forth over the pads of her fingers. "That's my woman." There was pride in his voice.

The hotel phone rang. The room went still. Stefano, keeping possession of her hand, tugged until she went with him across the room to answer it. It was the front desk telling him he had a visitor, a friend from out of town, Barry Anthon. Could he come up on such short notice? Yes, he was alone. Stefano answered easily. "Sure, tell him we're just finishing dinner and Emilio and Enzo will bring him up."

Time slowed down instantly for Francesca. There was a strange buzzing in her head. She could see the kitchen counter from where she stood and her gaze fixed on the butcher block of knives. They weren't just any knives. They were a chef's weapons in the kitchen, precise and sharp beyond measure.

Stefano's fingers closed around her upper arm like a vise. She hadn't realized she'd taken a step toward the kitchen when he pulled her up close to his body. His hand spanned her throat, thumb tipping her head back, forcing her eyes to meet his.

"You trust your man, Francesca. You put yourself in my hands. You committed to me. That means I have your trust. It may not be the latest trend, or the modern concept of what a partnership is, but you chose me and I chose you. I will never be anything less than the man in our relationship. Trust me to take care of you properly. I will always do my best for you. You do what I say in this matter—do you understand me?"

She moistened her dry lips with the tip of her tongue. "What are you saying?"

"You don't ever do violence, Francesca, not unless it's self-defense or in the defense of our family. I won't have that on your soul. You're going to be my wife. The mother of my children. You're about love and softness. Not killing. Never that. This man has harmed you. He murdered a woman who would have been my sister. When we're ready, the family will strike. Until then, you do *exactly* what I say." He turned and gestured toward his silent siblings. "What they say. This is our field of expertise."

She closed her eyes, not wanting to see the killer in him, because it was right there, exposed, his eyes flat and cold. Impersonal, when she could never be. She could kill Barry Anthon, but she could *never* be that objective or detached about it. She might regret taking a life later. She didn't know, but she feared she might.

There was silence in the room. Waiting. Stefano was patient. His revelation came as no surprise. She'd known all along what kind of man he was. He controlled his world and would expect to control his household—especially his wife. A million objections ran through her mind, but she really didn't feel them. She knew Stefano now and she knew him to be a fair man. He wouldn't be a tyrant or dictator, but he would definitely expect her to follow his lead in their marriage.

Her eyes searched his. His gaze was steady. He didn't even blink. She had no doubt that he would take care of Barry Anthon, but he would do it safely. Much safer than she could ever manage.

"I hear you, honey," she said softly. "Tell me what you want me to do."

"Sit between Ricco and me. Keep your hand in mine. No matter what he says or what any of us say, you stay quiet. Try not to look at him triumphantly, or with anger. If you can't do that, and I don't expect you to be a great actress, then just keep your eyes down. Barry would never buy a change of heart from you, but don't go as far as open hostility. We aren't quite ready to take him down. If things are too difficult, look to Emmanuelle. She'll pull you out."

Francesca took a deep breath. Inhaled Stefano. She feared once Barry entered the room she wouldn't be able to breathe properly. She didn't want to take the chance of drawing him into her lungs. He was in her nightmares; he didn't get anything else from her.

She took a slow look around her at Stefano's siblings. All

of them stood as still as statues. Beautiful, gorgeous specimens of human beings, tough and dangerous, waiting for her signal, completely prepared to protect her at any cost. Her gaze drifted back to Stefano's face. The angles and planes could have been immortalized in stone. She saw everything there, everything she ever wanted.

"Okay." She hesitated and then was compelled to issue a warning. "Barry Anthon is a monster. He'll give you his innocent face and all the while plan to stab you in the back."

"We have a lot of practice at this, Francesca," Emmanuelle reassured. "We've been playing to the public for years. We cultivate the paparazzi, feeding them the stories we want them to publish, giving them the pictures and images so we're controlling everything for our own purposes. We've got this."

"Barry is on the racetrack, trying to throw his weight around frequently," Ricco added, his voice low, contemptuous. "He likes to be the big man, but let me just say this, little sister: that poor excuse for a human being has nothing on us when it comes to manipulation or playing to the camera. He'll believe us. Just follow our lead and look to us if you get in trouble. You're *famiglia*. Sacred to us."

She was finally getting that the entire Ferraro family actually felt that way and it gave her a very much needed warm feeling. She smiled at them all, rubbing her hands up and down her arms, grateful to them. "I really appreciate you all."

The cold, frozen place inside of her that knew Barry Anthon would try again to destroy her was beginning to thaw a little. "I don't actually believe he's that afraid of me or the evidence I have against him. That's one of the reasons I didn't take Cella's phone to the FBI or another law enforcement agency. There's evidence of wrongdoing, but nothing really connects him other than his handwriting. Any competent lawyer would get him off if that's all they had against him."

She pushed a hand through her hair. "I think Barry likes terrorizing people. It gives him a feeling of power. He likes

destroying lives just because he can. Just like he wants women
to fall in love with him so he can destroy them that way."

Ricco and Stefano exchanged a long look. Ricco grinned.
"You're correct, Stefano. She's not only beautiful—she's a
gift."

Francesca had no idea what that meant, but it was sincere
and made her blush.

"That's exactly right, Francesca," Stefano agreed. "He's
a sociopath. He can be charming to get his way, but anyone
who crosses him is going to be mowed down one way or
another. He's been destroying others ever since he was a little
boy. I think his own mother is afraid of him. If he hadn't
been born into the Anthon family with their money, he'd
already be in jail."

The elevator *pinged* a warning and Stefano's arm swept
around her, bringing her front to his side, locking her there
under the protection of his shoulder. Francesca pressed her
hand to his rock-hard abdomen. She could feel his heat and
the reassuring muscles beneath the thin tee. Her throat went
dry and her heart pounded when she heard Emilio's voice
announcing Barry Anthon. She couldn't look. She didn't
dare. She did trust Stefano and the others to take care of
Barry—eventually. That didn't mean she didn't have the
compulsion to jump on him and beat him with her fists. It
would hurt like hell, but it would be satisfactory.

"Barry," Stefano greeted. "What a surprise. I had no idea
you were in town."

Stefano's voice was calm, matter-of-fact, not at all as if
just minutes earlier he had been assuring Francesca that he
would be taking care of a murderer in a very permanent
way. Keeping his arm tightly around her, he walked into the
foyer to greet their guest.

"Good timing," he added. "The family's here tonight."

"I didn't mean to interrupt your dinner," Barry said.

Her stomach lurched. She would know that voice anywhere. He sounded so normal. Genial even. She knew evil

lurked under that first layer in his tone because she heard it. The snide contempt for everyone around him. She wondered if the others could hear it as well. Cella hadn't been able to, and in the end she paid the ultimate price.

Stefano's fingers bit into her waist hard enough to hurt. She forced her lashes to lift and found herself looking directly into Barry's eyes. There was speculation there. A watchful, sardonic smirk for her alone. She refused to rise to the bait. She didn't smile in welcome; she couldn't manage even a sarcastic smile and he would never believe it anyway.

"I believe you know my fiancée," Stefano said.

Barry inclined his head. "I do. I was in love with her sister, Cella, a beautiful woman. I'm afraid Francesca didn't approve of the match. I had hoped, over time, to win her over, but unfortunately Cella was murdered and Francesca had to place blame somewhere. It fell squarely on my shoulders. I'll admit I was surprised that you two had met, let alone gotten engaged. Francesca and her sister didn't exactly run in our circle."

There was no faulting anything he said, or even his tone of voice, but he still managed to reduce her to the jealous, younger sister who refused approval of her older sister's relationship for petty reasons. He also had subtly pointed out that Francesca and Cella weren't members of the elite upper echelon and she didn't have his money or education. She didn't belong.

That did make her smile. She belonged to Stefano. With Stefano. She felt the others moving closer, taking her back. She belonged to the Ferraro family, and no one fucked with a Ferraro. She lifted her chin. "There is some truth in there. My sister and I certainly never have run in your circle, Barry. As for blaming you, I blame the man who murdered my sister so viciously and I always will."

Stefano's fingers bit down again. He waved toward the great room. "Come sit down and tell us what you're doing in town."

Barry followed Stefano and Francesca into the spacious

room and, after greeting the other Ferraros, took the armchair closest to Emmanuelle. Of course he would choose the one female Ferraro. Barry believed himself to be irresistible to women. He would flirt with Emmanuelle and try to get an ally in the enemy's camp. Francesca wondered if that was what Valentino Saldi was doing and if that was what made Emmanuelle so angry with him whenever they met. No one wanted to be used.

Stefano directed her to the long sofa. He sat close to her, keeping her tightly against him, her hand pressed to his thigh. Ricco sat on the other side of her, almost as close as Stefano. She could feel his body heat and the wave of menace pouring off him. It was tangible enough that Stefano sent him a quelling glance. Secretly, Francesca wanted to hug Ricco. He didn't like Barry's subtle attack on her.

"What brings you to town?" Ricco asked, sounding every bit as pleasant as Stefano. He gave Barry a shark's smile, all white teeth and politeness.

"There's a company in town I was looking into," Barry admitted. "It might be worth my time to either turn it around or sell it off piece by piece. I heard about the engagement and saw some of the really nasty articles written about Francesca. I thought I might speak on her behalf so none of you would jump to the wrong conclusions about her. After all, she could have been my little sister."

It took every ounce of discipline she had not to launch herself at Barry. Her fingers curled into claws, nails digging into Stefano's thigh. He didn't wince, but he did smooth caresses over the back of her hand. The nerve of Barry Anthon, to act like he would or ever could "speak on her behalf."

Vittorio laughed softly. "No one has to speak on Francesca's behalf, Barry. We're all in love with her. How could anyone help be anything but in love with her? The things the paparazzi dug up are all in the past. It's just enough to feed the frenzy and to be interesting, but not enough to be a huge scandal, although we've never shied away from that."

The siblings all laughed. Francesca managed a faint smile. Stefano grounded her with his absolute confidence. The family helped with their unconditional support.

"That's good then. Great," Barry said. "Such a relief. Francesca is a great girl. I had hoped we'd become good friends since we shared the love of her sister." He lifted his eyebrow at Francesca. "Perhaps one day. Have you set a date for the wedding, Stefano?" Clearly he didn't believe for a moment that Stefano was really marrying her. It was there in the subtle sneer.

Emmanuelle clapped her hands together. "I've been seeing to all the details. Francesca feels a little railroaded, I'm sure, but my mother and I are following Stefano's orders to the letter. He wants to marry his lady immediately and since we're all in total agreement, we can't put the wedding together soon enough."

"Do you feel railroaded, Francesca?" Stefano asked, his eyes meeting hers. Voice soft. Low. Intimate. He brought her fingertips up to his mouth and nibbled, looking for all the world as if he might devour her right there in front of everyone.

She shook her head, allowing Barry to see the truth—that she was absolutely mesmerized by Stefano, completely in love with him. Barry would never have that kind of devotion and love from anyone because he couldn't feel it himself. He could never sustain his interest long enough for a woman to find herself completely and utterly in love. He needed power over and then the destruction of his pretty toys long before true devotion ever happened.

"Will you be in Chicago long, Barry?" Taviano asked.

"Enough that I rented an estate for the month. I'd like to close this deal." He winked at Emmanuelle. "Plenty of time to hit the clubs and maybe have a dinner or two with your sister." His voice held complete confidence.

"Barry, you're such a flatterer." Emmanuelle batted her eyelashes at him. "And so brave with all my brothers sitting around you like a bunch of hawks. The last man who tried to take me out ended up in the hospital for two weeks. He had thirty-seven stitches in his head and no one was altogether certain if he would ever be able to function properly, if you know what I mean."

Barry's smile slipped. Her voice was very bright, almost as if she was teasing him, but she sounded serious enough. Francesca looked up at Stefano. He grinned, as if the memory was a happy one. Ricco cracked his knuckles.

Giovanni sighed. "We're not taking the blame for that one, Emmanuelle." He shook his head at Barry. "She did that one all on her own."

"Seriously?" Barry looked Emmanuelle up and down. She was small, almost slight. She had a good figure, but she was much smaller than her brothers. "I can't see that happening."

"It's true," Emmanuelle said with a casual shrug.

"He attack you or something?"

"He did that, he'd be dead," Stefano said.

"Then what?" Barry insisted.

Emmanuelle rolled her eyes. "I was PMSing, okay? No big deal. I told him to back off a couple of times and he wouldn't. He should have listened. I warned him twice."

Barry looked around at all her brothers and then he laughed nervously. "Good one, Emmanuelle. I almost believed you."

"Where are you staying, Barry?" Giovanni asked.

"The Mardsten estate. It's very private. I brought my own security with me. I've had a few threats lately. Someone's been after my design for a new racing engine."

"That's right," Stefano said. "Your company has been in the developing stages for a few years now for a new engine. Is it finally finished? Are you ready to debut it on the track?"

"Not quite yet, but we're close."

"You stole Martin Estee away from Aeronautics, didn't you? That was quite a coup. As a designer, he's the top in the business," Ricco stated. "You got lucky, especially if he manages to design you something new. We've been working on our own for a while now."

Vittorio nodded. "We'd give anything to be able to lure Martin away from you."

"Although you, Taviano and Emme have done a good job for us," Stefano pointed out to his brother. "Our last cars have kicked ass."

Barry shifted forward, his brows coming together. "You three designed your engine?"

"Mostly Taviano," Ricco said. "He's our ace in the hole."

Francesca watched Barry's face closely. His facial expression had frozen, his eyes going killer cold. She shivered and wanted to protest, to do anything to draw attention away from Taviano. Didn't they all realize they were painting a target in the middle of Taviano's forehead? Barry didn't like to be bested, and the Ferraros were winning races. Ricco was an excellent driver. He'd won race after race and more than once he'd left Barry's car in the dust.

Giovanni glanced at his watch and excused himself, heading for the elevator after brushing a kiss on first Emmanuelle's forehead and then on Francesca's. His siblings gave him a brief wave. Barry didn't even seem to notice. He was frowning at Stefano.

"I had no idea Taviano liked to design and build engines," Barry said.

Stefano shrugged. "He doesn't like the spotlight much."

"It isn't just me," Taviano objected modestly. "Vittorio and Emme fixed a few problems for me. Ricco managed to add more power when we thought we were already at max. So it's a group effort."

Francesca allowed the talk of the racetrack and cars to flow around her. Stefano and Ricco stayed in charge of the conversation, expertly slipping in a question every now and then and keeping Barry from addressing Francesca. Their siblings followed their lead, providing interesting conversation and asking questions that followed most naturally. None of them seemed as if they were conducting an interrogation, but Francesca was certain they were learning all sorts of things Barry didn't have a clue they were getting out of their casual conversation.

Taviano served the drinks that Vittorio made, and they kept Barry's flowing, while they only appeared to be keeping up with him. Francesca nursed the one drink Stefano had insisted she take. She was afraid that if she got a little tipsy, she'd tell Barry just what she thought of him and then she'd go after him with teeth and nails.

Barry liked his alcohol and Vittorio was being generous in mixing his favorite gin and tonic. Within an hour and a half, he was slurring his words and getting a little belligerent toward Stefano and especially her. He kept getting in little digs. Suddenly he went silent for a few minutes while the talk between the brothers and Emmanuelle swirled around him and then he jabbed a finger toward Francesca.

"What?" She couldn't keep the belligerence out of her voice.

"How'd you like being locked up in the mental hospital?" he challenged with a sneer. "Did they put you in a strait-jacket? I would have given anything to see that. Beautiful little perfect Francesca, all wrapped up like a gift. I heard some of those orderlies love to fuck the patients when they're all tied up like that. That happen to you? Did one of them sneak into your room at night? Maybe you enjoyed it . . ."

Stefano hit him at the same time Ricco did. Hard. The sounds were so loud Francesca cried out. She hadn't seen Stefano or Ricco move, but they were across the small space and both simultaneously punched Barry on either side of his face. She swore there was an audible crack and then Barry was screaming and throwing wild punches.

Emmanuelle stood up calmly and held out her hand to Francesca. "Let's go in the other room while the boys are playing."

She pulled Francesca out of her seat while Francesca stared with horrified eyes at the two brothers beating Barry to a bloody pulp.

"You have to stop them, Emmanuelle."

"Why in the world would I do that?" She kept tugging determinedly on Francesca's hand until they were in the kitchen. "Drunk or not, that moron is responsible for what he says. Taunting you like that is totally unacceptable, and doing it in front of my brothers is like waving a red cape at a bull. Seriously stupid. He deserves everything he's going to get."

"I don't want to have to visit my husband in jail. Or any of his brothers. I don't give a damn what Barry says. He took away my sister. Saying crap to me is *nothing*. Stefano is only going to make him angry. Really, really angry. Barry Anthon is all about being superior, and pride is everything to him. He'll retaliate . . ." She broke off, her hand to her mouth. "Oh. My. God. They're beating the crap out of him, poking sticks at a rattlesnake to stir him up."

Emmanuelle grinned at her. "They never do that sort of thing without a really good reason. In this case, they had two very good reasons, aside from the fact that it's going to make them all feel happy, beating up a monster like that. Barry won't go to the cops because he'll want to retaliate and he won't want a record of this." She glanced at her watch. "Giovanni should be back anytime with a full report on Barry's rented estate. We'll have the layout and maybe even an idea of his plans."

"Giovanni went to the place where Barry's staying?"

"Did you think we were getting him to talk about where he was staying because we were interested?" She slid onto one of the tall chairs at the counter and leaned her head into her hand. "Let's talk weddings. That's so much more interesting than Barry Anthon."

CHAPTER TWENTY-ONE

Stefano stood between his brothers, searching out the best shadows that would lead him to his chosen destination, the Bronx. He had a very bad feeling about this particular job. Something inside him kept urging him to move faster, to get it done. A shadow rider couldn't afford to make one mistake. He was the protector of his family—the *entire* family in every city or town around the world. He was their key to survival.

Each move was planned carefully and meticulously. They never cut corners and they never hurried. They never made anything personal. If anything happened to a member of their family, they called in cousins—investigators and riders—from another city. That way, there was never any blowback or suspicion. Still, if he weren't so disciplined, if it wasn't so ingrained in him to check and recheck every single fact before entering the tube for the ride to the final destination, he would have given in to the urgency pushing at him so hard.

"I'm not feeling good about this one," he confessed to his brothers. He stood just behind Giovanni and Taviano as they blocked him from the possibility of prying eyes as well as any cameras the paparazzi might have on them.

Below them, their New York cousins had arrived, music blaring, ready to take Stefano's two younger brothers to several clubs, where the members of Salvatore's family would be gathered publicly so there was no way, come morning, anyone would suspect them of having anything at all to do with any deaths in the city. No one would ever be able to connect the New York family, even in the event the social worker who had originally gone to the Ferraro greeters in New York and had laid out the problem of the seventeen-year-old girl changed her mind and went to the police. The chances of that happening were slim, but still, the Ferraros paid attention to every possibility and planned for it.

"I can get 'sick' or drink too much and have to go to my hotel room, or back to Salvatore's," Taviano offered, frowning straight ahead. They didn't make amateur mistakes like looking over their shoulder while talking to their brother. "I'll meet you there and back you up. The gang her uncles belong to is one of the bloodiest in New York."

There was worry in his voice and Stefano couldn't blame him. Not once had he ever admitted to the feeling of urgency and that something might be wrong, because it had never happened before. He hesitated, wondering if he should have his brother come along. The feeling in his gut was very, very strong. He'd never once ignored his built-in warning system. Still, the high-profile visibility of his family members partying with local family members was what kept their family safe from suspicion.

"We stick to the plan," Stefano said after a moment's pause. "I'll contact you the minute I'm clear and back on the plane."

"We'll be waiting," Taviano murmured. "Have you chosen your ride?"

"It's a go. I'll be slipping out right behind you. Franco will take care of the plane so we're ready to get back home as soon as possible. I don't like leaving Francesca with Anthon in town."

Giovanni smirked at his cousins as they hurried toward the plane, waving their arms and shouting to hurry up. "Anthon bit off more than he could chew. He's not going anywhere for a few days."

"Ricco, Vittorio and Emmanuelle will make certain she's safe," Taviano added.

Stefano knew that, but they weren't going to be in bed with her when the nightmares came. He didn't like her being alone. He also didn't like being away from her whether Anthon was in town or not. He wasn't about to admit that to his brothers. He'd never hear the end of it.

"Let's get this done," he said, signaling his brothers to descend the stairs to the tarmac below.

He'd chosen his shadow. It was one that was wrenchingly fast. He would begin the ride into the city, heading toward the Bronx as quickly as possible. His gut feelings had always proven to be true and he wasn't about to ignore this one. He had a sense of urgency that told him something wasn't right and he needed to move.

He stayed close behind Giovanni until his shadow connected with the one he needed. The stripes in their suits, so thin as to be barely discernible, helped to camouflage the brothers as they stepped off the plane onto the stairs. The specially made suits blended with every shadow so that the Ferraro riders disappeared, making them indistinct.

Stefano stepped into the mouth of the tube and allowed it to absorb him. The pull was tremendous, that terrible pulling and twisting as his body was literally wrenched into the shadow. Then he was moving, sliding fast, thinking of Francesca. He didn't want this for her. She was capable. Her shadow proved that, but he didn't want her to be a rider. He wanted her to be safe. He wanted a life for her. Most of all he wanted her to make a home for him and his children.

New York City flew by. He didn't try to see the events happening around him as he moved from shadow to shadow. He couldn't save the world. That wasn't his job. He could only help a select few. Only when asked. Only when they were certain. He was certain about this girl, and on some level, Francesca had recognized that the situation was dire. She didn't flinch when he kissed her good-bye and left her, knowing Barry Anthon was in town.

His mother had been born a Ferraro, a shadow rider. She was trained from the time she was two, just as he had been, just as his children would be. She hadn't found the man she could love and her marriage had been arranged. Her partner had been a rider as well, from Sicily, but he'd never been trained. The moment he found out about his wife's legacy, he thought riding the shadows was glamorous, a powerful skill he was determined to acquire.

Phillip took the Ferraro name, caring nothing for the strict code they were taught. He had no intention of building a home with Eloisa. He married her thinking to acquire power and money. Eventually, he came to understand what the family was about, but that didn't make him want to stay home with his children or participate in their lives or training in any way. The shadows allowed him to keep his affairs discreet, although Eloisa knew what he did.

Their marriage deteriorated even more after their youngest son, Ettore, died while riding a shadow. Phillip spent less and less time at home, and Eloisa wrapped herself up in charity events and stayed away from everyone but her sisters and brothers.

Stefano couldn't understand why her children never interested her. She always demanded a report the instant they returned from a job. She made certain she was involved in every aspect of the family business and she and Phillip had taken over the job of greeters after her parents died.

Neither Eloisa nor Phillip wanted a divorce. In their world, once two shadows were connected and totally interwoven, breaking those shadows apart was a frightening prospect. The riders would lose all ability to ride the shadows and the departing non-Ferraro partner would lose all memory of the family and what they did.

It was imperative that Stefano have Francesca's full commitment. If she left him after finding out what they did, if they were already connected, their shadows tightly interwoven, she wouldn't suffer because she wouldn't remember loving him. But he would. He would never ride again—something he was born to do—and he wouldn't forget her and the love he had for her. He wouldn't forget what it was like to ride inside a portal. Interwoven shadows couldn't just be ripped apart without consequences, once they were joined together. Stefano was born a rider. It was a hard life, but it was who he was. What he was. He couldn't imagine living a half-life, remembering, but without the ability. He knew the few riders who had lost their partners that way had suicided or disappeared, unable to stay around the family.

Stefano changed tubes again, this time in the Bronx, finding the one that would get him closest to the home of Diego, Alejo, and Cruz Gomez, the uncles of Nicoletta. Nicoletta's mother and father were both from Sicily. Nicoletta's father died when she was two and her mother remarried when she was four. Her husband, Desi Gomez, adopted Nicoletta. When she was fifteen, her parents were killed in a car accident and she was sent to live with her three uncles. Her life had turned into a nightmare.

Diego, Alejo, and Cruz were all members of a very violent gang. The gang was notorious among law enforcement for running drugs, prostitution and human trafficking. They fought turf wars continuously, always looking to expand and to swallow other gangs. A young, innocent girl from a completely different way of life had no business being thrown to the wolves.

The sad part was, he knew he was already probably too late to really save her. Nicoletta had been living a nightmare for two years. That would take its toll and there was no going back from those kinds of scars. The investigators' report had been long, listing the numerous beatings, the suspected rapes and abuse the girl had received at the hands of her three stepuncles. How was she supposed to recover from that?

The tube brought him nearly to the very side of the house where a narrow strip of weeds separated the Gomez home from the one next door. The houses all along the street were run-down, paint faded and chipped. The front steps were sagging. There were bars on all the windows and bullet holes in the siding. The front porch had old, worn furniture covered in sheets and blankets on it. A couch. Two chairs. A lawn chair.

Stefano took a careful look around, up and down the streets. The overhead streetlamps had long since been shot out. No cop was going to be patrolling the street. Debris swirled in the gutters and rushed down the street in little eddies. Several men were gathered on various porches, talking, drinking, and in one case, shooting up with a needle.

He could hear them talking, and one of them said the name Nicoletta. He chose a shadow that would bring him close to the group of men he knew were members of the same gang the Gomez brothers were in. He recognized the big man sitting on the stairs, his hand wrapped around the neck of a bottle of whiskey, his eyes on the Gomez house.

"They'd better fucking bring her out soon, or I'm going in after her," he snarled, wiping at his mouth with the back of his hand. "I told Diego to turn her over to me or the three of them are dead men."

The man was Benito Valdez. He was all muscle and scars from the years he'd spent in and out of prison. A great brute of a man, he scared most people just by looking their way. Even in prison he'd remained the leader of the notorious gang, running it from his prison cell. No one crossed Benito Valdez and remained alive. He had four brothers who were just as brutal as he was.

It didn't surprise Stefano that Nicoletta had caught Benito's eye. Even at seventeen she was beautiful. Every single picture clearly showed her physical beauty, the full, lush curves of a woman rather than of a girl. Every report had included the word *beautiful* in front of *girl*. Evidently Benito had waited long enough, or he was worried the Gomez brothers would eventually kill her. There was no doubt that Benito wanted the girl for himself. It was no wonder he had a feeling of urgency.

Stefano rode the tube back to the Gomez house and studied

the layout in front of him. He couldn't rush, no matter the growing sense of apprehension. He slipped out of the tube into the shadowy depths between the two houses and used the burner phone. "In position." His gut churned. Anxiety burned through his nerve endings, the sense of urgency increasing. For the first time, he had to take some deep breaths to restore his normal calm. The wait seemed as if minutes ticked by slowly while in reality it was no more than a few seconds.

"You have a go."

He snapped the phone shut, knowing he would have entered the house to check on the girl even if the answer had gone the other way. There was no payment on this one. A favor in return, but no payment. The social worker had no money, but she was willing to provide information when needed to the family. Stefano knew the New York family probably would never need to collect, but it didn't matter. The problem had been brought to them and they had taken it on, investigated and sent for riders out of Chicago. The family charged their criminal clients enough to compensate for all those they didn't ask monetary pay from.

Stefano looked the shadows over and found one that ran up the front steps, beneath the door and into the house. There were lights on, but not a lot, not overheads, which meant there would be shadows inside the house. Movement caught his eye and he whirled to face the threat. Taviano stood just inside the shadows beside him.

"What the hell are you doing here?" Stefano didn't know whether to be relieved or angry. No one went against his decisions, yet there was his younger brother.

"I had the same bad feeling, Stefano," Taviano said. "It's getting worse and there's no ignoring it. Don't worry. I covered my tracks. I'll tell you about it back on the plane when we have this done."

Stefano nodded. He wasn't about to waste time arguing. He found he was grateful for Taviano's presence. If his younger brother had the same bad feeling, something was definitely off.

Stefano had already chosen his tube and he stepped into the shadow, allowing it to carry him inside. Taviano rode the shadow next to the one he was riding. The moment they were in, he knew they might be too late. He heard voices. Three men, very distinct. Taunting. Amused. Cats playing with a mouse.

"Put it down, Nic. You wave that thing at me, I'll cut your throat with it." Low. Furious. Didn't mean what he said, but capable of great violence. Stefano was certain that was the one called Diego. He had a reputation for enjoying his kills.

"Stay away from me." A sob. Nicoletta sounded young and very scared.

"I told you, bitch, you don't cooperate with Benito, he'll sell you. You'll end up living the rest of your life flat on your back, chained to a bed, fucked by every man sent up to you. Better Benito than that. You choose." That voice rang with honesty. With authority. He was the leader of the three. That one had to be Cruz. Cruz knew if he didn't turn over the girl to the leader, he was a dead man.

"Nicoletta, put the knife down," the third voice, probably Alejo, said. Coaxing. Amused that she thought she could defy them. A worried undertone that Benito was already going to be angry because they hadn't brought Nicoletta to him immediately.

"I can't do this anymore." The desperation in the girl's voice caught at him.

Stefano took the shadow right through the house directly to the room where all four Gomezes were grouped. Taviano rode his shadow completely across the room. Both shadows instantly connected to the shadows playing throughout the room. The men felt the jolt of connection. Small feeler tubes ran from Nicoletta's shadow to merge with theirs. They could feel every emotion. Her terror. Her determination.

Nicoletta pressed herself against the window. Her clothes were torn. Her face was swollen and bruised. Blood trickled down her cheek from a cut over her eye and more dripped from her cut lip. There were bruises on both arms. Fingerprints around her neck. She'd been beaten repeatedly, but she'd fought back. He could see defensive wounds on her arms and hands. Even her knuckles were bruised. She had fought them hard.

"Nicoletta." Cruz stepped closer. He was worried, his eyes on the knife. "You can't fuck around with Benito. Put the knife down and just come with us. Alejo packed some of your favorite clothes. In a few days, Benito will let you come get the rest of your things. Put the knife down."

She made a single sound. Despair. Horror. Desperation. Stefano knew it was too late to stop her. He wasn't close enough to her. She lifted the knife, turned it toward her own body, ready to plunge it into her chest. Stefano's breath hitched. He read the determination on her face. The three men must have seen it as well. Alejo reached toward her imploringly, as if he could stop her that way. Cruz, the leader, leapt for her. Diego remained absolutely still, a look of horrified fascination on his face. If she died, all three of the brothers knew Benito would kill them.

Taviano got to her first. His shadow had taken him behind her and he emerged, catching her wrist from behind, fingers ruthlessly finding pressure points so that she had no choice but to drop the knife. She cried out and struggled, fighting desperately as Taviano subdued her, trying not to hurt her. He was completely exposed, out of the shadow and all three of the brothers saw him clearly.

Stefano burst from the tube behind Diego, catching his head between both hands and wrenching hard, in the most basic kill move he'd been taught since he was a child. He dropped the body on the floor and entered the tube to slide up behind Alejo. He killed him in the same manner. Quick. Without mercy. Completely impersonal, although he had to work to keep himself under control.

Cruz heard the bodies fall. It had only taken seconds to kill both men while Cruz's attention was centered on Nicoletta and Taviano. He whipped out a gun and pointed it at

Nicoletta's head even as he looked frantically around the room. He'd caught flashes of the intruder, but only that, a shadowy figure that moved too fast to see.

"I'll fuckin' kill her," he snarled, meaning it.

Taviano shoved Nicoletta behind him, using his body as a shield. She let out a soft little cry, a protest maybe, a shocked gasp that anyone would stand up to her uncles and deliberately put their body in front of a gun for her.

"Who the hell are you? How'd you get in here?" Cruz demanded, the gun rock steady. His eyes kept darting to the two bodies on the floor. Neither moved. Neither made a sound. They looked dead, but no one else appeared to be in the room. He'd watched Taviano struggling to keep Nicoletta from killing herself. They'd both been right in front of him so who had killed his brothers?

Stefano came up behind him, emerged from the tube and locked onto his head. The moment his hands fastened on Cruz's skull, the man pulled the trigger, but Taviano had already dove for the floor, taking Nicoletta with him, covering her body with his own.

Cruz tried to fight back, to turn the gun on the opponent he couldn't see, but Stefano had been practicing the move since he was two years old. It was as easy for him as breathing. He snapped the man's neck and dropped the body. "Justice is served," he murmured.

Silence fell, broken only by Nicoletta's ragged breathing. Taviano rolled off of her and stood up, reaching down for her. She cringed away from him, lifting her hands defensively. He caught her wrists in a gentle grip and pulled her to her feet. Her horrified gaze went to the bodies on the floor.

"Don't look at them," he ordered softly. "Look only at me."

Her eyes jumped to his face. She stood, her body trembling, breathing labored, her gaze caught and held by his. The light from an overhead bulb, dim now from age, threw out shadows. He could see hers, a dark shape on the wall and floor, tubes running from it to connect with every shadow in the room, including theirs.

His heart slammed hard in his chest. He could feel her every emotion. Fear was uppermost, but there was relief, not commendation. Mostly, she was confused. Disoriented. In shock. Very, very painful.

"She's a rider," Taviano whispered aloud.

She was a rider, a woman capable of riding shadows, of bearing children who could ride shadows.

"It changes everything," Stefano said. The plan had been to leave without her ever seeing him. She would call the social worker and the family's responsibility in the matter would be over.

"We can't leave her behind." Taviano's voice was firm. Absolute.

Stefano frowned at him. "Damn it, what the hell are we going to do with her?"

"She has to come with us. We have to make certain they can never find her."

Nicoletta began to inch toward the door, back flat against the wall. She made herself as small as possible, as if by pressing against the wall they wouldn't be able to see her. Had they not been riders, they might not have. The move on her part was instinctive. She'd become part of the shadows.

Taviano stepped in front of her, blocking her path. "We'll get you out of here, *angioletto*," he said softly. Talking as if she was a wild animal, trapped in a corner and about to bolt—and maybe she was. "Benito and his crew are close by. Just give us a minute and we'll have you safe."

She shook her head but she halted, clearly terrified.

There was no leaving her. Staring at her, Stefano pulled out the burner phone and punched a number. "She's one of us. Hurt. We're bringing her home. L and A will take her in. Make the arrangements tonight." He made it an order, no room for arguments. "Doc. Counselor. They'll need money for her needs. Arrange that as well. I'll take responsibility for her."

Nicoletta shook her head, her tongue touching her swollen lip to ease the ache. "Not for me. I've got to go before the others come." She took a step back, away from Taviano as Stefano put his phone away.

"We're not going to hurt you," Taviano said softly. "We were sent to get you away from them." He indicated the bodies.

She drew in air and shook her head. "They belong to a gang. They'll never stop looking for either of you . . . or me."

"They won't find any of us," Stefano assured her.

No one could be brought into the tube unless they were a rider. Nicoletta didn't need to know how to ride, not if one of them was carrying her, but she couldn't be aware. She wasn't a Ferraro. No one had claimed her. He was doing something completely unprecedented, but it didn't matter. She had to be saved. Somewhere in the back of his head, he had known, unless they got her all the way out, her uncles' gang members would track her down and kill her. To save her life, this was the only way.

He signaled to Taviano and moved to check the window. He'd known they were in trouble all along. Benito was making his move. He flung the whiskey bottle against the side of the house and stood up, staring at the Gomez house, the others standing immediately to join him.

"They're coming, Tav," he announced.

"I know you don't know me," Taviano said softly, stepping close to Nicoletta. "But I also know you're capable of feeling the truth when you hear it. If you stay here, even contacting your social worker to relocate you, you're going to die. If she helps you to try to disappear, she and her family are going to die. That's a fact. You know it and I know it. You have one chance and in taking that chance, you'll be giving your social worker a chance at life as well. She contacted us to help you. This is me helping you."

Tears ran down Nicoletta's face, but Stefano was fairly certain she wasn't aware of the fact that she was weeping. She just kept shaking her head. Still, she didn't take her eyes off of Taviano.

"We can't take you with us without your consent, but if

.you want to live, say the word and we'll get you out of here. They'll never find you—or us. You'll have a new life with a wonderful couple who will treat you like a princess. My family will watch over you and protect you for the rest of your life. But you have to choose now. Right this minute. I can hear your uncles' friends coming up the front steps to the porch."

Her face visibly paled. She jammed her fist into her mouth, her gaze darting from the bodies to his face and then to Stefano's. She nodded. Barely. The movement almost imperceptible. Taviano moved fast, not waiting for her to have second thoughts. She had to be terrified. Stefano had just killed three people in front of her. They were total strangers. Still, they had to look like a better bet than her uncles' friends. He had the syringe all of the riders carried in the event they had to cope with an innocent civilian to get them out of their way. He had the needle in her neck in seconds, his arm around her waist to keep her from falling as the drug hit her system.

Her fingers clutched at his suit jacket, terror on her face, but the drug was fast acting, a good thing, as loud voices and pounding on the front door announced they'd run out of time. "Okay, *angioletto*, let's get you the hell out of here."

Stefano took her from his younger brother, lifting her slight body, cradling her tightly against his chest, wincing a little as he looked into her bruised, swollen face.

"I'll take her, Stefano."

Stefano shook his head. It wasn't that easy riding with another person, one unknowing. He wasn't taking a chance with Taviano or the girl. The one and only other time he'd ridden a shadow with another rider in his arms, it had been his brother Ettore, already lost to them, so far gone there was no bringing him back. His chest tightened. He couldn't go there.

He held a young girl. A child really. She was important to all Ferraros and she'd been hideously violated. That alone went against everything he believed in. He was taking her home to the best parents he knew. The most loving. The ones that needed a daughter when they'd lost so much. They would give her the understanding and compassion she needed to overcome what monsters had done to her.

"Let's get the fuck out of here, Tav," he snapped.

Stefano held Nicoletta tighter. He wasn't losing her. Not to the shadows, not to the gang members breaking through the front door and not to the shame and despair she felt. He stepped into the portal and let it take them both. He flew past the men rushing through the house toward the bedroom, and out the open front door. He'd chosen a larger tube, one that connected with the shadows in the streets and he rode it as far as it would take him, blocks away from the Gomez house and the angry mob gathering there. He felt Taviano moving in the shadowy tubes parallel to him.

They jumped easily from one portal to the next, heading back toward the airport and the safety of the private jet waiting. Franco had the door open, lights spilling on the stairs so that they had shadows to ride all the way to the interior of the plane. The moment they emerged from the shadows, Franco closed the door and turned toward them.

"Emmanuelle called and told me to be prepared. She's alerted Giovanni. He'll return as soon as possible. He has to play his role out, though, just to be safe." Franco pulled the medical kit out and handed it to Taviano. "I have the bedroom ready."

On the private jet, there was a small room they kept for the family members who needed to sleep. The seats were comfortable and laid all the way back to provide more space if necessary, but the room had a double bed inside of it. It was kept made and ready for their late-night escapades.

Stefano carried Nicoletta into the room and laid her on the bed. "She'll wake soon. We have to clean her up before that happens. She's not going to want a bunch of strange men touching her after her ordeal."

"I'll do it." Taviano made it a statement. "Franco, I'll need warm water. Washcloths and towels. Did Emme leave any clothes on the plane? If not, I have a couple of flannels in my go bag. Bring me one of them."

"Tav," Stefano said. "You don't want to invest too much in her. We're turning her over to Lucia and Amo. Our family will watch over her, and we'll provide for her, but we can't stay involved with her. You know that. It's too dangerous. Especially you. She knows our faces. She saw me come out of the shadow and kill her uncles. She could burn us. Bury us. If she goes to the cops . . ."

"She won't," Taviano said. "You're afraid for me, not you." He took the bowl of water Franco handed him, dipped a cloth in it and sank down on the bed beside Nicoletta. "You connected with her. She's too afraid of Benito Valdez to ever do something as foolish as going to the police. She can take the name Fausti and be Amo's niece come to live with them. We can give her a new identity. She's not going to turn on us."

Stefano watched Taviano dip the cloth into the water and gently dab at the blood on Nicoletta's face. His youngest brother wasn't nearly as easygoing as he liked to appear to the world. In spite of trying to bring his brothers and sister a little joy in their childhood, all of them bore the scars of absentee parents as well as whatever vicious handling had taken place during training overseas. Their father was gone most of their lives, doing whatever he chose to do, while their mother became a brutal trainer, snapping orders, demanding perfection and snarling coldly at them when they weren't perfect.

Each of them had been sent away for a year at a time to train elsewhere in the world. Ricco had come back scarred, tough and cold as ice. He lived on the edge all the time and Stefano regarded him as a ticking time bomb. Vittorio was a peacemaker, but something burned bright and savage under all that cool. Giovanni was the most volatile. One moment he was rational and the next his temper burned out of control. Taviano appeared to be gentle. Kind. He had a sense of humor. But he wasn't any of those things as a rule. Stefano had tried to find out what had happened to each of them in those years they'd spent with other trainers, but none of his siblings would answer him.

He'd managed to keep Emmanuelle home by insisting on training her himself. When his mother insisted she go abroad, he went with her. He stayed glued to her. It was too late to stop whatever was happening to his brothers in their training, but not what might happen to her.

Stefano had been too strong, too ruthless even as a teenager, to put up with any of the trainers putting their hands on him. He'd earned the reputation of being dangerous before he was fifteen. His brothers were every bit as dangerous as he was now, but it had taken those years away to shape them into the killers hiding behind their handsome faces.

"She belongs to us," Stefano said. "We'll look after her, Tav." It was a concession to his brother, and they both knew Taviano would have defied Stefano's authority and just done what he thought was right. "I wouldn't have put her with Lucia and Amo if I hadn't meant to put her under our direct protection."

"I know that," Taviano said. "I'm going to get rid of her clothes and I would appreciate both of you leaving the room."

"You want me to do that? I have Francesca and I'm not in the least bit looking at her like a woman," Stefano said. "She's a child that needs help."

"I know what she is. Just go."

Stefano shook his head but didn't protest. He needed to hear Francesca's voice, but he couldn't call her. He'd gotten rid of the burner phone. They never kept them once they reached the airport. There was no talking to her, not even from Franco's phone. He needed her tonight. The things done to that child. She was a beautiful girl who would forever bear the scars of three sick, very brutal men. Had they not gotten there in time, she would be in the hands of Benito Valdez. The social worker who had contacted them thought she owed them, but in fact, Stefano knew it was the other way around. They would be forever in her debt. Nicoletta was a shadow rider just as

Francesca was. She was invaluable to his family. That included the various extended family they had.

It seemed to take forever for Giovanni to get back to their private jet. By that time the girl had awakened and she was very scared. He'd tried to go into the cabin to help Taviano with her, but that only agitated her more. He couldn't blame her. The gang her uncles had run with had prostitution rings, and it was rumored they were involved in human trafficking. She clearly thought she was being transported to some foreign country where she'd never be heard from again.

Taviano was patient with her, his voice low and gentle as he continually reassured her. He clearly was afraid to leave her alone, afraid of what she might do to herself.

"We'll need a doctor waiting," he told Stefano.

"Already done. Emme has already talked to Lucia and Amo and explained things. They're willing for her to live with them and they'll share their last name. Emme said Vittorio is working on the papers tonight. We'll have a new identity for her and a background no one will be able to shake within a few days. Benito Valdez will never find her."

"He'll keep looking," Taviano said, looking down at Nicoletta. She was exotic looking, with thick, luxurious hair and very large, heavily lashed eyes and a generous mouth. She would haunt Valdez. He'd seen her, watched her blossom into a woman. He'd acquired a taste for her, and he would keep looking.

"Let him look. She'll be safe, Tav. No one will find her in our neighborhood, especially not Benito Valdez."

That small exchange seemed to comfort Nicoletta. Stefano couldn't imagine what she was going through. They were perfect strangers to her. She'd seen them emerge from the shadows and kill her uncles. They'd been fast and just as brutal as the gang they'd taken her from, no matter how elegantly they were dressed. She had no idea what they were going to do with her.

"You'll be all right," Stefano assured her from the doorway

when her gaze jumped to his face. She looked pale and defeated, so bruised it hurt to look at her. "You're never going to have a normal life, not with what you've gone through, but you'll know love. Lucia and Amo are two of the best people we know. I know you're afraid, but we'll see you through this. And we'll watch over you. That I can promise you."

CHAPTER TWENTY-TWO

Stefano stepped off the elevator into his apartment, exhausted, nearly forty-eight hours without sleep. It had taken time to get Nicoletta settled. The doctor had examined her thoroughly and then sedated her. She would be all right physically given a month or so of resting and healing, but he admitted the emotional scars weren't going to be so easy to rectify.

He'd done the best he could for the young teen. She was safe in Lucia and Amo's home, not quite as scared, but definitely apprehensive. He was certain she'd give them a chance rather than try to run. Vittorio was keeping an eye on her while Taviano and Giovanni slept.

Stefano wished he'd called Francesca to make certain she would be home. He needed her. Really needed her when he'd never needed anyone. There was something incredibly soothing about her. She felt like . . . home.

He inhaled her scent and everything in him settled. He hadn't known his belly was in knots or that the relief could make him weak. He hadn't consciously worried that she might have left him, but he was asking a lot of her. She had learned things about his life—their life. She'd overheard his mother say ugly things, and Barry Anthon was in town. She'd seen him become violent and then he'd left her to go out of town.

She came out of the kitchen, her gaze moving over his face in a slow, careful perusal. Then it drifted lower, taking him in, looking for injuries. She stepped close. "Honey." Just that. One word. Her hands slid up his chest and around his neck so that she linked her fingers together at his nape. "Thank you. She's safe. Nicoletta. Emme said you got her out."

She *thanked* him. For doing his job. She looked at him with stars in her eyes and a soft, killer smile that was going to be the fucking end of him. She looked at him as if he could solve the world's problems in a few hours, fight the bad guys and still be home in time for dinner. He liked that look a lot.

He framed her face with both hands and brought his mouth down on hers. She tasted like love. Like sex. Like perfection. Once he started kissing her, he couldn't stop. He found himself devouring her. Exchanging breath. Telling her without words that forty-eight hours without her was too damned long.

For the first time in his life that he could remember, he allowed himself to sink into someone else's strength. Seeing a seventeen-year-old girl beaten and abused physically, sexually and emotionally had torn him up far more than he wanted to admit to himself. He'd held himself aloof, keeping under control, using his rigid discipline to keep from seeing the look in her eyes when she'd turned the knife on herself. Had Taviano not been there, she would be dead.

His eyes burned and he couldn't breathe because of the raw lump blocking his throat. He lifted his head, looking down at her, into her eyes. He saw only love there.

"It was bad?" she whispered, pressing closer.

"It was bad," he agreed. "I don't fucking understand. I'll never understand how anyone could do that to a child. Any child. Any woman." He touched his forehead to hers. "I'm wiped, *dolce cuore*, absolutely wiped."

"Go take a shower," she whispered. "I'll fix something light and then you can go to bed. You need to sleep."

Fussing over him. Taking care of him. Stefano enfolded her in his arms, keeping her close to his heart. Burying his face in the luxury of her thick, silky hair, he just held her, needing to feel her soft body imprinted on his.

Francesca didn't pull away or try to hurry him. She held him. Tight. Breathing him in the way he was breathing her in.

"I missed you, Stefano," she said softly, the murmur nearly lost against his suit jacket. "I couldn't sleep at night without you."

"I worried about you," he admitted, one hand sliding up the curve of her spine to bury his fingers in her wealth of hair. "I knew you wouldn't be able to sleep, or if you did manage to sleep, you'd have nightmares. I'm sorry I couldn't call you." He'd never thought much about that mandate until he'd wanted to reach out to his woman.

"No." She tipped her head back to look up at him. "Emme explained how important it was that everyone think you were here, with me." She went up on her toes and pressed kisses along the line of his jaw. "Your safety is the most important thing. I'm just so grateful that you do what you do so that girl is safe."

His heart clenched hard in his chest. "*Amore mio*, this is the first time in my entire career I've done something like this. Mostly, what I do is eliminate someone like Barry Anthon. Someone untouchable by the law. Or I recover an elderly woman's purse with her last few dollars in it. I'm not a hero. Don't think I am," he warned.

She laughed softly and pulled out of his arms. "You're *my* hero, Stefano, and you always will be. Go shower. We can talk when you're lying in bed and drifting off."

"When did you get so bossy?" He wanted to hold her forever. Take her into the shower with him, which would lead to interesting things. His cock jerked at the thought.

She dodged his outstretched hand. "Someone has to take care of you." She reached out and trailed her fingertips over the growing bulge in his trousers. "I'm a full-service kind of woman. Go shower, honey, and let me take care of you." Her eyes met his. "I *need* to. You always take care of me. It's my turn."

He fucking *loved* that. He watched her go into the kitchen before turning to the master bedroom. He'd wanted a home his entire life. He hadn't known love or laughter until he'd visited his aunts and uncles and realized his cousins had something important and valuable in their lives that his siblings and he didn't. Until he'd gone home with Cencio and been introduced to his mother and father. Lucia and Amo were loving and warm all the time. Stefano wanted that for his brothers and sister. He wanted that for himself.

"Francesca." He murmured her name aloud as he stepped under the soothing hot water. It poured over him and pounded into his aching muscles. He didn't know what he'd ever done to deserve her, but he had her and that was all that mattered to him.

He took his time because the water felt good, washing his sins away along with his exhaustion. He dressed in loose-fitting drawstring silk pants and a tight, ribbed wifebeater before padding barefoot into the kitchen.

Francesca was humming softly to herself, her back to him, long hair flowing almost to her waist, as she mixed the pasta. His shadow connected with hers and she looked up instantly with a smile. "Hey, honey. Feel better?"

He nodded and kept going straight to her. "You brought in groceries." She had made pasta with grilled tiger shrimp and fresh parmesan cheese. A salad sat on the smaller dining table in between the dishes already set out. There was an open bottle of red wine on the table along with two wine-glasses.

"I had to get groceries if I was going to be cooking for us. I really enjoy cooking, Stefano." She flashed a smile. "It gives me a chance to show off."

He swept her hair off her neck and over one shoulder so he could bend down and kiss her neck, sending a little shiver down her spine. "I like the idea of you cooking for us. Feels like home." He took the bowl of pasta from her and carried it over to the table. "What have you been up to while I've been gone, other than grocery shopping?" He narrowed his eyes. "And you took Emilio and Enzo of course."

"Actually, Emmanuelle and Enrica went with me," she

corrected, sliding into the chair across from his. "Enrica is all business when we're out somewhere, but so funny when we're alone. I really like her."

He nodded as he served both of them pasta. "Emilio, Enzo and Enrica were always getting into trouble when they were teenagers. Enrica used to sneak out her window to go on a date, because if her brothers or cousins knew, she always had a noisy escort with her."

Francesca laughed. "I can't imagine how awful you all were. You boys seem to have the girls outnumbered."

"Thankfully. We like to keep an eye on our women and we can't do that if there's too many of them."

"Such a chauvinist. Emmanuelle was helping me learn what you all do for those in the neighborhood."

His head jerked up, the smile fading. He was going to strangle his sister with his bare hands. "What the fuck does that mean?"

She winced. "Seriously, Stefano, you're going to have to clean up your language before we have children. We just answered some of the calls and checked on people. There's a flu going around and it hit some of the elderly hard. We went to their homes and brought them medicine, or whatever else they needed. Don't tell me you don't do that, because Emme gave you away. My big macho badass takes soup to Agnese Moretti, the schoolteacher, and the homeless woman, Dina, as well as Mr. Lozzi and Theresa Vitale. I sat with each of them and heard all about my man and what a saint he is." She grinned at him. "Actually, Agnese didn't mention the word *saint*—that was Signora Vitale. I believe Agnese said there was hope for you yet."

He couldn't help himself; he leaned back in his chair and laughed. That was exactly what his old schoolteacher would say about him. And she'd say it in her prissy schoolmarm voice that told everyone they'd better not contradict her because she was always right. *Dio*, but he was happy to be home.

"That woman. Is she very ill?" He couldn't help the concern.

He had a special place in his heart for Agnese. Most of the neighborhood did. Especially those she'd taught with such gruff compassion.

"Not as sick as Signora Vitale. I had Enrica call a doctor just to be safe. She's in her eighties and the flu can be difficult on the elderly. The doc said with a little care she should be fine. Her grandson is staying with her. He promised to heat up the soup and feed her every two hours, even if she takes just a couple of bites."

Stefano shook his head. "So you met Bruno. Was he disrespectful? Did you get the impression he'd actually take care of his grandmother?"

Francesca nodded. "Absolutely. Your 'talk' with him must have helped, because he really listened to the doctor and seemed genuinely concerned. I have no doubt that he loves her."

"There was never a doubt about that, only that he was a selfish brat. She gave him every damn thing he ever wanted, even when she couldn't afford it and had to sacrifice. He never seemed to notice. I just pointed that out to him—that and explained the consequences of dealing drugs in our neighborhood or anywhere else for that matter. I also promised him that if he went to prison on a drug sale charge, I could still reach him there."

"Could you do that?"

"I'm a shadow rider, *bambina*—of course I could get to him in prison." He took a second helping of pasta. "This is good, Francesca, really good."

"So explain to me all about riding shadows. What that means. Why you can't say anything until we're married. Clearly we're going to be married."

He put down his fork and studied her face. She wasn't looking to bolt. She was unafraid and very accepting. She already had an idea of what he did and she not only accepted it; she made it clear she stood behind him all the way. He either trusted her or he didn't. He had asked her to trust him blindly and she'd done so.

"You have to be certain, *bella*. There's no going back from this. There would be . . . consequences."

"I think I got that, Stefano." She put her fork down as well. "Are you finished? If you want, we can lie down and you can tell me."

He had the beginnings of a headache, mostly from being tired. He was usually good at forty-eight hours without sleep but anything beyond that could start taking its toll on his body, especially if he'd been shadow riding. "Thanks, *dolce cuore*, the bed sounds great."

"I'll just get these dishes done. It won't take me long."

"Leave them. The service will do them."

She smiled and shook her head. Stefano knew she wasn't comfortable with his money or anyone waiting on her. The elevator *pinged*, his only warning. He snagged the gun taped beneath the table and was on his feet. "Were you expecting anyone?"

She shook her head, fear creeping into her eyes. He hated that. Hated that she would ever need to feel afraid of anything. She was his. His woman had a lot to contend with, but fear shouldn't be one of them. "Get behind the counter and stay there until I tell you it's safe."

Francesca didn't argue with him. She nodded, her face pale, her eyes haunted. Anger churned in his gut as he stepped out from behind the table and moved with the shadows through the dining room toward the entrance. If Barry Anthon or any of his men had managed to penetrate his security, he'd be shocked. The hotel was a fortress. Getting up to his penthouse without detection was nearly impossible unless you were family and had the codes to the elevators.

His breath hissed out of his lungs, and his anger boiled to the surface. He stepped into the great room, locking his gun on his target, uncaring that his mother gasped and took a step back.

"What the fuck?" he demanded. "You don't even have the common courtesy to call first?" He raised his voice. "It's Eloisa, Francesca." He didn't tell her to join him because he could see his mother's agitation. She'd worked herself up to one of her self-righteous lectures and was fully prepared to be cutting, rude and ugly, just as she'd been about his future wife. Francesca didn't need to hear any more.

"How dare you, Stefano?" Eloisa snapped. "I understand now why you and Taviano skipped the briefing altogether. You endangered *all* of us, the entire family, with your recklessness, and now you're hiding up here in your little love nest, afraid to face me because you know what you did was careless and stupid."

"How dare *you*?" Francesca's voice came from behind them. She walked right up behind Stefano and slipped her arm around his waist. "Stefano is not reckless and you know it. He isn't hiding up here afraid to face you and I think you know that, too."

"Stay out of this," Eloisa snapped. "You have no right to interfere in family matters. You don't have a clue what we're talking about."

"Be very careful how you speak to my woman, Eloisa," Stefano warned, his voice dripping ice, but his heart had turned over at the show of absolute support from Francesca. Even his siblings didn't interfere when Eloisa was raging at him for some infraction. He'd always been the head of the family for his brothers and sister. He fought their battles with Eloisa, not the other way around. It felt good to have someone stand with him, even though he didn't need it. He had been arguing with his volatile mother from the time he could talk. "We're to be married, in spite of your objections, in a couple of weeks. She'll be my wife and with me, the head of the *famiglia*."

"Perhaps it would be best to start again," Francesca suggested. "Would you care to sit down, Eloisa? I'm Francesca Capello. We haven't been formally introduced."

Eloisa stood for a moment, obviously struggling with her temper, but to Stefano's surprise she nodded her head. "It's nice to meet you, Francesca. Please excuse my rudeness the other day. I had no idea you were in the house and would overhear the things I said to my son, things I believed at the time. Since then, I have read the numerous reports gathered on Barry Anthon and I know I was mistaken. I should have done what we always do and gathered the facts first."

Stefano opened his mouth to agree with her, but Francesca dug her fingers into his side hard and he refrained from blasting his mother in the way he normally would have. He glanced down at his woman. He fucking loved thinking of her that way. She was . . . magnificent. Her head up. Her arm around his waist. Her eyes clear. There was no fear now, only a confident woman standing beside her man. Yeah. He loved that.

Francesca gestured toward the armchair across from the couch. "Thank you for that, Eloisa. I appreciate it. Emmanuelle tells me you've been helping with some of the wedding details. It's all happening so fast I'm a little overwhelmed, so I'm thankful for any help at all."

Eloisa took the chair across from them. Stefano tucked Francesca close to him, his thigh pressed against hers. He'd missed her. Really missed her. It was strange to think of a woman night and day, to worry about her and look forward to being with her. To inhale the scent of her and know you were home. To crave her body like an addiction and need the sound of her laughter and the sight of her smile. He'd never had that before and now it seemed as natural to him as breathing.

"We really do have to discuss this mess, Francesca," Eloisa said. "I don't want to distress you, but Stefano did something that wasn't protocol in our business and it could have gotten someone killed. I can't let it go by without saying something."

"If you're talking about Nicoletta, I'm fully aware of the situation," Francesca said. "By all means talk to Stefano about it, but get all the facts before you get upset. He had a good reason for doing what he did."

Eloisa's face flushed with anger. Her eyes went hard. Stefano had seen that look a million times. He could have told Francesca that Eloisa wasn't reasonable when she was emotional. Her temper was legendary in the family. Even her siblings trod lightly when she was upset.

"First of all, Stefano, Francesca shouldn't be burdened with the knowledge of our work until *after* the wedding." She bit out each word, her teeth snapping together, as if she might take a bite out of him if she wasn't so controlled.

"Eloisa, you don't get to tell me how to handle my personal business, not when it comes to my woman." Stefano kept his voice as mild as possible. His family could get loud in their disagreements, but with his mother, it went from bad to worse very quickly.

Eloisa's breath hissed out in a long stream of disapproval. "When it comes to you being careless about family business, Stefano, someone has to, and there's no one but me. Everyone else is afraid of you." She leaned toward him, narrowing her eyes, her finger stabbing toward him. "I'm not. You had no right to bring that girl to our neighborhood. She should have been left there. And Taviano had no business being there. His job was to be seen. To be photographed. Both of you left the *famiglia* vulnerable."

Stefano shrugged. "Fortunately, Eloisa, I'm the head of the *famiglia*, and I make the rules, not you. It was my call. Taviano was there when he was needed, thanks to him acting on his instincts, which is what we're trained to do. I don't know why you're upset when we all did our jobs."

Eloisa leaned even closer, her eyes alive with anger. "Because deviating from protocol, something that has been in existence for a hundred years for good reason, at the last minute will get you killed. It will get your brother killed. You're both more important than this girl, whether she's a confirmed rider or not."

There was a shocked silence. Stefano counted his heartbeats, trying to control his temper. "Why would that be, Eloisa? Why would you think Taviano and I are more important than a seventeen-year-old girl? One being brutalized, raped and beaten nearly every fucking day since she was fifteen? If that isn't reason enough for you, this girl can provide children—riders—for our family. She could be a much loved wife to one of your sons. How is she not just as important if not more so?"

Eloisa's face turned red. She blinked rapidly, repeatedly, as if she had something in her eyes. Her fists clenched. "Because," she hissed, both fists clenched tight. "She is not my son. She is not Taviano. She is not you. I don't care if you and your brothers and Emmanuelle hate me as long as you're alive. As long as I know I did everything I could to make you the best riders out there. I sacrificed my entire life, my happiness, *everything*, in order for you and the others to live. To be prepared for a life you were born into. I wouldn't have chosen it for you, but I had no choice, just as you have no choice. I won't see you dead, Stefano. Not another one of my children before me. I won't."

Francesca's fingers bit into his thigh in warning. His gaze flicked to her face. He could see she was desperately trying to tell him to be cautious, to hear what his mother was saying, the underlying message. To hear the desperation and fury in her. He'd seen that a time or two in other mothers. Protective tigresses when it came to defending their children. He'd just never seen it in *his* mother.

She'd always been as cold as ice. She'd overseen every aspect of their training in the United States, even when they went to other families to train. She'd made frequent surprise visits to ensure they were working as hard as she deemed necessary. She couldn't go abroad with them, but she kept in touch, was just as demanding. His father had never shown any interest in their training. He'd never really shown any interest in them at all.

"Why don't you divorce him, Eloisa? You're retired. It won't matter whether or not you can ride a shadow. It won't matter to him if he doesn't remember any of us." He spoke as gently as possible. "He's never been anything but hurtful to you."

Eloisa held up her hand. It was shaking, but she kept it

there, a barrier between them. "If I can't ride a shadow, I can't get to one of you when you might need help. I don't care what Phillip does. It isn't like I'm going to find the love of my life at this late date, but I can continue to make certain my children are as safe as I can make them."

Stefano regarded his mother, wondering at her strange reaction. She sounded . . . caring. "Did you want to have children, Eloisa?"

There was silence. Francesca's fingers dug deeper into his muscle. He stroked the back of her hand with his thumb, needing to touch her. Grateful she was so close to him, leaning into him, staying by his side in spite of the way Eloisa had spoken of her earlier. She kept his temper under control and allowed him to listen to his mother's voice, judging it for honesty. He would never have asked his mother such a question, would never have gotten far enough in a conversation with her to even consider finding out more about her.

Eloisa was a very controlled, disciplined person, much like he was. She was also extremely private. She kept all emotions—other than anger—locked down. Now, she just looked vulnerable. He almost wished he hadn't asked. Eloisa never appeared vulnerable or fragile. She looked almost as if she might shatter.

Twice she licked her lips and her gaze shifted away from his, but not before he thought he caught the sheen of tears. She shook her head twice. "I wanted a husband and children just like most women, but that wasn't my reality. My reality was to give them a legacy they had no choice but to fulfill. I had gone through the training."

A bitter smile twisted her mouth, one difficult to witness. Francesca's palm stroked this thigh soothingly, as if she could feel his reaction and at the same time, keep him grounded and balanced.

"I know you think *tua nonna e il nonno* were loving, wonderful people, but they adhered to the old ways. They were taskmasters, far worse than I could ever be. The masters

we were sent to were brutal, and I know you think the training was too hard on your brothers and sister, but that was
what was drilled into us, that training was everything." She
shook her head, a little shudder going through her body.
"Some of the trainers were cruel, but a necessary evil."

"Is that what you think?" Stefano snapped, visions of
Ettore rising up, sharp and murderous in his mind. His gut
knotted and it was only Francesca's restraining hand that
prevented him from leaping up and pacing with restless
energy to keep from shouting insults at his mother. "You knew
the trainers were cruel and yet you sent my brothers to them
anyway. You sent me but that didn't turn out so well for the
family, did it?"

"Stefano, you can't ignore the fact that training is necessary. Without it, none of you could do what you do. It's
difficult, yes, but all other riders have gone through it."

"It's necessary, Eloisa, but it doesn't have to be at the hands
of brutal trainers. Cruelty has no place in what we do, so those
of us who ride shouldn't be subjected to vicious trainers just
for the sake of inflicting pain for their pleasure."

Eloisa gasped. Her hand crept defensively up her throat.
"Is that what you think? That I sent all of you to them so
they could be cruel to you?"

"You are our parent. It was your job to protect us." Stefano made it an accusation.

Francesca pressed closer to him, under his shoulder, her
body warm and soft and giving. Comforting him when he
hadn't known that was what he needed most. The memories
of his childhood were close—too close. Of his sister screaming night after night with night terrors. Of his brothers
returning from other countries cold and hardened, with hell
in their eyes. Of carrying Ettore's body through the shadows.
Rage moved in him and he tightened his arm around Francesca to help keep it at bay.

"I followed tradition, Stefano, just like every other parent
of a rider. I sent all of you to the best trainers around the

world. I went, and every other rider goes. When you were away from me here in the States, I went to ensure there was no cruelty, but I couldn't go to Europe with all of you." Eloisa's voice was low. Choked. Strangled.

"You *knew* what would happen, Eloisa, or you wouldn't have gone to the trainers here in the States."

"It's *tradition*." Eloisa all but shouted it, but there were tears in her voice.

"Years ago, the women were nothing, Eloisa. They had no rights. They couldn't own property. They *were* property. That changed because it wasn't right. Children were beaten regularly by parents. That changed because it wasn't right. Just because something is tradition, handed down from one generation to the next, doesn't make it right."

"Don't you think I know that? Don't you think I learned that when Ricco came back from Japan and he was so changed? There's death in his eyes. There's emptiness when before there was such life. All of them came back changed. Even you, and you're so strong, Stefano." Her voice broke.

"All of them are strong, Eloisa. Every single one of them. Dump Phillip. We can take care of one another in the shadows. Let yourself live. Let yourself enjoy your children instead of making yourself crazy, trying to protect us when we no longer need it."

Eloisa took a deep breath to steady herself. "I'll think about it. I can see you're tired, Stefano, so I'll go now and let you get some sleep." She shook her head and stood, raising a hand to keep either of them from giving her sympathy of any kind.

Stefano stood as well, taking Francesca with him, locking her tightly to his side. She immediately pressed her palm to his abdomen so that her warmth burned right through his thin shirt and into his skin. It went deeper still, so that her heat spread through his body, making him very aware of how lucky he was to have her. To have found her. His mother was a shell. She presented a cold, calculating woman with little emotion to the rest of the world and even he had believed it. Instead, she was a woman with dreams of being loved. She had been forced into a loveless marriage with a man who cared only for the power of shadow riding. Of the ability it gave him to carry on his affairs. She'd sacrificed the love of her children in order to carry on the traditions her parents had forced on her.

Stefano looked down at Francesca as the elevator doors slid closed. "Our children will know love, *dolce cuore*. If I become too harsh in their training, I need your word that you'll stop me."

She smiled up at him. "I would hit you over the head and knock sense into you if you dared to be too harsh with our children."

She was smiling at him, but there was truth in her eyes, honesty in her voice and steel in her spine. He had no doubts that she meant what she said.

"Let's go to bed," he said, turning her toward the bedroom. He wanted to lie down and just hold her. "That was a surprise. Eloisa has never talked about her feelings. Not once. She's never showed emotion, not even when Ettore died." His death was too close. Far too close. He felt as if the walls were pressing in on him.

"What she said about Ricco. The training. What was that?"

He stripped, tossing his clothes aside and then stretching out on top of the sheets, hands behind his head as he watched her take her clothes off. When she reached for one of the many sexy camisoles he'd bought her, he shook his head. "Not tonight, Francesca. I don't want anything between us. Not even something that gives me great pleasure in taking off. Just come to bed."

She was beautiful. More than beautiful. Her body was lush and inviting, just the way she was. "You give all of us hope. Did you know that? Do you have any idea how important you are to my brothers and sister? Not because you're going to give me babies, but because you represent something beautiful and amazing. None of us believed we'd ever have the chance to love someone. Or that we'd be loved."

Francesca stretched out beside him, her body turned toward his, one arm slung around his waist, her head on his shoulder, one leg thrown over his thighs. She did that a lot, he realized. Turned her body toward him. She never protested when he locked her to his side, or at night when he draped himself all over her. She just snuggled closer to him.

"You need to explain all this to me, Stefano," she urged. Her fingers moved over his chest, tracing his heavy muscles. "I need to know. I want to understand."

He shifted just enough that he could wrap an arm around her. The lights were off, but he could see her easily through the bank of uncovered windows that were one wall of his room. Up so many floors, there was no one to see in, yet he could look down on the city with all the lights. He loved his city. He loved his neighborhood. More than anything he loved his family.

"I've told you some of it. We go back hundreds of years. The Ferraro family always had riders born into it. Men and women capable of connecting with shadows and entering them, like a tube, an expressway. When we're inside the shadow, no one can see us. In the old days, our ancestors took on the task of protecting family and friends and then, eventually others in our neighborhood."

She nodded and turned her head just slightly to press a kiss into his chest. He'd told her this before, but he needed to start somewhere comfortable. She was patient with him, but then he knew she would be—just like she would be patient with their children.

"When the Ferraros refused to join the Saldi family or reveal to them just how they were able to protect so many, the head of the Saldi family issued orders to wipe them out. Every man, woman and child. Only the riders escaped. A few cousins off on a holiday. Those remaining alive went into hiding. Because the shadow riders were able to get away, the family began to rebuild in secret."

Her finger traced his ribs. "I know where you get your tenacity."

He captured her hands and brought her fingertips to his mouth, his teeth scraping seductively along the pads. "They spent years building an empire. Branches of riders were established in major cities throughout the world. Every rider had to be familiar with languages and geography so they're sent to each city to train while teens. The other family members began legitimate businesses. Solid ones that would bring prosperity to the family. Banks, hotels, casinos, nightclubs. Each business was carefully built up before another was added."

"All of them are capable of handling any money a shadow rider would get for his services that aren't so legit," she murmured. "Like the rescue of a seventeen-year-old girl."

"No money for that job. Some jobs are bartered for favors. Others small things. Taking on work that involves executing someone"—he deliberately used the expression to see her reaction—"requires a great deal of money unless, as in the case of a brutalized child, the petitioner can't afford it, isn't a criminal and the need is justified."

"That's why you have such a process. The greeters, and then the investigators."

"Yes." He bit down again on her finger, wanting to kiss her, warmth spreading through him because she didn't even flinch when he used the word *executing.* "We have to be certain before we take a job. There can be no mistakes. Both sides are investigated, the petitioner as well as the target and the incident itself. We protect the family at all costs. We make certain our own riders don't take down anyone who can draw attention to us in our own city. We don't do our own personal work. Nothing close to us. We use the paparazzi for alibis. Because we play so publicly, few people ever consider that we would do anything that they can't see."

"And you're careful." She made it a statement.

"And we're careful," he confirmed. He was silent a moment before continuing, his fingers delving into the silk of her hair. "It's difficult to find others outside the family with the ability to ride the shadows. There just aren't that many. Men have a little longer to find someone they truly want than a woman, because in the end, we serve the family and that means producing riders. Riders keep us safe. If the Saldis or anyone else ever try to wipe us out again, retaliation would be swift and brutal. They know that. They don't know how we do it, but they know we can get to them."

He had to make her understand. "The riders are important to the family, Francesca. Our training, training the children, it is necessary for us to continue. It's difficult but very rewarding. But . . ." He trailed off.

"Tell me."

He could because it was Francesca. His woman. She seemed to understand everything he needed or wanted. "I will train our children and they'll go to other trusted trainers, but Francesca, if this life isn't for them, I don't want them not to have a choice. I don't want arranged, loveless marriages for them. I'll teach you to shadow ride because I want you safe, but I never want you to do the work or see the violence. I don't want it touching you. I need you to understand that. It isn't because I don't want to share power with you. It's because . . ."

She rolled over, sprawling over his body, her hands framing his face. "You don't have to explain. I know you want me home, to balance out the training. There's nothing wrong with that."

"I want to come home to clean. To something wonderful and warm. To love. I want that for my children. I need that."

"I know you do," she murmured, and pressed a kiss into his throat.

"You have to know there are consequences to being with me, Francesca. I wasn't exaggerating when I warned you what kind of man I am. I expect to lead. I expect you to follow. I'll give you everything I can. I want you happy. But I need you safe. That's something in me I can't change. There will be a lot of demands. That you let me know where you are every minute. That has nothing to do with trust, and everything to do with my issue to know you're safe."

"I know that about you, Stefano."

He took a breath. He had to let her know everything. He had to know if she could live with the real consequences of being married to a shadow rider. "That's nowhere near the worst." He took a breath. Framed her face to look into her eyes. "The truth is, Francesca, once we're married and our shadows are completely merged, if things didn't work out and we divorced, the shadows would tear apart and there isn't any repairing them. I would lose my ability to ride the shadows. That's what my mother was talking about tonight. You would lose all memory of me, our life and even our children together. You wouldn't remember anything to do with shadow riding. You wouldn't suffer, because you'd have no memory of it, but you would lose your children. That's why it's important to know for certain before we're married, that this life is for you."

He felt her sudden stillness. The swift inhale. She started to roll off of him, her first retreat. He didn't allow it, his arms locking her to him. "Don't, *bambina*, don't leave me. Just listen. Hear the truth in my voice. I love you with everything in me. There will never be a time that I won't. I'm incapable of cheating on you. I'm too loyal, and I know you have that in you as well. We'll work things out. I know I'm difficult, but I swear, with every breath in my body, Francesca, I'll work at our marriage."

"It's a huge price, Stefano, if something goes wrong."

"I know that. I know what you're risking. It seems I have less to lose, but it isn't so. I would be half a man without you, and I wouldn't know who I was without the ability to ride. Marry me, be my wife. Be my partner. Take the risk with me. I need you in a way I've never needed anything or anyone." He was giving himself up to her. He'd never felt more vulnerable. Never felt more terrified. "Every fucking word I said to you is the truth."

She brushed her mouth across his. Looked into his eyes,

searching for something. She must have found it because she nodded. It was slow in coming, but in the end, she did nod her acceptance. "Yes. The answer is still yes."

Stefano woke Francesca three hours after he fell asleep and he made love to her. Gently. As gently as possible for him. He made certain she was gasping and ready before he took her, driving her up again and again, giving her three orgasms before he emptied himself in her. He fell back asleep to the sound of her taking a bath. The woman loved the fucking bathtub.

CHAPTER TWENTY-THREE

Stefano woke with the dawn creeping into the bedroom and urgent need clawing at his belly. His cock was hard and thick, desperate to be inside Francesca's warm, wet channel. Francesca's long hair moved in a sensual slide over his thighs and belly, so much silk, building a wild urgency as her mouth moved between his legs. Up his thighs, spreading kisses and little bites right up to his aching balls. She licked his sac and his cock jerked hard. Her fingers found him, rolling and caressing his tight balls even as her tongue slowly bathed them in warmth. She made little moaning sounds that added to the dark fantasy.

"Dolce cuore." It was all he could manage when she licked up his shaft. Greedy. Hungry. He reached down to bunch silk into his fist. Her mouth slid over the wide, flared head of his cock and she engulfed him. Completely. Taking him deep. Unexpectedly. The inside of her mouth was wet and slick, hotter than hell. "Fucking paradise." He groaned. Tugged at her hair to raise her head. He wanted to see her eyes. He loved holding her gaze while she went down on him.

"Gotta look at me, *bambina*. I have to see your eyes." He loved how she was ravenous for him in the same way he always felt insatiable for her. How her eyes conveyed her excitement and her love of what she was doing. He needed that almost as much as he needed her mouth on him. Her hair, moving over his thighs and belly, made him ultrasensitive so that every nerve ending in his body leapt to life. Fire danced over his skin, adding to the sensations her mouth and hands created.

He waited for the impact, holding his breath. When it came, when she lifted her lashes and her eyes met his, his heart contracted in his chest and deep inside, where no one could see, she shattered him. That look. So full of love. So full of lust. For him. The man. Not the name. Not the money. Not for any other reason. Just for him. His fists tightened in her hair. He wanted to jerk her up to him, but she chose that moment to take him in her mouth.

Watching him watch her, she parted her lips and slowly, inch by inch, took him deep. It was the hottest thing he'd ever seen. She kept her gaze on his, letting the hunger burn in her eyes as she hollowed her cheeks and sucked hard, her tongue lashing him with strokes that felt like white lightning.

Her mouth felt like a fist of scorching velvet wrapped around his cock. Hot. Tight. Wet. Perfect. He knew what paradise was, right there in his woman's mouth. She slid her mouth up his shaft and then engulfed him again in a tight, wet hold that rocked him.

"*Fuck.*" It burst out of him. Crude. But still. He couldn't think with his blood thundering in his ears and roaring through his shaft. Her hands were doing wicked, sinful things to his balls while her mouth did them to his cock. He gripped her hair harder and began to tug. "You gotta stop, *bella*. Right. The fuck. Now." Because if she didn't, he was going to pour everything he had in him right down her throat, and he didn't want this to end.

Francesca showed no signs of stopping. Her mouth tightened even more, the suction stronger than ever, sending heat waves storming through him. Desire tightened his thigh muscles, drew up his balls and danced in his belly. He held her head in place with her hair, his fists on either side of her head, guiding her now, his hips thrusting into that hot, wet tunnel.

Stefano stared down into her eyes, sinking there, letting her take him, the fire consuming him. He thrust deep and held himself there, locked in that paradise, her mouth closing around him like a vise. He didn't pull back until he saw the first hint of panic in her eyes. He let her take a breath and he thrust again and couldn't believe when her tongue lashed him with the lightning streaks, she suckled hard and once again took him deep, all the while her gaze clinging to his.

His breath caught in his throat. Not only was she giving him fucking paradise, but she looked at him with adoration, as if he was the only man in her world. He held himself there a beat or two longer, watching her take it, seeing the trust in her eyes. With a crude oath, he withdrew, transferred his hold to under her arms and yanked her up.

"Get on your knees—face the headboard," he commanded.

Already he was up on his knees, his cock in his fist, using rough strokes to keep that fire hot and burning. It wasn't that difficult when she rolled onto her belly and crawled up the bed toward the headboard. She looked the epitome of sensuous, her beautiful ass in the air for him, her head bending toward the mattress.

"Reach behind you with your hands."

She did so, turning her head to peek at him through the mass of hair tumbling on the sheets. He caught up his belt and used it to secure her hands behind her back. "I love the way you look right now. That's not too tight?"

"No." Excitement or trepidation made her voice tremble; he wasn't certain which, but she pushed back her hips in invitation.

He waited a few moments, jacking his cock while he watched her in silence, allowing anticipation to build. He loved that his woman gave him this—gave him everything he asked for and more. Her breathing turned ragged and he slid his palm up the inside of her thighs and then opened her wider with his knees. She shivered. He reached between her legs and found her wet and hot. He knew she would be. She'd enjoyed going down on him. Lusted after him.

She gave a low moan when his palm swiped over her slick entrance, but she didn't move. She just waited. Giving herself to him. He slapped her ass hard, a sharp sting and then rubbed the red spot soothingly. He bent and pressed a kiss right in the middle of his palm print. His tongue found her entrance and he licked up, all the way, a long stroke of heat searing her.

Francesca cried out, and he repeated the entire sequence on her left cheek. He spent time there, building the heat in her, using his hands, his tongue, varying the rhythm and strength, making certain to soothe her and keep her honey spilling into his mouth, onto his tongue, down her thighs so he could lick them clean.

She sobbed his name over and over, her breath hitching on every moan or cry he elicited from her. He took his time, enjoying building that heat in her body. His cock pulsed and throbbed with every single smack and caress to her beautiful rounded ass. He couldn't resist taking a bite out of her, his teeth finding the center of his palm print on her right cheek and then stroking over his mark with his tongue.

She exploded, screaming his name, her entire body shuddering. He drove into her, using her hips like handles, dragging her back into him so he could slam deep and hard, feeling the viselike grip of her body as she clamped down on him, stroking and strangling him with her inner muscles as she convulsed around his cock.

He didn't make love to her as he often did. He fucked her. Hard. Deep. Rough. He reached down and caught her hair, dragging her head up and back while he jackhammered into her, pistoning hard. All the while fire streaked through him, raced up his spine and boiled like a fury in his balls. It was exquisite. Fucking perfection. Her body responded to his rough treatment with another strong quake, rippling with shocks, gripping and teasing his cock as he drove into her over and over.

He dragged her up farther, using her hair, so he could see her breasts swaying through each hard jolt of her body. He wished he had two cocks so he could be in her mouth at the same time as he fucked her sweet, scorching hot tunnel. He didn't let up for a minute, a kind of sexual fury riding him hard. He drove into her again and again, nearly lifting her up off her knees with each stroke.

"You want more?"

She nodded.

"Harder? Rougher?"

She nodded again. Cried out when he complied.

"You're going to give it to me again, Francesca." He made it a command. "Come for me right now."

She did the moment he told her to, her body already his, exploding around him, clamping down hard so the friction was nearly unbearable. He rode through it, his teeth clenched, the fire building and building until he thought it was impossible to get any hotter. "Again," he demanded, not stopping. Not letting up. Driving as deep as possible, as fast and hard as possible.

"I can't," she gasped.

"You will." He made it a demand once again, knowing she'd comply. *"Now."*

He felt his balls tighten to the point of pain. The fire rushed down his spine to his hips and buttocks, up his toes and calves, into his thighs. The two fires came together, crowning in his cock as her body suddenly gripped him hard. Her sheath was scorching hot, burning him with a fiery strangling clasp. She screamed as her body milked his, and her orgasm tore through her and his through him in a vicious, brutal climax that rocked both of them. His seed jetted deep, filling her, pouring into her, triggering more aftershocks nearly as brutal as the original orgasm.

He loosened his hold in her hair, locked his arm around her waist and both of them collapsed onto the mattress. He breathed deeply, trying to recover, floating in a kind of bliss, his heart pumping wildly and his cock still jerking deep inside of her. "Give me a minute," he managed to rasp out. "I'll get your hands free."

He couldn't move for the longest time, a fine sheen of sweat covering his body and dampening his hair. He felt great. Better than great. After a few minutes he slipped from her body, the sensation sending another heat wave coursing through his veins.

"You still with me, *bella*?" He pressed a kiss into her back. She hadn't moved, hadn't made a sound, not since that ragged scream that tore through her along with the fury of her orgasm.

She nodded her head, but didn't speak. He gathered her hair and twisted it, getting it off her back so he could sweep his palm down the curve of her spine and over her buttocks. He liked seeing his marks there. He pressed kisses all along her spine, down to the small of her back and then over both cheeks of her bottom. Undoing the belt buckle, he freed her wrists and rubbed at them gently, inspecting them for marks before rolling onto his back, taking her with him.

Francesca lay up against his side, curled into him, one hand on his belly, fingers splayed wide. "I don't think I can move."

"Me either," he admitted.

"I'm glad you're home."

"I noticed. You can wake me up anytime," he added.

"You've really never done the tying the hands with any other woman?"

"Nope. I wouldn't share my fantasies with any woman who wasn't mine. They don't belong to another woman, only you."

She turned even more toward him. Her breast slid along his rib cage, sending a curl of heat spiraling through him. "And if you never found the right woman?"

"Then my fantasies would go to the grave with me."

"I'm glad you found me. I like everything you do to me."

"Tonight," he stated, "I'm going to fuck you with a vibrator while you suck me off. If I don't, I'll be waking up every night with that particular fantasy. I'll use handcuffs this time. Ones that are padded so there are no bruises. When I was fucking you, all I could think about for a few minutes there was how I wished I had two dicks instead of just one."

"I don't think I could handle two. As for your intentions for tonight, I don't have any objections," she said, licking along his rib cage. "Not that I mind you waking up every night with a fantasy. I'm more than happy to oblige you in all things. And I don't mind the handcuffs, but don't think I'm not well aware my ass is bruised, so don't sound so self-righteous."

He laughed and flicked her nipple with his tongue. "I want my mark on you. Not some object's mark." His hand found her bottom and he caressed her with his palm. "Are you sore?"

"A little."

"Good." There was a wealth of satisfaction in his voice he didn't try to hide. "I want you thinking of me every time you sit down today."

"I think you're imprinted so deep inside me, Stefano, I'm going to feel you there for weeks."

He used his arm to sweep her in closer to him so he could lean over her and look into her eyes. "You tell me if I ever get too rough or if our play gets too much for you."

"I will. You weren't too rough. I loved it. My body loved it. Couldn't you tell?"

"That was why I kept going. But you stop me if you don't like anything I'm doing to you."

"I will. I promise." She pressed a kiss to his throat. "I need a shower. So do you. And food. This time, I might even order us up something."

"I'll carry you if you can't walk," he offered.

"We're going to shower together?"

"Yes. I'm a conservationist. Conserving water is high on my priority list."

"I'll just bet it is. If you shower with me, we'll never get to breakfast," she pointed out.

"You will. You started something earlier that I want you to finish."

She laughed, her eyes sparkling. "I'm all for that. Carry me."

He was all for it, too. She took him right back to paradise with the hot water pouring down on him, her eyes clinging to his as he took her mouth. He thought himself well sated after riding her so ferociously, but the moment she began to suckle him, he was lost again. Hard and thick and needy again. This time she finished what she'd started.

They ordered up breakfast and ate it in the room Stefano liked to call his "sunroom." It was all glass on one side, the sliding doors opening onto a balcony that was wide and long. The walls jutted outward on both sides to help with wind and there was a small table and two comfortable chairs where they took their food and ate. He had sex on the brain, because he'd decided he'd have her out on the balcony and inside the sunroom, pressed up against the glass.

She sipped at her coffee and teased him about being an exhibitionist. He just sent her a grin and began to run through his morning reports while she opened the tablet he'd bought for her and read the local news. He liked sitting beside her, reading together, sipping coffee and being locked away from the rest of the world. He reached out and caught her hand, bringing her knuckles to his mouth.

"I can't wait for our wedding."

His phone chimed before she could respond. He knew by the ringtone that it was Lucia or Amo. He could feel Francesca's eyes on him as he talked on the phone, reassuring Lucia he would come. It was what he did, not what he wanted. When he snapped the phone closed, she let out a little sigh and shook her head.

"I was hoping you could stay home today, Stefano. I feel like we haven't been able to talk or spend time together, and this wedding . . ." She trailed off, and his heart jumped.

"I want to stay home with you, *bambina*," Stefano said, "more than anything. I'd like a day for us as well. Just the two of us." He stood up and pulled her to her feet, leaving the dishes for the maids. She would have to get used to that; if he wasn't mistaken, she'd probably gather them up the moment he was gone.

She smiled at him, that smile that always took his breath.

The one he'd always wait for. "Me, too. But I can tell from your tone it isn't going to be today."

He shook his head, walking them into the great room. "No. Unfortunately. Lucia called and needs me to get over there. Nicoletta is having a difficult time believing we aren't some human trafficking ring, or worse, that Lucia and Amo are the real thing, wonderful good people, and she's going to get them killed by staying with them."

"Oh no. I know what that feels like. It's the worst feeling ever. Of course you have to go." She licked at her lower lip for a moment and then lifted her chin. "I could go with you. I want to meet her. Don't you think feeling as if she had a friend would help settle her?"

He detested disappointing her. And was she getting cold feet? Was that what this was about? He sank into the wide armchair and beckoned her with his finger. "Come here, *dolce cuore*."

She hesitated, just for a second, but it was there. He was very good at seeing every detail. He'd been trained from the time he was two. All those years of having to describe everything he saw in rooms or outside. All those years of looking at people and having to describe them and every emotion that crossed their face. There was no way he would ever miss hesitation on his woman's part.

He pulled her onto his lap and locked his arms around her. "Relax, Francesca. You're upset about something and you need to tell me."

"I'm not upset. I'm really not."

It was a denial, but her eyes didn't meet his. She did settle into him, relaxing enough that he slid one hand up her back to the nape of her neck. He loved holding her like this. Close. Feeling her body melting into his as if they shared one skin.

"Tell me, Francesca." That was a command, and if she didn't comply, he wasn't going to be responsible for any words slipping out of his mouth she didn't like. He'd been making an effort for her, although, he had to admit, he didn't always succeed.

"I'm just nervous, that's all. We haven't known each other for very long, and this life you lead is very overwhelming."

He sighed. He knew once she thought about it, the idea of living outside the law was going to get to her. "Being a shadow rider is a responsibility I can't . . ." He broke off when she shook her head.

"It's not that, Stefano. It's the money." She made the confession in a little rush. "All that money. Living in a hotel. Having bodyguards. The clothes. I don't know how to act the way you and Emme act. I'm not sophisticated and I can't handle the paparazzi on every street corner waiting to snap pictures of me. It makes me sick to my stomach to think I'm going to embarrass you or your family."

"Fucking Eloisa." He burst out with it, fury moving through him. "You overheard the shit she was throwing at me and it got to you." So much for his resolve to not use foul language, but really, what the fuck? Why the hell would his own mother undermine his woman's confidence? He wanted to strangle Eloisa.

"Stefano. Really."

That was her little prim-and-proper-schoolmarm voice and he fucking loved it. He thought it best to keep that knowledge to himself.

"Not really, *bella*. You know damn well she put that shit in your head. You could never embarrass my family or me. I'm marrying you because for me you're as perfect as a woman could possibly get. I don't give a flying fuck if the rest of the world doesn't see you the way I do. And neither does my family. You don't seem to get this, Francesca, but you're nearly as important to my siblings as you are to me."

She raised her face and pressed it into his throat. "See? Right there is why it's important to spend time with you. You have a way of making me feel beautiful and confident."

"Let me take care of this thing with Nicoletta. I want you to become her friend. Hell, *amore mio*, you're more her age than mine, but not right now. She's overwhelmed and needs to settle with just Lucia and Amo for now. I've called Taviano—

he stayed with her on the jet. I think she's feeling shame for all that happened to her. Apparently Benito Valdez actually raped her on more than one occasion. He was very brutal and he made certain she knew he would have her permanently. His obsession with her was worse than we first thought. She's terrified he'll find her and that Lucia and Amo will be hurt or killed. I've got a counselor and a doctor who will be looking in on her daily."

"That poor girl. Thank God you and Taviano got her out of there."

"You understand why we're limiting the people she's around for now. She's overwhelmed. I promise the next two we'll introduce to her will be you and Emme. Just a few new people at a time."

Francesca sighed, and nodded her agreement. "That makes perfect sense, Stefano. Actually, it's best anyway. I would have been going for the wrong reasons. I do want to meet her and hopefully become friends with her, but I really wanted to go to be with you."

"I'm sorry, Francesca." He was disappointing her and that was the last thing he wanted.

"No, don't be. I'll be staying in today, so come back as soon as you can. Take Emilio and Enzo with you. They've been doing women things for the last few days and they're pouting. I'll be safe here in the penthouse."

He threw back his head and laughed. She could do that so easily, make him smile. Make him laugh. His arms tightened around her and he nuzzled her neck. "The idea of Emilio in a dress shop or shopping for china is hysterical. I should have asked you and Emme to take pictures or a video of his face."

Her laughter joined his. "The expression on his face was priceless. In all honesty, Emme and I worked really hard to come up with a dozen places the boys would have to go with us, just so we could see that look on their faces. Enzo was just as bad, if not worse. They looked like a couple of bulls going to their doom."

"I can imagine the places Emme decided to make them accompany you."

"We hit every single sexy lingerie store close to us. Emilio and Enzo did a lot of groaning. They were quite the hit in a couple of stores. At one of them, two women insisted on coming out of the dressing room in their sexy getups and asking the boys their opinions. I swear we didn't pay them to do that, but Emilio and Enzo think we did."

"Emme probably did behind your back. It's something she would do. She was always getting the two of them. She likes to get back at all of us for being what she calls 'overprotective.'"

Francesca laughed at him, her arms circling his neck. "Stefano, you know full well all of you are overprotective of Emme. You probably made her teenage years a nightmare."

"Ha. She made our lives a nightmare when she was a teen. She's a rider, *bambina*. That means she could get out of her room whenever the mood struck her. On top of that she's a little on the wild side."

Her eyebrow shot up. "Emmanuelle is wild? I don't think so. You don't see her picture splashed in every magazine with two women hanging on her arm. That's Ricco and your brothers."

"If she had two men hanging on her arm"—Stefano couldn't keep the menace or the grim out of his voice—"they'd find those same men in the morgue the next day."

"That is *so* not fair," she declared. "You really are chauvinistic."

"That's right," he said without apology. "Keep that in mind when we have a daughter. You might want to warn her."

She rolled her eyes at him. "I'm sure she'll figure it out very quickly. With you for a father and her four uncles as well as cousins everywhere, she'll most likely know it by the time she's three."

"You certain you aren't going anywhere today? No fittings for your wedding dress? No looking at cakes or flowers?"

"No."

Francesca was decisive about it, so much so that he had a hard time not laughing. She wasn't thrilled with all that making wedding plans entailed, especially on the scale Eloisa and Emmanuelle were making them. There was no point in fighting his mother and sister for control of the wedding, not even for his woman.

"Emmanuelle said she'd drop by and check on Theresa Vitale today, see if she needs more soup, or anything at all in the way of medicine. I think she's on the mend, but even with her grandson watching over her, we decided not to take chances. With Emme taking care of that, I don't have a thing to do but veg out."

"All right, *dolce cuore*, I won't be gone too long. I'll take Emilio and Enzo with me and we'll drop by the office to collect everything I need on the way back so I can work from here for a couple of days."

"I'd love that," she agreed instantly.

Stefano changed to his three-piece suit, standard wear when outside his home. It was a drawback at times being a rider and always wearing the suit, as classy as it was. Wearing it meant he could disappear at any time into the shadows, but it also meant he was overdressed on occasion.

"Walk me to the elevator, Francesca."

Francesca reached up to straighten his tie, leaning her body into his. "Don't be long, but make certain Nicoletta feels safe, Stefano. You did that for me—even when I was a little afraid of you, you managed to make me feel safe."

He kissed her thoroughly. "I'm really sorry I have to go," he repeated.

"It's for a good cause." She wrapped her arm around him as they walked together toward the elevator. "Are Emilio and Enzo waiting for you downstairs?"

"Yes, I texted them. I'll be safe. Don't worry."

Francesca took a deep breath and nodded, watching as the elevator doors closed and she was alone again. She really didn't want him to go. She'd felt strange the last couple of days without him. The wedding preparations had become extravagant as far as she was concerned. Neither Eloisa nor Emmanuelle seemed to know how to put the brakes on when it came to the wedding, not even when she objected to things. She had envisioned a very small wedding, with just his family. She didn't have any family of her own, but suddenly there were tons of aunts and uncles who had to be invited as well as cousins. First cousins. Second cousins. And then there were the people in the neighborhood. She had wanted to talk to Stefano about it, but he was so exhausted when he'd first gotten home and then they were all over each other. Now he was gone again.

She sighed again and found her way back to the sunroom to collect the dishes off of the balcony. She liked the penthouse, but living in a hotel wasn't really her idea of a home. She'd seen his "office." It was inside the family home. His family home was extremely intimidating. It was a huge estate, even by Chicago's elite standards. Just the front door was intimidating. It was thick and wide and painted a violent red. It should have been ugly, but instead, it managed to be elegant, just like the Ferraro family.

She stood for a long time staring out over the city. The family as a whole had many respected businesses. Each business was legitimate and made them millions, some more than millions. Still, the one small branch of the family—the shadow riders—wasn't at all legitimate; in fact, their activities would be considered criminal. Within the family they were almost revered. Outside the family many people, just as she had, assumed they were part of a crime family. She was one of them. Or she would be in a couple of short weeks.

Her phone went off, a musical melody that told her Emmanuelle was calling. She sighed, considering not answering. She didn't want one more discussion of flowers or cake. Still, she liked Stefano's sister a lot, and truthfully, it was nice to have someone be excited about the wedding and seeing to all the details.

"Hey, girl, what's up?" she greeted.

"I'm on my way to see Signora Vitale. Then I'm heading to the family home. I've been summoned by Eloisa." Her voice changed from annoyance to speculation. "She sounded . . . upset. She never sounds that way. In any case, I had planned to come to see you today to discuss music, but Stefano called and said you needed the day off."

Francesca realized there was a question in there. "Yes. I'm sorry. I do. I'm just going to rest and read and try not to think too much about everything happening so fast."

"Bridal jitters. They say it happens to everyone." Emmanuelle laughed as she hung up.

Maybe she was right and the restless feeling that just wouldn't leave her alone was just that—cold feet. After all, committing a lifetime to a man like Stefano was a little daunting. She would always have to work to stand up to him. That crazy protective side of him would be difficult. He'd want to build a fortress around her and their children. She was well aware that she would have to temper that quality in him for all their sakes.

Francesca took a deep breath and let it out, sweeping her hair back from her face. She'd dressed in a pair of vintage blue jeans. They were soft and molded to her body nicely, but were very comfortable. They weren't from a thrift store and she didn't want to know what Stefano had paid for them. It seemed like her clothes multiplied on a daily basis. She never saw him put things in her drawers or hang them in her closet, but she was fairly certain Stefano had someone shopping for her.

Still. She ran her hand down her thigh. The jeans were perfect. She wore a T-shirt, equally as soft, that was more fitted than she would have chosen for herself. Her underwear was the best part of the shopaholic who seemed to never quit. The lingerie was absolutely beautiful and she loved the way it made her feel sexy, even in a pair of jeans and a tee.

She made herself a cup of tea, flooded the house with soft music and sank into one of the luxurious, overstuffed chairs to read. She lost herself in a book for a long time, grateful for the chance to just be still. It was the phone that brought her back from the grand adventure she was on along with the characters in the book. This time it was the Vitale home.

Bruno, Theresa's grandson, told her that Emme had just left and Theresa had taken a fall. She was in the bathroom and refusing to come out. He'd heard her fall but she'd locked him out and was asking for Francesca. His grandmother was crying and upset and nothing he said or did would make her budge. Francesca assured him she would come immediately.

Francesca immediately texted Enrica to let her know that she would be needed after all, and to meet her downstairs. Then she called Stefano and told him what had happened. She was very proud of the fact that she remembered already to have her bodyguard in place so her man wouldn't lose his mind. She promised she'd text him the minute she got to the Vitales' and let him know what was going on.

Enrica was waiting at the elevator and escorted her out to the car. "I don't like driving and watching over you. We should have a two-man team on you," she said as she slipped behind the driver's seat.

"I could drive," Francesca offered. She hadn't driven in a very long time and traffic in Chicago was intimidating.

Enrica sent her a look and Francesca grinned at her as her bodyguard started the car. "We could have walked. The house isn't that far."

"There's a big storm coming." Enrica indicated the sky. "It's supposed to be bad. Thunder and lightning. Pouring rain. I don't want to get caught in that, but more, I don't want my cousin to kill me, which he would if I let you walk around with only one bodyguard. Believe me, Francesca, he wouldn't like that."

Francesca rolled her eyes. "He has a serious problem and needs help. I think for his birthday I'm getting him a counselor."

Enrica laughed. "You're good for him. He didn't smile much before he found you. Now he's more relaxed and he laughs a lot. I love that for him. I love that he has you. We're hoping the others will find someone to love them."

Francesca thought it was a very odd way of putting it. "Why do you all guard them so carefully? They're so well trained."

"So are we," Enrica said. "Don't you understand how important they are? Not just to our family, but to the world? Things have changed so much, and the laws allow criminals to slip through the cracks all the time. The gangs keep getting more violent and claiming more territory. The cartels are recruiting our young kids and using them to assassinate anyone in their way. The riders can slip in and out of anywhere without being detected. No one knows how they get in or who they are. They can get to anyone at any time. That's important. It's important to someone whose family has been wiped out by the cartel and just as important to someone like Signora Vitale. We *revere* the riders."

"Every life is important, Enrica, including yours. I'm uncomfortable with having bodyguards. I'm not a rider, you know, and I never will be."

Enrica pulled the car into the Vitales' driveway. "You're not a rider, but you're going to marry one. You complete his life and can give him children. They sacrifice all choices when they're born. Their lives aren't like ours. I have a choice in what I do. I can marry whomever I please. If they don't find the one they can love, they're forced, through duty, to be with someone they don't. They don't have normal childhoods. Stefano and the others had crap childhoods. So bad. You can't imagine."

She slid out of the car and went around to the passenger door before Francesca could answer. Francesca knew enough to stay in the car until Enrica decided to open the door. She waited, contemplating the idea of having children and making certain their lives were happy and filled with love. She was beginning to realize she had no real knowledge of what Stefano and his siblings had gone through, but she knew

Stefano was absolutely determined that his children wouldn't suffer the same fate. She loved him all the more for that and for the fact that he trusted her to make his life and their children's lives wonderful. She knew he was counting on her.

They hurried up to the front door, Enrica one step behind her, her gaze on the rooftops, the garage, the street itself. Francesca couldn't imagine what it would be like to be a bodyguard responsible for the safety of another human being. Bruno opened the door and he looked . . . terrible. He was pale and sweating. There was a bruise by his eye and his lip was swollen and cut. He stepped aside to let them in.

"What happened to you this time, Bruno?" Francesca asked. "Where's Theresa?"

Bruno closed the door and turned to face them. "I'm sorry, Francesca. Really sorry. I tried to refuse and they beat the shit out of me, put a gun to my grandmother's head, and Emmanuelle told me to cooperate with them."

Enrica spun around, her hand going to the gun tucked beneath her shoulder in a holster, but it was too late. A man stepped out of the coat closet behind her and struck her over the head with the butt of his gun. She dropped to the floor like a deadweight. Francesca rushed to her, but the man caught her arm in a tight grip.

"Mr. Anthon requests your presence at a very special event, Francesca," he greeted.

She recognized him immediately and her heart began to pound. She knew she went pale because the blood drained out of her face. "Harold McFarland. It appears Barry can't even come to Chicago without bringing his entire entourage. Where's Theresa?"

"The old lady? Don't worry about her. You should be worried about yourself and your new friends." He spat on the floor. "I'm going to enjoy burning down that bullshit deli you worked in. Your boss seemed to think you're some kind of saint. And the old lady thinks the same. They haven't seen the havoc you create yet." He laughed. "I'm going to enjoy showing them just what you're famous for."

He put a hand to her back and shoved her toward the bedroom. Another man—one she recognized from Barry's crew, Arnold Sumi—thrust Bruno in front of him. As he passed Enrica's crumpled body, he kicked her hard in the ribs.

Harold laughed. "You're such a prick, Arnold. Get Jimmy to tie the bitch up."

Francesca had seen the blood coating Enrica's dark, sleek hair and had been worried they'd hit her too hard and killed her, but they wouldn't tie her up if she was dead.

"There isn't any need to hurt anyone, Harold. I'll go with you."

"Damn right you'll go with me," Harold said. "You don't have any choice, not with a gun to Grandma's head. And then there's your friend. I've had a difficult time keeping the boys off of that one. You don't see bitches like that every day. We're bringing her along. She's going to be the main entertainment for us while you entertain the boss."

Francesca turned her head to see Emmanuelle slumped over in a chair, hands tied behind her back and blood trickling down her face from a laceration on her temple. There was a bruise on the side of her face and her dark gray shirt was torn beneath her pin-striped jacket, revealing the swell of her breasts.

On the floor, groaning, was another of Barry's crew, Marc Jonsen. He had pushed himself up into a sitting position and was holding his face. Blood poured from his nose and both eyes were swollen. Clearly he'd been the one to tear open Emmanuelle's blouse and she'd head-butted him.

"Are you hurt?" Francesca asked Theresa. The elderly woman was crying and clutching rosary beads. The blanket was pulled up nearly to her neck.

She shook her head. "Bruno . . ." She trailed off with a little sob.

Francesca turned to Harold. "What are you going to do with them?"

"Lucky for them the boss wants a message delivered to your boyfriend. You and the other bitch are coming with us."

Francesca glanced at Emmanuelle. Her nod was almost imperceptible, but there was no mistaking the wink she gave Francesca. She appeared nearly out of it to their captors, but clearly she wasn't as bad off as she was making herself out to be and that made some of the knots in Francesca's stomach loosen just a little.

CHAPTER TWENTY-FOUR

The wind slammed into the cars as they made their way toward the estate Barry Anthon had rented. Emmanuelle was in the car behind Francesca and that made Francesca very uneasy. She knew Stefano's sister could take care of herself far better than she could in the situation, but Barry wouldn't want Francesca killed, not until he had Cella's cell phone safely in his hands. But Emme was vulnerable.

Stefano and his brothers had humiliated Barry in front of Francesca and Emmanuelle. He wasn't a man who would forgive such an insult. He believed himself to be superior to everyone else. He felt entitled to take anything and every-thing he wanted. Barry would retaliate against the Ferraro family, and what better way than to humiliate Emme? His men were animals. Monsters. They destroyed lives at Barry's whim and enjoyed themselves immensely while doing so. Francesca had no doubt that those men were tormenting Emme in the car, especially Marc. He would want retribution for Emmanuelle defending herself.

As the cars drove through the heavily guarded gates under the archway, Francesca spotted at least ten more guards roaming around the property. Those were the ones she could see. Her heart sank. Four guards at the gate and ten more roaming just the grounds in the front, how many more were there? Even if Stefano brought his brothers with him, the chances of all of them being able to slip through that many guards unscathed seemed nearly impossible.

They drove right up to the front door. Harold's finger bit deep into Francesca's arm as he yanked her out of the car. As she stumbled out, the dark clouds above their heads opened up and slammed them with rain. It poured down in long silvery streaks, falling from the sky to hit the ground in great splashes. Harold swore and dragged her up the two steps to the wide porch with its marble columns and over-head roof. Just those few steps out in the open had them soaked from the downpour.

Francesca looked back toward the other car. Emmanuelle was pulled out of the car and shoved hard against the hood, Marc behind her. Her hands were zip-tied in front of her and clearly he thought she was helpless. He reached around and caught her breast, squeezing hard through the open jacket, humping her from behind while the others watched and laughed.

Harold paused to watch as well, grinning and rubbing his crotch. "I get a turn at that," he announced to Francesca. "And if Barry doesn't kill you first, I'll be taking my turn with you, too."

Emmanuelle kicked up hard between Marc's legs, driving the heel of her boot into his balls and then slamming her head backward to smash his nose again. He screamed, a high-pitched shriek that had his friends howling with glee as he dropped straight to the ground. Arnold, the man who had driven the car Francesca has been in, bent over Marc to try to help him to his feet. Marc shoved at his hand and continued to writhe on the ground.

Jimmy stepped over him and grabbed Emmanuelle's arm. "Come on, wildcat. Let's get you out of here before he can move. He'll shoot you, and we've got plans."

If anything, the rain came down harder, making it diffi-cult to see through the silvery bands. The wind howled an ominous warning, sending the sheets of rain straight at the house. It blew so hard the windows rattled and the porch itself was instantly drenched in the downpour.

Harold cursed more and thrust the door open, nearly

running through it and dragging Francesca with him. "I hate this fucking place," he snarled. He hadn't taken the time to wipe the soles of his boots and he nearly slipped on the marble tiles. He had to let go of Francesca in order to keep from falling.

She stopped where she was, just inside the door, holding it open so she could keep her eye on Emme. Jimmy was hurrying her up the steps, head down to keep the rain from his glasses. Francesca didn't have her hands free, but she stuck out her foot and tripped Jimmy as he hurried inside. Stepping close to Emme, she looked her over carefully for signs of abuse.

Stefano would lose his mind if he could see his sister. Emme was very small, and the men had clearly slammed her around. One eye was showing signs of swelling shut and there were two more cuts on her face, one on her right cheekbone where someone had hit her with a fist and the other on her chin.

"I'm okay," Emmanuelle assured her. "Just getting to know them." She flashed a wan smile. Her bound hands were up by her breasts her and her jacket was once more in place, covering her tattered shirt and what lay beneath it. "He'll come, Francesca."

"That's what I'm afraid of." Because Stefano would walk into a lion's den for the people he loved, or the ones that needed his protection—or justice.

They were taken through the great room, and it was enormous. All marble floors and hanging crystal chandeliers. The furniture was velvet, and a gleaming grand piano sat at an angle, dominating one side of the room. A man played, the music swelling through the house, a haunting melody that seemed obscene as a backdrop for what Barry and his men had planned. The piano player looked up and winked as they were shoved past him. His leering grin revealed two metal teeth shaped like fangs. Francesca recognized him as one of Barry's immediate crew that had destroyed her apartment when she lived in California. Everyone called him Fang for obvious reasons.

They moved through a wide hallway with wainscoting and arched doorways opening into other various rooms. Two men played pool and both straightened from where they were bent over the table and smirked at the women, all the while rubbing their crotches grotesquely, deliberately showing both Francesca and Emmanuelle what was in store for them. She knew them from San Francisco when they'd helped destroy her apartments. Denny and Si were brothers and notoriously nasty.

Francesca glanced at Stefano's sister. She appeared completely calm and she made no move to wipe away the blood on her face or mouth. She kept her head up, but her gaze took in every detail of the house and the men in it as they passed. Francesca followed her lead, although her heart pounded like mad. Barry had a crew of ten men that he kept close to him. She'd recognized seven of them so far. That meant the other three had to be close. If so, that was ten men used to killing for Barry. There had been too many guards to count outside and she assumed they were local muscle Barry had hired.

Barry's right-hand man, Del Travers, stepped out of a room as they passed. He was dressed in his suit and tie. Francesca knew he was a lawyer and he'd gone to school with Barry. He stared at Francesca without expression. That was one of the things she always detested about him. He was cold, like a fish. She always wondered whether or not under that perfect suit he had scales.

Harold shoved her hard in the back, making her aware as she stumbled forward that she'd stopped for a moment to stare at Del. A slow burn of anger began to rise in her. She was tired of Barry taking her life apart piece by piece. She didn't want them touching Emmanuelle. They were sick, perverted men and they had no business being close to a woman like Emme. She hated that they'd put their filthy hands on her, that they'd slapped and punched her.

Barry Anthon had surrounded himself with men just like him. He walked over people, a monster, charming those he wanted to manipulate, and hurting those he thought he could. And he did it for fun. Emmanuelle bumped her slightly and she glanced at Stefano's sister. Emme shook her head, as if reading her thoughts of open rebellion.

"Don't provoke them," she whispered.

Francesca clamped her mouth shut and continued down the hall into a large room where Barry sat at a bar, waiting for them. The last two of Barry's crew were with him. All ten men. Stefano would have to face them all if he came for his sister and her. And he would come.

Larry Fort was behind the bar. He was one of the worst. He'd laughed when he'd shoved her to the floor and torn the sink out of the wall so water sprayed throughout her apartment. Then he'd smashed the toilet and systematically shattered everything she owned. His partner, George Hanson, stood to the back of the room, his gaze immediately going to Emmanuelle. He glanced at Francesca and then at his boss.

Barry sat in a high-backed chair, much like a throne, a glass of bourbon in his hands. He looked terrible, his face swollen and distorted so that his usual good looks were impossible to see. He had stitches in three places. On his cheekbone, above his eye and along his jaw, all on the right side of his face. His lips were grotesque, triple their normal size. Both eyes were black and his nose had tape over it where it had been broken.

He stood up slowly, every movement stiff. "Put them in those chairs." He indicated two straight-backed wooden chairs. One was set in front of his "throne" and the other was toward the end of the room, back in the shadows. The room was well lit with bright overhead chandeliers, just like in the great room. The floors were the same marble, but this room was quite a bit smaller in size.

The lights flickered several times as the storm raged outside. The rain beat continuously at the window and the wind shrieked in fury. Harold dragged Francesca over to the chair, pushing her nearly up against Barry, who stood very close— on purpose, she was certain—staring at her through the slits of his eyes. Yellowish goo clung to the corners of his eyes and up close, he looked even more ghastly than he had from across the room. Harold shoved her hard and she fell back into the chair. It nearly went over backward and neither man lifted a hand to keep her upright. She was just lucky that the chair didn't go all the way over.

"Welcome to my home away from home, Francesca," Barry said. He placed his hands on the arms of the chair, bending down to peer at her closely. "It's a far cry from what you're used to. That pissant Stefano doesn't know how to live with all the money he's got. You shouldn't have crossed me and neither should your bitch of a sister. I would have had more fun with her, showed her the good life before I turned her over to my boys. They're patient. Aren't you, boys?" He lifted his head to look at the men in the room.

Six of them. The four that had brought them from Theresa Vitale's home and the other two waiting with Barry. His other men were still scattered throughout the house. Francesca kept counting, hoping for better numbers, but any way she looked at it, Stefano was going to be in trouble because he wouldn't bring his cousins to this fight. Just his brothers. She knew that instinctively.

She didn't look away from Barry or react to his vile statement. She didn't doubt for a moment that Cella would have been turned over to his men after Barry was done with her. She was certain he'd done that very same thing to countless other women. They feared him too much to ever testify against him in court.

"I would have taken you in front of her. Her baby sister, so sacred, yet you gave yourself to the highest bidder at the first opportunity. I should have offered you money. You're a slut just like all the rest of them, aren't you? You'd do anything for money."

She lifted her chin. "You know better than that, don't you, Barry? You know Stefano will come for me because he loves me, that's what you're counting on. The fact that he loves me. And he loves Emme. You don't have that and there's a part of you that hates everyone because you don't. You're not capable of real love, Barry. You're just not. You'll never know what Stefano has. I love him unconditionally. With everything I am and I'd do anything for him. What woman will ever give that to you? You pay these men to be loyal. They aren't loyal out of love. You trick women and then you throw them away because you can't feel anything. Ever. I'm sorry for you."

As she talked his face reddened, the stain spreading across the swollen bruises. "I'm not the one sitting in a chair, tied up like a fucking turkey, dessert for the men after they kill Stefano Ferraro."

"He's hard to kill," she said softly. "That's what you're worried about, isn't it? You have ten men inside this house, maybe more. You have another dozen outside. What does that say to your crew and me? You're terrified of Stefano." She leaned closer to him, her gaze steady on his. "And you should be."

"He's going to find his sister and you the center of attention. That should distract him just a little if he has such love for you both." He sneered at the word *love*.

She didn't answer him. Just watched him and prayed Emmanuelle wouldn't draw attention to herself. If she did, Barry would do something terrible. She felt the hatred pouring off of him every time he made a reference to Stefano. More, he was just a little insane. There was something very scary in his eyes.

Thunder roared outside, close, shaking the house, rattling the windows. The lights flickered again and went out, the room going dark. Barry swore. "What the hell?"

"The generator will kick in, boss," George assured. "Give it a minute."

There was a short silence. Francesca could hear Barry's labored breathing. He was much more afraid of Stefano than he wanted anyone to believe. When the lights flickered back on, dim and yellow, casting shadows all over the room, she could see sweat beaded on Barry's face.

"I want you two guarding the door," Barry instructed, waving his hand at Marc and Jimmy.

"I've got a score to settle with that little bitch," Marc said, indicating Emmanuelle with a chin lift.

"Yeah, boss, his balls are swollen," Harold said gleefully. "She dropped him twice. Smashed his face. With her hands tied."

"Little thing like that and he's not man enough to handle her." Arnold took up the taunt.

"Shut the fuck up," Marc raged. "I'll show you I can handle her."

"Get out and guard the door. Do it now before I put a bullet in your head. I said you'd have your chance at her, all of you, and I meant it. Her fucking brother will come. He'll want to look like the brave hero for his fiancée. I want you waiting for him. Kill him on sight." As he issued the order, Barry kept his gaze fixed on Francesca's face.

She didn't blink. Didn't look away. Inside, her heart stuttered dangerously, but she didn't give any visible sign that she was in any way worried. She wasn't about to give him that kind of satisfaction.

"You're so sure he'll save you," Barry said bitterly. "Maybe it will be too late and he'll come in here and find your throat cut." He stepped close to her and shoved a knife against her throat, the blade biting in.

She didn't pull back. "Like this hasn't been done a million times to me already, Barry. You need new material." Francesca forced boredom into her voice. She even gave a slight yawn. "My first week or two here in Chicago, I had this happen to me twice."

"You want new material?" Barry snarled. He pulled the blade away from her throat, his yellow slits for eyes reddening along with his face. "You want to see new material?" he repeated, his voice swinging out of control. High-pitched. Insane even. He gripped the knife in his fist and brought it down hard into her thigh.

She screamed as the blade tore through the outside of her thigh and came out the other side. The pain burned through her, leaving her breathless, raw, her heart pounding hard enough to hear. Her blood roared in her ears. She'd heard of men being tortured, stoically not making a sound and she couldn't imagine how they did it. She couldn't catch her breath, or take her eyes from the knife handle sticking out of her thigh.

Barry pulled the knife free and wiped the blood on her jeans, grinning at her. "That new enough for you, bitch? Do you want more? I can show you more." Hatred burned in his eyes. Maniacal glee. He got off on her fear. Her pain. She saw the truth in his eyes. He needed to see those things. She'd been too calm and hadn't given him his fix, or the respect he felt he deserved.

Mesmerized by the look on his grotesquely swollen face, and the red-yellow of his eyes, Francesca watched him touch the tip of the blade to her left shoulder. He placed one hand on the hilt of the knife, ready to drive it through her flesh there. All the while he smiled at her. George laughed. Harold cleared his throat. No one else made a sound, just waiting. All of them watching as mesmerized as she was, while Barry drew out the torment by forcing her to wait.

"Why is it that when a man doesn't like something a woman does, something he would do himself, he calls her a bitch?" Emmanuelle asked, her voice as calm as ever. "I've always wondered about that. Is it because you're such a little bitch, Barry? Always whining to Mommy when things don't go your way? I saw you at the racetrack when your car didn't win and you threw that little fit. That was bitch behavior. Did anyone call you a bitch then? Because I thought you were a total bitch. You moan and groan and complain, but act like a mean girl in high school. Petty and cruel just because you're one of the popular kids. But you really were only popular because Mommy and Daddy had money."

Francesca risked a look around the room, her breath hitching in her throat. Emmanuelle was playing with fire. Barry would kill her for that. A blow to his pride would be worse to him than a physical beating. The men were all smirking, not daring to look at their boss, but obviously enjoying the fact that Emmanuelle had taunted Barry.

Barry turned his head slowly toward the shadows where Emme sat in the chair, her hands bound in front of her. He reminded Francesca of a snake with his red slits for eyes and his cold expression. She moistened her lips, terrified for Emmanuelle. Barry stepped back away from Francesca, never taking his eyes from Emme.

Francesca timed her moment, waiting until Barry was within five feet of Emmanuelle. "Actually, Emme," she said. "He isn't a bitch—he's a pussy. You're really just a pussy, aren't you, Barry? You always have to have your big bad men around because you can't get it up yourself so you need them to take care of a woman while you can only watch." She'd never said that word in her life. Not once. But she'd had to think of something to get his attention off Emme.

Her leg burned and blood stained her favorite pair of blue jeans, but she'd all but forgotten about the stab wound in her fear for Stefano's sister. Barry would kill her for certain.

Barry made a sound in his throat. A snarl. Like a dog might snarl at something or someone provoking it. He spun around, moving back toward Francesca. Lightning zigzagged across the sky, lighting the room for a second, throwing their shadows across the floor and up along the walls. The dull yellow lights flickered. All attention was on Barry. No one could look away, hypnotized by the crazed expression on his face. Two lines of shiny saliva hung in strings from either side of his mouth. He looked almost as if he was foaming at the mouth, like a rabid animal.

"You're dead. That sanctimonious son of a bitch is going to find his sister and his fiancée dead. And then I'm going to kill him." He rushed toward Francesca.

"You can't kill Stefano, you moron," Emmanuelle taunted. "I'm tied up, and you can't kill me. How do you think someone as inept as you could possibly best my brother?"

Barry spun around, this time only feet from Francesca. She could smell the sweat pouring from his body. Feel the heat of his anger. She looked toward the shadows where Emme sat, as did everyone in the room. In the dim lighting Francesca could no longer see anything but the chair legs. The rest of the chair and even Emmanuelle's legs had disappeared into the shadows. Barry took three steps toward the other side of the room, desperately seeking to find Stefano's sister.

Francesca felt hands on her upper arms. Emmanuelle helped her up, forcing her to step forward right into the mouth of one of the shadows. There was a terrible wrenching sensation at her body, as if she was flying apart, and then Emme went still, arms around her.

"Don't move," Emmanuelle said very softly in her ear. "They can't see you. Don't make a sound and don't move."

Francesca nodded, clinging to her, afraid she'd fall, knowing Emmanuelle had taken her inside a portal. Her leg throbbed and burned. It felt like rubber, but she was determined to stay upright. The zip-ties were gone from Emme's hands, although Francesca's were still on, binding her wrists together, so she had to curl her fingers into Emmanuelle's jacket.

Barry rushed over to the chair where his men had shoved Emmanuelle Ferraro. The zip-ties lay on the floor and she was no longer there.

"Boss . . ." Harold said. Caution in his voice.

Barry spun around and to his horror, Francesca was gone as well. "Where are they?" he demanded, gripping the hilt of the knife, holding it in front of him as if he could defend himself against an unseen attacker. "Where the hell are they?"

His men shook their heads.

"Well, find them," he screamed. "Find them right fucking now. If you don't bring them back here in five minutes I swear I'll cut your heads off."

Harold, Arnold and George rushed toward the door. Larry remained leaning his weight against the bar, grinning like a maniac, not obeying a direct order. That was fine with Barry. He needed a target to take out his wrath on.

"I'll carve my fucking name in your throat," he promised, and stalked across the room. The urge to kill was strong. No one humiliated him and lived to tell about it. He was going to carve those women into little pieces, but first every one of his men was going to do them as many ways as possible and he'd film it all and make Stefano Ferraro watch the film before he died.

The Ferraros had always acted so high and mighty, everyone was afraid of them. Well, everyone feared the wrong man. He reached the bar and stepped around it, coming up on Larry's left side. The man hadn't moved a muscle. Hadn't looked at him, when he'd been staring so intently just moments earlier. Larry was *too* still. A chill went down Barry's spine and he stepped back. He could see that Larry's head was at a peculiar angle, as if his neck was broken. Barry backed away from the bar. The man was definitely dead. But how? No one had come into the room. No one had been close to Larry.

He'd heard rumors about the Ferraro family. Stupid, ridiculous, *impossible* rumors, about how they could make things happen to people without ever leaving their homes. That their enemies just died or disappeared. It was nonsense. They weren't part of any crime family. He'd had his connections check several times, just to be certain he wasn't stepping on toes when he'd gone after a couple of drivers on the track. He'd been assured they weren't in organized crime, although the rumors persisted.

Lightning lit up the room and almost simultaneously, thunder boomed, shaking the house again. It was a huge, well-built house and shouldn't be shaking. The rain lashed at it and the wind shrieked and howled. Shadows lengthened and grew, throwing out strange-looking tubes from every direction. The tubes looked like arms reaching for him. Out of the shadow a knife appeared, the tip biting deep into his forearm.

He screamed. Eloisa Ferraro was suddenly there. "You shouldn't have stabbed her, Barry," she said, and then she was gone again, as if she'd never been. As if she was a ghost. A fucking phantom.

With an oath, he turned and ran toward the door, toward the safety of his men. Yanking the door open, he tripped over something heavy lying on the floor. He went down hard.

Very hard. His body rolled and with a sob of frustration he pushed himself to his hands and knees, looking quickly around to see where his crew was, to see if any of them had witnessed this further humiliation.

Marc sat on the floor across the doorway, his body tied in a web of intricate knots, his head drawn back at an impossible angle. It looked as if he'd struggled and the ropes around his neck had tightened until he'd strangled. The knots formed a strange, elaborate harness. Several feet from him, suspended from the ceiling by his wrists, was Jimmy. The knots formed what appeared to be long sleeves that went up his arms to his shoulders and formed a circle around his throat. Staring up in horror, Barry could see where Jimmy had held himself as long as possible, but then his strength gave out and he'd hung himself.

Barry swore and crawled backward, scrambling fast. He'd heard of such knots, but he'd always associated them with erotic bondage. He'd gone to a demonstration once, but it was an art he didn't have the patience to learn. During the demonstration, he'd heard a bit of history and knew the knots had originally been used to restrain prisoners and sometimes torture them. He hadn't listened too closely because he was only interested in watching the naked woman get tied up.

A shadow moved on the floor where the body swung and once again those strange feelers reached toward him like arms. A knife plunged into his thigh, a fist around the hilt. It emerged from the shadows just as the one before it.

Then Ricco was there, shaking his head. "Shouldn't have touched her with a knife, Barry. You're not going to be in one piece by the end of this." Then he was gone.

Gone. Disappeared. The knife was still in his leg, blood bubbling around the blade. Barry was afraid to pull it out, but it was grotesque there. He was losing his mind. There was no other explanation. Still, he was bleeding from two knife wounds, but shadows didn't come alive. That couldn't happen. Not in real life. Was he hallucinating?

"George! Arnold!" He called out for the two men who had been with him the longest other than Del. Del was a great lawyer and he loved to indulge himself with women, but he wasn't as good at kicking ass as George and Arnold.

No one answered him. Other than the howling wind and the sound of the piano, he couldn't hear a sound coming from any room. No one was coming to help him. He had to jerk the knife out of his leg on his own. Taking a deep breath, he wrapped his fingers firmly around the hilt and yanked hard. For a moment the world spun and was edged in black. The pain was excruciating, worse than when the blade had gone in.

Barry dropped the knife and ripped his shirt to wrap the wound up. It hurt like hell but there were no signs of arterial bleeding. The stupid son of a bitch couldn't even find an artery. How stupid were the Ferraro brothers anyway? Bringing a knife to a gunfight? He tossed Ricco's knife away and then his own to pull his gun from its holster under his arm. He'd all but forgotten it. He didn't generally do any of the strong-arm stuff—those were his men's jobs—but he could if he had to. This was a case of if he wanted the job done right, he'd have to do it himself.

Del. Del was close, in the next room. His lawyer didn't want any part of what was going to happen to Stefano. He didn't like getting his hands dirty. He claimed he was the law and he needed deniability, but he was a fucking coward. He liked to participate with the women. In fact, he was one of the worst, beating the crap out of them while he fucked them before going home to his wife and children. He especially liked young girls. Teens. More than once Barry's men had had to clean up his messes, but he was a damn good lawyer so Barry kept him around. This time, the bastard would use a gun.

Barry pushed himself to move. He was shaking and that just pissed him off more. The door to Del's room was open and he stepped inside. Del had draped himself on the bed, hands behind his head, staring up at the ceiling. The rain slammed against the window so hard the window rattled. Shadows played along the walls and across the bed.

"Get up, you lazy fuck," Barry snapped, impatient with the way Del always chose to stay out of the muck with the rest of them.

"He can't, Barry," Emmanuelle's soft voice said in his ear. She was right behind him. Close. He could feel her breath against his neck. "He's dead. So sorry. His neck broke when he tried to rape me."

Before he could turn, before he could make a move, a hot blade sank into his side. Low. Between his ribs. Fire flashed through him. His breath left his body in a concentrated rush or he would have screamed the house down.

"You shouldn't have stabbed Francesca, Barry. It was very stupid of you."

The knife retreated and he spun, one hand clamped to the wound, the other clutching the gun. He whirled, cursing. Tears leaking out of his swollen eyes. There was no one there. Nothing but shadow. Breathing heavily he leaned against the wall, trying to think. The stab wound in his leg was the worst. Ricco had really nailed him. Eloisa barely scratched him. Emme's knife hurt, but really, how bad was it? He could still breathe. He had the gun. Fuck the damn Ferraro family.

He just needed to rally his men. Denny and Si were in the poolroom. Lazy bastards. They were always clowning around, oblivious to what was happening around them. He'd shake them up. He paid them damn good money to do what he said. He hurried down the hall, dragging his leg, cursing every jarring step. He slammed his fist on the poolroom door and it sprang open.

Denny was on the floor. He had marks across his face, as if he'd been caned. His pool stick was still clutched like a weapon in his hand. Si was on the table, the same marks on him, his pool stick broken. Barry's heart began to pound. Hard. He tasted terror for the first time in his life. The wind rose and drove the rain at the bank of windows. Outside the trees swayed macabrely, the shadows dancing through the window onto the walls and floors, even across Denny's face as if laughing at him.

"Shouldn't have stuck that knife in her, you fuck," Giovanni said, and slammed a knife into Barry's good leg.

Up high. In his thigh. Almost an identical wound to the one his brother Ricco had made. Barry screamed. He couldn't stop screaming as he fired the gun repeatedly at Giovanni. But Giovanni had vanished as if he'd never been. As if he wasn't human. A phantom. A ghost. Barry wiped his eyes with his gun hand and slumped against the wall. He had to get out of there. He could hire someone to kill Stefano and his entire family. Wipe them out. He would get satisfaction from that. He didn't need to see it done, just so long as it was done.

He wrapped the wound on his leg and headed for the kitchen, intending to go out the back way. There was a car waiting outside. There was always a car. He'd sent Arnold and Harold out to hunt the women down. If he was lucky, they were still alive and they could get out with him. He stopped just outside the kitchen. There was no door, only an archway. The room seemed quiet—so quiet he could hear the piano. Fang stilled played. He was still alive. The music sounded better than it ever had—but bizarre, as if the drama unfolding in the house was nothing more than a theater play that he was stuck in the middle of.

Arnold sat at the kitchen bar, a sandwich in front of him. There was a whole ham cut into thin slices on the bar beside the plate with the sandwich. Harold was against the wall behind the bar. Barry stepped inside and hurried to them. "Get up. We've got to get out of here. The Ferraro brothers are every . . ." He trailed off.

Arnold was pinned to the chair by a series of knives, his eyes wide open and staring in horror. Harold was held to the wall by knives going from his belly to his chest. Barry staggered back, reaching for the archway to hold his trembling body up. He looked wildly around. There was no one. Only silence. The shadows played across the back door as if daring him to enter them. He shook his head, sobbing. No way was he going out that door, not with the shadows moving across it.

"I like knives, Barry. Learned to cook in Europe when I

was training there," Taviano said, his voice close to Barry's neck. "And to use knives for all kinds of purposes."

Barry brought up the gun and Taviano slapped it away. Easily. So easily. Barry closed his eyes, knowing what was coming, trying to steel himself.

"I gave them a little demonstration, but they weren't impressed, or at least they didn't say so. You know you shouldn't have stabbed her. She's ours. Dumb, Barry, but then you always were a dumb prick."

The knife went in on the other side, in the same spot where Emmanuelle had stuck him. He knew there was no sense in looking for Taviano. He'd disappeared, just as all the other Ferraros had disappeared. Like ghosts. Barry stayed very still, leaning against the archway, sobbing. He had no idea how long he stayed there, blood running down his clothes, his mind uncomprehending.

This couldn't really be happening to him. He always won. He was always in control. Now he was staggering through this mausoleum, bleeding from multiple stab wounds, his men dead inside.

The sound of the piano penetrated through the lashing rain and shrieking wind. Lightning still lit up the sky, as if the storm stayed crouched over the estate he'd rented. *Fucking Ferraro family. Think they own Chicago.* He pushed off the wall and stumbled down the hall toward the great room and the sound of the piano. Fang was still playing, seemingly unaware of the deaths taking place around him. More, the concerto he played was intricate, difficult, something Barry wouldn't have thought in Fang's repertoire. Barry had gone to several concerts with his mother and heard the greatest pianists in the world play. Fang wasn't one of them, yet his playing now was superb. The beautiful music sounded so incongruous as a backdrop for the ugliness happening inside the house.

Barry burst into the great room and the first thing he saw was George. The man was lying beside the piano bench, his neck at an odd angle, his eyes open and staring in horror.

Fang was facedown, just on the other side of the piano. The man playing was Vittorio Ferraro. He turned suddenly, one hand lifting from the keys. In one movement he picked up the small throwing knife, turned and flung it at Barry, all the while his other hand still played. Then his second hand joined, even before the knife sank into Barry's shoulder.

"Shouldn't have stabbed her, Anthon," Vittorio said, and dismissed him, keeping his back to him as he played the concerto.

Dismissed him. As if he were of no consequence. It was humiliating. If he'd still had his gun he'd have killed the son of a bitch. The knife barely hurt, not with the wounds in his thighs throbbing and burning. Not one knife had touched a vital spot. Not one . . .

Barry looked around him, his heart pounding hard. He felt hands on either side of his head. Almost gentle.

"You're dead, Barry. Justice is served." Stefano broke Barry Anthon's neck. He stepped back, dropping the body to the floor. "Did you call Sal? He'll need to really clean this place."

"It's done. Get your woman and let's go home."

Stefano nodded and went back to get Francesca. He stepped into the portal where she was waiting for him with Emme. Emme had wrapped up the wound in Francesca's thigh, but Stefano lifted her into his arms. "Put your arms around my neck and your face into my shoulder, *bambina*. Keep your eyes closed. I don't want you to see any of this."

"Okay," she agreed softly.

"It's over, Francesca—he's dead. He'll never hurt another woman."

"Thank you, Stefano. All of you. Let's go home."

Stefano stepped into the next shadow and took his woman home.

EPILOGUE

Stefano stood at the altar, his heart pounding. He had never really believed this day would come. He glanced at his brothers and saw the same look on their faces that he knew was on his own. Disbelief. Awe. Raw hope. They were shadow riders, men and women with responsibilities that didn't allow them to choose what they wanted. Finding someone who could love them, someone willing to share their lives, was rare and nearly impossible to believe could be true.

But there she was. Francesca. His woman. Walking toward him, looking like a vision, too beautiful and ethereal to be real. Dressed in white lace, her gown clinging to her figure, showing her curves and that ridiculously small waist he liked to put his hands on. Her hair was down, just as he'd requested, when his mother and sister were insistent on her putting it up. She'd done that for him, argued and won just to please him. Her veil was intricate lace surrounding her face. She was on Pietro's arm.

Emilio and Enzo had vied for the privilege of walking her down the aisle to him, but Pietro had asked, and in the end they decided that she needed family of sorts. Joanna stood up for her. Enrica and Emme as well. Enrica's concussion hadn't kept her out of the wedding party. Stefano couldn't see them. Only Francesca. Only his woman, walking toward him, giving not only him, but his brothers and sister the promise of a future.

The church was overflowing. Family. Cousins from New

York and San Francisco. The branch in Los Angeles had drawn the short straw and had to stay away. The entire neighborhood, everyone in their village, had been invited, and most came. He'd even spotted Dina, wearing Francesca's coat, seated at the back of the church.

Nicoletta made her first public appearance with Lucia and Amo, sitting between them, looking pale and a little frightened, but she was there. Still, Stefano could only really see his woman. He took the steps down to her, took her hand from Pietro and tugged until she was beside him, right where she was meant to be.

They turned together and faced the priest, his heart swelling with joy as he said his vows to love and cherish her. He would . . . for all time.

Keep reading for an excerpt from the
next Carpathian novel by Christine Feehan,

DARK CAROUSEL

Available August 2016 from Berkley Books

Charlotte Vintage pushed the stray tendrils of dark auburn hair curling around her face back behind her shoulders and leaned toward her best friend, Genevieve Marten. Icy fingers of unease continually crept down her spine. There was no relaxing, even with a drink in front of her and the pounding beat of the music calling to her.

"We know they followed us here, Genevieve," she whispered behind her hand. Whispering in the dance club with the music drumming out a wild rhythm wasn't easy, but she managed. They had accomplished what they'd set out to do, but now that they had drawn their three stalkers out into the open, what were they going to do?

"We must have been crazy, thinking we could do this, Genevieve. Because we have no business exposing ourselves to this kind of danger." Mostly Charlotte didn't think she should have exposed Genevieve to the danger. At least not both of them together. Not when they had a three-year-old to consider.

She made a slow perusal of the club, trying to take in every detail. The Palace was the hottest dance club in the city. Everyone who was anyone went there. In spite of the fact that it was four stories high, every single story was packed with bodies, as well as the basement underground club. Men tried to catch her eye continuously. She wasn't going to pretend she didn't know Genevieve was beautiful, or that she wasn't so hard on the eyes either. The pair of them together drew attention everywhere they went—which was a bad thing.

"We're acting like normal women for a change," Genevieve said a little defiantly. "I'm tired of hiding. We needed to get out of the house. *You* needed to get out of the house. You work all the time. Honestly, Charlie, we're going to grow old hiding away. What good has it done us? We're not any closer to finding out who is doing this to us."

"I can't afford to be bait," Charlotte pointed out. "And I don't like you being bait either. Certainly not both of us together when we have to look after Lourdes. She can't lose everyone in her life. It goes against everything in me to hide away, but I've got to consider what would happen to Lourdes if I was killed. They already murdered her father. She has no mother. I'm all she's got." When Genevieve sent her a look she hastily amended, "*We're* all she's got."

Charlotte wasn't the hide-from-an-enemy type any more than Genevieve was. They'd met in France, both studying art. Genevieve painted and she was good. More than good. Already her landscapes and portraits were beginning to be sought after by collectors. Charlotte restored old paintings as well as old carvings. Her specialty and greatest passion was restoring old carousels.

Genevieve was French. She was tall with long, glossy dark hair and large green eyes. Not just green, but deep forest green. Startling green. She had the figure of a model, and in fact had had several major agencies try to convince her to sign with them. She was independently wealthy, having inherited from her parents and both sets of grandparents.

Genevieve's maternal grandmother had raised her. A few months earlier, that grandmother, her last living relative, had been brutally murdered. Several weeks later, a man Genevieve had been dating was murdered in the same way. His blood had been drained from his body and his throat had been torn out. Charlotte's mentor, the man she was apprenticing under, was murdered a week after that.

Twice, when they were together, the two women had

become aware that someone had tried to enter their house late at night. They'd locked all windows and doors, but whoever was after them had been persistent, rattling the glass, shaking the heavy doors, terrorizing them. The police had been called. Two officers were found dead in the courtyard, both with their blood drained and their throats torn out.

Charlotte received word a couple weeks later that her only sibling, her brother, had been found dead, murdered in the same way. He was in California. In the United States. Far from France. Far from her. He'd left behind his business and his daughter, three-year-old Lourdes. Lourdes' mother had died in childbirth, leaving Charlotte's brother to raise her. Now it was up to Charlotte. Genevieve had decided to come with Charlotte to California. Whoever was after the two of them was in the States, and Genevieve wanted to find them.

Genevieve laid her hand over Charlotte's. "I know Lourdes is your first priority. She's mine as well. She's a beautiful little girl and obviously traumatized by what she saw. Her nightmares wake me up and I'm not even in the same house."

Charlotte knew Genevieve wasn't exaggerating. Genevieve always knew whenever Lourdes had nightmares, even if she wasn't staying with them. At those times, she always called to make certain the child was all right. Lourdes had been present when her father had been murdered. The killer had left the child alive and sitting beside her slain father. She'd been alone in the house with his body for several hours before he was found by the child's nanny, Grace Parducci, a woman who had gone to school with Charlotte and had known her brother and his wife.

"The police aren't any closer to solving the murders, Charlie. Not here and not in France. Lourdes is in danger, just as much as we are. Maybe more." Genevieve leaned her chin onto the heel of her hand as she hitched her chair closer to Charlotte's in order to be heard above the music. "I've been thinking a lot about this and how it all got started. What we did to draw some crazy person's attention."

Charlotte nodded. She'd been thinking about it as well. What else could she think about? Both of them had lost every family member with the exception of little Lourdes. Charlotte didn't want to lose her, and lately, in spite of taking every precaution, she hadn't felt safe. At. All. Grace had reported being followed and feeling as though someone was watching her as well.

Charlotte knew there was a part of her that had come with Genevieve to the nightclub in an effort to try to draw the murderer out. She'd certainly come prepared. She had weapons on her. Several. Most unconventional, but she had them. She honestly didn't know if the men stalking them were the same ones that had murdered her brother, but it seemed likely.

Charlotte wasn't the type of woman to run from her enemies, and it upset her to think her brother's murderer was going free—that he or she was trying to terrorize them. No, not trying. She was terrified for Lourdes. She had no idea why the little girl had been left alive, but she wasn't taking any chances with her. Coming to the nightclub without her was a chance to draw the killer out without endangering Lourdes.

"That stupid psychic center we went to together for testing," Charlotte murmured. "It gave me the creeps."

Genevieve nodded. "Exactly. The Morrison Center. We went for a lark and it wasn't in the least bit fun. They got interested in us way too fast and kept asking very personal questions. When we left, I thought we were followed."

Charlotte had thought so as well. The testing site had been a little hole in the wall but in a high-traffic area, so neither thought anything of it. They both often said they were "psychic" and thought it would be so much fun to go in and test, just like having their palms read. Something fun to do. It hadn't turned out to be so fun.

Charlotte looked into Genevieve's green eyes and saw the same pain she was feeling reflected there. Who could have known that something they'd done on a whim would have such horrific consequences? It was like that with them.

They both thought along the same lines, knew what the other was thinking.

"Ever since going there, I feel like we're being watched," Genevieve said. "And not in a good way. When we were still in France, before *Grandmere* was murdered, a couple of men asked me out and I got this really creepy vibe from them. When they talked I just kept having the image of the testing center crop up in my mind and I couldn't help associating them with it."

Charlotte nodded her understanding. The same thing had happened to her more than once. And then the murders happened. Since then, they'd been much more careful. No dates. No fun. No strangers in their lives. Charlotte ran her brother's cabinet-making business, and she did a little art restoration on the side, but she hadn't really been working at her own business for months. Not since she'd returned to the United States.

"What are we going to do, Charlie?" Genevieve asked. "I can't live like this for much longer. I know I should be grateful I'm alive, that *we're* alive, and I don't want to do anything that might endanger Lourdes, but I feel like I'm suffocating."

Charlotte knew how she felt. "We've taken the first step by coming here. We weren't all that quiet about it either, Vieve. We've attracted a lot of attention. Those men, the ones who keep asking us to dance, they give off that creepy testing vibe to me. What about to you? And do they look familiar to you? I swear I've seen them before. I think in France."

Genevieve followed Charlotte's gaze to the three men who had continuously asked them to dance and sent drinks to their table. They winked and flirted and stayed close all night. They were good dancers. They'd asked other women and Charlotte had watched them. All three knew what they were doing on a dance floor. All three were exceptionally good looking. They seemed like men who frequented the dance club and picked up their share of women there. Still, there was something off about them.

"Same here. The one named Vince, Vince Tidwell, touches me with one finger every time he gets close enough. He just runs it over my skin. Instead of giving me any kind of cool shiver, I get the creeps and the image of the testing center is right there in my mind. I keep telling myself we tested in France, so would they really follow us here? But I'm fairly certain they did."

"So maybe we should leave and then wait for them outside and try to follow them," Charlotte suggested. "Lourdes is safe for tonight. I've called half a dozen times and Grace assures me all is quiet on the home front. We could track them tonight and find out where they're staying and who they really are. Maybe we'll find out what they want from us."

Genevieve's vivid green eyes lit up. "Absolutely. I need to do something to make me feel like I'm not sitting on my thumbs just waiting for someone to murder me. I have to do something positive to help myself."

Charlotte nodded. She knew better. She had Lourdes. Responsibilities. One *huge* responsibility. She'd always been adventuresome. She pursued her dreams with wide-open arms, rushing headlong where others were afraid to go. She hadn't stayed home with her brother. She'd worked hard from the time she was very young so she could finance her trip to France, where she'd always wanted to go. She'd learned French early, and worked hard at it until she could speak like a native. She'd left behind her brother and only come back to help him when his wife died. And then she'd left again.

"Selfish," she murmured aloud. "I've always been selfish, doing the things I wanted to do. I want to go after them too, Vieve. I swear I do." She had to put her mouth close to Genevieve's ear to be heard over the music. She wasn't the type of woman to hide in a house with the covers over her head, but what was the right thing to do? She honestly didn't know.

"Lourdes would be a lot safer if we figured this out, Charlie," Genevieve pointed out.

She wasn't saying anything Charlotte hadn't already told herself, but she still didn't know if she was making excuses to jump into action because she wanted to justify taking the fight and shoving it right down the throat of their enemy.

Charlotte made up her mind. She couldn't just keep hiding. It wasn't in her character, and Genevieve was so right—Lourdes needed to settle into a normal life. They couldn't keep moving and trying to cover their tracks. "Let's do it then, Vieve. We can follow them and see if we can find out what they're up to. You can't look like you, though. You draw way too much attention."

Charlotte risked another quick look at the three men. The one named Daniel Forester appeared to be the leader. His two friends definitely deferred to him. He was tall and good looking, and he knew it. He was staring at her even as he danced with another woman. The woman looked up at him with absolute worship and he was ignoring her to look at Charlie.

She raised an eyebrow at him to let him know she thought he was being rude. He grinned at her as if they shared a secret. "He is an arrogant prick," she hissed.

"So are his friends. Players. All three of them," Genevieve said. "They know they look good and they use their looks to pick up women."

Charlotte couldn't help it; she laughed softly, breaking the stare with Danny to look at her best friend. Genevieve was in full makeup and looked like a runway model. "Seriously? We're really getting bad here, Vieve. We both know we look good and we came here hoping for a little fun."

"I don't know what you're talking about, Charlie," Genevieve protested, all haughty. "I look like this all the time. Waking up, I look like this."

Charlotte blew her a kiss. "Truthfully, you do look like that when you wake up. It makes me sick."

"Uh-oh, here they come. They're bringing drinks. Vince and his friend Bruce at your nine o'clock. They're carrying one for their friend Danny as well." Genevieve lowered her voice until Charlotte could barely make out what she was saying over the music.

Both women plastered on smiles as the two men toed chairs around and sat at their table without asking.

"I know you must have missed us," Bruce Van Hues said.

"So we came bearing gifts." He put the drinks down in front of them, flashing them smiles as if that would convince them he was merely joking.

"Pined away," Charlotte said. "Could hardly breathe without you."

Vince laughed, nudging Genevieve playfully with his shoulder before pulling his chair very close to hers, making a show of claiming her. Charlotte saw Genevieve's eyes darken from her normal vivid emerald green to a much deeper forest green, like moss after a rain. That was always, always a bad sign with her best friend. Genevieve had a bit of a temper. She flashed hot and wild, but it never lasted long. Charlotte could hold a mean grudge. She wasn't happy about it, but if she was honest, she could. For a long time.

Charlotte knew Vince was genuinely attracted to Genevieve. Most men were. She was gorgeous. But she was fairly certain the three men had followed them to the club. They hadn't just picked them out of the crowd of women. Four stories' worth of women. Many were beautiful; most were hungry, looking to take someone home. Genevieve and Charlotte had made it clear to the trio of men several times that they weren't there for a casual hookup. That hadn't deterred them in the least.

Danny sauntered over, pulled out the chair beside Charlotte's and dropped into it. "I think I've done my duty for the night." He picked up the drink in front of Charlotte, grinned at her and took a sip. "You haven't done yours, though, woman. You've hardly danced at all. Think of all the disappointment that's caused so many men."

Charlotte shook her head, flashing a small smile at him. He really thought he was charming. He pushed the drink toward her and she deliberately wrapped her fingers around the glass, automatically finding the exact spots where his fingers had touched as she lifted it to her mouth and tipped some of the contents down her throat. The jolt hit her like it always did when she opened herself up to a psychic connection. Her mind tunneled and she found herself in the void, looking at the fresh memories of the men who had touched the glass before her.

The bartender first. His touch was imprinted there. He was worried about his mother and didn't like his father. He wanted a raise and was very tired of drunken women coming on to him. He wished he could come out openly and declare he preferred men, but his father had made it clear if he did so, it would ruin his family and he would be disowned. The bartender wished he had the guts to tell his father to go to hell and just walk away from his family instead of living a lie.

Charlotte felt bad for the man and risked a quick look in the direction of the bar. There were too many bodies dancing to the music to see the actual bar, and she knew she was putting off the inevitable—allowing herself to "read" Danny's memories. Quick flashes of horror movies pushed at her vision. A stake driven into a man's chest. Blood erupting, spraying like a fountain. The victim's eyes wide open, revealing shock and terrible suffering. Danny swinging a hammer to drive the stake deep. Voices urging him on. Distaste for the task but determination.

Charlotte gasped and let go of the glass, leaping up, knocking her chair over in the process as she backed away from the table. Not a horror movie. Reality. She couldn't breathe for a moment, couldn't catch a breath. There was no air in the room. He had done that. Had killed a human being by driving a stake through the man's heart. Vince had been there. So had Bruce. She recognized their voices.

She was aware of the men standing, of Genevieve grasping her arm. Danny's fingers settled around her neck, pushing her head down, afraid she would faint. His touch only made matters worse. She didn't get anything off human beings, only objects, but she imagined she was right there, watching him hammer a stake through a man's heart. Torturing him while he was conscious. The idea of it made bile rise and she pushed one hand over her mouth.

"I'm going to be sick," she whispered.

Genevieve caught her around the waist and began moving

her away from Danny and the others, toward the restrooms. "What is it, Charlie?" she whispered. "What did you see?"

"He killed a man." Charlotte choked the words out. "*Tonight.* Before they came here. He drove a stake through his heart while the man was alive. Awake. The other two were with him. And then they came here, drinking. Dancing. *Laughing.*"

Genevieve stopped right outside the ladies' room and glanced over her shoulder. "They're watching us, Charlie. Let's get inside, out of sight."

Charlotte nodded. She had to pull herself together. "It was just a shock. They killed a man and then came here to dance." She let Genevieve lead her into the ladies' room. "Or pick up women."

"Specifically us," Genevieve pointed out. "I get the vibe off of them that they're totally targeting us. Not just any woman. They certainly had their choice. Several women made it clear they'd be willing to go home with them tonight, but they keep coming back to us." She glanced around the crowded ladies' room and lowered her voice even more. "Do you think they could possibly be the ones who murdered your brother and my grandmother?"

Charlotte frowned and forced herself to quit leaning on Genevieve. Her stomach still churned, but she had it under control now. "I'm sorry, Vieve—it was just so shocking. I let go before I could get any more. I shouldn't have, although the murder was so fresh that it probably would have covered everything else." She rubbed the frown off her mouth and sent Genevieve a wry halfhearted smile. "I panicked. I've never done that before in my life. It just goes to show what happens when you have a child. You get soft."

"What are we going to do, Charlie?"

Charlotte took a deep breath and then squared her shoulders. "We're going to get as much information as possible in as little time as possible and then we'll leave. See if they follow us. If I can figure out the location of the body, I can call in an anonymous tip to the cops and name them as the murderers."

"You want to go back to the table and sit with them?" Genevieve asked, her eyes wide with shock.

Charlotte nodded. "We can't let on that we're onto them. We have to just play it off like I was suddenly sick or something. I'll think of an explanation."

Genevieve took a breath and then slowly nodded. "Okay. I can do that if you can. But let's leave as soon as possible."

"Agreed. We'll have to get out in front of them and then find a way to watch to see if they try to follow us out. Turning the tables on them is going to be dangerous, Vieve. If they're following us, then they want something. Murdering that man has to be connected."

Genevieve swallowed hard. "Did you recognize him? Was it someone we know?"

Charlotte tried to focus on the murdered man. He'd been about forty. Dark hair. His face had been twisted with pain. His eyes alive with terror and excruciating agony. She would see those eyes in her sleep. She shook her head, trying to still the shudder that ran through her body. "I don't know. He looks vaguely familiar. It's possible he was on Matt's crew. My brother had a lot of employees. When I sold the company, some of them were laid off and they were angry. I got a lot of threats." She ran her hand through her thick hair. "I just can't place him. He looked . . . terrified. In so much pain. I don't understand what they were doing to him."

"They drove a stake through his heart? You mean like they do to vampires in movies?" Genevieve asked. "Because when *Grandmère* and your brother were murdered, the blood was drained from their bodies and their throats were torn. Someone might interpret that as being killed by a vampire."

Charlotte's eyebrows shot up. "Now we're really getting outside the realm of possibility and into the realm of complete fantasy."

"I didn't say there are vampires, only that someone nutty might think there are." Genevieve sighed. "Okay, I'll admit, when I saw *Grandmère*, for a moment I entertained the idea that there were such things."

Charlotte put her arm around her friend in an effort to comfort her. "I'm sorry, honey. I know that was horrible for you. Anyone would have thought the same after seeing her like that. Let's hope there isn't any such thing out there like a real vampire, because the way our luck has been going, it would be after us." She tried for a little levity, although with the bile still forming a knot in her throat, she didn't feel in the least like laughing.

Danny, Vince and Bruce, the three handsome men who had spent the evening flirting with every woman in the place and with Genevieve and Charlotte in particular, were vicious, cold monsters. She took a step toward the door.

Genevieve caught her arm. "Wait. Wait just a minute, Charlie, and let me rethink this. I know I was the one pushing for us to get out of hiding and try to find whoever murdered your brother and my grandmother, but maybe I was wrong to make us a target. These men clearly are murderers, and if you don't think they're the same ones who killed our families, then we shouldn't draw their attention any more than we already have."

They were staying in the restroom far too long. "We don't run. That's what we promised each other," Charlotte reminded her. "We're never going to be free if we don't find out who murdered the ones we love. Lourdes will never be free. You were right, Genevieve. I was the one trying to hide. Being responsible for a child threw me, but we're strong. We've stuck together through everything so far, and we can do this."

"They aren't going to get away with it, are they?" Genevieve said, trying to pour steel into her voice. "We'll find out who took our families, and we'll do it together."

Charlotte looked up at her friend's beautiful face. There was determination there. Fear, but also courage. She nodded. "Damn right, we will. Let's get out there and take back the control. They think they have it, but we're good at what we do."

Genevieve glanced at herself in the mirror. "Charlie?" She hesitated. Long lashes veiled her eyes. "What if there is such a thing as a vampire? What if these men are killing them?"

Charlotte opened her mouth and then closed it. Genevieve didn't deserve a derisive response. She needed to think about what she said carefully. Logically. "First, honey, if there were vampires, after all this time, wouldn't the world know about them? And secondly, the man they killed was no vampire. I saw his death. I saw him. I felt him. He was just as human as the two of us. Maybe they believe they're killing vampires, but I don't see how. And driving a stake through someone's heart, vampire or human, while they're alive and conscious, is just plain sadistic. We can't take any chances with these men. We have to find out what they want, and we need to be very careful. If they've targeted us, we need to know why."

Genevieve took a deep breath and then nodded. She'd been the one to insist they come out of hiding and act like they were alive again, but it was Charlotte who was more the warrior woman. When it came down to facing danger, it was Charlotte who stood in front of her.

The two of them made their way back to the table, threading through the crowd. All three men waited for them, eyes examining them carefully as they approached.

"Why is there always a line in the ladies' room and not the men's?" Charlotte asked and threw herself into the chair beside Danny. "Every time. It's crazy and makes me tempted to march into the men's room and do a takeover with a bunch of other like-minded women."

"What happened to you?" Danny asked. He sounded charming. Solicitous. Worried even. He couldn't hide the cold alertness in his eyes. The suspicion.

She had to touch that glass again without a reaction. Charlotte flashed an embarrassed smile. Deliberately she inched her fingers toward the glass he'd drunk from. "I'm violently allergic to something they put in some of the alcohols. I should have been more careful." She wrapped her palm around the glass right where she thought his prints were and began to slowly push it away from her, making a show out of it.

Much more prepared this time, when the jolt came, she

rode it out, seeking to go deeper into the tunnel to find more memories. To see if these men had murdered her brother. She caught images of Danny following Genevieve and Grace from a store. That was how he had found their home. The three men had changed places frequently while following the two women so that no one car had been close to them at any time, which explained how Genevieve, always so careful, hadn't spotted a tail. It also explained how they had come to follow Grace.

There, in the tunnel, Charlotte found that there were two older murders, both committed by driving a stake through a man's heart. All three men were present. She didn't feel anything but a grim hatred emanating from them. Her brother wasn't one of the victims. Still, one of the murders took place in France. She recognized the gardens where Daniel had staked his victim.

The three men were serial killers. The bodies couldn't have been found or the murders would be splashed across every news station imaginable. She knew she couldn't keep her hand around the glass much longer and maintain her embarrassed smile. Genevieve looked so anxious, her face pale, her gaze studiously avoiding the three men, but centered on Charlotte as if her life depended on it.

As if she knew the men would see her desperate fear, Genevieve leaned toward Charlotte. "Are you certain we shouldn't leave? The last time you drank something that affected you so adversely, I had to take you to the hospital."

Charlotte was very proud of her. Genevieve might be terrified, but she was thinking all the time. She'd said the perfect thing to reinforce Charlotte's explanation. Slowly, she let go of the glass, having pushed it halfway across the table.

"I'm all right, Vieve. I just took a little sip and knew instantly something was wrong." She shrugged. "I should have spit it out, but I didn't want Danny to think I was spitting all over him."

The men laughed, although she could tell it was forced. She wasn't certain they were buying her little charade. She leaned back in her seat. It was time to change the subject and do a little digging. "Vieve and I met in France and have been best friends ever since. Where did the three of you meet? You obviously have been friends for a long time."

"School," Vince answered immediately, turning his attention to Genevieve. He ran his finger from her bare shoulder to her wrist. "Grammar school. I love that sexy little French accent you have."

Bruce nodded and leaned toward Genevieve. "How long have you been in the States?"

Charlotte was grateful for Genevieve's French accent. It always managed to be a conversation changer. As a distraction, it worked very well.

"We met while working on art projects in Paris," Genevieve supplied, deliberately taking the attention away from Charlotte. "Charlie was interning, learning art restoration from some of the greatest in the world, and I was painting. We became great friends."

Charlotte casually reached for the napkin in front of Danny, the one he'd been resting his hand on. She crumpled it up slowly, finger by finger, dragging it into her palm as if doing so absently, smiling and nodding to indicate the introduction in France was a good moment for them both.

It was difficult to keep her smile in place, and she welcomed the opportunity to change her attention from Danny to Genevieve, because even with the object being new and fresh rather than older, as her talent preferred, she was getting enough images to know that Danny and his friends had been stalking Genevieve and Charlotte for a long while. And they'd definitely been in France.

Her heart pounded hard. She saw flashes of the building where she'd gone to test her psychic abilities. She and Genevieve had gone in laughing, determined to have fun. It never occurred to either of them that they might be in danger, or that the danger would follow them and possibly hurt others they loved.

Danny and Vince had followed them back to the little studio they were renting together. She didn't see them anywhere near where Genevieve's grandmother lived, nor was there even the faintest memory of standing over the body after or during the time of the murder. She didn't see them near her brother or his home either.

Taking a deep breath, she let go of the napkin. The three men had been in France, followed them from the Morrison Psychic Testing Center, where they'd done the psychic testing, and now had followed the two women to the United States. They were Americans, but from where she wasn't certain. She was frustrated with the fact that she didn't get clear, detailed information like she did from older objects.

Vince continued his conversation with Genevieve, all about her painting and what she liked to paint, volunteering to be her next male model if she was looking for one. Danny and Bruce seemed to be concentrating on her, and Charlotte was afraid for a moment that they might have asked her something while she was trying to gather information.

"You restore art?" Danny asked, hitching closer to her, extending his arm along the back of her chair, fingers gliding along her bare skin, tracing the spaghetti straps on her top.

She forced herself not to pull away, instead flashing him a small smile. "Yes. I specialize in restoring very old carousel horses, the wooden chariot and entire carousels. I can restore American carousels, but the ones I'm most interested in are from Europe. There isn't a lot of call for that sort of thing outside of museums or private collectors, and even fewer here in the States, but it's my first love."

Danny looked puzzled, as most people did. She couldn't explain to them why she liked touching the old wood and feeling every groove in it, every carving. She loved knowing everything there was to know about the carver, long gone from the world, but so familiar to her once she'd touched their art piece.

She laughed softly at his expression. "I can see you don't get it. The horses are unique, each one carved differently, some more than three hundred years ago. How cool is that? I was able to work on one that was carved during medieval times. To prepare for the jousting competitions for young knights, a rotating platform was used with legless wooden horses so they could practice their skills." She couldn't help the enthusiasm pouring into her voice in spite of the situation. She loved the fact that the carousel could be traced all the way back to the twelfth century, when the Arabs and Turks had played a game on horseback with a scented ball. Italians and Spanish had observed the competition and referred to the game as "little war," or *carosella* or *garosello*.

"Keep talking," Danny said gruffly. "I thought it was kind of silly, but it's actually interesting."

"Right?" She nodded her head, which helped her to avoid looking straight at him. She didn't want to see the image of him driving a stake through a man's heart. "A Frenchman got the idea to build a device with chariots and carved horses suspended by chains attached on arms attached to a center pole. It was used to train noblemen on the art of ring spearing. Ladies and children loved the device almost as much as or more than the noblemen." She glanced at Genevieve. The strain was beginning to show on her friend's face. Charlotte gave a little exaggerated sigh. "We should be going. We have to get up early tomorrow."

She stood up before the three men could protest. She needed to get Genevieve out of there as quickly as possible before she gave away the fact that she was terrified. Charlotte was afraid of them as well, but she was determined to find out what was going on. The fact that the three men had followed them from France, found where they were staying and followed them to the club meant Lourdes wasn't safe anyway. They had to change tactics. They needed to quit burying their heads in the sand and find out what threatened them and why.

"Thanks for the drinks. We'll see you around sometime," Genevieve said, flashing her million-dollar smile. She stood up as well, taking a step back as Vince climbed to his feet. Genevieve was tall, but he still towered over her.

"Give me your cell. Let me program my number in," he said, all charm.

Genevieve's gaze shifted to Charlotte's and Charlotte's nod was nearly imperceptible. The last thing she wanted was for sharp-eyed Danny to realize they were onto them. They'd been discouraging at first because they weren't looking to pick up a man, so they had that going in their favor. The three men were very good looking and clearly used to easy conquests. Twice Charlotte had indicated to Danny that she wasn't looking to hook up with anyone and he should move on to a sure thing. She had hoped, in the beginning, that he was interested in her only because she presented a challenge. Now she knew better.

Genevieve reluctantly took out her phone, but instead of handing it over, she programmed Vince's number in herself. Charlotte caught her arm as she passed her, already on her way out the door. She lifted a hand at the three men as Danny protested, pulling out his phone.

"Seriously?" Charlotte smiled at him and waved. "You have an entire smorgasbord of hot women fawning all over you." They had to move and they had to move fast. She knew the men would follow them, and that meant disappearing before they got outside. They'd have to get to their car, get out of the parking garage, find a place to hide and then wait for the men to come out.

"I didn't spend all evening sitting with them," Danny protested.

"Maybe we'll see you next time," Charlotte said, and deliberately hurried into the crowd, heading for the door. "Come on, Genevieve. We have to get the car and fast. We don't have much time."

Genevieve nodded, already fishing for her keys in her purse.

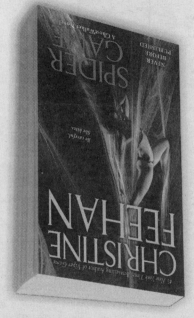